INK

INK

JONATHAN MABERRY

ST. MARTIN'S GRIFFIN
NEW YORK

First published in the United States by St. Martin's Griffin, an imprint of St. Martin's Publishing Group

INK. Copyright © 2020 by Jonathan Maberry. All rights reserved. Printed in the United States of America. For information, address St. Martin's Publishing Group, 120 Broadway, New York, NY 10271.

www.stmartins.com

Designed by Jonathan Bennett

"Kindling" © 2020 by Jezzy Wolfe. Used by permission of the author.
"Tangled" © 2019 by Leza Cantoral. Used by permission of the author.
"A Series of Images to Convince You That She Is Dead" © 2019 by Leza Cantoral. Used by permission of the author.
"Faces: A Monk Addison Bonus Story" © 2016 by Jonathan Maberry Productions, LLC. Originally published by Borderlands Press in *A Little Bronze Book of Cautionary Tales*.

Library of Congress Cataloging-in-Publication Data

Names: Maberry, Jonathan, author.
Title: Ink / Jonathan Maberry.
Identifiers: LCCN 2020028405 | ISBN 9781250765888 (trade paperback) | ISBN 9781250200952 (ebook)
Subjects: LCSH: Paranormal fiction. | GSAFD: Suspense fiction.
Classification: LCC PS3613.A19 I55 2020 | DDC 813/.6—dc23
LC record available at https://lccn.loc.gov/2020028405

Our books may be purchased in bulk for promotional, educational, or business use. Please contact your local bookseller or the Macmillan Corporate and Premium Sales Department at 1-800-221-7945, extension 5442, or by email at MacmillanSpecialMarkets@macmillan.com.

First Edition: 2020

10 9 8 7 6 5 4 3 2 1

This is for Abigail Smith (1941–1996)

Librarian, reader, enabler of
creative behavior, superhero

Thanks for introducing me to my mentors:
Ray Bradbury, Richard Matheson,
Harlan Ellison, and L. Sprague de Camp

I wish you could have seen
what's happened since then.
Well, maybe you can . . .

And, as always, for Sara Jo

PROLOGUE

"Will it hurt?"

Patty Cakes paused, the tattoo needle in her hand, looking at the man who lay facedown on the table. He was as white and hairless as a worm.

She could have lied to him, but she never did that.

"Yes," she said.

The man took a long time before he said, "Good."

PART ONE
WELCOME TO PINE DEEP

By the pricking of my thumbs,
Something wicked this way comes.

WILLIAM SHAKESPEARE

All that really belongs to us is time;
even he who has nothing else has that.

BALTASAR GRACIÁN

1

There are towns like Pine Deep.

A few.

But not many.

Luckily, not many.

2

Monk Addison rolled off the iron bridge and slowed to a stop on the two-lane blacktop. He sat idling in front of a sign that was mounted fifty feet inside the town limits. His car was a twenty-year-old piece of shit that growled like a sick dog. A Chevy something-or-other with reflector tape on one of the taillights, duct tape holding the seats together, and an ashtray filled with butts. The CD player worked, though, and Tom Waits was growling at him about chasing the devil through the cornfields.

Monk studied the billboard on the right-hand side of the road. It told two stories, one old, one a little less old. Neither new, and he read something into that.

The old sign was an advertisement for the Pine Deep Haunted Hayride—biggest on the East Coast, it claimed. There was some art, but it was so faded that it was impossible to tell what it showed. Looked like shadows in a glaucoma sufferer's eyes.

It was the new sign that made Monk stop and look.

Someone had gone to some effort to paste a big white banner across the billboard's face. Glued it down flat, no bubbles or wrinkles. And then used spray paint to write two words. Elaborate, in a mix of old English and cartoon; 3-D, with lots of color. Like one of the better graffiti taggers in New York. The message was just two words.

GO HOME

The message was obscure and it was clear.

Go home . . . because this isn't it.

The sign was stained from rain and snow, scraped by stuff blown by wind; torn a bit here and there, maybe by birds looking for something to line a nest. Monk didn't think anything torn from that sign would ever make it to a nest, though. The smarter birds would have dropped the paper before wrapping it around their eggs. The dimmer ones might have gotten all the way home with it, then their mate would have balked and kicked it away.

"Go home," said Monk.

There was a U-Haul hitched to the back of his car. Everything he owned was in it.

He slapped his pockets for his smokes, didn't find them, and remembered he was four days into his hundredth attempt to quit. Cigarettes were a bad habit, and he'd picked it up for the same reasons cops did. Monk spent hours, sometimes days, sitting in cars watching closed houses or apartments for the right person to come through the door. For cops it was someone they wanted to arrest. For Monk it was someone who'd already been arrested, charged, and who'd skipped out on his court appearance. The bail bondsmen who hired Monk to find those people paid him well, but the waiting was a bitch. Smoking gave his hands and mouth something to do. But he needed to stop killing himself one death stick at a time. All that said, he decided to find a store and buy a carton. He wasn't that far down the shitter that he was going to dig an ashy butt from the tray. Give that a day or two in this place.

Go home.

"Well, fuck me," he said and put the car into gear, pulled onto the road, and drove toward the sunset. Behind him, across the river on the Jersey side, it was already getting dark. There were moody clouds bullying their way into the sky.

He drove along the blacktop.

He drove to Pine Deep.

He drove home.

3

There were hundreds of black birds on the power lines along Route A-32.

Most were crows. Some starlings and grackles. A few were so thin and threadbare that it was impossible to tell what they were. Maybe they didn't even know. It was that kind of town.

Only a few of those birds were old enough to remember what

happened the night Pine Deep burned. All of the birds—the black ones, the nightbirds—knew it, though. It was the lore of their kind.

The birds sat there in the fading light of the first of October, rustling their feathers, gossiping the way birds do, watching the old car with the trailer drive past. They stopped whispering and watched with black-within-black eyes.

They knew trouble when they saw it.

One by one the nightbirds fell like suicides from the cables, plummeting until they flapped their wings, and then flew along the road behind him. The bruised clouds in the east reached for them with fingers of rain, but they outflew it.

The car and the nightbirds followed the long road as it snaked and turned, rose and fell, rolling like a black promise through the endless fields of corn and pumpkins, of apples and garlic. Farmhouses, remote as ships on the ocean, stood amid oceans of green that rippled in the freshening storm breeze. Farm roads cut off north and south, seemingly at random. Every signpost was pocked with bullet holes, old and new. Every now and then the car passed a house or barn that was nothing more than a blackened shell overgrown with creeper vines. There were several houses being built, but the green wood bones looked naked and vulnerable.

Four miles from town the car passed a man who leaned a shoulder against a fence, his face shadowed by the visor of a ballcap embroidered with PINE DEEP SCARECROWS. He wore layers of filthy clothes—sports coats and fishing vests and tropical shirts and flannel shirts and windbreakers. There was no scheme to the clothes except they all had pockets. Lots of pockets. A fanny pack sagged around his narrow waist, and the pockets of old cargo pants bulged with things he'd picked out of garbage cans and gutters and elsewhere. No one in town knew his name. They called him Mr. Pockets. He watched the car pass with eyes older than the trees, and a smile whose lips seemed to ripple and writhe. He spoke a single word as his eyes watched the car roll away.

"Delicious."

Night was falling hard, and as the clouds devoured the sun, the car rolled on.

4

Patty Cakes remembered the man. The customer.

Remembered him coming in. Stripping off his shirt.

She remembered his skin. Like a mushroom. Cool to the touch and spongy. He smelled like yeast from a bakery Dumpster.

She could not remember his face, though.

He paid in cash, so no credit card receipt.

She half-ass remembered his name. Owen something. The last name was a blur, if he'd said it at all.

What she remembered most—what she remembered with an odd clarity—was his touch. It wasn't deliberate, she was pretty sure. He hadn't tried to cop a feel or accidentally brush against her breast, the way some guys did. He hadn't laid his hand casually over the wrong part of the armrest in hope of the backs of his fingers brushing her crotch. That was an old trick, but he hadn't done that, either.

No.

What he did was so casual, so accidental.

It was after she took off the black pearl latex gloves she wore when sinking ink. She'd given him a punch card. Five sessions and a sixth free. The tips of his fingers just ran along the back of her hand as he took the card. Easy, no pause, nothing forced. Just that touch. Then he was gone, taking his name and his face with him. Taking the blowfly with him. The newest member of a swarm, he'd said, though there were only two others on his skin. Looking real, like it was crawling on his back. Her stuff always looked real.

That touch was real.

She hadn't imagined it.

Had he meant to do that? Patty wondered. Had he? Or was it her being weird about being in a new place? New store. New town and state.

Patty stood looking out of her storefront window. Not knowing. She held her left hand—the one he'd touched—in her right, massaging the point of contact with a thumb that went around and around and around.

Will it hurt?

That was what he asked. She'd told him it would. It didn't hurt that much. Not to most people, but if you said it did then they were usually happy it wasn't as bad as they thought. They felt braver, stronger. That strength made them feel validated for having chosen to get a tattoo in the first place.

Will it hurt?

"Yes," she said aloud, as if answering that question again now.

Good.

That's what he said, and then he didn't say anything at all until the blowfly was done. He was a cadaver in the chair, one of those people who go so far into their heads during the process that they might as well be dead. Patty preferred new customers to be chattier, because it gave her insight that might affect the kind of colors she used, or to inspire remarks that might bring them back. With a good conversationalist in the chair she could double the job in one sitting, or get them back as regulars and build some sleeves, or get them to buy the chest pieces or full-back work. Good money but also jobs that would allow Patty's artistry to shine. Jobs that would make her fully alive.

Not this man, though. He asked the one question and then said, "Good." Nothing else. Not a word.

She was quick with him, but only as quick as art allowed. After the blowfly was done, she gave him a printed aftercare sheet to which was stapled a 10 percent-off coupon for any new purchase.

He said nothing. But he'd sniffed the paper like a dog sniffing a patch of ground he wanted to roll in; then he folded it carefully and put it in his pocket. He left without saying a word. That word, though, echoed in the empty shop after he was gone.

"Good," Patty said, repeating it, trying for the same weight and inflection. Getting too close. The word tasted wrong in her mouth. Like someone else's spit.

5

The first time Monk tried to call Patty, while he was still in New York, it had gone straight to voicemail.

The second time, while he was way out in some part of Jersey that seemed to be nothing but strip malls, there was no signal. One flickering bar that simply refused to push through his call. Or didn't give a fuck. He wondered how the hell people who owned, worked in, or shopped at all those stores got through the day without Wi-Fi. He realized that he was being way too twenty-first century about that, and it soured him.

He called a third time as he was cruising along through

farm country on the east side of the Delaware, while motoring between fields of corn that seemed endless. The corn was hypnotizing. Every mile seemed identical to the last. It was like being in one of those old *Twilight Zone* stories about being caught in a time loop, driving forever with no chance of ever getting where you needed to be. He was positive he was passing the same fence posts and the same damn scarecrow over and over again.

He called Patty again. Fourth time? Fifth? It rang three times and then she picked up.

"Monk . . . ?" said Patty Cakes in a voice filled with sleep. It was early evening on a long workday.

"Hey, there," said Monk, slowing to a stop on the shoulder for fear of driving out of cell range. "I'm here."

"Here . . . ?"

"Yeah."

"Where?"

"Here. In town. Or almost. Still way the hell out in farm country, but I'll be there soon."

There was a pause. A little too long, even for someone who just woke up. "In town . . . ? You're here in Brooklyn?"

"Huh? No," he said, "I'm in Pine Deep."

Another pause. Then, in a voice that was more dreamy than sleepy, Patty said, "Oh. Sure. Good. See you."

And the line went dead.

Monk stared at the phone as if the screen display would provide an explanation. Or translation. Or something. He frowned, not liking that conversation one little bit. Patty was going through some shit—that's why she left New York. This place was supposed to be a dial-it-down move; zero stress in rural America. But she sounded out of it. Or high. He put the pedal down.

The speed was posted at thirty-five. He didn't give much of a fuck about that.

6

The big cop in the shiny black-and-white cruiser was tucked behind a billboard advertising the Pinelands Fringe Festival. He sipped a Diet Dr Pepper and felt the day get older one dying molecule at a time. There had been five cars in two hours. All of them local, none of them breaking any laws he cared about.

Then he saw the old Chevy blow past. The cop didn't have a radar gun pointed out the window, but it didn't matter. Guy had to be doing sixty in a thirty-five zone.

The cop reached out a hand and got as far as the switch for the lights and siren, but stopped there. It wasn't the car that stopped him, or the profile of the big man behind the wheel. He hadn't seen either before.

No, it was the birds that made him pause.

In the air, fifty or sixty feet above the car, a flock of nightbirds followed that car. More birds leapt from trees and joined in. All of them dark. No pigeons or finches. He wasn't even sure they were crows. He knew those birds. Had for a long time. Birds *like* those anyway.

This was, after all, Pine Deep.

The cop leaned back and let the car go. Thunder rumbled off to the east. Very close. Maybe already on this side of the river. There had been a lot of clouds lately, a lot of rain. The early October crops were getting fat, but there was a weird feel to things. People seemed a little jumpy. The nights were colder than they should have been. Lots of roadkill on the highway. The cop didn't like any of that because it reminded him of another autumn back when he was a kid. That started with storms and nightbirds, too.

There was a sudden bang of thunder accompanied by a supernova of lightning. The cop winced and covered his eyes; the cruiser shuddered.

"Jesus Christ," he hissed and then fought to blink his retinas clear. The storm seemed to have suddenly leapt across the river and now crouched over the farm fields, its underbelly heavy with ugly udders filled with rain. The next bursts of thunder were loud, but not as shocking, as if the storm—having gotten his full attention—was settling down to business. The cop saw lightning reflected on the curved leaves of the corn, making them look like polished porcelain, and when the lightning flashed they looked cracked and ready to break. The cop ran the pad of his thumb along the red-gold stubble on his chin. A habit he had that he didn't know he had.

Then his radio squawked.

"Base to four," said the voice of the dispatcher, Gertie. "Base to four, over."

The cop picked up the handset. "Four to base. Go ahead."

"Mike, honey," said Gertie, "are you off dinner yet?"

This was a small town and they weren't all that formal.

"Copy that. Skipped dinner. I'm watching by the Fringe billboard on A-32. What've you got?"

"A 10-54 out on Barkers Farm Road."

Officer Mike Sweeney smiled. That ten-code was for "livestock on road."

"Walking or hit?" he asked.

"Hit. Tourist car plowed into a cow."

"Anyone hurt?"

"I think so."

He smiled up at clouds. "Then," he said, "it's a 10-52."

"Oh," said Gertie. "Right. But there was the cow thing, too."

"Is the cow dead?"

"No. Messed up, though," she said. "I've got some EMTs in-bound. For the people, I mean."

Gertie was a nice-enough person—though Mike was aware that he was the only one who thought so—but she was not cut out for police dispatch. She gave Mike the make, model, and color of the car, and the name of the tourist who'd called in.

"Gertie . . . ?" said Mike.

"Yes, honey?"

"You don't really need to use the ten-codes. You can just tell me a car hit a cow."

"Trying to be professional," she said defensively. "Crow likes us to act like real police."

"We are real police, Gertie. But we can talk plain . . . and trust me when I say that Crow doesn't give much of a damn about how we 'act.'"

There was a silence. Not exactly sullen or stony, and—he was sure—not all that contemplative. Gertie was Gertie. More of a fixture than a part of the team.

He heard her clear her throat. "You going out there?" Her voice was a little stiff.

"On it," Mike said and ended the call.

The old car pulling the U-Haul was gone and the road was empty. The locals would have read the sky; the tourists wouldn't be flocking in too heavily midweek. Mike started the engine and pulled away from the curb, did a U-turn. Rain began splatting on his windshield. He turned on the wipers and his light-bar, kept the siren off, and went in the opposite direction.

He thought about that old car, though. There was something about it that he did not like. No, sir, not one little bit.

7

Dianna Agbala selected a deck of tarot cards from the scores lined up like books on her kitchen shelf. She waited for that flash of coldness that told her it was the right deck for the moment, and slid it out and set it on the table.

Her tummy was warm with two cups of coffee and for now, at least, the sky was dark with storm clouds visible through her kitchen windows. She was on the evening shift at the store and adjusted her day accordingly. Sia and Dua Lipa had gotten her through dinner, but now she was shifting her energy and asked Echo to play "Aud Guray" by Deva Premal. Soothing, elegant, miles deep.

The cats were already settled down. They were intuitive and knew when she was going quiet, going inward. Toby Oscar was stretched in a patch of sunlight, and Zoey lay on the top of the fridge. She liked to survey the world like an imperious senior lama.

Dianna's sensitivity varied in its manifestations. Nothing was ever a lock, and even with all of her experience there were surprises and mysteries everywhere she looked. Being confident in her world was not the same as knowing the complete shape and size of it. No one did, and anyone who said otherwise was running a con game on the tourists.

The music was already doing its work, tugging her gently away from concerns of the moment—the need to check Facebook and Instagram, the desire to check emails to see if her mother or—more dangerously—her ex had written. Her mood softened as she sat down at the table and picked up the boxed cards. Her touch had responded to the traditional Rider-Waite deck. It was so familiar that it made her smile. This was the deck she'd learned on, which was not at all uncommon for people like her. Rider-Waite was first published in 1910 and was a classic. Pamela Colman Smith's paintings were enduring classics that had been painted using instructions by the mystic A. E. Waite. They looked simple, almost primitive, but there was so much subtlety in terms of hidden symbolism that the cards were highly valued more than a century later. Dianna had worn out at least five decks over the years, and one antique set was in a shadow box on her bedroom wall. The store where Dianna worked even sold sets of coasters with the images of the Magus, Empress, Emperor, and Fool on them.

She settled herself in her chair and took some long, cleansing breaths. Not trying for any deep level of tranquility, but instead a soft and receptive state. When the calm gathered around her like a comfortable bathrobe, Dianna opened the box and slid the cards into her hands. They were so old now, so worn from thousands of readings. Because customers often picked trendier or newer-looking decks, these cards slept for long periods of time. Even during this morning ritual they were not the deck that spoke to her very often.

While she shuffled she disconnected as much of her consciousness as possible, letting noninvolvement permit the right cards to find her and match her need. Then she dealt three cards facedown and set the others aside. Those three represented the past, present, and future. She had no specific question in mind on mornings like this, but the town had been on her mind a lot lately. The Fringe neighborhood was growing very fast and it was very much her kind of crowd—artistic, a bit wild, complex, outside of normal definitions. The first Pinelands Fringe

Festival was coming up soon and there was a bit of friction with the longtime locals. They didn't want the festival, despite all the money it would bring with it. There was some validity to their pushback. The Trouble had happened during a Halloween festival, and since then the "events" in Pine Deep tended to be apple festivals that lasted an afternoon, and Santa arriving on a fire truck on Black Friday. Dianna had enough locals as clients to know that they thought having another big festival was asking for trouble. Tempting fate. Invoking the wrong kind of spirits in a town known to have troubling energy going back centuries.

So it was the town that formed the basis of her three-card reading, even if unintentionally. Dianna never swam against the current in her readings.

She turned over the first card. The Ten of Swords.

The image showed a man lying facedown with ten swords stabbed into his back. Dianna stiffened, reading both the traditional meaning of that card but also experiencing a sharp stab of instinctive awareness. And the old line from Shakespeare flickered through her thoughts.

By the pricking of my thumbs, something wicked this way comes.

Clients often thought that the Devil or Death cards were the worst or direst, but for Dianna the Ten of Swords was far worse. But it was also maddeningly nonspecific. The people in town should be on the lookout for betrayal, painful endings, loss, wounds, and crisis. Some unforeseeable pain was on the horizon, something that could not be avoided. A pain that would cut deeply, leaving some of her neighbors feeling like they had been stabbed ten times over, and completely leveled out emotionally, mentally, and spiritually.

Her heart stopped for a frozen moment when she saw that card.

It was an ugly card to get at the start of a new day.

It was an ugly card to have, ever.

She almost stopped to reshuffle. Almost. But Dianna took a breath and plunged ahead.

"What is the outcome of this?" she murmured.

She turned over the second card.

The Magician.

She chewed her lip. The Magician was not inherently a bad card, but its meaning was conditional on the other cards. Sometimes it was an empowered and uplifting card. However, if something bad was coming to Pine Deep, or was already there, then the cause of it was whomever the Magician card referred to. Because the card was part of the Major Arcana, unlike the Ten of Swords, it represented an actual individual person. Minor Arcana cards—those of the swords, cups, wands, and pentacles—represented situations that would happen to someone. Major Arcana cards represented the people or individual that created those situations.

Most often, and in most decks, the Magician was male. The image on the card was a man in white robes with a red sash holding a sword aloft while a snake coiled around his waist. The infinity symbol hovered over his head, showing that he operated outside of time and space. The snake and the symbols in front of him meant he was able to use anything to create anything. The Magician wielded real power. He turned energy into matter and took matter and converted it to energy. He saw the essence in all things and could use it to do what he wanted with it. Good or ill.

When accompanying the Ten of Swords, the Magician card spoke of a pernicious intent that chilled Dianna to her core.

The desire to end the reading was very strong, but her need to know was stronger still. She had to know what the implications were of such a person being present and doing such things.

"What is to come of this?" she asked and heard the tremble in her voice.

Dianna licked her lips and steeled herself before turning the last card. There were plenty of cards in both higher and lower Arcana that could change the meaning of this reading.

The one she turned, though, was not one of those.

The picture was that of a building crumbling as lightning struck it. Flames erupted from its window and two people leapt for safety but were too far from the ground. The fall would kill them.

The Tower. Another of the higher Arcana cards.

The card of total destruction.

She recoiled from it. Depending on when it appeared in a reading, the Tower could represent physical structures being destroyed. Dianna knew of a psychic who'd had that card appear in every reading leading up to when the planes hit the Twin Towers. But it could also represent so much more. It could represent systems. It could represent people. Lives. The Tower represented the greater body of anything—physical or metaphorical. The Tower represented the dismantling of those systems or structures.

She pushed her chair back from the table. A sound made her turn and she saw that both of her cats were now standing together, trembling with fear, their hair raised and stiff along their spines. Toby Oscar made a sick mewling noise. Zoey bared her teeth and hissed.

8

Sergeant Mike Sweeney saw the cow as he topped the rise.

It was standing in the middle of the road, staring bemusedly at the blocky ambulance that had stopped a few yards from its nose.

A silver Kia Sorento squatted on the shoulder; its hood had an expensive dent in it, and there was a head-size crack on the passenger side of the windshield. As he slowed to a stop, Mike could see a smear of blood on the inside of the glass. He kept his lights on and parked at an angle that would force all traffic to share the opposite lane. As soon as he opened his door he could hear the yelling. Part of him wanted to get right back into the cruiser and drive over to the Harvest Inn for a couple-three beers.

Three men and one woman, all of them screeching at each other at the top of their lungs from behind the ambulance. Mike sighed and trudged around to see a woman standing with her knuckles on her hips and a man seated in the back of the ambulance as two EMTs took vitals. The man wore a foam cervical collar and held a compress to his forehead. There was a lot of blood—typical of scalp wounds—but the man didn't appear to be hurt all that badly. The EMTs were yelling at the man to let them put him on a gurney and transport him. They wanted to strap him into a back-and-neck immobilizer. The woman was also screaming at the man—shrieking, really— telling him that it was his own goddamn fault for not wearing a goddamn seat belt. The bleeding man was yelling at everyone, but because he was outnumbered he wasn't finishing any sentences.

Mike girded his loins and plunged in.

"Folks, please," he said in what he thought was an appropriately loud and authoritative voice. They all ignored him. It wasn't clear they even saw him. So, Mike slapped the flat side of the ambulance with a hard palm, a booming whump that sounded like a hand grenade. Maybe louder. The blow was hard enough to rock the vehicle and everyone suddenly shut up and gaped at him.

Mike Sweeney was conspicuously large. Six foot four, with the massive arms and shoulders of someone who spent some part of each day clanking free weights. He had dark-red hair and fierce blue eyes and there were all kinds of scars on his face and hands. He knew he was imposing as fuck, and so he deliberately loomed.

Into the ensuing silence, the cow mooed.

Mike cleared his throat, identified himself, and asked what happened.

Everyone started talking at once. This time all he had to do was hold up a hand. They instantly became as silent and attentive as kids in a country day school. Mike pointed at the woman.

"You first."

She actually bristled and her eyes became immediately reptilian. "Why? Because I'm a woman?"

"No," he said slowly, "because you were driving."

There was a beat. "Oh."

Mike gave her a small nod. "Start at the beginning." Before she got a word out, though, thunder rumbled overhead. "Long story short," he encouraged.

There were, he knew, no short stories in anything related to couples in crisis. Not on domestic disturbance calls. Not in traffic incidents. He was philosophical about it, though, because he still thought that was all this was.

9

Dianna Agbala hated the term *psychic*, even though it was on her business card and in neon in the window of Nature's Spirits, where she worked.

She was more than that, but the word was a convenient catchall label. Good for business, and a lot of people who came to the store did so because of Dianna and her gifts. Personally, she preferred "sensitive," which is what her grandmother called it. Her mother called it "Satan's curse," but that was Mom—the quintessential church lady. BFF of our lord and savior. Not like Nanny, who was much more than open-minded. She'd been completely open. Every sense, not limited to the five physical ones. Mom was a sensitive, too, but spent all those years begging Jesus to save her soul from the demons who possessed her.

So often growing up Dianna wished Nanny had been her mother. Would have been a happier life. Nanny would have loved Pine Deep for all the reasons Mom said she'd never come back.

"Lady Di," said a voice and Dianna turned to see the assistant manager, Ophelia—all frizzy blond hair and enormous glasses—coming into the reading alcove, a schedule sheet held out. Dianna accepted the sheet. "You're going to be busy tonight."

"Idle hands . . ." murmured Dianna. Her schedule varied between daytime, ten to four, and evenings until nine o'clock closing. Card readings, some palmistry, or simply reading a client and discussing the forces at work in their lives. She preferred the later shifts because after a long self-imposed drought Dianna was back in the club scene. Drinking, dancing, and hunting for the kind of woman who matched her energies and her needs. Size, shape, age, and color didn't matter, but there had to be that spark. A bit of magic.

There was a huge bang and the windows shuddered in their frames. Both women jumped and then looked at each other and laughed. Outside the rain was falling softly, but Dianna wasn't fooled. It started this way every day lately—thunder for hours as the storm clouds came to a boil out over the farmlands, and then the rain would march into town. Then, as it had since the end of summer, it would rain all afternoon and well into the night.

"Maybe we'll get the afternoon crowd," said Ophelia doubtfully. "Tonight's going to be a bust. If it's like last night I might close up early."

"Sure," said Dianna. "Whatever you want."

She used a bottle-green fingernail to run down the list of names. It was a nearly even split between her regulars—mostly older locals who just wanted to know that this was not going to be another Black Harvest year—and new names she didn't recognize. Some of the names were the kind of nicknames or stage names that immediately marked them as people from Boundary Street. The Fringe. Or whatever it was called, depending on who you asked. Kiki LaOomph had to be a burlesque dancer, and Dianna figured, either transvestite or actual trans-woman. The name made her smile, made her want to read her cards but also catch the act. Other names included Skinz, Brutal John, Yo-Yo, Jellicho, and Tammiduck. Names that defined the metamorphic identity and true persona of each, rather than the birth names that often carried baggage. Dianna had once considered changing her own name after the divorce from Jaden, but hadn't. She'd kept her so-called maiden name when they'd gotten hitched, and Dianna was Nanny's middle name. So . . . she kept it. But she understood the desire to reinvent oneself all the way down to the birth name.

"First one'll be in soon," said Ophelia, which was also not her real name. She'd been born Mary Janowitz but shed that skin twenty years back to become Ophelia. Just Ophelia, except on social media, where she was OpeheliaUndrowned.

"Thanks," said Diana, folding the schedule and tucking it under the stack of tarot cards. "I'll play for a bit."

When Ophelia left, Dianna considered the decks of cards. She had over a hundred decks at home and always selected seven at random—as much as anything a sensitive does is truly random—and brought them to work. Standard Arcana as well as oracle cards of different kinds.

The reading she'd done half an hour ago at the kitchen table hovered around her like a cloud. It had been so intense, so threatening that it felt like a betrayal, as if the cards had decided to turn on her. But when she looked through the window the town was not crumbling down and no one she knew was in any kind of real crisis. Dianna told herself it was a hangover reading. Last night had been a bit wild, with a few too many exotic vodka drinks at Tank Girl and more than her share of a big bottle of wine with Nellie, a petite blond with piercings in very interesting places.

Just a crazy night, she told herself. Only that.

Dianna took a cleansing breath and then ran her fingers lightly down the stack, eyes unfocused, letting the cards speak to her. They always did.

Her fingers slipped off the edge of the last deck and thumped the tablecloth.

Dianna blinked in surprise.

Not only had none of the cards given her that tingle, none of them even felt cold. Warm cards were nothing, they were asleep. When a deck went cold it was like opening a window to look out into another world. There was always one deck or another that was like touching an ice cube, especially when she was doing her own morning three-card reading.

She leaned back in her chair and studied the cards, her fingers resting on the curved edge of the table. The cloth was a deep purple velvet and embroidered with birds, insects, and flowers stylized to suggest pre-Colombian art. She'd had it since college, when it had been a wall hanging. Like the cards, the cloth was an old friend. As were the crystals Dianna often handled to cleanse her energy between clients. Now, though, the cloth felt oddly rough beneath her fingertips.

"Don't be that way," she said. The cards, being cards, managed not to look contrite. She wasn't fooled, though. They could hear and understand her.

A shadow crossed the weak sunlight, rubbing it out and casting the storefront in dirty gray shadows. All the colors seemed to drain from the amethysts and turquoise and apophyllite on display in the window. And even the Lemurian seed points and heulandite clusters looked washed out. By itself she would never have taken particular note. After all, the rain had been almost unstoppable in town this fall. However, Dianna was not the kind of person to ignore patterns, especially when she was as open and receptive as she usually was at the start of a long day.

The cards, the cloth, the crystals, and the clouds.

"I—" she began, but the jangle of the bell above the door pulled her immediately out of the pattern of thought that had begun to form. Not just the bell, but the man who came in.

He was not big, not impressive-looking, not handsome, not in any way pleasant to look at. At the same time, there was nothing specific about him that made Dianna recoil. Except, maybe, that he was completely hairless. Totally bald, no mustache or beard, and as he approached she saw he had no eyebrows or eyelashes. A cancer patient? Maybe. There was definitely something sick about him. His skin was pallid, doughy, tending toward gray-white. Like something grown in the dark when no one was looking.

Lord of flies.

The three words flashed into her head, unbidden, unconnected to any deeper thought.

Don't be here for me.

For a moment the man stood there, looking around at the store layout. The shelves of spiritual books, the many tables of stones and crystals, the displays of statues—Ganesha, Buddha, Kokopelli, Quan Yin—and all of the other items for sale. Things to uplift, expand, deepen.

She watched the slow smile that formed on his mouth. No, not formed. Crept. As if the smile were an insect sneaking out from under the fridge, ugly and knowing.

Don't come over here.

She thought it, pushed at the thought, tried to load it like a bullet into the barrel of her desire. But even as she thought it, even before he turned that smile in her direction, Dianna knew that he was here for her.

For her.

For her.

His grin widened but did not brighten. It was as gray as the dirty clouds. His eyes were pale, the color of spit. He walked toward her, his body lumpy, his gait awkward. Dianna looked away, then down at the schedule sheet. Her fingers shook as she pulled it out and opened it. The first name was one she did not know, one she thought was someone from Boundary Street.

Owen Minor.

Lord of flies, hissed her inner voice.

And then his shadow fell across the table.

10

The story the couple—Corinne and Andrew Duncan—told Officer Mike Sweeney confused the living hell out of him.

"Wait, wait," he said, interrupting the wife's second telling of her side. "Go back to the part where you hit him."

"Of course I hit him," she yelled. "You would, too. You'd have probably shot him if he did that to you. Are you married? No? Well, if you were married and your wife went through cancer—twice—and your husband, the man who is supposed to love you until death do us part—"

"For Christ's sake, Corinne," bleated the husband, "of course I love you."

"—but then does something as mean and callous and cold-hearted as that, you'd hit him, too. I mean, he pretended that he never even had it in the first place."

She was crying now, and Mike felt deeply uneasy. He was never good with people crying. He cleared his throat again and gave the husband a hard look.

"May I see your arm?"

"Why? I told her and I'm telling you," said the husband, "that I never had any damn tattoo. Don't you think I would remember if I had a fucking tattoo?"

"Please watch your language, sir," said Mike automatically. "Now . . . may I see your left forearm?"

The man, Andrew Duncan, swore again and thrust out his arm. His sleeve was rolled up and he rotated his forearm so Mike could see the pale skin above his wristwatch. There was no tattoo.

But there was . . . something.

Mike bent closer. "Is that a scar?"

"Of course it's a scar," hissed Corinne. "He had it removed. Burned off with lasers or however they do it."

"It's not a scar because I never had a tattoo," insisted Andrew.

"It does appear to be a scar of some kind," said Mike, and he could feel himself shifting to take sides. There was something on the husband's arm. It was small, about the size of a thumbprint, but faded, almost smeared, the way a watercolor looks after it's been soaked. Mike could see no trace of any specific pattern, and certainly not the pink ribbon emblem of breast cancer or the black ink of the two dates when Corinne was declared cancer-free. All he could make out was a faintness of pink and gray, but the effect was of a scar that was so old it had nearly vanished.

"It's been there for six years," said Corinne and now tears were rolling down her cheeks. A fly buzzed around her face and she slapped it away in irritation.

It was drizzling, with the droplets moving in misty waves as storm winds came sweeping along the road. The clouds promised much heavier rain, and soon. A tow truck had arrived during the narration and the driver was busy hooking the Kia to the tow-bar, throwing frequent looks at the sky.

The story was a strange one. While they were driving, Corinne remarked that tomorrow was the sixth anniversary of the call from the oncologist to tell her that she was cancer-free. It was a big thing, because this time they were sure they'd gotten it all. After the first bout, the cancer had crept back in and was more aggressive by the time it was discovered. But the partial mastectomy, the radiation, and the chemo had done the job. Andrew had gotten the ribbon tattoo with the date of her first all-clear the day she got the first good news, and had added the second date two days after the next remission. The tattoo was small and generally covered by his sleeve, but since it was Andrew's habit to wear his wristwatch with the face on the inside, he'd chosen the placement so that whenever he checked his watch he would see it. See, and be reminded of the blessing of healing.

While they were driving, however, after Corinne made her comment about the anniversary, she asked to see the tattoo.

Andrew had looked at her, frowned, half smiled, and asked, "What tattoo?"

She thought he was making some kind of joke, but when she pressed him on it, Andrew thought she was making a weird and ugly joke. He asked, "What cancer? What are you even talking about?"

They went back and forth like a bad comedy act, and that disintegrated into accusations, yelling, and finally she started crying hysterically and slapping at him. At his bare wrist. He tried fending her off, pulling his arm out of reach, and when she leaned over to try for another smack, there was the cow.

Mike had all the details but none of the story made sense, unless Andrew was a lying piece of shit. And a seriously cruel lying piece of shit at that.

There was more thunder and the rain began falling in earnest.

"Mrs. Duncan," he said, "I'm going to let the EMTs take your husband to the hospital. Pinelands Regional Medical Center is in town. They're going to want to take some tests and maybe an X-ray and a CT scan."

"They should test him to see if he has a fucking heart," she said, trying to make it sound bitter, but it came out broken and sad.

Which is when Andrew Duncan, looking genuinely confused, started crying.

The EMTs put him on the gurney, strapped him into the back brace, and were about to close the door, when Corinne suddenly climbed inside. She wrapped her arms around her lying piece of shit husband, and they both disintegrated into truly awful tears. The EMTs gave Mike puzzled looks. He returned a meaningless nod and stepped back as they drove off, siren wailing like a despairing ghost. The tow truck followed.

Mike stood in the rain, watching them go. The storm intensified so quickly that the ambulance vanished from sight before it even topped the hill. Wind gusts slanted the rain like scythes, but Mike ignored it. Rain didn't bother him. He had other things on his mind.

Then he turned to the cow. She had been munching roadside grass, not looking hurt or even bothered by the collision with the SUV. But as he began walking over, the cow gave a last moo and fell over. Dead as a stone.

"Ah . . . fuck . . ." breathed Mike. He squatted down, letting the rain soak him to the skin, as he stroked the cow's cheek and neck.

INTERLUDE ONE	THE LORD OF THE FLIES

His name was Owen Minor, and life was never kind to him.

He saw no reason to be kind in return.

Some lives are like that. It's a roll of the cosmic dice, and as Owen always saw it, those dice were loaded. He was born too early and born wrong. That's how his mother described it when she complained to one of her friends, and she complained a lot.

"Carrying him was awful," she said once to a girlfriend while they were drinking at the kitchen table. His mom thought Owen was upstairs asleep, but he'd crept downstairs to listen. As he often did. "Bad enough the condom broke. Or it had a hole. Or some damn thing. Thought I was doing the whole safe sex thing—and it's not like the son of a bitch I was banging was the great prize of all time. Sure, he had a pretty face. Like Brad Pitt, if someone had taken a ball-peen hammer to his face. Good body, though. Biggest cock you ever saw on a white man. Maybe that was it. Even those—what do you call 'em? Magnums?—are a size too small for that kind of meat."

Owen knelt in the shadows of the adjoining dining room, in a niche between the china cabinet and a stack of boxes filled with old issues of *National Geographic, Soap Opera Digest,* and *Entertainment Weekly.* He shivered there in the darkness, even though the house was warm.

"So, anyway," continued his mother, her words a little slurred from the combination of white zinfandel and hits of Godfather OG, which she chain-smoked, filling the whole house with the skunk stink of ultrapotent marijuana, "he banged me cross-eyed right here on this table. Hand to God, Gracie. I didn't even know the rubber broke and I didn't give a damn."

The laughter was shrill. Like jackals Owen had seen at the zoo.

"Anyway, he went off to Afghanistan about two weeks later and got killed."

"The Taliban get him?" asked Gracie.

"Nah. Got his stupid ass run over by a truck. No great loss of a person, but a real waste of a good dick."

More laughter. Then the scalding steam hiss as one or the other of them took a deep hit on the joint.

"So, here's me with a bun in the oven. Try to explain that to a husband who hasn't had a stiff dick since Clinton was president. Fucker beat the shit out of me. I threw him out and filed a paper on him, but damn if he wouldn't have earned a little bit of thanks if he'd hit me in the guts instead of the mouth. One miscarriage and a lot of things would have been better, you know?"

"I heard that," agreed Gracie. "Heard it was a bad pregnancy . . . ?"

"Oh, god . . . this is why I'll never have another damn kid. Got every symptom you could get. Swollen ankles, hemorrhoids, mood swings, my tits blew up like balloons but they hurt, nipples leaking through my blouse, threw up every fifteen goddamn minutes, and when I wasn't hurling I was pissing."

"Damn, girl."

"Only blessing there was, was that the bun popped out of the oven just over seven months in. Just a red wrinkled piece of almost nothing. They had him on ventilators and incubators and all that. Always sick then and still sick all the damn time. Asthma, psoriasis, heart stuff—and you know I'm still paying off those bills. Health coverage in this state sucks the big one."

"He's a good kid, though," said Gracie, and Owen leaned out just far enough to see his mother's face. Looking for a smile. What he saw was the hard line of her mouth turn down into the ugliest of sneers. Then his mother looked away, so all he could see were her slumped shoulders and the curl of smoke reaching up above her untidy hair. He heard her take a hit, saw her back go rigid as she held it in, and then the long exhale.

"I wouldn't ever say this in church, Gracie," she said slowly, "but between you, me, and the wall . . . I wish the little fucker hadn't even taken that first breath. No, don't look at me that way. Not saying I wish him ill—not really—but there's something wrong with that kid. He's not right. Everyone sees it. You see it, and don't lie . . . it's just that you got a good heart and you won't say a word against anyone. You see it, though. Owen was born wrong in every way you can mean that."

Owen's shiver turned to a tremble as he waited for Gracie's rebuttal.

Which never came.

11

The storm wasn't predicted. It came out of nowhere and got big and loud and it pissed Monk off.

The skinny blonde on *Channel Six Action News* out of Philadelphia said it was going to drizzle and then mostly clear. But it was raining harder than hell as Monk drove toward town. Big fat drops at first, splatting onto blacktop behind him. Monk saw them in the rearview and tried to outrun them. They caught up.

By the time he passed the sign for Dark Hollow Road, the rain was rapping on the hood like a million knuckles. The car was too old to have automatic headlights, so he punched the button and then turned on the high beams. The storm that had chased him out of New Jersey now barraged him here in Bucks County. Within minutes it was raining so damn hard he couldn't see five feet in front of his headlights. On a twisty country road like this there were too many ways to get killed, so he pulled to the verge to wait it out.

He tried Patty's cell again and got voicemail. Left a message. He popped the cassette and found a bootleg tape of Buddy Guy killing the crowd at his Legends blues club in the South Loop of Chicago. Singing about dying of a broken heart in the rain.

"Preaching to the choir, brother B," murmured Monk.

The sky outside the car was raining hammers and nails, so Monk turned the sound all the way up. Then he sat there eyeing the stale butts in the ashtray. Weighing his options and making bad choices.

On either side of the road, the nightbirds stood in lines on the fences, huddled into their wings. Cold but curious.

12

"Um," said Dianna, momentarily flustered, "have a seat."

The man smiled an oily smile, hooked a foot around the leg of the guest chair, and slid it halfway around the table so he could sit closer.

"You don't need to do that," she said quickly.

"I'm a little hard of hearing," he said. "And I don't want to miss a thing."

It was a normal statement but the way he said it was not. He almost sang those last eight words in an imitation of Steve Tyler from Aerosmith. He wasn't loud or forceful about it, and he even half whispered it, as if making a joke for himself. He settled onto the chair and wriggled a little as if adjusting his buttocks down deep in the thin padding. That movement, like everything about Owen Minor, was faintly repellent. Not openly offensive, nothing she could comment on or bring to Ophelia. Nothing to cancel the session over. Merely wrong.

She immediately chastised herself for judging a total stranger—a reflex that warred with her trust in her own ability to read energy. But the whole day was a bit off anyway, so her instant dislike could be flavored by that. This man could just as easily have run afoul of someone else's negativity and simply be carrying it around with him like a bad smell. That happened. The first time she met Chief Crow there was a whole cloud of darkness around him, and a bigger one around his adopted son, Mike. Both were, she learned over time, very good men, which meant that her initial reaction was spoiled. Untrustworthy.

Be in the moment, she scolded herself. Be fair and be open.

Dianna pasted on a pleasant and entirely meaningless smile. Like Ophelia's customer service smile, bright but offering no actual insight.

She consulted her list. "I see you want a standard three-card reading?"

"Yes," said Mr. Minor. "That would be . . . wonderful."

An odd pause, and a bit of emphasis on the first syllable of *wonderful.*

"Is this your first time getting a reading?" she asked.

"No," said Minor. "I've had many readings before." He paused, then repeated, "Many."

"Well . . . that's great, then."

"Yes."

"I mostly use a standard layout," she explained, hiding behind routine. "First, I'll pick a deck for us to—"

"No," said Minor quickly, touching her arm as she reached toward the stack of boxed cards. His fingers circled her forearm for just a second—less than a second—and then he withdrew. "Oh, dear . . . my apologies. I didn't mean to do that."

Dianna pulled back her arm and wished she could rub it down with hand sanitizer. Even though his action was fast and light, she could still feel his fingers on her. It wasn't anything painful. More like an awareness of a smudge of dirt. She heard a buzzing and saw a fat fly on the stack of cards and waved it away in disgust.

The action sent the insect hurrying away, and also chased the memory of his touch from her mind as surely and completely as if it had never happened. She was distantly aware of the sensation that there was something on her skin, but that was all.

"First, I'll pick a deck for us to use," she said, unaware she'd already said this. Owen Minor smiled and nodded.

"Of course," he said and watched as she ran her fingers down the stack of boxed cards, paused, moved on, paused again, and then finally settled, with a tremble of hesitation, on the Rider-Waite deck, identical to the one she had at home. She shook the cards from the pack and held them in her hands for a moment, then took a small breath and offered them to Minor.

"Please shuffle them any way you want. Don't look at them, of course. Shuffle and think about any question or problems you have."

"Of course," said Minor.

Dianna frowned and looked around, trying to locate a faint sound, but unable to place where it was coming from. "Must be a couple flies in here."

"I don't hear anything," he said, and Dianna had the odd feeling he was lying. He kept on shuffling and shuffling.

Dianna covertly studied his face. Or, at least, tried to. Despite the strangeness of his skin and the oddness of his energy, his face was so completely ordinary that it was hard to categorize any detail. It was as if the moment she remembered the size, or shape, or orientation of any of his features, the memory was canceled out. As if no short-term or working memories could be anchored. Dianna knew she should be worried about that, but wasn't able to focus on worrying about it.

The only detail that stuck with her was his tattoos. He wore a dress shirt buttoned at the wrists and all the way to the Adam's apple, but peeking out from collar and cuffs were flies. Very lifelike. As beautifully rendered as the roses on her inner forearm, but deeply ugly. A rose inked so vibrantly that it seemed to bloom before the eyes was a thing of wonder; flies that looked like they could lift from that pallid skin and fly directly at her was another.

As he shuffled, Dianna rubbed at the spot on her forearm where he'd touched her. Near her rose. It repulsed her as much as if it had been one of those flies crawling on her. The odd sound intensified for a moment and she had the sudden, irrational thought that it was the buzzing of blowfly wings. Which was impossible. Silly, really, and she forced the idea away. Then Owen Minor tapped the deck on the table to smooth the cards. Before he handed it back he put it to his nose and sniffed. Not merely a quick sniff, but he ran his nose along the long side of the deck, taking a deep inhale. His eyelids fluttered as if the smell gave him an erotic thrill.

Dianna felt a flush of disgust and wished she could just end the session, but that was against store policy and her own professional integrity. It was not required that the customer be likable or even nice as long as they did nothing that was overtly and inarguably offensive. Most often with male customers they spent a lot of time looking at her chest. Having very big breasts came with challenges. Apart from being a source of frequent back pain, they were an eye-magnet. During puberty that was humiliating. As a young woman hunting her way through the club scene it had been fun, but the novelty wore off very quickly because her breasts became a way-obvious focus of attention, comment, and groping. Guys would find ways of standing so close to her that a brush of their arms or hands against her breasts was inevitable. Hugs were often wraparound so that there was some side-boob touching. All perfectly innocent. Right. And the stares. She even once had one of those novelty T-shirts that said My Personality is Up Here, with an arrow pointing to her face. It backfired. For a couple of years she wore clothing that covered her chest and blocked any hint of cleavage, but that felt like a defeat, it felt cowardly. Over time she reclaimed her sense of clothing style, and tried to just ignore drifting gazes and obvious lustful glances. Once in a rare while someone would make a deliberately crude comment. If it was in a club—and it happened in lesbian bars, too—she would either freeze that person out of her awareness or wither them with a biting comment. If it was here at the shop, she reserved the right to end any sessions that smacked of sexual harassment. Ophelia accepted that, but they differed a bit on where the line was. Staring was not really actionable. Sniffing tarot cards wasn't, either.

All of that said, this man skeeved her out on a deep level. Everything about him felt transgressive, though it was hard to land on exactly what was wrong with him. Maybe it was those blowfly tattoos.

Maybe only that.

She held the cards and went deep into herself. Listening with senses not listed among the standard five. Unnamed senses that connected her with energies that flowed subtly or dramatically all around her. Then she dealt three cards facedown on the table, took a breath, and turned over the first card.

"This card represents you," she said.

"Yes," he said, "I know."

"Dianna . . . ?"

She blinked and looked up at Ophelia, who stood a few feet away, hands clasped as if nervous.

"What?"

"I asked if you were ready for your next client?"

Dianna blinked again. "Next . . . ?"

It took her a moment to come back to the moment. To be where she was. She looked around at the store, and it was as if the overhead lights were just now coming on, though they had been on all along. The client chair was empty, placed orderly across from her. Her deck of cards stood in a neat tower. A few customers browsed, talking with one another in low voices. Rain pattered on the window.

"What?" she asked.

Ophelia gave her a queer look. "You okay, sweetie?"

Dianna nodded vaguely and glanced down at her client list. The first name was Owen Minor. Odd name. She wondered who he was or what he'd be like.

"Um . . . yes," she said. "You can send Mr. Minor over."

Ophelia's expression changed into one of confusion, with half a smile as if she was trying to figure out a joke. "You mean Gertie Swanson. She's in a hurry, too. Has to get back to the station."

"No," said Dianna, tapping the list. "Owen Minor. He's the first . . ."

Her voice trailed off as she caught sight of the clock above the window. The hands had moved and the time was wrong.

"Mr. Minor left already," said Ophelia.

"What?" asked Dianna again.

"Sure, he was very pleased with the reading." Vertical lines now formed between Ophelia's brows. "Are you sure you're okay?"

"I'm fine," said Dianna quickly. "Right. Gertie. Sorry, I guess I had a hard time coming back from . . . well, you know."

Ophelia nodded, but looked unconvinced.

"It's good. It's fine," insisted Dianna. "Everything's fine."

But it wasn't fine. Nothing was fine. Forty-nine minutes of her life was gone and she had no memory at all of the customer whose name was at the top of her list. No memory of him, of the reading, of anything. She sat there, rubbing the inside of her forearm, listening internally for even the echo of a memory. Finding nothing. A fly, trapped inside the picture window, buzzed faintly.

No, she thought, *nothing is fine at all.*

13

Monk sat in his car and wondered if he was going to get storm-surged the fuck back to the Delaware River.

Streams of muddy water came running out of the fields to fill the gullies on either side of the road. A torrent slapped its way past his car, gurgling along the doors. He had the heater on but didn't know if he had enough gas to keep the engine running until the storm let up.

"Should have gassed in goddamn Doylestown," he told the night.

The perverse and contrary voice that lived inside his head told him he should have stayed in New York. He told that voice to shut the hell up, but it only laughed at him.

Monk thought about Patty and tried her cell four more times. Got nothing. Nerves made him try to get to her, but his car never made it off the muddy verge and back onto the road. The wheels spun mud into the storm and accomplished exactly nothing beyond digging him deeper into the muck. Monk slammed it back into park and glared through the *slap-slap-slap* of the wipers. Thunder was continuous, as if the storm had parked itself overhead and simply refused to move on until it had beaten Pine Deep to a pulp.

"Fuck you," Monk snarled.

The storm just laughed, just rained harder.

14

Patty stood by her window for a long time, trying to remember if Monk had actually called, or if that had been a dream. She was almost positive she'd fallen asleep in one of the chairs. The time on the wall clock didn't match her memory. If it was right, then the customer was gone and out the door three hours ago. She was pretty sure it had to be less. Half an hour. That's how long ago it felt like he'd been there. The clock kept being an asshole and telling her different.

"I'm tired," she said to the empty room. "I'm blown out and burned down."

Even her voice was tired. A slur.

Time for a catnap?

Her body needed one, but Patty hated naps. They always left her feeling like she'd been mugged—logy and stupid and usually a bit anxious. Like she hadn't prepared for a test in school and now the teacher was handing out papers.

The clock on the wall was an ancient retro Marilyn Monroe. It, along with the three barber chairs and some termites, had come with the place. A spike was drilled through the bridge of Marilyn's nose and crooked black hands kept telling Patty the wrong time. The motor hummed and the second hand ticked.

Had Monk called?

She could have picked up her phone, checked the call log. Or, fuck it, called him back. Didn't.

Just stood there.

Her tattoo shop was on a corner and both streets seemed empty even though there were a lot of people out. But she wasn't feeling particularly social. Never had felt *less* social, in fact. So they were just figures in motion. Not real in any way that seemed to matter.

If her store had been something other than a tattoo studio, then maybe people would do that small-town thing—stopping by to introduce themselves. To say hi. To be neighborly. The exact opposite of how people were in New York.

Not the same as back home in Tuyên Quang, where she'd grown up. In small-town Vietnam everyone was pretty much born knowing everyone else. You never went very far from home. She hadn't been farther away than ten miles until she was nineteen. After that . . . well. After that she'd gone to hell. And back, just not all the way back.

After that was the fire and everything that went with it. The big soldier. The other tattoo women. The little girl—what was her name? Patty tried to remember as her thumb went round and round on the back of her hand.

15

Owen Minor stood in the shadows and the rain. That fact that he kept shivering had nothing to do with the cold or wet.

He was so goddamn turned on he couldn't bear it.

Owen leaned against the alley wall behind Patty's store, his coat pulled tight around him, head cocked to listen. Blowflies, some as thick as the last joint of a woman's little finger, crawled all over his face and throat and down into his clothes. His hands deep in his pockets, pushed through the slits he'd made so he could touch himself. As he did now. The wind had been blowing steadily all day and into the evening, but the shivers began as soon as he'd touched her hand. The little Vietnamese woman. That broken doll with all those memories inked onto her skin. And after her, the psychic. He had so many things to play with, so many memories to devour.

First, though, was Patty Cakes. Her. Her. For sure, her.

His hand moved frantically beneath his clothes.

Her memories were wonderful. So deeply awful. So beautiful.

The shivers continued all the way through his orgasm.

Aftershocks of it lingered long after Owen Minor got into his car and drove away.

16

It took Patty a long time to shake it off. Whatever it was. She couldn't come up with any label for the fuzzy, detached way she was feeling.

Focusing on the town helped, because moving here was part

of a personal salvage operation. Raising her sunken hopes from the bottom of the muddy river that was New York.

Pine Deep was nice, but she wasn't sure it was home. She desperately wanted it to be, because New York had never really been that. Or, maybe, it had been home for a while and stopped. Like a battery running dry. Wherever she lived and worked had to matter to her on a lot of deep, important levels. And so far, Pine Deep seemed to hold that promise. The street where she'd set up shop seemed like it might be the kind of street in the kind of town where Patty felt she could breathe.

Moving here hadn't been an accident. When she lived in New York, there always seemed to be a reason to come down to Pennsylvania, to Bucks County. It always seemed to be autumn in this part of Bucks County, as if the rest of the year and all the other seasonable changes were nothing more than garments it wore briefly and then discarded. It was an October kind of place, even when the sun was blistering its way through an August sky or snow heaped up on the pumpkins left unharvested in remote fields. October people lived here, and although Patty was born in a place where it was never cold and always green, even during the grayest monsoons, that climate had never defined her. It was always October in her heart.

Bucks County, and particularly towns like New Hope and Pine Deep, felt like they should have been where she was born. Maybe Pine Deep more so because it was a little strange. Darker and less obvious than her town in Vietnam. Beautiful, too. It invited the artist's touch, drew the artist's eye. She drove down here at every opportunity. To shop at the organic farms and coast the fringes of happy crowds at the apple festival. To drum up business at the biker rallies and the fringe festivals. To be where there were people who were all alike because none of them was alike. It was the first place where she didn't feel like she was actively fleeing from somewhere else.

Life in New York had been a lot like washing your hands in acid. You got clean, but there's such a thing as too clean. Her tattoo parlor there had been a refuge, but Boundary Street was home.

Cold, strange, broken, but home.

The sign in the door was turned to CLOSED, but Patty didn't notice. She hadn't done that. Had not seen the customer do it.

She stood and watched the rain.

It was like the downpours back in Tuyên Quang. The kind of rain that looked like a wall. Her mother once said that it was like ten thousand arrows falling, but that was too poetic for Patty. To her it was a wall. Gray and unbreakable.

The kind no one could get through to touch her.

As she had been touched.

She liked the wall of rain.

But this wall, in this town, was translucent and Patty could see lights come on in clubs that opened early and stores that closed late. She turned off her own neon, except for the one right above the door. INK was all it said, in harlot red. The color was named that in the vendor's catalog, and though Patty tried to explain to the salesman that it was offensive and old-thought bullshit, the man's eyes glazed and he had no good comeback. She bought the sign anyway. It wasn't harlot red to her. She was Vietnamese and that color represented happiness, love, and luck.

Putting it up over her door was like a talisman. It was like putting up a cross in vampire country. And it made her happy to know that it was burning bright, night and day, clear weather or storms.

Where was Monk? she wondered. But she still didn't check her phone. It kept not occurring to her to do that.

She turned away and went through the studio, through the beaded curtain, past the customers' bathroom and then into her apartment. Her bright-red raincoat and hat were in one of the unemptied boxes and she found them, pulled them on, and went out into the storm.

The rain smelled like tilled earth, moss, incense, and ozone. With her hands buried deep into pockets, drops pattering on the broad hat brim, Patty began walking down the side street. Down Boundary Street.

Boundary Street.

The fact that Pine Deep had a street with that name was a big part of the draw for her. There'd been one in New York, though try and find it on a map. GPS couldn't. Uber drivers back in the city could, though, which was weird.

The street wasn't on MapQuest, Google Maps, or GPS here, though. She'd had to ask, and the first five people she'd stopped when she first arrived didn't know. It was a guy with a lot of skin art, a flannel shirt, and a lumbersexual woodsman's beard who gave her directions. Boundary Street was just off the main drag, which made her wonder why the other people didn't know.

Maybe it was because this part of town was new, built since the Trouble. Maybe nobody bothered to tell the people at Google Earth about it. Or however that worked. She didn't know and really didn't care. It was here, that's what mattered. And, sure, there were some sideways mentions of it in the kind of downbeat indie documentaries hipster filmmakers concocted for their thesis. Strange, but then there were a lot of strange things in life, Patty knew. She was one of them. Monk sure as hell was another.

At times, when she was really drunk, Patty wondered if Boundary Street wasn't on the map because it was more a state of mind. Not always a good one, but that spoke to perspective. The kind of place that Tom Waits had to be talking about when he said you couldn't find it unless you started out with bad directions. Maybe every big city had a place like Boundary Street.

Probably. After all, the debris has to wash up somewhere.

It was home to her in New York, and now it was home to her here.

She passed a small knot of drenched twenty-somethings huddled under an awning. Short skirts, push-up bras, makeup applied with a trowel, and a lot of money wasted at the hair salon during the rainy season. Patty hated them and feared them. Every single one of them was prettier than her. Prettier and younger, and there wasn't a single person on the street who didn't know it.

Patty had one really good trick, though. Most Americans can't read an Asian face worth a damn, and she went full Vietnamese as she passed. Eyes that said exactly nothing, mouth that offered no emotion, teeth locked together to create the wax mask. It had been foiling white people for thousands of years and it gave these women nothing to go on. No lever for the scorn in their eyes.

Even so, they shared conspiratorial grins as she passed, but Patty could see shadows lurked in their eyes. Trying to fool each other that this—whatever tonight's plan was—was still a good idea. The Joker grins were plastic but necessary, because none of them had reached the point where fiction was going to buffer them from the realities of life down here. The shadows in their eyes told Patty that they were each feeling it. The Boundary Street vibe. That look must be similar to what young zebras showed when they realized that being a young, tough herbivore didn't mean a whole lot to the tawny cats smiling at them from the dark shadows beneath the trees.

She walked on.

Seeing the women started Patty thinking. The Fringe had become a destination, drawing people from New York, Philly, and elsewhere. It was a place you wanted to find, because art and music and acceptance were exploding there. But Boundary Street? No. People who came to Boundary Street seldom understood how they got there. It was not even the real name of the street, though it's what everyone called it. Somebody—an artist, maybe, or a drunk—made up a bunch of street signs and glued them over the official ones. The department of streets kept taking them down, but they were always back up a day or so later. After a while, the town stopped trying.

Pine Deep didn't try to do much else down there, either. Took so long to get the gutters clean that people used persistent items of trash as meeting points. The rain washed some of it away, but even Mother Nature wasn't trying all that hard.

Patty Cakes was chewing on all of that as she aimed herself in the direction of the package store. Morty's Cold Beer. The wind drove the rain at her like needles, opening raw spots on her cheeks and nose. It made her eyes hurt. On nights like this the wind was hungry for blood.

She walked along, listening to the clicking of her heels in the hope that the beat would conjure a song in her head. Music was everything to her. She had an iPad crammed with songs, and if that ever failed her it was linked to Pandora, Amazon Prime, Sirius, and Spotify. There wasn't enough music in the world for Patty. Music kept the doors locked and shades drawn; it kept the monsters in their closets.

There were plenty of monsters. Always monsters.

Beer helped, too.

The window was crammed with beer signs and they painted the wet pavement in Christmas colors. Corona blue and Budweiser red, Stella orange and Heineken green. Patty paused outside, looking up and down the street. To the left of Morty's were three clubs in a row. The Bonesman's Blues, named after a local ghost legend. Hopalong, which was a gay cowboy place. And the lesbian bar, Tank Girl. To the right was a piercing place, a queer bookstore, and the inevitable Starbucks. Nondescript EDM pulsed out through the open club doors and was crushed by thunder and rain.

Closer to this end of the block was a storefront that always seemed to be rented out for some kind of twelve-step. Everyone she could see through the window looked bent over. Like people at a kid's funeral. She couldn't tell if they were crying or reading or praying. She turned away. Whatever was going on over there hurt to look at.

"Beer," she said to the night.

The neon signs glowed with happy colors. *It's safe in here,* they seemed to say.

So she went in.

INTERLUDE TWO	THE LORD OF THE FLIES

It was so sad that Theresa Minor died.

Gracie Thompson said it to everyone she knew, because she was the kind of person who said those things. The neighbors on the block, all of whom liked Gracie, nodded and murmured meaningless things. They said they were sorry for her loss. Much less so for Theresa, who few of them liked and no one respected.

Very few of them ever mentioned the Boy.

Owen.

They all knew his name, but they mostly called him "the Boy."

Did you hear about the Howard's cat? It went missing, just like the Bucker's dog. I heard the Boy was hanging around the yard.

Someone said the Boy was looking in Janie Cooper's window. Stan Simmons saw him all hunkered down on a limb of that old olive tree outside her room, and her not even thirteen.

The fire inspector's been asking about the old Anderson place. Poor Lyddie burned to death—God bless her soul. She used to have the Boy mow her lawn but fired him when he stole some stuff off the clothesline. Bras and underpants and stuff. Then the house burns down? You can't tell me there's no connection.

And on and on.

The Boy.

Now he sat alone in the middle of the front row of the Lensky Funeral Home's smaller viewing room. Sitting there like a lump. Pale and blotchy. Smelling of things no one wanted to put a name to. Didn't matter that his clothes were clean and he looked like he'd washed. The smell was always there. An earthy, wormy thing.

No one sat near him. Not for four rows behind him. And no one on the front two rows on the other side of the aisle. They didn't want to meet his eye, even if they weren't aware of that need.

He sat there, fists clutching the crotch of his jeans, flexing and clutching his erect penis. That hardness wasn't obvious, but the minister saw the hand motion. He tried not to look at those hands, but did anyway. Whatever was happening there was easier to see than looking at Owen's face. At those eyes.

At that knowing little smile.

17

Mike Sweeney sat in his cruiser, staring out the window at the dead cow. The rain was so dense it nearly obscured the animal, but Mike could just make out its shape there in the tall grass. The sight of it bothered him more than it should. It felt ominous in some undefined way. Mike scowled through the windshield at it.

No one could ever accuse him of being overly cheerful. Not at the best of times. The police chief, Malcolm Crow, made a lot of jokes about Mike being an Olympic-level brooder.

"Mike can brood the ass off a thing," Crow would say.

That was true enough. Life wasn't a happy bunch of puppies to Mike. Life had started with an abusive and violent stepfather and then slid downward from there. Considering everything that had happened to him over the years, and what was going on inside of him, brooding seemed reasonable. Even imperative.

Looking at the dead cow was not what depressed him. It wasn't even the cold rainwater that had wormed its way into his boxers and puddled in his shoes.

The story the Duncans had told bothered him.

The tattoo.

Corinne Duncan was so unwaveringly certain that her husband had, for some reason, gotten the ink removed.

The husband, Andrew, was equally sure that he never had a tattoo. Mike was good at reading people, and when that man insisted that his wife never had cancer, and he had certainly never gotten a pink ribbon tattoo . . . there was no lie in his voice. Or his eyes.

The scar, if it was a scar, looked old. Years old.

"What the hell?" he asked the dead cow.

The cow, being both dead and a cow, said nothing.

His windshield wipers slashed back and forth and the rain fell.

"What the hell," Mike murmured again.

And again.

18

Patty bought a case of beer and lugged it home. She was tiny but a lot stronger than she looked. Even so, her muscles ached by the time she unlocked the door and staggered out of the storm.

The iPad was singing to her when she came in, though Patty didn't remember turning it on before she left. Didn't matter. It was good stuff, and with all those singers it meant that she didn't have to drink alone. The beer was cold and the first sip was better than any kiss she'd ever had. Adele was singing "Set Fire to the Rain," which always killed her.

Patty raised her bottle to the storm outside. "You can kiss my ass."

And sang along with the brokenhearted lyrics.

As she lowered the bottle, Patty saw the tattoo on the back of her left hand. Where he'd touched her. The spot she had rubbed and rubbed and rubbed with her thumb until it was so red the image looked faded. The image—the tattoo—which she'd inked there herself years ago in a conspicuous spot so she could not get through a day, not an hour, without catching a glimpse.

Of her.

Of Tuyet.

Sometimes seeing the sweet little face made her smile.

Sometimes it drove a spike of ice into her heart.

Now . . . ?

She raised the bottle and took a very long pull.

"Mommy loves you," she said softly.

19

Nobody in Pine Deep knew his name.

He couldn't really remember it, either. Doug, maybe. Dave? Don? He wasn't sure. Nor was he sure about the last name. Could be Anderson or was that the last name of the last guy to give him a ride? Was he also the Dave or Doug or Don?

Yeah. Maybe. It was all a gray jumble.

Which meant the man on the Crestville Bridge wasn't sure of either first or last name.

The car—was the driver Don Anderson?—had dropped him by the entrance to the bridge.

"You're sure this is where you want to get out?" asked the driver. Don or Dave or maybe Denny. "I can take you into Doylestown. It's no problem."

The fellow had a kind face. Lots of lines and creases as if he'd been there and back. The nameless man thought it was the face of someone who might have understood. Only if there were some way to tell him, though. Some way to say it.

"I'm good here," he said, opening the door.

The driver looked at him for a long three count. "You need a couple bucks? Get yourself a hot meal?"

"Really, I'm good."

They looked at each other, and the man thought the driver might have understood what was happening. Like the guy could read the conversation. There was a lot of sadness in his eyes. He kept starting to say something, but didn't have the words. That made sense to the nameless man. He couldn't put it into words, either. Not now, and not the dozen times he'd tried to spill it out before. To other drivers. To that old black guy who ran the PTSD circle group who'd bought him a plate of eggs and sausage the other day. Like remembering his own name, there didn't seem to be enough words left in his head to make sense of it.

So, he got out and stood in the autumn weeds and watched the car go over the bridge and out of sight. Curtains of rain closed over it and the car was gone as if it never really existed. Like so many things.

Like all the memories.

God, the memories.

He walked out onto the bridge. Not too far. Not over the water.

He stepped over the rail and ducked under the supports. The storm was breathing on him. Whispering in a language he had never understood before now.

The nameless man turned and leaned his forehead against the cold metal, feeling the sharp edges where thick paint had peeled back.

"Please," he murmured. Not to the storm. No. The storm was not his friend.

Please.

All he wanted, all he was, all he had ever been was knotted up in that single word.

Please.

If he could only have one memory back, that would be an anchor that held him to the world. Any memory of something that mattered, something that defined him. Even a small thing.

Anything.

All that was left was the sure and certain knowledge that those memories were gone. Not merely gone . . . that they had been stolen. He knew that for sure. The truth of it seemed to leer at him from the shadows of his mind. He could see it. A pallid face with empty eyes and a laugh that sounded like the buzzing of insect wings. Polluted and awful.

Stolen.

Gone forever.

Please.

The rain drilled holes in him. The wind laughed at him. The storm drew back its fist. The man cringed, cowered, nearly hugged the strut. *Please.* Just one memory that mattered.

The wind and the storm and the day and the coming night spoke a single word in response to his.

No.

Tears boiled out, cold on his cheeks because he could no longer stoke the fires of anger, of fury, of outrage. Of loss. When he leaned into his head and looked down into the bottom of the box where everything he ever was and had ever done was stored, there wasn't even hope left. There was nothing.

"Please," he said again, meaning something else now as he leaned back.

And back.

Until gravity took him in her arms.

The rocks below were a kindness.

20

It rained for hours and hours. It rained as if the storm owned the world.

"Screw this," said Monk, and turned the car off except for the hazard lights. Patty still wasn't answering the phone. She must have called it a night and gone to bed early. Couldn't be many customers out on a night like this. Patty took the occasional pill, or smoked a lot of weed. Anything to hush the voices in her head. Monk could relate. So, maybe he should just let her sleep.

If the storm wasn't so bad he would just head over to his own new place. Sack out, unpack in the morning after he checked on Patty.

Through the slanting rain he saw the ranks of birds and had to spend some time thinking about that. He was familiar with them, or something like them. There had been a thing back in New York where black birds—nightbirds—played a part. Those fuckers had been evil as shit and Monk felt his heart racing as he struggled to get a read on the ones here. He was pretty good at reading people, always had been. Useful in his trade. If you can't read people then you're no damn good as either a PI or a skip-tracer, and he was good at both.

How do you read the black-within-black eyes of birds, though? Especially seeing them through a downpour and at a distance.

And yet . . .

There was something he could feel. Actually, quite a few things, most of them not so good. He was worried about Patty. He didn't dig the vibe of this town one little bit—though he had to admit the town's reputation was probably coloring that. He didn't like the storm at all. It felt wrong in some unspecific way.

The birds, though. When he looked at them he didn't get the feeling he usually got when there was maybe someone out in the tall grass, watching him through a sniper scope, adjusting for windage and elevation. An itchy spot between his shoulder blades. None of that.

The birds did not feel like a threat. If anything they felt like they were on his side. But that thought itself was weird, and Monk didn't have a mental hook to hang it on. So he left it for now. His doors were locked and the windows up.

"I'm so goddamn tired," he told the storm.

It rumbled in reply, sounding like someone dropping fifty bowling balls. Monk pulled his leather jacket out of the backseat, put it on, zipped it to his chin, stuck his hands in his pockets, and went to sleep. Dreams were waiting and they took him with cold, pale fingers and dragged him under.

The nightbirds stood vigil around him.

INTERLUDE THREE   **THE LORD OF THE FLIES**

"When you say that you can't remember your mother, do you mean just her face?"

Owen Minor shook his head, annoyed because this was the fifth or sixth different way the therapist asked the same question. The woman simply could not get the idea straight.

"No," he said with the kind of false patience foster kids learn for all such sessions. The key was always to walk the line between calm self-assurance and acceptable emotionality. Never too cold, never too enthusiastic. Not too much grief, or love, or anger, or anything. The key was to be, or at least appear to be, balanced. In control. Safe. "No, it's just that I don't remember much about her at all."

The therapist, Mrs. Green, was a goat-faced forty-something with too much nose, not enough chin, and ears that stuck out like open car doors. Her face might have been comical if she had a shred of personality. Mrs. Green glanced at his file.

"She passed away three years ago?"

"Yeah," he said and then corrected it. "Yes, ma'am."

"And you were nine?"

"Yes, ma'am."

Mrs. Greene nodded. "Do you have photos of her?"

"Sure," said Owen. "I have a bunch of them."

"Then how can you not remember what she looked like?"

Owen clenched his fists in his lap, careful that his crossed leg hid them. He wanted to punch her, to slap her. Instead he took a breath, adjusted his tone, and said, "I know what she looked like. But I can't remember her."

"What about her can't you—?"

"Everything," said Owen. "I know I had a mother. I know I lived with her until she died. I know there was a funeral and all. I know what I should know, but I don't remember her. I remember where I grew up—the house, my bedroom, the living room furniture, the color of the kitchen walls. I can remember going to school. I remember my teachers. I can remember the lady who lived next door—Gracie Thompson. But I don't remember my mother being any part of all that." He paused, fishing for what he thought she would want to hear. "I want to remember her. Why can't I?"

Owen was happy with the amount of emotion he put into his voice. He watched her eyes and saw when her professional detachment turned to compassion. That would influence her report for the foster agency.

He was twelve but he understood how the whole thing worked.

He was not particularly upset at the loss of all memories associated with his mother. They had been fading since she died, and from what he read in his diary, she'd been a slut, a drunk, and a shit. It was better not to have to lug around any memories that related to the stuff in that journal. The beatings. The nights he had to spend in the closet because of something he did that she didn't like. Or when she made him sit in the cold parked car while she had a guy over. Sometimes she gave him a blanket and a box of Trix to munch on, mostly she forgot to even bother. He remembered sitting in the car, but he didn't remember her. Not even a moment of her. Nothing.

Owen sat and listened as the therapist explained traumatic memory loss, and variations on the stages of grief, and all of the other stuff she'd been trained to say. He'd read up on what to expect from people like her. He was prepared and had rehearsed what to say and how to inflect it.

She talked.

He sat.

She tried to reach him.

And he let her think she had.

The only hard part was trying not to smile.

21

Orson Hardihey sat in his car and did not even hear the rain.

He should have, because it hammered down furiously on the metal roof above him and the windshield through which he stared. Should have. Did not.

He sat there, hands on the curve of the steering wheel, looking at the fly crawling across his knuckles. It was fat and gleamed with an oily opalescence. Tiny legs picking their way delicately over his calloused knuckles. Multifaceted eyes somehow mirrored, showing hundreds of different miniature versions of Orson's face. That's how Orson saw it anyway. Hundreds of reflections, and in each one his own mouth smiled at him. Smiled with his own mouth but not with his own smile.

The smile was oily and sickly and wrong.

The fly crawled, making sure never to turn its eyes and those smiling mouths away.

Orson looked at the house at the end of the driveway. His headlights only reached as far as the porch steps, but that was enough. He could see the house. The locked door. The drawn shades against which shadows moved like images from some antique camera obscura. A woman shape. Children shapes. Cavorting, distorted by angle and distance and the vagaries of flickering light from a fireplace. Goblin shapes. Orson saw them and hated them and loved them and wanted them and despised them.

He looked at the fly and saw all of his faces looking back.

"Yes," he said as if in answer. "Yes, of course I will."

Orson got out of the car. No umbrella, no hat, not even a collar turned up against the wind. He walked to the trunk, opened it, removed the brand-new Remington 20-gauge and the box of buckshot. The gun had a four-shot capacity. Orson didn't think he'd need more than that, but stuffed his pockets with more shells.

He stood for a moment looking at the weapon. A Model 870, with a receiver machined from a solid billet of steel, with a custom-quality satin finish on both stock and fore-end and walnut woodwork. The receiver and barrel were richly blued and highly polished. The rain plopped on the gun, beaded, and rolled off.

"Nice," said Orson aloud.

Before he racked the slide he watched the fly crawl down from his knuckle and flatten out against the back of his hand. It flattened and flattened and flattened until it was thinner than a dime, thinner than a postage stamp, and then no thickness at all. It was part of him. A tattoo of a fly on the back of his hand. The eyes, though, they were still mirrors.

"Nice," he said again.

He did not bother to close the trunk. Nor had he turned off the engine or closed the driver's door. None of that mattered. Orson slogged through the mud toward the house, climbed the steps, paused to wipe his feet, and then knocked on the door.

When it was opened an inch, he saw an inquiring blue eye. A voice asked something, but Orson could not really hear her, or understand. That part of Orson was going away. Nearly gone.

He raised the barrel very quickly—a round black eye to stare into that blue eye—and then he fired.

There were screams from inside he did not hear. There were voices begging, but he couldn't hear those, either. The shotgun boomed and boomed and boomed. A silence while he reloaded, and then a last boom.

The door stood open. The lights stayed on. The rain fell.

Everything else was utterly still.

22

Monk dreamed himself into hell.

There were a lot of nights like that.

Iraq had cooled off for months and there was a lot of talk about the United States pulling its troops out.

Talk. There was always a lot of that kind of talk. Mostly it was either someone on a campaign trail, some pundit misreading the political moment, or some handwaving to distract the public eye from something else no one wanted seen.

That was Monk's world, once upon a time.

Back then, of course, Monk wasn't Monk. Not yet. He was just Gerry, or Big Ger. Twenty-four years old. One of the youngest ever to join Delta Force, and they kept sending him to combat hot zones, mostly in the Middle East. Pulling triggers and cutting throats for Uncle Sam. When he walked away from that, he got picked up as a PMC-private military contractor. Running ops in Iraq, Syria, and Afghanistan, and some off-the-books gigs in Syria, Yemen, and Iran. Small jobs, the kind that don't make headlines in any way that reveal what really happened.

Monk was part of a cleanup crew. Go in, eliminate a target, and wipe out all traces. Collateral damage was part of that.

He dreamed about the night before he left.

The op looked simple. Go into a small village and take out a team manufacturing a more sophisticated version of roadside IEDs. This new design was almost certainly Russian, though no one was ever going to be able to prove it. No materials traceable back to Russia were ever found. Instead, local teams used their own metals, plastics, ceramics, and explosives based on designs emailed to them from dummy accounts. All instructions were in Pashto, even down to idiomatic phrasing. These new explosives were made to look improvised but were actually quite sophisticated—a lethal subtlety—and they were racking up more kills than should be possible during a troop drawdown.

Monk's team had a really good sniper and spotter on overwatch, nestled into a weedy cleft in the hills. The rest of the ten-man team went in by squads, moving like ghosts through the darkened streets, night-vision goggles turning the village into a funhouse of green and gray and black. The intel was that all civilians had been moved out more than a week ago, and that everyone here was a tango. A terrorist.

Although that made the job more dangerous, it simplified the math. No friendlies. No worries about collateral damage.

They deployed from their vehicles more than a kilometer out and then proceeded toward the objective—a large house off the town square—making maximum use of cover, following a route they'd memorized from the briefing. None of them were virgins about gigs like this. The entire team had done jobs exactly like this one eight times before. Not a single injury sustained and a body count of hostiles that kept the CIA and the officers higher up the food chain very happy.

The spotter's voice came over the team channel and the lieutenant raised a fist. They all stopped and sank to one knee in
banks of shadows thrown down by town walls, weapons tucked
into their shoulders, fingers laid along trigger guards, eyes
watching.

"Seeing two armed sentries on the top of the target building
on the southeast corner of the square. Rifles slung."

"Take them," ordered the lieutenant.

Monk could not see the sentries from where he crouched behind a withered bush, nor did he hear the shots, muffled as they
were by sound suppressors. But the spotter said, "Clear."

And they moved on, entering the square and running along
the sides, still clinging to the cover of the buildings. There were
only a few small lights on inside the building, though they were
likely left on all night. With the sentries on the roof, the people
inside probably thought they were safe.

In some cases a target like this would simply be erased by a
drone strike, but the orders were to bring back laptops, papers,
cell phones, and at least one person with a pulse who might be
induced to answer questions. Once the entire hostile presence
was accounted for and eliminated, helos would come in for ex-
traction. Charges would be remote detonated and good luck to
whoever had to sift through the ashes to determine what the
hell happened.

That was the plan.

Even while he slept Monk remembered that old phrase.

Man plans and God laughs.

Or maybe it was the Devil who laughed at what happened
that night. The last night he had been truly Gerald Addison.
The night before he began the journey to become who—and
what—he was.

Monk, dreaming, twisted and writhed as memories tore at him.

The nightbirds on the telephone wires twitched at the sound of gunfire and explosions. And the awful screams from long ago and far away . . .

THE LORD OF THE FLIES

Owen Minor lay in a ball in the upper corner of his bed, which he'd pushed against the walls. He loved the security of that nook. There were a dozen pillows of various firmness, and big blankets. The TV was on, but he wasn't watching it; he merely liked the noise and motion on the big flat-screen. Sometimes he had music playing on his iPad in the other room, and even the TV in the living room. He did not like silence. It scared him. Silence was when you thought about things, about people and places. About memories. And he had very few of those left. Already everything before his mother died was gone. Completely. Photos didn't trigger even so much as a flicker or a shadow on the walls of his mind.

He had some school memories left, but only a fraction of what he knew he should remember. Pieces of those days seemed to peel like paint and flake off, falling away to leave bare spots in his life. There was a girl he liked once, a little redhead in the seventh grade. He searched for her on Facebook and found her page to see how she grew up. Very cute. Biggest green eyes. Owen saved some images from her photos section and printed three of them out. They were on his corkboard in the basement, but early last week he lost every memory of her that he ever had. All of it . . . just gone.

He wondered what would happen when all of his memories were gone. Would he simply go away, too? Would he fade like a mist and simply not be there anymore. There, or anywhere?

Would it hurt?

Would it be like falling asleep?

Would he vanish from other people's memories?

Or would he exist only in the eternal now, like a monk or a lama?

Owen lay curled like a grub in his bed and wondered what would happen when his mind was emptied of everything.

23

Dianna stood outside the tattoo shop, rain hammering down on her umbrella. The lights were on, including the WALK RIGHT IN sign in neon, but the door was locked. No little sign with a clock saying BE RIGHT BACK. If Patty was planning to close early, she could have texted.

"Well," she said, "damn."

She was feeling tired, a little sick, and glad to be away from the shop. After that first client, the day had canted sideways and fallen off the rails. No psychic was right all the time—if they were, all they'd do would be to play the damn lottery—but sensitives like Dianna were right more than they were not. Especially with her regulars. Not today, though. She'd been so completely off that she'd had to fake her way through readings, relying on the face value of the tarot cards, rather than interpreting their meaning. Most of the newbie customers couldn't tell the difference, though she doubted they'd come back because the readings had had all the energy of a dead battery. The regulars, though, had given her odd looks. They knew she was off. It felt like she was cheating them, and some of them had that awareness in their eyes. No one said anything, but they knew.

They knew.

Maybe Patty would cheer her up. She was a new friend, but

Dianna felt like she'd known the tattoo artist forever. Not her type in a romantic way—skinny to the point of looking emaciated—but kindred. They both had baggage and even though that was never the topic of their conversations, it was there. To a degree that was a comfort. Fellow travelers through the storm lands.

Plus, Patty was a real artist. Dianna had several tattoos, but until she'd met Patty Cakes, the ink was just symbolic. Phases of the moon, an LGBTQ rainbow. That sort of thing. She'd come into the shop the day it opened, stopping by on a whim, or maybe pulled there. Guided there. The small Vietnamese woman had been cleaning her equipment and simply stopped, turning to look up as if Dianna had called her name. Then Patty walked over to her and held out a hand. Not to shake, but palm up, nodding toward Dianna's left arm. Without even a flicker of confusion Dianna placed her forearm on the upraised palm. There was no tattoo there, but it was where Dianna wanted one.

Patty placed her other hand over the unmarked skin and then began rubbing it very gently. It was in no way sexual. It was so much like the way Dianna held crystals or an unshuffled deck of cards. Reading potential. Letting the moment speak to her.

"The moon," said Patty.

"I have the . . ." began Dianna, but trailed off, embarrassed because she'd spoken before listening to her heart. There was even a flicker of disappointment in the artist's eyes. There and gone.

Patty let her arm go. "Show me the one you have."

Dianna hesitated, momentarily losing her grip on her confidence. She glanced at the big picture window. Patty nodded, walked over and lowered a privacy shade, then turned, hands clasped lightly.

"Show me."

Dianna nodded. She felt her throat and cheeks burning a little, which was odd. She was never embarrassed. Not anymore, and not in this town. But she felt oddly naked. Exposed. Her fingers moved to the top button of her blouse, trembled, then Dianna took a breath and undid the buttons. All of them. She slipped out of her blouse and turned to show her spine. She reached back to unclasp her bra, but Patty made a small dismissive sound.

The tattoo of the phases of the moon ran from midback to a few inches below the nape of her neck. With anything more than a tank top it was hidden. The work was good and the job had been very expensive.

"Brooklyn Jack?" asked Patty.

"Yes, how did—?"

"It's good work," said Patty, "but it's a man's art. Jack tries, but he isn't . . ." She let the rest hang, then after a moment added, "And it's in the wrong place. Not the back for the moon. Never there. It should be on your arm. Left arm. Heartline."

"Yes," said Dianna.

"Put your blouse on."

Dianna picked it up from the chair where she'd dropped it. She buttoned it quickly.

"It's not the phases," said Patty. "You know that, right?"

Dianna nodded. "I know it now. Didn't then."

"Phases are transition. You're not becoming something. You're there. You're not bi, you're pure."

Pure. The word was so beautiful. Once, long ago, her mother accused her of not being pure because Dianna liked girls. That was high school. Later, after a disaster of a marriage, Mom had told her she was impure because she'd left her husband for a woman. That was six years ago, when Dianna had realized she wasn't bisexual but a lesbian going through the motions of being bi in order to try and fit in and make an ill-considered marriage work.

"Pure," said Patty again, nodding as if in agreement with her own judgment.

Dianna held out her arm and they both looked at the pale skin.

"What do you think?" she asked. "There are other symbols . . ."

Patty made that face. "Are you campaigning?"

"What?"

"Are you looking for a slogan? 'Come join the lesbian army'?"

Dianna laughed. "No."

"No," agreed Patty. "You're not recruiting and you're not uncertain anymore, are you?"

No," said Dianna, "I'm really not."

"Right."

"So . . . ?"

Patty held out her left hand, palm down, to show the exquisite tattoo on the back of it. It was of a lovely little girl with huge eyes and a smile that could melt all the ice in the world. But when Dianna glanced at the artist's eyes, she saw a sadness so deep that it clawed a hole all the way down to the blackest darkness. Dianna did not have to ask. She did not need the details. Her sensitivity clicked on like a switch had been thrown and she felt the pain, heard the echo of screams—the child's and the mother's, but not screamed at the same time. Separated by a wall of horror that was too high for anyone to climb. In that instant Dianna knew that this little girl was dead, and that she had died apart from her mother; and that she had died in the most ugly way possible.

Just as she knew it was her mother who had, through a process of heartbreak, need, and the deepest artistry, inked that face on the back of a hand that could never touch the lost girl.

Dianna felt her heart break and tears burned in her eyes. But Patty said, "No."

Patty took the hem of her T-shirt and pulled it up to just below her chin. Around her neck she wore a small glass vial filled with a pinkish liquid. Her breasts were tiny, the nipples dark. But between the areoles was a flower Dianna recognized—a white climbing rose. Or a Cherokee rose, as it was known in the States, whose history was forever tied to the Trail of Tears, the forced and brutal migration to a reservation in Oklahoma. The delicate petals were believed to represent the tears the women had shed along the way. But Dianna knew that it was an invasive species, brought to the United States by travelers from China and Vietnam.

The flowers on Patty told their own story. The ones closest to the nipples were withered and crumbling as if they, like the milk that once fed the little girl, had dried up never to blossom again. But as the other flowers got nearer to the small woman's heart they burst with color and detail and looked so real that Dianna could almost smell their fragrance. She slowly raised her eyes as Patty let the shirt fall. They stared at each other for a long time. Some conversations didn't need words.

Dianna held out her arm again, and Patty smiled.

The artist turned off the OPEN neon, locked the door, and began. It took hours. They talked some, but not of the tattoo. They talked about the town of Pine Deep, about its energies. The ley lines that ran like streams of power—light and dark—along irregular paths through every part of the town, the farms, and the state forest. They talked of the new streets that had been built, and which had come to form the Fringe. Boundary Street, which ran like the main street of the growing community. Mercy Street, where the best music could be found. Autumn Lane, with all of its specialty shops. Coyote Court, where the children played, with different members of the community volunteering to watch them, including one of the locals—the big, red-haired cop named Mike. He wasn't inked or pierced, was a straight white male, didn't even drink. But he wasn't a Norm. He was accepted there more than in the town he grew up in.

They talked about seeing and knowing. About the burden of understanding.

There were tears and laughter, and a few pauses to hug or hold hands.

It took four hours for Patty to finish, and when she was done, they both wept.

A green vine, delicate with the sweetness of early spring, seemed to sprout from a blue vein near Dianna's wrist. It curled and coiled up Dianna's forearm, sprouting roses in dozens of shades, as if all of the colors of nature were gathered there, part of that single vine. Each flower was larger and more vibrant than the last, and also subtly different—more realistic, more defined—until a final rose, whose lush petals brushed against the tender inside of her elbow. This final rose was ripe and full, with a red so deep that it was black in places, and so luscious that it seemed to rise from her skin and perfume the air, insisting on its own immutable reality. Not a flower in transition, but one that was so clearly itself that seeing it was a celebration of joy.

They both stared at the tattoo, smiling, sobbing, as tears ran down their faces. Dianna kissed Patty on both cheeks and the lips. A sisters' kiss, but the kind of kiss only real sisters could ever hope to understand.

That had been how Dianna met Patty a couple of months ago.

Now she stood outside, rain hammering on her umbrella, staring in through the glass at an empty room.

She wore a long gray trench coat over her clothes, a burgundy scarf wound around her throat, and gloves that matched the scarf. But she was cold, and only some of that was because of the rain and wind. She was angry and confused and scared. Her left arm hurt.

She wanted to show the tattoo to Patty, to get some answers. Maybe to yell at the woman. Her heart wanted to break, too, because that beautiful tattoo had lost its luster. The vibrant colors were washed out, and that big, beautiful rose now looked like it was withering. What the hell? What the actual fuck?

She pounded on the door.

Nothing.

She pulled her cell and called the store, got nothing. Texted Patty. Same result.

"Damn, damn, damn," she said. The tattoo throbbed very faintly. And not in a good way. After five furious minutes she turned away and walked through dirty puddles to her car.

Dianna did not see the flies clustered around the light under the small awning above the parlor door.

They, however, saw her.

24

A fly crawled on the glass outside of Patty's bedroom. It was a fat blowfly speckled with green and purple, and not the prettier shades. There was a soiled quality to it. A garbage heap stain on the wings and too much red in the multifaceted eyes. It was the kind of fly that would look more at home crawling over the face of a dead animal on the side of the road.

The insect scuttled between the lines of rain that ran crookedly down the pane.

It had watched the woman inside open her first bottle of beer.

Her second. Her eighth. It watched her throat bob as she swallowed, swallowed, swallowed. It watched as she stared at the dead face inked on her hand.

It watched her punch the wall, punch her own thighs, punch her face.

The fly watched her all through the storm.

25

Eileen Sandoval worked four days a week in the Pumpkin Patch, a quilting supply and fabric store on the corner of Main and Whippoorwill. She was eleven days shy of her fifty-third birthday, and all but three of those years had been spent in Pine Deep. She'd moved to Philadelphia for three years to attend the Tyler School of Art and Architecture, but eventually had to accept that her dream of being a high fashion designer was bigger than the talent she actually possessed. It was a hard thing to know about herself, but in time she made peace with it.

Since then she worked at the Patch, as everyone called it, Wednesday through Saturday, and had three days off to look after her mother. During those days her sister, Maria, was able to have a bit of a break. Mother was a handful. Alzheimer's was a monster of a disease, and things had progressed to stage-five severe decline. Because their mother was so physically fit, the math was skewed for how long she would live. The sisters never voiced their shared feeling that death would be a mercy, but it was always in the air between them. They'd been to the support groups, watched the videos, read the website information. There was no happy ending and death was the closest thing to mercy they could expect.

The four days at the Patch were merciful in their way, too. The place was fairly busy, especially once the temperature began to drop. Rain also increased business because the knitting and quilting circle ladies came in nearly every day for the supplies they'd need on cold and wet autumn nights. And there was a back room for small groups and classes, some of which Eileen taught.

Tonight was slow, though. The shoppers were all gone and the rain was just plain awful. Eileen stood looking out through the glass front door, her cardigan pulled tight around her and the heat turned up, but she couldn't shake the chill. Everything outside looked like a bad impressionist painting—smears of car and traffic lights, indistinct shapes of things that moved in the darkness.

A buzzing sound made her turn and when she did it was with sharp irritation. That damn fly was back.

Eileen hustled over to the counter and snatched the flyswatter from the hook. Three times today she'd seen the little beast and gone hunting with the swatter, and three times the fly had found some place to hide. Waiting for her to forget about it before it snuck out and began buzzing its little wings.

Eileen hated flies. Not as much as spiders, but flies were high on her list. She'd pick up a praying mantis or let a ladybug crawl onto her hand to take it outside. Lightning bugs, too. And grasshoppers or crickets could share the store or her home because they were good luck. Spiders . . . ? No. They were dead as soon as she could whack them with a shoe, a rolled-up catalog, or the swatter. Flies, ditto.

Ugly, dirty, nasty little bastards.

Buzz.

Eileen whirled, raising her weapon, as ready to strike as any knight facing a dragon.

But the fly was nowhere in sight.

She froze there, poised, watching and alert.

Nothing.

Not even a buzz.

Eileen did not even feel the fly land on the back of her neck. She didn't feel it crawl under the collar of her blouse, or wriggle down along the line of her spine. None of that registered.

Nothing, in fact, registered.

She was not at all aware of standing in the store with the fly-swatter for nearly an hour.

She was only marginally aware of walking out, locking the door behind her, getting in her little Honda, and driving home. Those things were so routine her body did most of the work, requiring very little from her mind.

Parking outside the house, unlocking the front door, and going inside were even easier.

There were some flickers in her mind after that. Vagueness of movement. Of selecting the right knife. Of choosing the angle of thrust. Of wiping blood spatter from her eyes so she could see where to stab again. Marie's screams did not register, though. Nor did the vacant murmurings of their mother as Eileen pulled back the blankets and raised the blade.

None of that was in her mind. None of it was real.

One item did manage to lodge in her awareness. As the blade fell over and over and over again, she saw the fly. Not a real fly, of course. An artistic one. Tattooed with great skill on the soft webbing between the index finger and the thumb. Eileen had no memory of actually getting that tattoo. She had no interest in such things. It was there now, though.

Within seconds even that thought was gone because the fly tattoo was soon painted over with an even coating of rich, dark red.

A car idled down the street from the Sandoval house. Windows smoked to a vague nothing, lights off. The passenger inside was completely invisible.

The only sounds were his grunts and gasps as his hand worked and worked and worked. But the rain muffled all of that and no one alive knew he was there.

26

Staff Sergeant Gerald Addison and his Delta team walked through hell in Monk's dream.

In some firefights everything was so personal, so condensed to what was happening in a soldier's immediate vicinity, that there wasn't even the possibility of anything else. Bullets punching through the vain armor of clothes and deep into flesh, splashing life onto the walls. A grenade arcing through the air and the words *Frag out!* echoing through the halls of a shocked mind. The flex of a finger on a trigger, and that action defining all conscious control, except when the magazine ran dry and hands performed the swapping-out ritual without needing to be told. Shell casings, looking shiny and delicate, popping against doorframes and tinkling on the tiled floors. Faces yelling and then breaking apart as the gunfire dehumanized them into red nothing. Smoke and brick dust, red jewels floating through the air, and the screams.

Monk—the man who was almost Monk—kicked a door in and went inside firing. That was the drill, those were the orders. No friendlies. A target-rich environment and everyone a bad guy. His team were practiced killers, and the men here in this little town were the definition of evil. The kind who put IEDs even on roads used by civilians. The kind who strapped suicide vests to little kids. The kind who should have had bull's-eyes tattooed on their foreheads like the mark of Cain. Unclean.

The door tore free from its hinges and Monk followed the

muzzle flashes of his own rifle as he stormed inside. With each trigger pull he saw his immediate world in freeze-frame images. The man with the black beard and head scarf kicking free of his blanket, reaching beneath his cot for his AK-47. Too late. A heartbeat too late as Monk's bullets punched through his sternum. The dying man's scream buried beneath the shouts and gunfire. Movement in another corner of the room. Monk turning, firing. Chasing any shape and defining that form in the flame of the next shots. Seeing bodies twist and fall, arms flung up as if in prayer or supplication, loose clothing billowing in that odd slow motion that only ever happened this deep inside the ballet of slaughter. Each face forever burned into Monk's eyes as muzzle flame and bullet defined facial features, personality, expression, everything.

Which is when things began to fall apart.

The shapes rising up around him were not more men with rifles. They should have been. That's all there were supposed to be. Here and everywhere else in this town. Just an ISIS team. Seventeen men, ages seventeen through fifty-four. They had the names, the histories, the lists of soldiers and civilians murdered by these men.

Just men.

Only men.

Except in that little room.

The photo strobe of each gunshot captured the faces of the three women. One of them old. One younger middle-age. One barely an adult.

Torn by bullets.

And the other faces. The smaller ones.

Running backward like hell's clock—teenager, tween, young kid, toddler. Infant.

The bullets found them all.

Gerald Addison's bullets found them all.

It took no time at all to burn through a thirty-round magazine with a rate of fire of 950 rounds per minute. Each round traveling 2,900 feet per second. There was no time for errors and no take-backs.

There was a voice in his head, one of the other shooters, yelling the same thing over and over again. "The intel was wrong. The intel was wrong."

No shit.

That was when Gerry Addison died from his own gunfire. Not from any bullet. His flesh was unscratched the entire time. No. He died anyway.

Monk was still waiting to be born, but that could wait. The small room in the little town was not a place for birth. It was not a place for living. The angels of death had come and they held dominion.

In the now, in his dreams, shivering inside his leather jacket, Monk Addison sweated and writhed and wept and remembered. Joy was such a fleeting thing. Guilt endured.

27

"That was great, babe," Scott said as he rolled off her. He was a little out of breath. Gayle wasn't. "You're the best that's ever been."

Scott was asleep in under two minutes. The sex had lasted only twice that long. From the time he pulled off her panties and pushed up her T-shirt to when he came inside of her . . . four minutes.

Gayle Kosinski lay there in the dark and tried to analyze things. Scott wasn't rough, but he'd definitely forgotten how to be gentle. There was no tenderness anymore because that was part of love and Gayle knew, without doubt, she had moved into the category of "habit."

She lay unmoving, listening to his breathing deepen. She hadn't moved much the whole time. Scott didn't seem to require it. Or even notice. Not anymore, and not since Randy was born. Even after they were able to have sex again, for him it was a thing to do. Not because of any feelings of duty or obligation. He needed to come twice a week, and she was there in the same bed. That was the equation, the habit, the process.

In a bedroom in a comfortably middle-class part of Pine Deep, with all the lights off and the rain coming down so hard it felt like the house was under attack. Her husband's semen seeped sluggishly from her to soak the sheet. She was naked and cold, but did not pull the T-shirt down over her breasts. The underwear she wore to bed was somewhere on the floor. Where he'd simply tossed them. His boxers were, too, but that wasn't the point. Things went where they were thrown because he was in the moment. Once upon a time he would have either set any clothes he removed from her on the chair beside the bed. Or, if he was really in the moment, he would pick them up afterward and present them with a gallant flourish, and some kind of joke. *Your unmentionables, m'lady.*

Back then he'd been playful, generous, inventive, passionate, and, she thought, empathetic. That ship had sailed, hit an iceberg, caught fire, and sunk.

Gayle tried not to think about the four minutes of sex, but couldn't help it. Scott had kissed her, but it was perfunctory, his tongue like a dagger. His hands always went straight to her breasts. She had very large breasts with very sensitive nipples. He liked that. He made a lot of private jokes about how she had the best tits in Pine Deep. Nipples so hard they could cut glass.

And a pussy that was tight even after two kids. That was flattery from Scott. He used to be better at it but all of that was a long time ago. Now it was those kinds of comments and him pawing at her. He'd be hard as soon as he had her shirt up, turned on by her breasts far more than her face. Or by any crucial part of her. And when he removed her panties he was inside of her in seconds. No foreplay worth mentioning. No oral sex. No gentle touches. No pause to see if she was wet enough. Just a need to rut.

Her vagina felt bruised and there would be finger marks on her left breast where he'd clutched as he'd come. No one else would ever see that, though, and the marks always faded quickly enough. Gayle wondered if this qualified as abuse. He never forced her. Never, ever hit her. But he also didn't exactly ask. He even told her he loved her, but it sounded rote. Perfunctory.

But Gayle still felt like a victim.

Maybe not entirely of her husband's indifferent lust, but of her own choices.

There had been a phase of pretending she liked the spontaneity of it, the immediacy. But that had never really been true. Gayle could not remember the last time she'd had an orgasm with him. Three years ago? Four? Her pink plastic pal in the bedside table was a more dutiful and attentive lover.

Veni vidi vici. That was Scott's way.

I came. I saw. I conquered. More or less. *I groped, I fucked, I came, I went to sleep.* That was closer.

Gayle listened to the storm. It was as cold and angry as she felt. As alien as she felt. As lonely as she felt.

The conversation from three hours earlier played over and over in her head.

"You're really serious about wanting to go on a date with

another woman?" Scott had asked for maybe the tenth time since she'd brought it up.

"Yes. If that's okay."

Scott smiled and shook his head. "I never pegged you as a lezzie."

"Honey," Gayle said patiently, "I keep trying to explain this . . . I'm not a lesbian. I think I might be bi."

"But you want to fuck a woman."

"I never said I wanted to have sex with anyone. I want to have a date. If that's okay."

"It's weird."

"Why is that weird? You're the one who started bringing up the threesome thing."

"Oh, come on." He snorted. "That's hardly the same thing."

"I know. This would be a date and not you fucking two women."

"Hey, keep your voice down," he hissed. "The kids . . ."

"The kids are asleep and I wasn't yelling."

Scott poured himself some wine. Did not offer to refill her glass. "I was just joking about a threesome."

"Joking? Oh, come on . . . you know you weren't joking, Scott. Every time Carolyn was around you kept staring at her."

There'd been some back-and-forth with him claiming that he wasn't interested in her. Not per se. He was simply turned on at the thought of being with two women.

The remark was telling. He wanted to be with two women. Not with her and, say, Carolyn. Or not *us* and someone else. With two women. She'd been so tempted to ask how Captain Four Minutes could ever hope to satisfy two women. Gayle wasn't 100 percent sure he understood what a clitoris actually did.

The conversation about another woman had been after the

big July Fourth party they'd thrown. They were party people. It was something they both loved and were good at. It was his friends from the brokerage and her friends from school; Gayle was an administrator there. That night, while they cleaned up, and because Scott seemed to be in a mellow, happy mood, she mentioned that she'd like to see another woman.

Naturally Scott thought they were talking about threesomes again.

Gayle said, "No, honey, weren't you listening? I said I wanted to be alone."

"With some woman?"

"Yes. Maybe."

"With Carolyn?" asked Scott.

"No."

"With who, then? That blonde soccer ref? She's a dyke and—"

"Please don't use that word," said Gayle, realizing that the conversation was already sliding downhill. "And, no, not her. Not anyone in particular. It's just something I . . . it's . . ."

"You're asking permission to go fuck someone and want me to feel good about it?" he demanded, and the moment was lost right there. "That's what you're asking? Permission to fuck some woman?"

"Scott," she said, trying to keep things in neutral, "I keep telling you that this isn't about me wanting sex with some random woman. I don't really know if I want to have sex with any woman. But I need to be true to who I am."

"True to what? That you're a lesbian?"

"That I'm bisexual."

"Which is the same thing."

"No," said Gayle, "it's really not."

"That's bullshit."

"Okay, then how would it be any different if I did what you wanted and had a threesome with Carolyn? Don't tell me you'd expect us to just be all over you. I've seen your Pornhub history, Scott. You know I have. You watch a lot of threesome videos and a lot of girl-on-girl. You can't stand there and tell me the thought of me with another woman doesn't turn you on."

Scott made a noise that was neither a yes nor a no.

"So," persisted Gayle, "if you'd be okay with me and another woman having sex while in bed with you, how does that not bother you, but me being bi does?"

"It would be us with her."

"Again, how is that different?"

"It just is."

After that the conversation slid further downhill into a hushed yelling match. The kids were in bed so the two of them stood inches apart and had a fight with the volume turned down low.

That was the end of it for a while and they settled back into their routine. They watched movies at home with the kids. She worked afternoons and evenings at the high school. He played poker or golf with his buddies. One of the very few activities they did together was go to the gun range, but there they had to wear ear defenders and that killed conversation. If sometimes Gayle saw Scott's face—the version of it he wore when he came—superimposed over the target, then that was probably healthy on some Jungian level.

Then Scott came to her one morning and said that he'd thought about it and realized he was being selfish and said that she could go out on a date. One date, just to see. To get it out of her system.

"You're sure?" asked Gayle, truly startled.

"Yeah, but there's one condition."

Gayle braced herself. "Which is . . . ?"

"If it's just to see how it feels to be on a date with a woman, okay. If something happens and you guys, I don't know—make out—maybe that's okay, too. At least you can't get knocked up. But if you're looking for someone to be in a relationship with, then no way. No fucking way, actually. We're married. We have kids. We have a life."

She was tempted to correct him about the sex thing again, but left it. Things were good for weeks after that. He even encouraged her to open a Tinder account and twice they'd prowled the listings together. The fact that he fondled her breasts and the insides of her thighs while they swiped did not go unnoticed.

Then, in mid-August, Gayle met Carrie. A special ed teacher who also worked at Pine Deep High School. Carrie had the right politics. She also had the right look—dark hair, dark eyes, pale skin, generous curves. Not a stick figure and not brain-dead. Carrie was one of the smartest people Gayle ever met. Sharp, sophisticated, funny, mannered. A divorced mother of a grown son. Forty-three, but looking thirty-five.

It wasn't love at first sight, but it was in that same zip code. And Gayle was pretty sure it went both ways. They talked and talked. They texted. They shared. And they set up a dinner date.

She told Scott.

He smiled, nodded, and then said, "No."

Gayle blinked. "Wait . . . what?"

"No."

"But you said . . ."

"I know what I said, but now I'm saying no. No goddamn way."

"You said I could," Gayle snapped, hurt and confused. "You said you understood. That you wanted me to—"

"Yes, I did," he said, cutting her off, "but since then I thought about it and I don't want some dyke turning you queer. I don't want to raise the kids on my own while you're out there eating pussy every night."

It was then that she realized he'd come home from work drunk. And it was then that she knew he wanted a fight. Needed one because someone at work—probably the brokerage chief financial officer who was, admittedly, a total dick—had messed up his day. He needed to own the moment and so he dug in. *No. Absolutely and forever no.*

Scott wanted a fight and Gayle, unable to help herself, gave him one. It was big and bad and awful. They both knew he was going to end the fight, because he could play the divorce card and Gayle did not want to do that to the kids. She caved in the end, but she made him earn it. By then they were both in tears, but there was no makeup sex, no truce. All there was, was a silence so cold it withered everything. Even the animals hid from them, and the kids—sensing it the way kids do—crept around as if navigating a mine field.

Three days later Scott stormed into the bedroom while she was changing, her iPad held up in righteous triumph. On the screen was a photo of Gayle standing half naked in the bathroom. It was a photo she'd sent to Carrie via Instagram. Very private. She never did find out how Scott learned her password.

That was an even bigger fight. No hushed voices then. The kids woke crying. Gayle slept on the couch for a week. The silences were dreadful.

After that she watched Scott like a hawk. She didn't dare change her passwords because that would be like tossing a bottle of lighter fluid on a fire. The kids drifted through the days like little ghosts, afraid to say anything, unsure of where to look. Gayle sent Carrie a very brief, terse goodbye email. Scott watched her compose it. There was no response.

The drama built, built, and then faded.

Now it was October and they didn't talk about it anymore. By unspoken consent they acted as if nothing at all was wrong. Happy life. Happy home. With four minutes of thrusting twice a week, and self-engineered orgasms for her in the rare quiet times when the house was empty.

Gayle lay there, listening to the rain.

Thinking of Carrie.

But not of Carrie. Not her specifically. Thinking of what might have happened on that date. And on nights since. What would it really be like to be in a woman's arms? To have her arms around someone like her? Would it be strange? Awkward? Silly? Or would it be like finding a way home?

She absolutely did not know.

The rain hammered on the roof and pattered on the window and mocked her pain.

28

Monk, sat on the edge of his bed, bathed in sweat, his face in his hands.

The nightmare ended because all terrors, no matter how intense, can't last. They, like smiles and love and physical pain, can only endure so long.

Time heals all wounds, they say. But that isn't true. Nightmares end but memories endure, trapped in the biochemical envelope of flesh that is the human body.

Everyone who knew him when he'd been Staff Sergeant Gerald Addison was gone. Dead, or moved into different versions of the world that were particular to them and did not involve him at all. That last night, that raid, was not a bonding experience. His team killed nearly three dozen people. Not one of them was the target. Blaming it on bad intelligence did not change a thing. Blood was spilled, lives ended. Men, women, and children. All of them snuffed out in a confusion of gunfire and explosions. How much of it was Monk's to own was something he could never quantify. He did not try to stop his men in time. And he had pulled his own trigger.

He raised his head and looked at his hands. As lightning flashed and flashed outside he saw the bright-red blood dripping from his fingers and palms. He could smell the stink of explosives and that of burning flesh.

"God help me . . ." he whispered.

Around him the ghosts wanted to touch him, but they were spirit and he was flesh. Their faces were on his skin, and that was touch enough.

"I'm sorry," said Monk as once more he buried his face in his hands and wept.

INTERLUDE FIVE   THE LORD OF THE FLIES

The person in the casket was not anyone Owen Minor knew.

Nor had been the body in the last thirty viewings he'd attended. Viewings were rarely listed for family only. And it didn't much matter who it was beginning to rot in the box. Male or female, young or old, any race—it was all the same to him. He wasn't there to see the corpse. No, he liked the crowds. He loved going through the handshake line. Owen knew how to arrange his features to have that meaningless half wince people wore when shaking the hands of the grieving family members.

"So sorry," he would say. Or, "If there's anything I can do . . ."

leaving that hang because there was never anything anyone could do. And if the bereaved asked how he knew the dead one, he would have something cribbed. You could learn a lot from paying attention to the obituaries, doing some searching on social media, and also subscribing to a White Pages app that allowed him to search everything from old phone numbers to former street addresses. If the deceased was young, he could claim to have known them in school. Or if they worked at a big enough company, then he was someone from work. "Yeah, we were always gabbing. You know [fill in the blank] was so funny. Always cracked us up."

Everyone loved to hear that about the person they were burying. They were funny. They were sweet. They were really stand-up.

All lies. Sometimes—often, really—they were a comfort. A tiny Band-Aid on a huge wound. The comments were also generic and mildly vague, which prevented any real conversation. He made sure to position himself about halfway through the line of friendly mourners, picking up cues from what the folks in front of him said so as not to make any unusual or conflicting remark. One very useful thing was to troll the deceased's Facebook or Instagram page for pet pics. It was so easy to claim they'd "often met and chatted" while walking their dogs. He had Photoshopped pictures of himself and the dead dog owner grinning, just in case the conversation went that way. He'd only needed to use it once.

This was his hobby—well, one of them anyway—for years since his mother died. He began doing it while still in foster care and liked it too much to ever stop. He particularly liked funerals for children. If he got tears on his face or the side of his neck, it was an erotic thrill. More than once he had to hurry to the funeral home bathroom to jerk off in a stall.

Then, on a snowy evening at a well-attended viewing in

Denver, something happened that nearly screwed everything up. The dearly departed was a soldier who'd come back from Afghanistan with a headful of ghosts. From what Owen picked up by moving from one conversational group to another, the soldier had been in too many firefights, had lost friends to sniper bullets, IEDs, and other horrors. The man himself had not gotten a scratch, though, and survivor's guilt drove him into a bottle and then to a crack pipe and finally he put a pistol in his mouth. It was a closed casket and Owen stepped into a line of people who came up, placed their hands on the polished hardwood lid, and then shuffled off to shake hands with the family. His cover there was that generic neighbor from the block. The dead man lived and died alone, so there were no conversational bear traps, no way they would know he was lying.

But the older brother of the deceased was a big, gruff-looking guy who had the sleeves of his dress shirt rolled up over Popeye forearms. His skin was covered with sleeves of tattoos ranging from crude and moderately offensive—devil girls with improbable bustlines—to high-end nature art of vines crawling with flies, bees, and a praying mantis that came down all the way to his knuckles.

When it was Owen's turn, he offered both his hand and his condolences, and the big man gave him a nod and a powerful two-pump handshake. As soon as Owen's fingers wrapped around the man's hand and touched the edges of that ink a massive jolt of energy shot through him. It was like touching a live wire and Owen shivered, staggered, and would have fallen if the brother hadn't used his grip and his other hand under Owen's arm to steady him.

Owen was instantly terrified because he thought that somehow, in some unanticipated way, the big man knew that he was an imposter. He was going to smash Owen. Out him and beat him and humiliate him. He threw a frightened glance up at the man, expecting fury and accusation in the craggy face.

What he saw, though, was surprise and compassion. The man steadied Owen and then astounded him by giving Owen a hug.

"It's okay, brother," said the big man, the corpse's actual brother, "he's in a better place. Thank you for coming out, man. This is rough on all of us. Why don't you go sit down, catch your breath a bit? And again . . . thanks for being here."

Owen tottered away, dazed by that bizarre encounter, but more so by the power of that touch. He even took the man's advice and sat for ten minutes, catching his breath, trying to understand. His fingertips tingled where they'd touched the ink on the brother's hand. And the back of his own hand burned. Not horribly, but definitely.

By the time he got home, the burning on his hand had intensified and then faded, leaving behind a scar. Of a kind. He thought it was actually a burn, but then he held his hand up to the living room light and nearly screamed. There, curling around his wrist and spreading down onto the back of his hand, all the way to the knuckles, were vines. Rich and green, painted in a dozen subtle shades, with broad leaves on which walked honeybees and bumblebees and wasps and blowflies. Standing above them, imperious and regal, was a praying mantis. On his skin. Belonging to his skin. Inked as if he'd spent hours in some artist's chair.

It was the tattoo of the dead soldier's brother.

Or . . . it had been.

It was Owen's tattoo now.

The pain was gone, but the art remained. Owen took cell phone pictures to make sure he wasn't imagining it. Psychic fractures can happen, fugues can occur. Owen knew a lot about that stuff from courses he'd taken and websites he'd visited. His loss of the memories of his mother had led him to learn about all that.

The cell phone's camera took the photos. When he checked an hour later, they were still there. Too mundane, too static to be a hallucination.

He had those tattoos on his wrist and hand.

It wasn't until late that night, when Owen was in bed, that he had his first memory dream. If it was a dream. In the years since then he'd tried to give it a better word. *Fantasy* was totally wrong, and *dream* wasn't quite right, either. What it was . . . was a memory.

Just not his own.

He dreamed of a man, a tough soldier with a gruff face, falling in love with an Afghani girl. She was from a good Muslim family, but the girl wanted to leave them, her home, her country, and go to America with the soldier. They kissed when no one was looking, and made love in a bedroll out in the desert. He was gentler than he looked and even wore a condom so she wouldn't get pregnant. They spent hours talking about making a life together far from there. She said it was her dream to walk in a real forest, with thick leaves overhead, vines and flowers and insects and a thousand kinds of birds. The soldier promised that they would walk together in woods exactly like that. In North Carolina and Pennsylvania, in central California and Montana. Places he'd been where nature was always rioting with life and color. He told her that he loved her. He said he would put in the paperwork for her citizenship.

Then, one morning, the girl was missing. They found her after two days of looking. Out in the desert, sprawled in the bloodstained shreds of her clothing. She had been stoned to death by the men of her own family.

The soldier, torn by grief, had tried to avenge her, but military and local laws prevented it. His time in country burned off and he cycled back to Stateside. Heartbroken and bereft. He'd told the story to a tattoo artist, describing the things the girl had longed to see, and the artist—an exceptional craftsman named Malibu Mark—drilled the leaves and vines and insects onto the heartbroken soldier's skin.

In the darkness of his bedroom, Owen Minor lived those dreams as if they were his own. Every gasp and cry, every tear and drop of blood, were his.

Only and completely his.

29

A police cruiser sat under the sheltering arms of an ancient oak. The tree had nearly died when teeths of flame had gnawed at it during the fire that ended the Trouble. It clung to life, though, just as it had clung to the side of the drop-off for well over a century. Thick roots were dug deep into the flesh of the earth, holding the tree in place through storms and snowmelt and forest blazes.

Over those years a lot of cars had sought shelter beneath its twisted arms. Lovers gasping out promises in the dark. Criminals hiding until the bloodhounds lost the scent. A priest masturbating over memories of a very special altar boy. A man fitting the barrel of a pistol into his mouth in hopes the bullet would blow away the memory of a wife whose Humvee rolled over an IED in Afghanistan. So many lives. So many stories. The police car was a story still unfolding. It was parked there often. Sometimes the officer would sit behind the wheel and cry. Sometimes he would listen to music for hours, the radio and his cell turned off. And, occasionally, on nights like this, the car would sit empty. The officer's uniform folded neatly on the back seat, underwear, shoes, and all. On nights like this that car would be empty for hours and hours.

On this night, the officer came back, naked and trembling. He stood beside the car, leaning on it while the brutal rain washed the mud and blood from his pale skin. It washed away his tears. It removed everything except the memory of what had happened down in the swampy depths of Dark Hollow far below. The oak tree kept all these secrets close and did not even whisper them to the other trees.

INTERLUDE SIX   **THE LORD OF THE FLIES**

The memory Owen Minor dreamed did not belong to him. On some strange level, down deep where knowledge comes more from instinct or intuitive leaps than from rational thought, he knew it was not really a dream. Not a fantasy about something triggered by the tattoo.

It was an awful thing. All of the pain and passion, the cries and screams, the blood and tears.

It was a delicious thing. The pain and passion, the cries and screams, the blood and tears. Especially the tears.

And as he slept, he fed on every single drop.

30

They call midnight the witching hour, but no witchery happened. All of the sorcery had been done.

All the farmers were asleep by then, though their sleep was troubled by thoughts of what that much rain might do to the crops. Harvest was in full swing and torrential rains killed things, drowned roots, washed soil away, and glued the wheels of farm equipment to the ground.

In town, the clubs on Boundary Street pulsed and throbbed

and hammered and feasted long past the two o'clock cutoff. No cops bothered them. No neighbors complained because that was a new part of town and the only neighbors were either running their own clubs or drinking at the bars next door.

Patty was asleep by then, but it wasn't a good sleep. Not anywhere close to that.

Owen Minor was also asleep, smiling as he dove deeper and deeper. He kept getting hard and soft, hard and soft, in time with the things he saw. The things he did. His pale fingers clutched the pillows and tore at the sheets and his tongue tip darted out every now and then, clever as a snake's, and licked sweat from his upper lip. Flies crawled over his face and there were maggots down deep in the sweaty folds of his sheets.

Out on the road, Monk Addison was way down in his own dark hole lit by remembered flashes of guns. Ghosts stood all around his car, and some were inside, on the front seat, crowded into the back. Looking at him. There were always ghosts with him. Sometimes they screamed him awake. Tonight they let him sleep, and he slept all through the night. Monk stirred only once, when the rain eased and then stopped. He murmured a single word—a name—before sliding farther down.

"Tuyet . . ."

The ghosts and the nightbirds all heard that name. They heard him repeat it throughout that long night.

Slowly, smirking at a job well done, the rain and the storm went away.

PART TWO
LORD OF THE FLIES

For all that it was at its worst
And all that it wasn't at its best
The memory of us is a flame smouldering
In the aftermath of a monsoon
A flickering spark waiting
For a new moon,
A mourning sun,
And a soul to ignite
The fire of my next big blaze.

"KINDLING" BY JEZZY WOLFE

I shut my eyes and all the world drops dead;
I lift my lids and all is born again.
(I think I made you up inside my head.)

"MAD GIRL'S LOVE SONG" BY SYLVIA PLATH

31

It wasn't the first time Patty Cakes woke up on the floor.

Not even the first on a bathroom floor, hers or someone else's.

It wasn't the first time she'd fallen down the mouth of a bottle and tried to drink herself to the bottom. Life was like that sometimes. Maybe more than just sometimes.

At least it was her own bathroom this time.

The puddle in which she lay was her own spilled booze.

Her own blood.

She lay there, her cheek and hair in the wet. Her body was twisted into a boneless sprawl as if she'd been cut down from a scarecrow post and simply allowed to drop. No vomit this time. No piss. That was something. When you were that far out on the edge for this long, you took your comforts where you could find them. However small and cold.

Sound was the only thing that seemed to be alive, to have movement. A faucet dripped stubbornly, punching into the metal ring of the drain as if determined to erode it to nothingness, no matter how long it would take. Outside the window the crows of night gave reluctant ground to the morning pigeons. A cricket, who had no damn business being in a yard in this part of the city, whistled for attention, and got none. There was wind, too, but it was subtle and secretive, as if its sound belonged to someone else's experience and not hers.

Patty did not make any sound. She couldn't even hear her own breath. Nor did she move. She didn't want to move. Not yet. She'd learned the hard way that moving too quickly summoned the migraine demons and invoked the storms of nausea. No thanks.

The smart play was to try and assess the damage from where she was. It meant listening inside her body for damage, for misuse; separating new pain from old. Allowing wrongness to make its case. That process took time, whatever time it needed. She was in no hurry. Her tattoo parlor could not open without her, and there was nobody in town who needed to be inked this early. If it was early. Everybody could wait.

Awareness came creeping like a timid nun, whispering to her, tugging on the fabric of her consciousness.

She could see that this was her bathroom. The flowers and tigers and dragons painted on the wall. The soaps and shampoo bottles huddled together on the edge of the tub. She could see that without turning her head. The bunched-up blue bath mat pushed hard against the base of the toilet. All the beer bottles she could see were her favorite brand. Fat Pauly's, a craft lager from Iligan City in the Philippines. The bathroom smelled familiar. All bathrooms had their own smell. This one smelled of her and her habits and her stuff and her life.

Her iPad in the other room was playing its way through every song she'd ever downloaded, one album at a time. Last she remembered it had been somewhere in the *G*'s but had clearly made its way to the *N*'s. Right now it was grinding its way through Nick Cave and the Bad Seeds. *Murder Ballads.*

Well, she thought, that's a bit on the nose.

She closed her eyes for a moment and when she opened them the light had changed. Just a little. Enough, maybe, for the sun to have moved an hour's worth across the sky. Hard to tell, though—the bathroom window was tiny and it looked out to a shared alley. Across the way was the dirty brick wall of the back of Hucksters, one of those fashion places that sold upscale clothes no one would be caught dead in.

Patty's face was turned away from her hands. One hand was tucked under her, the other stretched behind. Awkward. Starting to hurt a little as the muscles woke up to these stresses of angle and reach.

Then, like a switch being flipped, her body told her it was time to move. Maybe it was the pain, maybe it was shame for finding herself like this again. Whatever. She had to move, and so she moved.

Sitting up was awkward. Her muscles were stupid and didn't know how to work. Her body had too many disconnected parts, and her brain had no blueprint for reassembly.

But she managed it.

After three or four hundred years, she managed it. Cursing was involved. No, it was integral to the process. In Vietnamese, because that was the language she spoke when she first learned about pain. In English, too, because the Americans—particularly the New Yorkers—were better at it than anyone.

Then she was up, sitting naked against the cold edge of the tub. Gasping, as if she'd run up ten flights of stairs. Sweating, despite the chill. She blinked away the fireflies that suddenly swarmed around her. She dragged the back of her hand across her forehead and cheeks.

Which is when she saw her hand and understood why there was blood in the puddles of spilled beer. She'd assumed she'd cut herself somewhere on broken glass. No. A cut, even a bad one, would be better than what she saw.

Blood leaked from the back of her left hand. Tiny beads, seeping through the crust of a heavier flow that had mostly dried. She looked around for the tattoo needle and saw it on the floor, over by the toilet. Not the big professional she used. This was something crude. A disposable syringe filled with black ink. The kind of makeshift tool street kids and squatters used because they couldn't afford to visit a pro. She'd inked over those kinds of tattoos a hundred times over the years.

Now it was the opposite. She'd inked a crude image onto her own skin.

It was a face, but there was no artistry to it. No skill. No trace of talent, of control. It wasn't much better than a monotone stick figure's empty features. Eyes, a dot for a nose, a smiley mouth. Heavy, wavering lines. Too much ink.

That was bad enough. If it had been on her leg or arm or anywhere else it would have been no big thing. A fuck-up done during an alcoholic blackout. She had fifty friends in the trade who could have fixed it and turned crudity into beauty.

No, the poor quality wasn't the thing that punched a cold

hand through her breastbone and began beating the shit out of her heart.

The tattoo was on the back of her left hand. Thick lines cutting through the delicate features of a face Patty had inked onto her own skin. A smiling, beautiful face. Drawn years ago, not from a photograph but from a mother's own broken heart.

But . . . whose face? Patty was positive she should know the name. That she should know everything about the little Vietnamese child staring up at her. But there was no name in her head.

Or . . . there was . . . but it was so far out of reach.

On her skin the awkward, clumsy lines of new tattoo ink tried to block those memories. Or trap them? The bars of a cage prevent passage either way.

"Don't go," she whispered to the face on her hand. To the place in her mind where the memory should have been. She looked at the original ink, and then at the stupid smiley face that covered it now. That little girl. Obliterated by her own hand. A crime, a sin committed in the emptiness of a drunken night.

Patty Cakes threw back her head and screamed.

32

Monk jerked awake and reached for his pistol, but his fingers hit the zippered front of his leather jacket. He looked around, searching for what had kicked him out of his dreams. An old Kenworth T600, heavy with grain, thundered past, shaking the whole car. But . . . that was happening now and whatever woke him had been then. Seconds ago.

He stopped trying to find his gun. It was locked in a safe in the trunk.

Monk blinked his eyes clear and watched the grain truck whip away, pulling a train of wet leaves behind it.

"Fuck me," he mumbled. The rain had stopped and the sun was shining so bright that it made his head hurt. All around the car water dripped from the leaves and glistened on the blacktop. It was pretty, like something from a painting. "Shit," he said and meant it.

Monk popped open the door and got out, unfolding himself and feeling every minute of all his years and miles. His joints sounded like someone cracking walnuts. There was a vile movie-theater-floor taste in his mouth and about a pound of sleep crust around his eyes, which he wiped away on his fingers, then wiped his fingers on the seat of his jeans.

"Shit," he said again.

The sky was broken into pieces. Clouds here and there and patches of blue. It reminded him of the way the sky looked way out at sea after a gale. Troubled, like it still had things to say.

On either side of the road the fields had a hammered-down look, and there were deep puddles everywhere. Those same chattering crows were still lined up on the fence rails and power lines.

"Yeah, yeah, yeah," Monk said, as if they'd made some kind of stinging observation. He walked up and down the road until his body felt like his own. His lower back hurt from the position he'd fallen asleep in.

The morning air was clean, though. It smelled of rainwater and mud, but there was nothing nasty about it. That was something.

"Shit," he said once more. It was an eloquent word at times like these.

Then he cut a look at his car, hurried back to it and called Patty. No answer.

"Shit," he growled, meaning something entirely different. He got in, started the engine, spent two minutes working his tires out of the drying mud, and headed on his way with the U-Haul thumping along behind.

33

It was the ringing of her cell phone that brought Patty Cakes back from the edge.

She was surprised to hear it, jerked backward into the now. She was sure she'd left the phone on her night table, plugged into the charger and with the ringer off. She'd done that deliberately before she started drinking last night because she didn't want anyone calling. Not customers, not her cousins who lived in the Bronx. Not even Monk Addison.

So how did the phone get all the way under the ancient claw-foot tub?

The ringing snapped her back so quickly and so completely that the echo of her last scream still seemed to bounce off the walls; and it no longer seemed to belong to her. More like the cry of a seagull far away down a windy beach. Even her tears stopped.

It kept ringing, refusing to go to voicemail.

Patty leaned down, her shoulder hard against the cold curve of the tub, and fished for it. Finding a wadded-up tissue that was soaked with beer, blood, and bathwater. Finding the lip liner she'd lost before Christmas. Finding the withered husk of an ancient roach. Then her fingers found the phone, clawed it toward her palm, caught it like a reluctant fist, and pulled it out.

The screen display was blank. No name, no text.

Patty punched the green symbol anyway.

"Yes?" she asked, surprised that her voice wasn't shrill. When no one spoke, she repeated the greeting.

Nothing. No sound. No rustle of someone who'd accidentally dropped their phone.

"Hello? Who's calling?"

There was a faint hiss, like the way open lines sounded back in the days of landlines. No one spoke.

She tried saying hello a few more times, and then punched the off button. As she did that, in the fragment of a second before the connection was completely dead. she thought she heard a voice. Two words. Small, faint.

"*Mẹ ơi?*"

Patty Cakes froze, staring in horror at the phone. She rarely spoke Vietnamese, though she often dreamed in her native language. Even after all these years living in America she had never forgotten a single word. And certainly not those two words.

Mẹ ơi.

Mommy.

And the voice. The voice.

Her voice.

Tuyet. Yes! That was it. That was the name of the little girl whose face was looking up at Patty from her own skin. Tuyet. Sweet Tuyet.

Or . . . was that her name at all? Doubt suddenly welled up in her. Was this little girl just a ghost from too much drink? She'd had the DTs before, and they always came with visual aids. Cruel stuff, with clarity to sharpen the edges.

"*Làm ơn, mẹ ơi,*" cried the little girl's voice. "*Làm ơn đừng quên tôi . . .*"

Please, Mommy . . . please don't forget me. . . .

The scream boiled up inside of Patty as she stabbed the buttons to hit callback. The phone rang. And rang.

And rang.

Her daughter did not answer. Of course she did not. Tuyet was ashes in an urn. She was memories sewn into the tissue of the past. She was seven years old—and had been seven for ten years. She would be seven years old forever, because little murdered girls do not age.

The phone rang and rang and then it stopped.

When she stared through tears at the screen display there was no record of any outbound call. Not since she'd called Monk yesterday afternoon. There was no record of an inbound call at all. Not in a full day.

She wanted to hurl the phone away. Instead she clutched it to her chest, where she could feel the beat of her heart through the skin of her tightly curled fingers.

"Please . . ." she begged.

The phone rang. Patty jumped and sobbed as she punched the button.

"Tuyet!" she cried. "*Tôi đây. Đó là mẹ.*"

I'm here. It's me. It's Mommy.

There was nothing for a million years as she strained to listen. Only the echo in her mind of those words. Those terrible words.

Please, Mommy . . . please don't forget me . . .

"God, no," begged Patty.

The voice on the other end said, "Patty . . . ?"

It was not her little girl, and Patty caved over the phone. The voice was male. Familiar. A friend, but right then she hated him. She hated anyone who could possibly have been on the other end of that call except the one person who could not be there.

"Patty?" called the voice. "Are you there? Are you okay?"

She raised the phone as if it weighed ten thousand pounds.

"Monk . . . ?" She wept. "Oh my god . . . Monk . . ."

She couldn't finish the call because the shakes hit her then.

They hit her like fists, like kicks, and the phone tumbled from her trembling fingers.

34

It was going to be a great day.

Owen Minor knew that before he even opened his eyes. The buzzing of the flies told him. He could feel them, too. Walking on his skin. Wriggling in his flesh. He'd sent so many out into the storm last night. Watching. Remembering for him. Playing some fun games.

Minor, eyes still closed, lay in his nest of sheets and murmured the names the flies had brought him.

"Eileen Sandoval," he said, smiling.

A fly crawled across his chin.

"Orson Hardihey."

Another fly fluttered its wings under his nose, tickling him.

"Andrew Duncan. Oh . . . and Mrs. Duncan, too."

Flies walked on his face, over his closed eyes.

"Dianna Agbala. Mmmm."

Minor felt himself getting hard.

"Patty Trang," he said softly. "Patty Cakes."

When he opened his eyes the blowflies scattered, then spiraled in the air above him. Beautiful and dark, colorful and sweet. His hand moved, faster than any snake, and he caught one and slapped his palm against his open mouth. The fly exploded between his teeth. The blood and ink tasted like heaven.

35

Monk found the address, but it wasn't easy.

Patty's new store was on Corn Hill, in a part of town that was as close to the rough side as artsy-fartsy Pine Deep ever got. He didn't know the cross street and his map didn't exactly match this version of town. He kept checking painted numbers on curbs and storefronts until he found the right area. She was in the 700 block and he was coming up on it.

But he nearly wrecked his car when he saw the crooked sign for the cross street.

Monk stamped on the brake and sat there for five full seconds. The car behind him gave him an angry honk, but he didn't care. He barely heard it. The sign said:

BOUNDARY STREET

His mouth went totally dry.

"No . . ." he said. "No . . . no, fuck no . . . no goddamn way."

One of the reasons he'd left New York was because of Boundary Street. Not on any map but there, sure enough. He'd left Chicago for the same reason. And Lisbon. And New Orleans.

Fucking Boundary Street. Did every goddamn city have a goddamn Boundary goddamn Street?

One of the nightbirds landed on the sign. It stared at him, head tilted. Then it opened its mouth as if to cry, but there was no sound. Even so, Monk thought he heard it. As clear as if it had been the billboard by the bridge.

Yes, it said.

Monk pulled the car to the curb, killed the engine, got out, opened his trunk and took his gun from the safe, slapped in a loaded magazine, shoved the weapon into his waistband, and went running to Patty's store. The echo of her sobs—of the destroyed sound of her voice—was a knife in his heart.

There was a guy standing outside Patty's trying to peer inside. He held a sample case and looked like a salesman of some kind. The man turned as Monk came running up.

"Say," he began, "would you know if—?"

"Fuck off," snarled Monk in exactly the kind of way that leaves nothing ambiguous. The man blinked once, and then fucked off.

Monk pounded on the door. Got nothing. He tried the phone. Not a damn thing. He was half a second away from kicking the door in when he thought to try the knob. It would be locked, of course. It was early, so no way it wouldn't be locked.

The knob turned.

He whipped the door open and went in at a run, yelling Patty's name. The place was small, his voice was big, but the shadows somehow swallowed the sound. He frowned into the gloom, not liking it worth a damn.

There was something wrong here. He drew the gun, racked the slide to put one in the chamber. There was someone here who should not be. Every instinct he owned told him that. Some motherfucker had come here to hurt Patty and they were waiting for him.

He stopped, alert, his body tensed, gun raised in a two-hand shooter's grip, finger extended above the trigger guard. Something was wrong. He looked around, pivoting on the balls of his feet. The room was washed in brown and gray tones. The three barber chairs, the stacks of boxes, some closets. The door to the customer bathroom ajar. No one in sight. No sound.

But . . .

Monk had spent most of his life in somebody's uniform, humping battle rattle through jungles and deserts, pulling triggers and cutting throats. He didn't do that now, but once a soldier, always a soldier.

He's watching me, he thought.

He. Whoever he was.

Wherever.

The gun barrel tracked with the turn of his head.

You want me, motherfucker, you're going to have to earn that shit.

And he went looking for something to hit.

The walls were covered floor to ceiling with sketches and photos of some of her best work. Patty's best was the best. Monk had been in tattoo parlors on six continents and he had strong opinions on the subject. Half of the ink on his flesh was hers.

He stopped by the small fridge in the corner. It stood open and there were empty, half-empty, and smashed beer bottles clustered around it like soldiers after a failed siege. There was some blood, too.

He called Patty's name again and got exactly the same nothing of a response.

Beaded curtains—cheap plastic and bamboo—stood motionless at the entrance to the hall. No. Not entirely motionless. They moved a little. Was it from the change of air pressure when he'd come in? Or were they settling to stillness after someone passed through?

Tough or not, he was scared to go into the black hallway behind. Tough never meant being without fear. Only idiots think otherwise.

"If you're in there," he said in a quiet voice, "I'm going to fuck you up."

The silence and the darkness said nothing.

It *did* nothing.

Except waited for him. His move.

Monk took one hand and hooked fingers around the last strand of beads. They rattled and he waited to see if the sound sparked movement.

Monk pushed through the beaded curtain into the black

hallway. He didn't turn the lights on, preferring darkness most times anyway. The hall was empty. A bedroom was empty of everything except boxes. What he guessed was Patty's bedroom was empty, and the bed hadn't been slept in. But there was a single handprint on the wall by the light switch. The print looked like it had been made with motor oil, but Monk knew different. He could smell the coppery stink of blood in the air.

The feeling of being watched was still there. Still strong, but he was running out of places for anyone to hide. The only thing that moved were a few flies crawling down the wall. Absolutely nothing else that he could see.

That did not make him feel better. Just the opposite.

The door to Patty's bathroom was closed. Monk put his ear to it and listened. He heard two sounds.

The slow drip of water. And . . .

A faintness of weeping.

He tried the door handle and this time it did not turn. But it was a cheap-ass Kwickset and he busted it open with a hard shoulder and a curse. The door banged inward twenty inches and then jerked to a stop.

Patty lay naked on the floor, curled like an island in a sea of beer and blood.

36

"Ah, Jesus," Monk said, forcing himself through the opening, kneeling down, bending close. "Ah, Jesus, Patty . . ."

His words were gruff, his tone gentle and sad. He gathered her in his arms and picked her up. She weighed nothing at all. Tears ran from her eyes but her lids were closed. She shivered constantly and her golden skin was patterned with goose bumps. Monk held her close, sharing his animal warmth with her. Patty was so cold. Like death, but not yet dead.

She turned her face into the cleft between his chin and shoulder and began to weep. Much harder and louder than before. Big, terrible sobs that punched jagged holes in the walls of the new day.

INTERLUDE SEVEN   THE LORD OF THE FLIES

After that first time, that first night, Owen Minor was convinced that he was insane. Given that he believed he'd somehow stolen someone's tattoo, had that tattoo appear on his skin, and then had dreams so vivid that they were as real as memories—just not his own—there was a case to be made.

When it happened the second time—after brushing the tattoo on the forearm of someone on a crowded elevator—he thought he was losing his grip on reality.

It wasn't until the fifth time that he wondered if he was a mutant, like in those X-Men movies. Someone born with extraordinary abilities that could only be explained away by weird science.

Those five times happened over a period of eleven months. Owen went to a therapist and tried to explain it. But when he showed the spots on his body where the tattoos appeared, the doctor started giving him the look. The skin was always bare, unmarked, without even the ghost of an image. He told the shrink that these borrowed tattoos always vanished completely after he'd dreamed his way through the equally borrowed memories. The result should have not surprised him—the doctor scheduled him for CT scans, blood work, and when all of that came back negative, the next step was a sheaf of prescriptions. More sessions and more drugs were to follow. Risperidone, Aripiprazole,

Olanzapine, Ziprasidone, Quetiapine, Pimavanserin, and the old fan favorite, Clozapine. Xanax was also a hoot. He enjoyed the drugs at times, even some of the more uncomfortable side effects. Explosive diarrhea, for example, broke up a slow day.

But the most recent dose changes made him sick and sleepy, dried his mouth out, and gave him such awful constipation that he developed hemorrhoids. He threw the rest of the drugs away and stopped going to therapy sessions.

He was afraid, though. The thought of going mad was terrifying. His mind was the only thing he liked about himself. His body was a disappointment. He'd grown from a pallid child to a pallid man. Fleshy and sickly. Going to the gym made him hurt, and it was also like sweating to little effect while in a spotlight. The only way he got dates was through a deeply phony set of details and doctored pictures on Tinder, and he'd already been reported twice for deceptive profiles. The only sex he'd ever had was with hookers, and they never kissed him. Owen had never once been kissed on the lips. Well, maybe his mother had done that when he was a baby, but he didn't remember.

Owen searched the Net for cases of any kind similar to his own. He found nothing on WebMD, nothing in articles or news stories. Lots about lost memories, but nothing about borrowing them.

Then he made a strange discovery.

One Tuesday night after working all day slicing deli meats at a Jersey Mike, he had the idea of looking backward to see if there were any clues. This all started with that big guy at the funeral of the soldier who'd committed suicide, so Owen pawed through the thick file folder of obituary and funeral announcements he'd kept. He found the obit, which listed the names of the deceased's surviving family. No parents, but there were two sisters and one brother, Grant Buckley. Owen put that name into the search windows for Twitter, Instagram, and Facebook. And he was there. Grant's Twitter comments were mostly retweets of Breitbart and Sean Hannity. Nothing personal. The Instagram feed was mostly pictures of Grant and his buddies in various places where the military sent him. He was some kind of sergeant in the army. Owen knew next to nothing about the army, and less about the various wars going on around the globe. On Facebook, though, he struck gold.

Very strange gold.

There were a series of posts on Grant Buckley's feed in the weeks following his brother's funeral. Some talked about the dead man, but they were soon completely overtaken by posts about Grant's tattoo.

Grant's missing tattoo.

The big man's first posts were of the "hey, guys, this is weird" kind, because the tattoo of vines and insects began disappearing over a period of days. There were tons of posts from friends and friends-of-friends who had thoughts, opinions, speculations, and solutions that solved nothing. Within a few days of his brother's funeral, the tattoo had vanished completely. All that remained on the man's wrist and hand were faint smudges, like a watercolor left out in the rain for too many days. Grant was amazed, pissed off, and, Owen sensed, scared.

He scrolled through the man's feed until he came to a post five weeks later, in which Grant went on a diatribe to say what a rotten tattoo artist Malibu Mark was. Grant was threatening a lawsuit, and some of Malibu Mark's other customers jumped onto the thread to tell Grant he had his head up his own ass and to basically fuck off and die.

Owen was puzzled, but there was a little tingle of excitement in his loins.

He could not find anything on the other four people whose tattoos he'd accidentally taken. They were random strangers. Owen thought long and hard about what to do next. How to research this.

The following morning he went looking for people with tattoos. There was a lot of skin art around, more than he thought, but he couldn't exactly walk up to perfect strangers and ask to touch them. And if he did, how would he make the touch? Some of the people in the tattoo world scared the hell out of him. Men and women. Nor did he want cops called on him.

He knew that there was a way, but he had to think it through.

He needed new ink. He craved new memories. And he wanted to know how the whole process—weird as it was—worked.

From that moment on, Owen Minor was on the hunt. Always. Every day, every hour.

37

Gayle Kosinski dropped her kids off with her mother. Mom had blocked out the day to bring the Halloween decorations down from the attic and turn her cottage into Spook Central. The kids were delighted.

As Gayle was leaving, her mother stopped her by the door. "You okay, honey?"

"Sure," said Gayle, forcing a smile. "Just tired. I need some me time. Maybe a little retail therapy."

Mom's brow furrowed and she almost asked a question, but didn't. Instead she kissed Gayle and told her to go melt that AmEx card. Gayle could feel her mother watching through the blinds as she got into her car and drove off.

She was, in fact, planning on burning through some money. There were so many new shops open along Corn Hill and down Boundary Street. Jewelry might make her feel better. It used to.

Gayle called two of her friends to see if either was free, but Joanie and Karen were busy. She debated calling some of the second-tier friends, the ones she only ever got together with once or twice a year, but decided against it. They would want to play catch-up and Gayle wasn't yet ready to discuss her sexuality with them. Maybe not even with Joanie and Karen. Joanie was a church lady, so she might be judgmental, and Karen was a bit of a gossip. Too risky in either case.

So she prowled around until she found curb parking at the outer edge of the new area everyone was calling the Fringe. The sky was patchwork, with bits of blue and clumps of gray. There was rain in the air, so Gayle stuffed a little fold-up umbrella in her shoulder bag.

Walking felt good, though there was hardly a spring in her step. Resentment is heavy.

She spent an hour browsing scarves and hats in a boutique staffed by an indifferent Goth girl who did not once look up from her phone. Gayle didn't buy anything and drifted out, certain she hadn't registered on the girl's radar in any meaningful way.

The next four stores were clothing, but most of them tended toward stuff in size zero. Stick-figure mannequins and equally emaciated shoppers turned Gayle away. The fifth clothing store, though, was perfect. The name above the door was Get Real, and the clothes ranged from size ten on up. Way on up. Gayle saw a pair of five-pocket skinny jeans in a stretch fabric with back yoke stitching. They were distressed and faded and looked awesome when she tried them on. She did not have a big butt and her legs were slim. She stood in front of a three-panel mirror, turning to look at herself, extending one leg and looking over her shoulder at her ass.

"Yeah," said a voice behind her, "those work real good."

Gayle jumped and turned to see another woman behind her. A truly gorgeous black woman. Also very curvy, with wavy black hair. She was heavier than Gayle, but it looked incredible on her. Full hips and very large breasts—much bigger even than Gayle's—so that the woman had a true hourglass silhouette. She wore black tights with swirls of glittery dark-purple coiling like smoke around her calves and thighs, and a long black tunic cami, over which was a complexity of interwoven scarves, draped like a shawl. All of it was off set with silver and amethyst jewelry. She had a tattoo of a vine of roses—from delicate buds to glorious bloom—on the inside of her left forearm. On her chest, just visible between the drooping curve of the scarves and her cleavage, was a flawlessly inked lotus flower, and on one delicate petal was a honeybee.

It was her deep brown eyes, though, that made Gayle's breath catch in her throat. They were so . . . knowing.

She's seen so much.

That thought, quick and irrational and unfounded, flashed through her mind. And yet she knew it was true. Just as she knew the follow-up thought was true.

She sees me.

"Um," she said, scrambling for something clever to say. "Thanks. I'm, um, just trying them on."

The woman smiled. There was amusement bordering on wickedness in that smile, then she turned away and vanished into the rows of clothing. Gayle caught sight of her own face in the mirror and saw how flushed she was. Face, throat, upper chest—all red as flame.

She hurried back into the changing room, put her skirt back on, and went out. She went up and down every row, but the black-haired woman was gone. Gayle crept to the front window and leaned toward the glass, craning to look left and right, but no one outside looked like her. Everyone else seemed paler, less real.

Feeling oddly defeated, Gayle walked back to the changing room where she'd left the jeans. They were expensive, an extravagance. And a bit too showy, too overtly sexy.

She bought them anyway.

On the way out of the store she paused, caught by a stack of glossy pamphlets on a free literature table by the door. A woman's eyes were the only thing on the cover of one pamphlet, but they were compelling. Dark, amused, knowing. Staring right at her. There was nothing written on the cover, so she opened it and saw a handful of stills of a crowded bar, of a singer with a guitar perched on a stool, of someone either doing stand-up or maybe reading poetry, of a sleek bar with gleaming bottles and smiling faces.

Every face was female.

The name of the place was Tank Girl. Gayle was only vaguely aware that it was a reference to an old comic book. Or a movie. Or something. Something postapocalyptic with a female punk lead character.

That didn't matter much to her. What drew her, compelled her, lit her up inside, was the total lack of men in the place.

A woman's place.

Would it be the kind of place she needed to find?

Gayle's pulse was hammering as she folded the pamphlet and tucked it into her pocket.

38

Patty let Monk pick her up and carry her into the bedroom. He sat her on the edge of the bed, and gently removed pieces of broken glass from the soles of her feet, her calf, and her left thigh. Before he picked up the tweezers, though, he helped her into an oversize NYU sweatshirt and a pair of underpants. There was no modesty in play, she knew. That ship had sailed a long time ago. No, this was Monk being Monk.

He also put a pot of water on the tiny two-burner stove and fished tea bags out of the belly of the big broken ceramic Buddha on the bureau. The head was designed to lift off and the body was hollow, but the head had been broken years ago. Now Buddha was fat and headless and full of good teas.

Monk squatted down beside the bed, refusing the offer of a chair. Patty watched him as he worked. The tweezers hurt but not because he was clumsy. He wasn't. Monk, for all his size, was very gentle. Those big, knuckly, scarred hands were deft and clever and they moved with practiced efficiency. She didn't even know her feet were full of glass splinters until he told her.

"Sorry if this hurts," he said.

Patty just shook her head. The splinters weren't what hurt. She slid her right hand under the edge of a pillow, watching Monk's eyes to see if he noticed. If he did, he didn't say anything.

Her room was small and cramped. It was decorated with no coherence or theme. Pictures were elegantly framed or thumb-tacked or taped, and hung with no thought to contrasting or complementary colors. A twin bed and two mismatched dressers. No built-in closets because the apartment was a barely converted commercial space. There were still some boxes in the basement, left over from long-ago tenants—a BDSM sex toy repackager and then a small independent printer who made homophobic religious tracts. The last tenant had been a barber shop, and the swivel chairs were still upstairs, though down here were stacks of hairstyle posters being eaten slowly by roaches. She hated going down there because it was musty, dark, and there were too many roaches. The only time she had been down there was to oversee the installation of a sturdy double-deadbolt lock. Patty did not want anyone breaking in. Intruders had done enough damage to her family.

Monk's face was set into a frown of concern and he winced as if each splinter were being pulled out of his own skin. The iPad was still playing; neither of them had bothered to turn it off, though for some reason it wasn't following the alphabet anymore. The Alan Parsons Project was singing a sad sweet song about being old and wise. For some reason the songs were on shuffle now. She wasn't sure how that happened, and it bothered her, but not enough to say something.

"This is going to be a patch job," he said, "but you're going to need an actual doctor. Couple of those are going to need stitches. I'll take you over to the ER soon as I'm done."

"No," she said. "Please, I don't want to go there."

"Not a debate, Patty," said Monk. He dried off her legs and feet with a towel, opened a package of Band-Aids, and began tearing them open.

"I can do that," she said, but he kept working.

It took sixteen bandages total. Five big ones and eleven smaller ones. Then he rocked back on his heels, arms hanging over his knees, hands loose. He wore a pair of ancient blue jeans and a white Ramones T-shirt. Someone who didn't know him would think he was, at best, a roadie for a band or at worst, a bouncer from a truck stop strip joint. He was neither, but his official job wasn't much of a step up from the latter. He was a bounty hunter who specialized in bail skips, working that gig for a string of bondsmen in New York and Philadelphia.

Patty believed she was the only living person who knew Monk's story. Or most of it, at least. She knew about the tattoos and scars on his body, and a good piece about the scars on his soul. Just like he knew her. Not all of her, but enough.

He stood up and fished a pair of sweats from a drawer and steadied her as she put them on. Then he stood there, looking at her with slightly raised eyebrows. Letting the bloody tweezers, the bandages, and the fractured morning ask the questions.

"I got drunk," she said after nearly half a minute.

"Uh huh."

"You going to lecture me?"

He tried on a smile. "Have I ever lectured you on the evils of either grape or grain?"

"No . . ."

"There you go," said Monk.

The song ended and the Monkees began singing "Last Train to Clarksville." They both turned their heads to look at the iPad. It wasn't the kind of song she'd ever have downloaded.

"I have no idea," she said, the faintness of a smile on her lips.

"Weird," he agreed.

They listened to the song all the way through. It ended and then Primus began howling about Tommy the Cat.

"I'm okay," said Patty, turning back to Monk and trying to sound confident. "Thanks for . . . well, for everything. But I'm good now. I'll just clean up a bit and then take a nap. Open the shop late."

Monk didn't move.

"Really," she insisted. "I'm fine."

"Uh huh."

"I just need some coffee and a muffin and I'm good."

Nothing. He just looked at her.

"I have two customers who . . ." Her words trailed off. "Why are you looking at me like that?"

Monk scratched his wrist and picked at a scab over a small knife cut. He cocked his head and peered up at her. "I'm kind of waiting for you to stop jerking me off here, Pats."

"I'm not."

"No? So, when were you planning to tell me about your hand?" He didn't even glance at the pillow, where she'd hidden it again. "When were you going to tell me about what happened to Tuyet?"

She said, "Happened to who?"

The frown on Monk's face deepened, the way a person's does when he doesn't get a joke or can't follow an obscure conversational reference.

"Tuyet?" he repeated, making it a question.

Patty smiled. "Who?"

They stared at each other and the moment felt like it was being stretched too taut. The pain in Patty's foot and leg suddenly flared as if the pieces of beer bottle were only now cutting into her. The room seemed strange. Stuffy. Close. Like the stagnant air of a basement.

"Tuyet," Monk said again, leaning on the name. When Patty shook her head, a look of genuine concern wrinkled Monk's face. "Did you hit your head when you fell? Fuck, let me check." He started to rise, but Patty flinched back.

"No," she said quickly. "I didn't hit my head. Who's this Tuyet? What's the deal?"

Monk straightened slowly but did not approach her. He looked big and clumsy and confused. "On your hand," he said. "Christ, Patty, she's on your hand. She's been on your hand for ten fucking years."

"What are you talking about?" she demanded. "Are you trying to make a joke or something? I don't have anything on my hand."

He pointed to the pillow. "Then why are you hiding it?"

She refused to look. "I'm not hiding anything."

Monk stared at her for a five count.

"Patty, what's going on here? You're starting to scare the shit out of me."

"This is ridiculous," she snapped and started to rise, but Monk shifted to block her. He did not touch her or physically restrain her. That wasn't Monk at all. But he stood there. Looking at her. Looking past her face down to where her hand was still on the bed but no longer covered by the pillow. She did not want to look. Patty did not know why, but it was almost as if she could not look. As if the action of looking wasn't . . .

Wasn't what?

It isn't allowed.

She heard her thought as clearly as if a clone of her had leaned in to whisper in her ear.

It isn't allowed.

"You hid your hand, Patty," said Monk. "I saw you do it. I saw you checking to see if I saw it. There's something wrong with the tattoo of Tuyet."

"Who is this fucking Tuyet you keep harping on about?" she snarled. Or tried to snarl. It came out weak and cracked and small.

It took a lot for Patty to raise her hand. It took much more for her to look at it. She could feel the simple action depleting her, like a knife draining an artery. She looked down at the back of her hand. She could hear Monk's labored breathing. He sounded scared.

Patty knew she had a tattoo on the back of her hand. She remembered inking it there. Doing the work one-handed took time. Getting the details took time. It took patience. It required so much of her thought and feeling and art.

It took . . . love.

Love . . . ?

She frowned at that thought. The frown became a wince as she looked at the tattoo. It was the same as when she was in the bathroom. A face—some girl—done in photo-realism style, and a crude and primitive one done over it.

"Patty," said Monk gently, fearfully, "don't you know who Tuyet is?"

She shook her head.

But her lips moved. Formed two words. They came out so small, so far away, as if the memory attached to that tattoo was moving away from her, fleeing down a long hall, running too fast to be caught.

"My . . . daughter . . . ?"

That was all she got out before she screamed.

39

There are so many kinds of screams.

A mother's scream as her whole body tightens like a fist and pushes a baby into the world, wrapped in blood and mucus, but no less beautiful for all that.

The child's scream as it realizes it is alive, awake, and alone—no longer part of the mother. Fragile and aware of temperature, sounds, smells, and pain. With no other way to articulate its reaction to everything, the soul in the tiny envelope of flesh screams.

The screams of erotic intensity that accompanied the copulation that created that child. The screams of lovers everywhere as all of their awareness is instantly distilled down to a moment of pleasure so exquisite that all other thoughts are shouted to silence.

The scream of a woman taken with no thought to producing anything but humiliation.

The scream of someone in such need that they masturbate over and over and over again and manage to conjure no lover, no tenderness, no touch other than their own.

The screams that take an angry person higher, past fury and into the blind purity of rage.

The screams of the dying who realize that they are so badly wounded that no amount of clinging to something physical—a hand, a rifle, a pillow, a Bible—will overpower the coldness that will drag them down.

The screams of grief of those watching their loved ones die, and in that moment understanding the gap between their perceptions of their own power and their control over the world.

The screams of children at play, that ultrasonic burst of pure joy.

The screams of someone suddenly accomplishing a thing that they—and everyone—thought was beyond their power. Pulling someone from under a car, defeating an impossible opponent, clambering over the last crag of a mountain, crossing the finish line an inch before a better runner, smashing that last overhand with such force the racquet strings break but the ball lands an inch inside the line.

The scream of sudden pain, sudden loss, sudden heartbreak, sudden joy, sudden despair.

So many screams.

And there are the screams that no ear can hear, from the sad and lonely and desperate who have lost their voices but scream all the same.

As the big man with the faces tattooed on his skin gathered the small woman into his arms, another scream filled the air. Only the nightbirds outside the tattoo parlor heard it, though. Only they could.

Them and a fat blowfly crawling along the inside of the store's picture window.

It was such a small voice, thin, fading. But the shriek rose into the air and sent the birds scattering.

"Làm ơn đừng quên tôi."

Over and over again.

Only the nightbirds heard it. Only they saw the thin figure standing in the street, reaching with bloodied fingers toward the figures inside the tattoo parlor. A little girl, broken and discarded. They saw her hands clawing the air as if it were somehow possible to pull the small woman and big man to her. To force them to see her, to know she was there.

"Làm ơn đừng quên tôi."

Even after it turned a corner and was lost to sight.

"Làm ơn đừng quên tôi."

Mommy . . . don't forget me. . . .

40 ▋▋▋▋▋▋▋▋▋▋▋▋▋▋▋▋▋▋▋▋▋▋▋▋▋▋▋▋▋▋▋▋▋▋▋▋

Owen Minor was at work—at his day job—when he felt the tremor build inside of him. It always began as a flutter in his chest, as if his beloved flies were somehow able to crawl over his beating heart. But then the feeling spread outward. Down to his stomach and loins. Up through his throat to his mouth, which began to water, and his eyes, making them wet.

He slipped into a bathroom and locked himself in a stall, then stood with his arms wide, palms braced against the cool metal walls, legs straddling the toilet. There, in safety and quiet, he let the visions come.

The woman from the tattoo shop was feeling it.

She was feeling it so goddamn much.

He was panting now, gulping deep breaths as the memories of Tuyet filled his hungry mouth and wrapped around his tongue and dripped down his gullet to his stomach.

"Tuyet . . ." he murmured. Drool hung from his rubbery lips and dripped onto his shirt.

41

Monk held Patty, rocked her, whispered nonsense words into her damp hair.

Later, he began touching her head, probing it for more cuts or bruises, anything hidden by her thick black hair. He found a lump that made her hiss in pain and surprise.

"You really cracked your head."

"I didn't," she insisted.

"Yeah," said Monk, "you sure as hell did. Can't see it but it feels like a fucking grapefruit. Did you fall?"

Patty didn't remember doing that and touched the spot he'd found. It was so intensely sensitive that she yelped in pain.

"You need to go to the hospital," Monk said. "You need an X-Ray."

"I already told you—"

"I know what you told me. I'm telling you that there's something wrong," he replied, keeping his voice down, keeping it all in neutral, the way you do around the sick. The way you do around people who are losing their shit.

"I'm just hungover," she insisted. "I drank myself into a blackout. Pardon the hell out of me for not having my shit together at the snap of a finger. Not everyone around here has superpowers. We can't all be like you."

It was a good jab, but Monk didn't flinch.

"First off," he said mildly, "cut the shit. Unless you're inking me, you can't get under my skin and you know it."

She mouthed *kiss my ass*. He ignored that, too.

"So, sure," he continued, "you got shitfaced and blacked out. So what? You're an adult, which makes you allowed to act like a juvenile delinquent any time you want. I'll even join you next time. But that's not the point. How many times have you told me that nothing—not one thing—matters to you as much as Tuyet? How many times have you told me that seeing her face on your hand as you work is the only thing keeping you sane? Like a million times? Christ, Patty . . . I can't believe you could get drunk enough to forget her name. To forget her. You need to go get a CT scan or MRI or something."

"I don't need one."

"You want me to call nine-one-one, 'cause I will." He pulled his cell phone out of his pocket and held it out like a threat.

She started to cry again. Then suddenly she burst from the chair and lunged for the holstered tattoo needle on the table. She jerked it free and raised it like a dagger as she slapped her left hand flat on the wood bench. Monk was ten feet away. He was not poised to move. He was big and she was small. She moved at the speed of heartbreak.

He moved at the speed of love.

INTERLUDE EIGHT　　　　　　　　　THE LORD OF THE FLIES

Owen Minor kept asking, "What's happening to me?"

He asked that of his reflection in the mirror.

He asked it of God, though he was pretty sure he was shouting into an empty room.

He asked it on social media through a dozen dummy accounts he created. Reddit and 4chan, and even some Facebook pages. He was good at creating false identities. Very good. He even found his way onto some sites on the Dark Web, but there were too many criminals and criminal wannabes.

No one had an answer. Most of the people he met online thought he was a freak. Owen couldn't fault that view, though he was not the kind of freak they took him for. He wasn't a sex stalker. No, his hungers were so very different from that, but he did not know how to identify or explain them.

On one late night, as Santa Ana winds blew through the trees outside, Owen wondered if he was a monster. An actual one. A supernatural thing.

It was such a strange conversation to have with himself.

What, after all, was supernatural? This was the real world. He still liked the idea that he was a mutant, the next stage in human evolution, but the more he fed on memories the less that felt likely. This was stranger than that. The hunger was so specific, and the need so urgent that it felt less genetically aberrant and more . . .

More what?

Unnatural felt wrong because it was clearly natural to him.

There had been no accident. No one had injected him with an experimental drug, he hadn't been bitten by radioactive spiders. Somehow he knew this ran deeper than DNA. It didn't feel at all like an accident.

No, it seemed to him as this was very much like a gift given, By whom, or why, was beyond him.

"I'm a fucking monster," he told the mirror one night, as tears ran like mercury down his face.

"I'm a monster," he said on another night, after feasting on fresh grief from a man who wore a tattoo with the faces and birth and death dates of his wife and two kids, whom he'd buried after they died in a car accident and he had lived. "I'm a monster."

That time he said it with a bottomless and pernicious joy.

42

Mike Sweeney winced as he sipped the truly appalling coffee he'd gotten from the machine near the waiting room. It tasted, as Crow once phrased it, like a sick lizard had pissed in it.

It was hot, though, and he was cold. He stood for a moment, feeling the warmth wriggle like a snake all the way down into his belly. He needed sleep, and a shower that was more cleansing than standing buck naked in a downpour. Luckily he kept deodorant and cologne in a gym bag in the trunk of his cruiser.

"You still here?" asked the duty nurse, Trish, coming out of a patient's room and nearly colliding with him. "I thought you were going off shift after you brought that couple in last night. The head injury and his wife."

Trish was a sturdily built woman in her late forties. The last of the summer freckles were fading from her cheeks and she smelled of hospital antiseptic and Walmart perfume.

"Stuff came up," he said, shrugging his big shoulders.

"Bet you haven't even been to bed yet."

"No, but it's in my immediate future."

Trish nodded and patted his arm as she passed. She was one of the good ones. Reliable, not too nosy, but with a knowing wisdom in her green eyes. She'd been here for the Trouble.

"Hey," he said before she got very far, "what happened with that couple? Was the husband admitted or . . . ?"

"The Duncans? No," she said, turning back. "It was kind of weird, though. One minute they're hugging and crying together, the next they're nose-to-nose screaming. I had to ask the wife to sit in the waiting room. She was freaking out about the tattoo thing. Kept insisting her husband had it removed, but . . ."

"Yeah."

The doctor had examined the tattoo and said there were no signs at all of laser surgery to remove it. No scarring. Nothing. The best guess was that it was an inferior tattoo job and the ink faded.

"And," Trish continued, "Dr. Argawal suggested a neurological follow-up. The CT scan was negative, so either the husband's lying or the head injury gave him a moderate dose of traumatic amnesia."

"Sure," said Mike dubiously, "but isn't it weird that the tattoo fades and he can't remember having it?"

Trish gave him a pitying smile. "Mike, honey, this is Pine Deep."

It was the answer to anything. In no way a denial that something was weird. Hell, weird was the town's most abundant crop. The question was always whether it would be good weird or bad weird.

Mike nodded and watched her walk away, but this time she stopped and came back to him. She wore a strange little smile.

"You like weird stuff, Mike, right?"

He shrugged. "Guess I do. Depends on what it is."

"That thing with the Duncans? That wasn't the first time I heard about something like that."

"Hitting a cow?"

"No, the tattoos."

"What about the tattoos?" asked Mike.

"Well," said Trish, her eyebrows raised, "you remember the homeless man they brought in yesterday suffering from malnutrition and exposure? The one the rangers found near the passion pit?"

That was the local name for a cleared-out section of woods between the big Guthrie farm and the edge of the state forest, where a drop-off plunged all the way down to the swampy, wormy bottom of Dark Hollow.

"What about him?"

"He's a John Doe. Won't give his name and didn't have a wallet. But he said he was a Vietnam vet. Clearly suffering from PTSD," said Trish, lowering her voice to a conspiratorial level. "He had tattoos everywhere. Two full sleeves, some on his legs, and a whole bunch on his back. But here's the weird part. He said that he'd lost the tattoos on his chest."

"Lost . . . ?"

"That's what he said. He insisted that he'd had a bunch of tattoos on his chest. All the best ones, he said. But they're gone now."

The hairs on the back of Mike's neck stood up. "Gone . . . how?"

"That's just it," said Trish, an odd light in her eyes, "he has faded blotches all over his chest and stomach, but they weren't actually tattoos."

Mike looked at her. "Like Mr. Duncan?"

"I guess. I didn't do the intake on him and only had a quick look when I took his vitals."

"He's still here?"

"Oh, sure," she said. "He'll be here a couple of days. He wouldn't give us his name or anything. No wallet or ID. Looked like he'd been living wild out there for a while, poor guy. You know how it is with some vets. They went off to fight for the flag and apple pie and all that, but when they got home nobody recognized them anymore. Happened in 'Nam and it's still happening with the kids coming back from Afghanistan. And the suicide rate is awful. Seventeen to twenty every day."

"I know," said Mike, shaking his head. He looked down the hall. "Say, what room's the John Doe in?"

"Three thirty-one. The one on the corner with the glass wall. We put him there to keep an eye on him, you know?"

Monk chewed his lip for a moment. "Can I talk to him?"

"About the tattoos?"

"About whatever he wants to talk about," said Mike.

She nodded. "I guess. You'll need to clear it with the attending."

"Argawal?"

"Yes. He's working a double."

"Thanks, Trish."

She lingered for a moment. "I mean . . . it is weird, right? Duncan and then the vet, both saying they're missing tattoos . . ."

"Yeah," said Mike slowly, "it's definitely weird."

43

Dianna Agbala stepped out onto her porch and looked up and down the street.

Ten thousand birds were singing in the trees, most of them hidden by rioting autumn leaves. The sound made her smile.

She wore an oversize sweater that hung nearly to the knees of her black tights. It was ugly, but it was thick and warm and an old friend. Her dark hair was still up in a lazy bun and she wore no makeup. Her shift at the store didn't start until that afternoon and there was nothing at all on her schedule until then. She needed the downtime, too, because yesterday was such a freaky day. Losing nearly an hour and forgetting nearly every detail about a customer worried her. Ophelia had tried to laugh it off, but it wasn't funny. It was scary. Dementia ran in her family, and although her mother and grandfather each got it in their seventies and she was only halfway there, the thought was terrifying. To lose one's mind? To have memories carved out of one's mind and discarded forever was obscene.

She sat down on the rocker and pulled the sweater tight.

People don't just lose an hour of their day. Sure, maybe after a concussion or some kind of bad shock, but not during an ordinary workday. Dianna had spent a lot of time last night thinking it through. She was too weirded out to go deep on the subject with Ophelia. First, Ophelia was her boss and second, they were friendly, but not true confidants. And this felt confidential. She wanted to talk with someone, to get out of her own thoughts, but . . . who?

The name Val Guthrie-Crow floated into her mind. Val was a friend, but mostly she was a customer. A semi-regular who came in for readings when the store was likely to be empty or slow. Val ran the biggest farm in town, was married to the chief of police and the adoptive mother of the senior patrol officer, Mike. By every Pine Deep metric she was solid, normal, practical, and grounded. And yet, Dianna knew Val had a spiritual side. Where once she'd been strictly Christian, since the Trouble Val had become more open-minded, and to a surprising number of things. Everything from energy portals in the forest to ghosts. And that was a crucial thing for Val: reinforcing her belief that death was not the end, but merely a doorway. Val and her husband had lost two of their four children. The youngest two. A brain tumor had taken the youngest before his first birthday, and the little girl had been consumed by leukemia ten months later. Not recent deaths, but the distance between that kind of loss and any true healing was measured in light-years.

Dianna was not a channeler, and was not able to actually speak to the spirits of the dead children . . . but she could feel them. She caught glimpses of them surrounded by light. When Dianna was down very deep in the middle of a reading for Val, she sometimes saw the two little tattoos that were hidden on Val's chest—a ladybug and a lightning bug—glow with golden fire. They were the symbols of the little ones, and Val never showed them to anyone. Val was a modest woman who usually wore T-shirts under her work shirts. No cleavage, no tattoos. Only her husband ever saw them.

Would Val be open to a conversation about losing an hour of time? Or would she measure that against what she'd lost and turn away? Dianna had a lot of respect for Val, but grief warped everything.

A big crow came and landed on the far end of the porch rail. She recognized her as one of the mated pair who lived in the oak tree separating Dianna's yard from her neighbor, Mrs. Sandoval. The bird was old, though, and her feathers bedraggled by age and last night's storm. The bird cocked her head and cawed very softly.

And just that fast Dianna had a flash image in her mind.

Not of Val, or Ophelia, or anyone else she knew. The image was of a very pretty woman about her own age, with long dark hair. A woman with a lovely face but haunted eyes. Trying on five-pocket skinny jeans in a stretch fabric with back yoke stitching, at Get Real.

Dianna smiled at the unbidden memory. She'd complimented the stranger on the way those jeans fit. A bold move on her part, because her comment had been phrased and inflected to be flirty and the woman had a wedding ring. Not that a ring made her straight, but she had the look of straight. Like she belonged to the PTA, went to church on Sundays, threw parties for everyone's birthday, knew how to make every kind of cocktail at home, and had a husband who didn't know whom he was sharing a life with. A lot of assumptions, sure, but Dianna was, after all, a psychic. Said so in neon at the store.

Why had she said something to the woman trying on the jeans? Gaydar was mostly a myth, especially with all of the many, many ways in which sexuality manifested. Usually gaydar was good for spotting the more deliberately dramatic queers. The ones who want to be spotted easily and accepted on their own terms. But, truthfully, there wasn't a "gay look." There wasn't even always a vibe.

Unless, of course, you were psychic.

Dianna smiled at the thought.

Had the woman bought those jeans? And, if so, could Jennifer at Get Real be convinced to share that information? Dianna looked at the lady crow, who bobbed her head as if nodding encouragement.

"Nice," she said aloud and decided to stop at the clothing

shop and ask. The decision felt good. Felt right. The day even contrived to look a bit brighter.

44

Monk got them both to the ER.

He had a bloody towel wrapped around his hand where her needle had stabbed him. The pain was bad, but his heart hurt worse.

Patty said nothing on the way. Not a word. She could not look at Monk, or at his hand. She couldn't look at her own hand. Her right hand was balled into a fist and every now and then she pounded it down on the top of her thigh. After the eighth or tenth time, Monk laid his palm on her leg, as much in the path of the blow as his other hand had been in the path of the needle.

It stopped her.

For the rest of the ride, and for the forty minutes they sat together in the waiting room, she looked away until the nurse came for her.

They were going to take Monk first because of the bloody towel, but then the nurse got a closer look at Patty's face. A moment later Patty was gone, whisked away by staff who kept throwing suspicious looks back at Monk. He tried to go with her, but they wouldn't allow it, and Monk knew better than to try and claim he was her husband.

So he sat down and waited.

A half hour crawled by, leaving shells of each long minute on the floor. During that time a cop came and looked at him from across the waiting room. Didn't say anything to Monk, but he spoke quietly to the intake nurse. Then the cop disappeared from sight, but Monk could feel him somewhere, maybe watching on a monitor.

Shit, thought Monk. He knew where this was heading.

45

Mike Sweeney watched the old Vietnam veteran through the big picture window. He'd told the nurses that his name was Joey Raynor, but he had no ID to back it up. No address, no social security card. Nothing. Mike ran the name through the system and got lot of hits for different Joseph Raynors, including more than thirty in the Philadelphia metropolitan area and seventeen in Bucks County. None of them came back as missing persons, though. Mike called Gertie to have her run a request through military channels, including the VA.

While he waited for that information, Mike watched Mr. Raynor sleep. He could always tell when someone was really sleeping or faking it. This guy was way down deep. Maybe so far down that he wasn't able to dream the kind of dreams that had driven him out of his life and into the woods. Mike hoped so,

Last thing he was going to do was wake the poor bastard up.

So he turned and walked away.

Then he stopped halfway to the stairwell and walked back. Something had registered on the outside edge of his awareness. Something off about the room. He opened the door very quietly and took a single step into the room.

He mouthed the words *What the hell* but didn't say them aloud.

Raynor shuddered in his sleep, like a dog dreaming of hunting. Or a rabbit dreaming of being hunted. But that wasn't what had brought Mike back.

It was the flies.

There were five of them. Big, bloated ones. Dark as bruises. Ugly. The homeless vet lay on his side, with the ties of his gown askew, the flaps open to reveal the ornate landscape of interlocking tattoos on his back. The flies were crawling over them. Mike edged forward and saw the little bastards licking at the man's skin.

Doing what? Tasting his sweat? Feeding off of something the poor bastard rolled in or slept on down in Dark Hollow? The flies kept crawling and licking, licking and crawling. It turned Mike's stomach. He wanted to swat them, smash them, squash them. But he did not want to wake the patient.

Instead he stood there, watching. Appalled and fascinated at the same time.

46

The ER was mostly empty except for an old woman who sat hunched over her many years, eyes staring at nothing, lips moving as if in conversation but she made no sound. An orderly came to help her into a wheelchair.

Monk sat alone for another few minutes, then a male nurse came to fetch him. On the way to the examination bay, Monk tried to spot Patty, but all of the curtains were drawn.

"I need to get your blood pressure," said the nurse. He was a soft, doughy guy somewhere in his thirties, but aging badly. Unhealthy complexion, watery-blue eyes, and a hypertensive flush on his cheeks like he'd run up four flights of stairs. The exact opposite of what you'd want in a medical professional. He looked like he should be having his own vitals taken. The name stitched on the pocket of his scrubs was O. Mäsiarka. Monk thought it should have been something like I. Schlub. The nurse held up the sphygmomanometer. "Mind removing your jacket?"

"I'm licensed to carry and am wearing a gun in a shoulder rig," said Monk. While the nurse sorted out how to respond to that, Monk fished the laminated card from his wallet and held it up, watching the nurse's lips form the words *licensed bail bondsman* and *fugitive recovery agent.*

Mäsiarka cleared his throat, and after a considerable pause asked aloud in an awed voice, "You're a bounty hunter?"

Monk put the card away and didn't answer.

"Like that guy on TV? Dog?"

Monk sighed.

"You here looking for someone?"

"I'm here because my hand's bleeding all over the goddamn place, pal," growled Monk, "so can we put some topspin on this?"

"Um . . . sure, sure, right. Sorry. Okay. Let's get those vitals. Still need you to remove that jacket."

"Sure," said Monk, resisting the urge to sigh again. No matter who was there when he showed more of his body there was going to be some variation of the same set of interlocked reactions. He watched the nurse's eyes when he slid out of the jacket. They damn near popped out of their sockets. Not because of the gun in the shoulder holster, but because of the tattoos visible on his arms and shoulders and chest. Everywhere the tank top didn't cover. All those pale faces. Most of them were photo-real, as if his skin were a window they looked out of. Others were more stylized and clearly done by different artists. In every case, though, the eyes looked real. They watched, and people could feel them watching. Certain kinds of people anyway.

"Nice ink," said Mäsiarka, but his voice nearly cracked saying it.

Monk said nothing, and the nurse finally busied himself taking his blood pressure, temperature, and also listened to Monk's heart with a stethoscope. He entered the numbers on a computer that swung out from the wall on a metal arm. Then he cleared his throat again and tried to sound conversational. "I got a couple tats. A devil I got in college. Frat thing . . . you know how that is. And others I got in Arizona when I went to visit the Grand Canyon. Other places, too. Some people get bumper stickers, I get ink." Like a lot of nurses he wore a long-sleeved Henley under his scrubs and didn't offer to show the tattoos to Monk. Which was good, because Monk truly could not have cared less. He also disliked the man for calling them "tats" instead of tattoos.

The nurse gave up trying to be social and lapsed into asking the usual medical history questions—health insurance, address, age, weight, if he was on any meds. Monk's answers were short, accurate, and left no conversational door open. The nurse typed it all into the computer, then went away, saying the doctor would be in to see him. Monk managed to forget Mäsiarka almost at once.

Instead he thought about what must be going on in Patty's head. How much does a person have to drink to forget their child? Especially after what happened to the little girl. And with that sweet face tattooed on her own hand. That math made no sense to him and there was no scenario he could build that offered a framework of probability.

"Come on, Pats," he said softly, "it's Tuyet. Come on, now . . ."

The triage bay was silent around him and he conjured no answers.

Fifteen minutes later a slim figure materialized outside of the bay.

"Mr. Addison?"

"Yeah."

"I'm Dr. Argawal." He looked like he was ten years old and

was clearly right out of medical school. Mild Mumbai accent overlaid with the nasal tones of Philadelphia. He flashed a bright smile that showed none of the erosion that would sand the edges off it if he worked that gig for much longer. The smile flickered as he came around and saw the gun, but he made no comment. Clearly Mäsiarka had mentioned it, and was likely sharing the news with the police stationed at the hospital. There would be drama. But not from the doctor, who kept everything in neutral.

Monk nodded but said nothing.

The doctor's eyes kept flicking to the faces on Monk's arms and shoulders. He so wanted to ask questions, but wasn't yet that kind of person. Monk watched him trying not to look as Argawal put on a pair of pale-blue plastic nitrile gloves.

"Let's see what's what," said the doctor as he peeled away the bloody towel. The puncture had stopped bleeding but Monk's whole hand was puffed and red and looked like it felt.

"How did you hurt your hand?"

"Working in my basement," said Monk, repeating a lie he'd told the nurse. "Was punching holes in some sheet steel for a shed I'm building."

Argawal frowned at the wound, flicked a glance at Monk, and then bent closer to take a second look at the puncture.

"Punch press?" the young doctor asked, trying his level best not to let a skeptical eyebrow rise, but he wasn't practiced enough at it. Monk kept a smile off his face.

"Yeah. Very fine bit, almost like a needle," said Monk. The punch press thing was a stupid idea that he'd pulled right out of his ass, but once it was said out loud he had to stick to it.

"There's quite a lot of bruising."

"Yeah, well, when I do something I do the hell out of it."

Dr. Argawal gave him a small smile and sent him for X-rays. When the pictures came back negative for broken metacarpals, the doctor put six stitches in, all the time telling Monk how lucky he was he didn't have a broken hand.

"Yeah," said Monk sourly, "people are always telling me how lucky I am."

"The stitches can come out in a week or so. I can prescribe something for the pain if—"

"How's Patty?" interrupted Monk.

"Miss Trang?" asked Argawal, suddenly very polite and formal. "We're running tests."

"Didn't ask what you were doing, Doc. I asked how she was."

The doctor's expression went from young and feckless to middle-aged suspicious in the space of a blink. Then shutters dropped behind his eyes.

"We'll know more when we get the test results," he said without inflection.

And that was that. The big nurse showed Monk to the waiting room and then Monk was alone again. For a long time.

INTERLUDE NINE   THE LORD OF THE FLIES

Owen Minor saw that the mail was scattered on the floor inside the door and he hurried over to it, smiling, because the latest issue of *Inked* was right on top. He snatched it up and saw that another magazine, *Tattoo Life,* was nestled under it. Now he was doubly happy.

He took both magazines with him, leaving the rest of the mail on the floor, and ran upstairs to his bedroom. The bed was littered with other periodicals, both commercial and industry. Apart from older copies of the ones that had come in today's mail, there were back issues of *Inked Girls, Freshly Inked,*

Skin Deep, Tattoo Energy, Paperchasers Ink, Urban Ink, Skin Shots, Rebel Ink, Tattoo Society, Things & Ink, Tattoo, and *Tattoo Master.* There were reams of printouts of people—men and women—from tattoo websites. Owen was not entirely sure he was heterosexual but acted as if he was, more out of habit than anything else. Photos of either gender, or the gender neutral, with tattoos turned him on. And not the people, exactly. It was the ink that intoxicated him.

Because ink was a pathway to memories. If he couldn't have his own, then he wanted any he could take.

Since going looking for people to touch, he'd found more than forty. All strangers, though, and the frustration level was mounting. The memories were so scattershot, and some were almost toxic.

When he brushed a waitress at a truck stop in Colorado he took a tattoo of a hummingbird. Because she had such sad eyes, Owen thought it might be tied to something important—a lost love or a lost child. But the woman simply loved hummingbirds and he spent a whole night trying to wave the fucking things away from him while he cowered under blankets. If he'd been able to actually touch them he would have swatted them out of the air and crushed their little bones in his fists. But he could not touch the dreams in that way.

Another time he took a shamrock from the shoulder of an old man on Venice Beach. The kind of guy who looked like he'd been all around the block and had some real stories to tell. Real memories. Owen pretended to lose his balance on the sand and grabbed the guy's shoulder for support. That night he thought he'd dream of maybe something like a bunch of Irish guys drinking and carousing. Instead he found himself sitting bedside as a small girl of about ten lay fighting for every breath.

The man, then a priest in a neighborhood in Chicago, held her hand and prayed with every atom of his being. He bargained with God for the life of the little girl. He staked all of his faith and all of his need against a tiny flicker of mercy from something vast and unseen. He believed completely that God would answer, would spare that fragile child. But, in the deep darkness after midnight, those small and weary lungs simply could not take the next breath. The frail chest settled back and the tension in her limbs evaporated, leaving a shell filled with nothing.

The priest's faith had been eroded for years, and this was his dark night of the soul. However, instead of a light of understanding or a rekindling of his sputtering faith, a black wind brought only cold darkness. His priesthood did not end that night, but his belief in a loving God did. The man fell away from the church in slow degrees, and twenty years later he was a bitter English teacher in an inner-city school in California. He drank but was not a drunk. He wept, but he was not entirely broken. The shamrock behind his shoulder was there to remind him of the luck that had failed him. In the dream, Owen could see that the green flower had once been a cross the man had gotten inked when he was contemplating the priesthood. It was modified into a four-leaf clover during one brief spell of optimism, but was now forgotten.

All through that night Owen fed on the memories of that little girl, and of others who had come to the priest hoping that he could intercede with the Lord or with saints. It was a symbol of loss that ran as deep as the soul.

And it was so fucking delicious.

Owen went back to the beach the next day and the next, looking for the old priest, but he never found him. The stolen dreams came and went. Some annoyed him. Some fed him. The best ones fed him. His only real regret was that once he'd devoured the memories, the tattoos faded entirely. No second helpings.

He opened the new copy of *Inked* and began reading. Learning more about the art and science of tattoos. About the politics of them. About the different frequencies of tattoo culture. People who got tattoos because they were into *Star Wars* or Pokémon or other pop culture stuff. People who get them because they belonged to a club, or a group, or shared an identity.

He read for nearly forty minutes before he found an article that literally took his breath away. The focus was on tattoos representing loss—people whose children had died, friends/family of murder victims, relatives of vets KIA, friends of suicides. The writer included fragments of interviews that cut right to the heart. One sidebar, though, cut even deeper. It was about a marine and three close friends who'd been through Parris Island with him, who shipped out with him in the early days of the 2003 invasion of Iraq, and who'd all died on the same bad night in Nasiriyah. The marine had their names inked onto his forearm and after that no bullet touched him, no mine killed him. Because his friends were there looking out for him, watching over. A brotherhood of ghosts. However, five years after he was discharged, the marine lost that arm in a farming accident, got it caught in a thresher. The lost of that tattoo absolutely crushed him, because he'd come to believe it was a very real connection with his dead friends. The man said he hit the bottle and then spent years in personal and group therapy, battling the demons of PTSD, survivor's guilt, and unrelenting grief.

Owen read that article ten times, back-to-back.

He was crying. He was laughing.

He had never been happier.

47

Gayle fussed around the house. That's all it was. Fussing.

She straightened pictures on the walls that didn't really need straightening. Chopped down on decorative pillows. Sent unimportant emails. She was aware that this was killing time, but that was fine. What mattered was tonight.

In the middle of the night she'd made a very important decision. A secret one. A dangerous one. When she was along in the house, Gayle removed the folded pamphlet from the back pocket of those skinny jeans.

Tank Girl.

She opened it and held the accordion pages to the natural light spilling in through the bedroom window. Women at the bar. Women behind the bar. Women performing. Only women.

Did that make it a lesbian bar or one welcome to bi-curious?

Suddenly Gayle realized that she didn't even know if the distinction mattered. Or existed. Then she paused and felt a chill of uncertainty. Would someone like her be welcome in a place like that? Would her total lack of experience shine like a prison break spotlight?

She almost tore up the pamphlet.

Almost.

Did not.

Instead she put it back into the pocket of those jeans and found more things to keep herself busy. She'd already contrived a credible escape plan for tonight—a seminar on meditation that was likely to run late. Scott's lack of interest in that could not be

more comprehensive. He called everything even remotely related to that aspect of her life "New Age woo-woo horse crap."

Gayle decided to sand and restain the patio furniture that
was currently sitting in the garage. It didn't need to be restained,
but it was that or scream as she climbed the damn walls.

48

Monk's cell rang as he was getting really bad coffee from a machine in the hall. The display read *S&T.* Shorthand for the bail
bondsmen who gave him most of his good-paying jobs. He debated letting it ring through to voicemail, but Patty would be a
while yet and he had to fill the time, so he punched the green
button.

"Yo," said Monk, "is this urgent? 'Cause I'm busy."

"Checking in to see if you've found our boy yet," asked
Twitch, one of the two partners in the bond firm. Sadly, his
real name was Iver Twitch. His parents were, Monk knew, total
assholes. Twitch's partner wasn't much luckier—his name was
J. Heron Scarebaby. Apparently it was something else before his
grandfather went through Ellis Island, and either the immigration clerk was a dick or clueless. Either way, the name stuck.
The universe pushed the two of them together and Scarebaby
and Twitch was a thriving bail bond business with offices in
several cities. Monk never bothered to ask why neither of them
changed their names, or used something less outright bizarre
for their business. Why not? Who the hell would forget bail
bondsmen named Scarebaby and Twitch? It was like something out of Harry Potter, but without the wit or charm. Just
the weird.

Monk shifted around to check both ends of the hall. Couple

of nurses at the station and a female cop with soft red hair and hard green eyes standing outside of the ER entrance. Those green eyes were staring at him but she wasn't close enough to hear any of the call. He lowered his voice anyway.

"No," said Monk

"Are you looking?"

"I just got to town, man," complained Monk. "Give me two goddamn minutes, will you?"

"We have this matter and then there's a couple of other skips we need you to find," said Twitch.

"*Day* ends in a *y*," said Monk.

"And let's not forget," continued Twitch, "there's a lot of money in play here. With the pending case, I mean."

"I know."

"A lot of my money if you don't catch this little cocksucker."

"I'll catch him. I have a few good leads."

"In Pine Deep?"

"One of 'em, yeah," said Monk. "But I think he's holed up somewhere nearby. Black Marsh, maybe. Somebody said something, and it feels like a solid tip. Don't worry, I'll find him."

"Are you looking right now?" demanded Twitch. "I mean, as we speak?"

Monk sighed. "No. Look, something else came up. Had to deal with it."

"Did I mention that this is a lot of my money? I mean, that has come up in our discussions, right?"

Monk sighed again. "I'm at the hospital with Patty."

There was a hard beat. Then, "Is she okay?"

Monk gave him a rough cut of the story, and finished with "They're running tests."

Another pause, and Monk could almost hear the gears

grinding as the small, fragile, decent part of Twitch warred with the lawyer-turned-bail bondsmen aspect.

"You mentioned some raised eyebrows. Local cops going to be a problem?"

"To be determined. Bet you ten bucks and my left nut they're going to think I knocked Patty around."

Twitch cursed quietly but with eloquence. "You need me to run interference, you call me."

"I won't let this get in the way of the job."

"That's not what I meant," said Twitch, clearly offended. "You and Patty are family. Anyone moves against you and I'll drop the house on them."

"Thanks. I'll keep you posted."

"Okay," said Twitch, and the line went dead.

Monk pocketed the phone, cut a last look at the red-haired cop, and went back to the waiting room.

49

Patty always thought that emergency rooms should be called waiting rooms.

Once they did their tests and dressed her cuts, they left her to wait. And wait. And wait.

It was not a kindness most of the time because it made the people in those triage bays remember how they got there. Those were seldom happy memories.

Memories.

Patty tried to understand what was happening. Tried to logic her way through it in hopes that a practical approach would keep the screams tamped down into the bottom of her lungs.

So she drifted back into the memories that were still anchored to her mind. Her life. Her family.

Patty was the middle daughter from a family of tattoo artists who'd been sinking ink since the fifties. A family whose needles had created some of the most intricate and beautiful artwork carried back to France, England, Australia, and the United States on the arms, chests, and shoulders of the young men who'd survived the rat holes and rice paddies of what became known as the Vietnam War. Dragons and tigers, pretty girls and laughing devils. And other things, too . . . beautiful flowers and the faces of girlfriends a world away.

When Saigon fell and the Communists took over the country, the family was decimated and scattered. Many were killed or sent to labor camps because other villagers labeled them as collaborators.

Patty was born after that. By then the family was much smaller and they worked the tourist trade. Their work was inspected at random and any infraction was punished with swift brutality—something the smiling tourists were not allowed to see. Patty's life had been hard, but with the irony of enthusiastic American tourism, there was more money flowing into even the smallest villages.

Patty fell in love with one of the tourists, the son of a Vietnamese national who'd fled the country in the stinking hull of a fishing boat. The son, a pharmacist, had always wanted to visit the country. When his parents talked of Vietnam they seldom mentioned the war. Instead their eyes would glaze over as if they were looking at the lush forests and endless rivers, the towering mountains and the ten thousand varieties of beautiful flowers. They spoke of its history and of the music and dance. His father would then roll up his sleeve and show the tattoo he'd gotten in a village outside of Ho Chi Minh City. A dragon and a phoenix in an eternal dance. It was the most beautiful piece of skin art the young pharmacist had ever seen, and when his father died of cancer, he made it a mission to find that village and get the same tattoo.

A knowledgeable tour guide had brought him to the small studio Patty's family shared with five other artists. The three oldest artists in the place all recognized the design and the work. Tattoos, like any other kind of art, were unique to the people who had made them. Any really experienced eye could see it. The artist had been Patty's grandfather, and now she was the last artist in the family.

He hired her to do the same tattoo on his back. She did, and everyone who saw it said that Patty was every bit as skillful as her grandfather. A few—including the hardest sell in the village—said she was better. The young man stayed in town longer than he intended and had other pieces of Patty's art inked forever onto his body.

That man was Patty's first real lover, and though they never married, she got pregnant. Sadly, the young pharmacist confessed that he had a wife and children back in the States. He fled, and Patty's family treated her like a whore. When Tuyet was born, they fawned publicly over the beautiful little child, and privately ignored her. A whore's bastard.

But as Tuyet grew, she charmed them. No one was as sweet as her. A light that shone all the time. A smile that could melt ice. A laugh that drew smiles even from the most stone-faced relatives.

Somehow Patty could remember some of that.

Fragments.

Mostly they were memories of the reactions of her sisters, mother, and grandmother. But those were borrowed. She lay there and fished for her own memories. Surely they must be down there in the dark. Misplaced, yes, but lost? That wasn't possible.

"*Làm ơn đừng quên tôi . . .*"

The words echoed in her mind, but even the voice was unfamiliar.

Please don't forget me.

Patty closed her eyes and balled her fists and refused—absolutely refused—to scream.

50

Monk felt the man before he saw him.

It was something in the way the air changed in the waiting room. A shift on a level that he could sense but not name. He turned fast, expecting trouble, the magazine falling from his lap to slap against the scuffed linoleum.

The man stood a few feet inside the door. He was short, lean, compact. Somewhere north of fifty, with streaks of gray in his curly black hair. Dark eyes. Some small scars on his face. And a warm smile that did not reach his eyes at all.

"Morning," said the man. He wore naturally faded jeans, New Balance running shoes, a flannel shirt in a lumberjack plaid, and a chief's badge. A gun belt was cinched around his narrow waist. Not the kind with pouches and slots for Tasers, pepper spray, or cuffs. Just the gun—a big old Beretta 96A1, a brute of a .40 handgun.

"I'm Malcolm Crow," he said, "chief of police here in Pine Deep."

Monk stood up slowly. He towered over the cop, who couldn't have been more than five-seven and maybe not that tall. Monk was a bit over six feet but knew he looked taller. People told him that. Probably because most of his mass was in his chest and shoulders. The cop did not seem particularly impressed.

"Okay, Chief," he said.

"People call me Crow."

"Okay, Crow."

"Welcome to Pine Deep," said the cop. There was a flavor of irony in his inflection that Monk could not identify. Like it was some kind of old joke, but he didn't know the context. "You brought in Ms. Trang?"

"Yes."

"Name?"

"Gerald Addison. People call me Monk."

The chief's left eyebrow lifted. "Monk? Like a gorilla, because of the shoulders?"

"No," said Monk, but he didn't offer any other explanation and the cop didn't press it.

"What's your connection to Ms. Trang?"

"Patty's an old friend."

"What kind of friend?"

"We go way back."

"That's not an answer," said the cop.

Monk thought about it. "We're close. Like family."

"You bust her up?"

"No," said Monk flatly, expecting the question, knowing this was the kind of cop who would try to blindside him with that sort of stuff. He had poker player's eyes and was looking for a tell.

"Lovers' quarrel?"

"No," Monk repeated, leaning on the word.

"She say no and you didn't hear her?"

"Fuck you."

The cop's smile widened a millimeter. But he also nodded. Then he said, "You look the type who'd know the drill. Will I have to insist?"

"I'm strapped," said Monk. "But you already spotted that. Or the doctor told you. I have a Sig in a shoulder rig and a backup piece on my left ankle."

"Yup," said the cop, "I can see the bulge. Let's do the dance."

"Me or you?"

"I need the practice," said the cop. Monk gave him three seconds of a flat stare, then turned around, placed his palms flat on the wall, and spread his feet. He felt expert hands pat him down. The cop was professional and thorough. He was not unduly rough.

Both guns were removed. As was a Buck 898 Impact folding knife Monk wore in a leather holster on his right hip. The questing hands also removed a small leather case from Monk's left front trouser pocket, unzipped it. Crow made a small, soft grunt. Not of surprise, more of appreciation. The set of lockpick tools was high end.

"You can turn around."

Monk pushed off the wall and turned. The cop had moved back out of range of a sucker punch or kick. The two guns—the big Sig Sauer P226 Scorpion and the .38 Smith & Wesson five-shot Chief's Special—the little zippered case, and the knife were on the far edge of the coffee table. The cop had removed the magazines and ejected shells from each weapon. The snap on the cop's own gun was undone, but he hadn't drawn.

"You can sit."

They both sat, facing each other across the table.

"Now," said the cop, "let's see your carry permit, ID, and anything else you want to show me. Put it on the edge of the table near you."

Monk complied. When Crow got to the fugitive apprehension license he gave that a small *tap-tap* with his forefinger.

"Yup," said the cop, "I figured you for a skip-tracer, hence the lockpicks. Besides, you have the look."

Monk shrugged.

The cop used his foot to hook a plastic chair over. "You can take the cards back and have a seat."

"What about my guns?"

"When we're done talking."

"Okay," said Monk, standing to gather the cards and put them back into his wallet. He settled into the chair.

Chief Crow studied him for a few moments. "Tell me what happened with Ms. Trang," he said. "Tell me all of it. And tell me why it was you who found her. Maybe tell me why you have a stab wound in your hand, and let's not pretend it was a punch press. Oh, and tell me why your car outside has a trailer hitched to it."

"Sure. But before I do all that, how about telling me how Patty's doing?"

The smile flickered just a little. "How about you go first?"

51

Patty stared at the ceiling, seeing the white speckled acoustic tiles in negative. The white became black and the dark holes became stars.

She ignored the sounds coming through the open door, just as she ignored the policewoman seated outside reading stuff on a cell phone. She tuned out the noises from the nurses' station and the small beeps and pings of the machines that lurked around her bed. None of it was entirely real to her.

Patty tried to ignore the pain signals from her hand. Not because she was afraid of pain—that kind of pain was nothing to her anymore—but the pain threw memories at her.

Just not enough of them.

Tuyet.

There was still a ghost of a little girl in her mind. Small, pretty, dressed in a pale-blue dress over darker-blue leggings. There were little white flowers on both. A matched set. A gift from *bà ngoại*—Grandma—on Tuyet's last birthday. She was starting to grow out of the leggings but cried every time Patty wanted to move them on.

"They're my favorites!" wailed Tuyet. "They keep me safe."

Safe.

The clothes still smelled a little like smoke after fifty washings. Tuyet had been wearing them when the house next door caught fire and then spread to their place. Tuyet had run around waking everyone else up and they all got out safely.

They keep me safe.

When they found Tuyet in the road she had been wearing that dress. The police found the leggings later, in a trash can behind the house where six men lay dead. A house where no one had been safe.

Patty's fists were clenched so tightly the IV port in the back of her hand stung like a wasp. Not that hand. The other one. The one she could bear to look at.

Why could she remember every detail of that dress and so little else?

Why?

How was that even possible?

There was a soft ping and the cop outside laughed quietly at something that popped up on her screen.

She's there to make sure I don't kill myself.

Patty looked up at the reverse star field on the ceiling. After a long time it seemed like the holes really were white dots against an infinity of black. The stars began to move. Slowly at first, then faster, swirling more like sparks.

But by then Patty was asleep, sliding down a long slanted tunnel in the floor of the world, toward a darkness so complete there was not a word for it in any human language.

She was just about to fall forever when there was a sound that pulled her back. Not a voice. Not a scream. Something more mundane. A knock. Then the soft creak of hinges as the door opened.

Patty forced her eyes open, suspicious that this was actually part of some trick of the demons in the dark. She opened her eyes, the merest of slits, afraid that if she saw a monster it would know, and then it would pounce.

A head and shoulders leaned in through the door.

"Ms. Trang?" asked a soft voice.

It was not Tuyet. It was not Monk.

It was a cop.

52

Monk gave Chief Crow a version of what happened. It wasn't exactly a pack of lies; more like a cluster of carefully sculpted half-truths. The cop seemed willing to let Monk tell it from the beginning, clearly appreciating context. There was no sense of urgency, which made Monk wonder about who was doing some other kind of checking elsewhere. Was there someone already at Patty's place? Or spooking his car outside?

He was acutely aware of Crow's dark-blue eyes and how closely they watched everything, while the chief's body language sold the fiction of a lazy, mildly dumb hick cop. Monk wasn't fooled for a second. Crossbreed a rat terrier with a Cavalier King Charles Spaniel and it's the laziest lapdog in creation until it decides your nutsack looks like something that needs biting.

Monk stuck to the truth for as far as it worked. He said that his friend Patty Trang—known as Patty Cakes—had moved her tattoo business from New York to Pine Deep. Looking for the quiet life.

"Why Pine Deep?" Crow asked when he was done.

"Why not? It's a nice little town."

"No," said Crow, "it's not. A tourist who doesn't know how to use GPS might wander this way thinking they just drove into an Andrew Wyeth painting, but anyone moving here would have a better take."

Monk shrugged. "Been quiet around here for a long time. The Trouble—isn't that what you locals call it?—was way the hell back, right? Only time Pine Deep makes the papers anymore is around the holidays or on slow news days when some reporter gets a Throwback Thursday itch and wants to drag it all back out. That was then, and this is now. Besides . . . Pine Deep's got a big fringe community, right? Got that Fringe Festival thing coming up. And, a big LGBTQ presence, too."

"Is Ms. Trang gay?"

"She's whatever she is. None of my fucking business."

"It is if you're sleeping with her."

Monk leaned back in his chair. "The fuck's that to you?"

"Maybe nothing. Maybe motive. Working on figuring it all out."

"Ask Patty."

"Someone is," said Crow.

The second hand chased some silence around the face of the big wall clock in the corner.

"Get to the part where you show up with a U-Haul," suggested Crow.

"Maybe I'm looking for the quiet life, too."

"And you've made so much money chasing bail skips that you can retire to the country and paint pretty landscapes."

"I'm not retired."

"People just visiting tend to pack a suitcase, not their whole apartment."

"That's my business, isn't it?"

Crow's eyes were hard as fists, but that little smile was still there. It made Monk itch. "To be determined," he said mildly. "Let's go back to your story. Tell me about the two of you moving from New York to here, of all places. I promise not to interrupt."

So Monk took a breath and explained how Patty moved to Pine Deep a couple of months ago and set up her shop, building it on the bones of a failed barbershop. He said that she lived alone and quietly and was building a clientele, mostly drawing on the people living and working in the Fringe. She ran a clean shop, was chatty and social during office hours, but after that she liked to turn the rheostat to whatever level she wanted. Hard to do that in New York; easier to do it out in the sticks.

"As for Pine Deep," said Monk, "for some reason Patty fixated on it as a place to reset her clocks."

"Even a broken town like this one?" asked Crow, and there was a hint of something in his voice that Monk couldn't quite identify. Some species of sadness, maybe; but if so it was the kind that came with the wrong kind of familiarity.

"Especially a broken town like this," said Monk. "Patty's been through some shit. She understands broken more than most. Don't know if she could live in a Polly Perfect town."

Crow nodded. "And you?"

"I get along wherever," said Monk. "But New York's used up for me. I needed a new start, too. Plenty of work for a cat like me in Bucks County, down in Philly, up in the Poconos if I want to go that far, and over in Jersey. I bought a place and moved down here, too. Took me longer because I had some open gigs that needed handling."

"She knew you were coming, though?" prompted Crow.

"Sure. And while I drove down I kept trying to call her. Got mostly no signal or shit-poor reception."

"Again I say, welcome to Pine Deep."

"Then the storm hit and I pulled over to wait it out." Monk described exactly where. Then he explained everything that happened at Patty's place, from the unlocked door to finding Patty to picking glass out of her and bringing her to the ER.

Crow listened. He took no notes and only gave the occasional nod. Monk wondered if the chief already knew this from Patty herself.

"And it's your opinion that she mutilated her own hand?" asked Crow after a long moment of reflection.

"Yes."

"Mangled the tattoo of her own daughter?"

"Tuyet. Yes."

"How did her daughter die?"

Monk met his eyes. "Badly."

Crow nodded. A tiny movement. "Tell me."

It took a lot for Monk to figure out how to tell it. There was so much sewn into the fabric of the memory. How he met Patty. How he became who he was. And what he was. It was odd that in all these years he'd never had to tell the story to anyone. Not a soul. But there was no way out of this room and out of the moment without telling at least some of it to this strange little cop. He looked Crow in the eyes and said the things that slowly wiped the smile off the man's face.

"Tuyet was abducted from her grandmother's house. The people who did it beat the old lady to death and shit on her corpse. Over the next eight days and nights, they gang-raped the little girl and then one of them choked her too hard while sodomizing her. Tuyet died. They left her body in the middle of a dirt road. Animals found her before the authorities did."

The room was utterly silent.

It was impossible to tell whether Crow knew any or all of this. His face showed absolutely nothing. No emotion of any kind.

Finally, Crow said, "When did this take place? And where?"

"Ten years ago," said Monk, and he heard the eroded sound of his own voice. It hurt to talk about this. So much. "In Tuyên Quang township, northeastern Vietnam, northwest of Hanoi."

"Who committed the murders?"

"Six guys. Local gang."

"Police ever catch them?"

"No."

"So, they got away with it?"

Monk just looked at him.

Crow said, "Ah." Then he asked, "Why were you there?"

"Tourist."

The smile flickered back. "Somehow you just don't look the type to be uploading tourist pics to your Instagram. You're too young to have been in-country during the war, but you do have the military look. PMC?"

Monk smiled. Private military contractors was a much less threatening term than mercenary, even with all the shit Blackwater and Blue Diamond did over the years.

"In Vietnam?" said Monk. "No. I was a tourist when I was there."

"But you've been in that line of work?"

"Once upon a time."

"Ever regular military?"

"Sure. So what?"

"Honorable discharge?"

"My tour ended and I didn't re-up. End of story. No drama."

That lie was easier to tell because Monk had told it a thousand times. The real story was buried deep in need-to-know files, and no country cop was ever going to get a whiff of it.

"How did you get involved with Ms. Trang and the murder of her mother and daughter?"

"It just happened."

"Nothing ever just happens," said Crow. "And don't try to dick me around. Please answer the question."

Monk shrugged. "Sure. Patty was working in a tattoo place. Her family's business. I had some ink scheduled but she didn't show up for work. One of the other women working there told me what happened."

Crow studied him for a while and Monk allowed it, meeting the cop's eyes.

"And you became friends?" asked Crow, one skeptical eyebrow raised. "Child molestation and murder aren't your typical bonding experience."

"It is what it is, Chief, and I don't need to explain any more about it to you."

"When did she move to the States?" said Crow.

"That year. Too many memories in 'Nam. Patty needed to start fresh." Monk paused. "But before she left she inked Tuyet's face on her hand."

"She did it herself?"

"Yes. I saw her do it."

"That could not have been easy."

"Fuck, man, nothing about that whole time was easy. She had to identify what was left of her little girl's body," said Monk bitterly. "That was the image she carried around. It's what she took to bed with her and what she woke up to. Doing that tattoo was the healthiest thing Patty could have done. I'm sure you saw the tattoo. There's enough of it left under the junk she inked last night. That's the face of a smiling, happy little girl. Alive and full of joy. It's the face Patty needed to remember, you dig?"

Crow nodded. He pursed his lips for a moment then nodded at Monk's hand. "You left that part out."

"When I got to Patty's place this morning she was totally freaked," said Monk. "She'd gotten smashed as all hell and de-faced the tattoo of Tuyet. I don't know why. She wouldn't talk about it. And when I was getting ready to come to the ER, she grabbed a tattoo needle and tried to stab her own hand with it. Not sure if she wanted to finish obliterating Tuyet's picture, or to destroy the new one. Or maybe punish herself. Either way, I got to her before she could."

"And took the hit yourself?"

"Better me than her."

"Atonement?" suggested Crow.

"No," said Monk. "And fuck you."

Crow nodded as if acknowledging that point. "And instead of telling the truth to the intake nurse and Dr. Argawal, you whipped up a crock of shit about a punch press?"

"Neither of those fucks needed to know. Not sure you do, either."

"It's my job."

"This is Small Town, USA. Your job is to give out tickets."

"Here's one of my problems, Monk," Crow said after a pause. "Ms. Trang says that she doesn't remember ever putting that tattoo on her hand."

"She did it last night while she was drunk out of her gourd."

"No," said Crow, "I mean the other one. The original one."

Monk said nothing and looked away for a moment. Then, "Yeah, I know."

"You tell me a horror story about a mother losing her child in the worst possible way, and about how the tattoo of her daughter smiling is her lifeline, but that doesn't really square with her defacing the tattoo and claiming she doesn't have a daughter at all. Or, at least has no memory of anyone named Tuyet. Any thoughts on that?"

Monk turned back. "Yeah. I think she drank a whole case of beer and got stupid shitfaced, hit her head on something in the bathroom, and is pretty damn messed up overall." He leaned forward. "Let me ask you something, Crow. You have anyone you'd do anything for? I mean absolutely anything? Take a bullet for? Not because you're a cop but because the person with a bull's-eye on them matters more than your life, your pain?"

Shadows moved like ghosts behind the police chief's eyes. "Yes."

Monk nodded. "So don't ask me why I took that hit rather than let Patty do any more damage to herself."

It took a moment, but Crow gave him a small nod.

Monk said, "You have any kids?"

"I had four," said Crow very softly. "Two died."

"Oh . . . fuck, man, I'm sorry. I hope they went out cleaner than what happened to Tuyet."

Crow said nothing. The ghosts were still there in his blue eyes.

"My point is," continued Monk, "that there's nothing and no

one in this world matters more to Patty than Tuyet. She kisses that picture every morning when she wakes up and before she goes to sleep. She talks to it—to her—because it's all she has of her baby. What do the MRIs say?"

"That she has a mild contusion consistent with a fall. No skull fracture and no concussion."

"Bullshit."

"X-ray and CT scan confirm."

Monk stared at him. "I . . ." he began but had nowhere to go with that. Then he cleared his throat. "Am I under arrest, Chief?"

Crow took a moment, then said, "Not at the moment."

"I saw a lady cop in the hall. My guess is you had her in with Patty. Why don't you go talk to her? Ask her what Patty actually said. Then either come back and arrest me or give me my shit back and let me go about my business."

As if on cue the female officer tapped on the door. Crow crossed to her and stood watching Monk as the officer spoke quickly and quietly in his ear.

While he waited, Monk thought about the chief. The man was small and somewhere in his fifties, but he had the look. The kinds of scars that come from conflict. If the scars were older Monk would have pegged him as a welterweight boxer or wrestler. All-State or maybe Golden Gloves. A tough little monkey who grew up rough. But the facial scars were relatively new, maybe earned in the last twenty years. Maybe from the Trouble. There were also calluses on the man's knuckles, the heels of his palms, and the edges of both hands. Those calluses were old, suggesting a lot of years in the martial arts. Since the knuckle calluses were the least defined, Monk pegged Crow for a student of one of the open-handed styles, like maybe jujitsu or aikido, or one of the animal styles of kung-fu. Mantis or Eagle. There was no bullshit bravado or dick measuring. This gun knew he was tough and had no need to sell that to potential bad guys. He was one to watch.

Crow came back and sat, blowing out his cheeks. He was no longer smiling.

"How's Patty?" asked Monk before Crow could speak.

"She's being admitted for observation. Her blood alcohol level is exceptionally high, but she's also dehydrated. Borderline malnutrition, too."

"Yeah, well, Patty's been dealing with anorexia for a long time," said Monk.

Crow nodded. "Doctor says the wounds look self-inflicted, so we'll put her on suicide watch for a day, and maybe two. Does she have a regular therapist?"

"No."

"Family?"

"Two sisters back in 'Nam she doesn't talk to. Not even birthday cards. Some cousins in the Bronx she never talks to. No one else."

"A friend we can call?"

"You're looking at him."

Crow nodded. "You understand that I'm going to check you out, Mr. Addison? If I get even a whiff of anything suggesting abusive behavior—"

"Yeah, I get it. You'll send some cops to arrest me."

"Not exactly. If I come to the opinion that you are responsible for what happened to that woman," said Crow quietly, "I'll pay you a visit myself."

There was no trace of a smile at all. Crow was half his size and nearly twenty years older, but his eyes chalked the odds on the slate.

Crow put a foot against the edge of the coffee table and pushed it three inches toward Monk. "You're free to go."

"I'd rather stay right here."

"I'd rather you didn't," said Crow. "Leave a cell number."

Monk digested that, then took a business card from his wallet and handed it over. Crow glanced at it, nodded, and tucked it in his pocket.

With that Chief Crow stood, gave Monk a tiny nod, and went out.

Monk sat for a moment, staring at the empty doorway.

"Yeah," Monk said softly, "welcome to fucking Pine Deep."

53

Owen Minor stood in a patch of sunlight that leaned into the room. He liked the feel of the smile that twisted his lips.

Outside was a beat-up old car with a U-Haul trailer attached. Out-of-town plates. A man stood on the pavement staring at the car and everything about his body language spoke of anger and tension.

Owen checked to make sure no one was looking at him and then reached up under his shirt, worming his finger along belly flesh until he touched his sternum. He could feel something there. Something new.

And . . . something different.

Wriggling like maggots through his skin.

He couldn't wait to get off work so he could go home and find out what it was.

54

Monk looked at his U-Haul and car. They were exactly where he'd left them. Locks were locked, everything appeared normal. Except nothing was normal in this damn town. He didn't even need to actually poke around to know that cops had already had a look. Smart, careful cops. This Chief Crow continued to impress and piss Monk off in equal measures.

He knew nothing would be missing.

"Asshole," muttered Monk, but he didn't really mean that. Or, more accurately, he wasn't sure. Crow could be a semi-corrupt small-town cop breaking rules because he liked being in charge and in the know. Or . . . Crow could actually give a shit about what had happened to a single woman living alone in his town. Either motive would explain the way Crow had kept the conversation going so his people could search the car and trailer. If it was the former, if Crow was a bad guy, then he was going to be a pain in the ass and maybe a real problem.

If it was the latter, then Monk would have to be careful not to become an actual problem. Crow was a small man, but he had very big power. What Patty called big energy. Tiger energy.

"Mucho cuidado," he told himself.

A rustle made him turn and look up. The birds were still there. Nightbirds looked different during the day. Less sinister, more vulnerable, somehow. Like old men who wanted to help but were aware they were past their physical prime.

Monk nodded to them, not sure why he did it.

One of the birds opened its mouth and made a low sound. Not a caw. More like a cough. Somewhere in a part of the sky Monk couldn't see, thunder rumbled in an "I'm not done with you yet" kind of way. He turned up the collar of his leather jacket, got behind the wheel, and drove home.

INTERLUDE TEN   **THE LORD OF THE FLIES**

Owen Minor drove to the tattoo parlor where Malibu Mark worked, but it was a bust. The studio was high end and did not take walk-ins. The receptionist, a tiny woman named Tink who was covered in some of the best ink Owen had ever seen in person, was a little snooty and asked why he hadn't called to book a session. Owen lied and said that he didn't know the rules because he'd never gotten a tattoo before. In truth, he didn't want his phone number in their records.

Tink's attitude defrosted a few degrees and she patiently explained the process and went over the cost structure. He made an appointment to come back and gave her the number to a disposable cell, a burner. He was already being cautious, following the rules of safety and anonymity he'd learned from reading crime novels and watching true-crime shows.

Waiting the eleven days for his appointment was excruciating. His imagination went into overdrive, swerving into deep desire and gut-twisting paranoia. He kept expecting a knock on the door and some kind of cop or agent to barge in. Some Scully and Mulder thing; taking him into custody for crimes that were on no books, but for which he'd be locked away forever. Or sent to some freaky government lab where they would study him, take samples, dehumanize and enslave him, forcing him to do some kind of spooky spy shit. Or, one of his victims would have tracked him down somehow, and come to cut his heart out for what he'd done. Not that Owen felt a flicker of remorse for what he was doing. No. None at all. He wouldn't have this gift if it wasn't meant for him to use. As he saw it, this was no different than someone being born with a beautiful voice breaking hearts by singing sad songs. No different than a soldier pulling a trigger because he was a natural killer.

In the moments when he was not filled with fear, he was turned on far beyond his ability to masturbate his way to a calm space. Even when he jerked himself raw on his third or fourth orgasm in a single night. He thought about how it would feel to devour the dreams of someone like Charles Manson or Ted Bundy. It was a rush reading about them, but to be them in dreams? Holy fuck.

One of his victims had been a biker who'd stomped a gay teen-ager to death after paying the kid twenty bucks for a blowjob. That had been a real head trip. All those complex emotions—the bik-er's desire, his shame and anger, his rage and the heartbreak he felt way down deep because he wanted to be the boy he was kill-ing. Those memories were so powerful, and sunk deep into the biker's soul via a tattoo that was a straightaway on a long desert highway. The road was straight, but the biker was twisted. The ink was intended as a statement—straight as the endless high-way, blah blah blah—but in his alone times that biker clamped a hand over the image and crumpled onto his shower floor, weep-ing, praying to God, begging forgiveness. Only when he was drunk, only when he was alone.

The days passed and finally it was time to see Malibu Mark.

The artist looked like Uncle Fester from the old Addams Family movies, except for wildly hairy Einstein eyebrows. He gave Owen an up and down inspection that was so penetrat-ing it felt like rape. Owen couldn't read his face, but there was some kind of magic in the man's eyes. Like he knew on some level. When he spoke, though, his words and tone were low-key, normal.

"Your first?" asked Malibu Mark.

"Y-yes," said Owen, stumbling over it.

"How'd you hear about me?"

"There was an article in *Tattoo Master*."

"Oh," said the artist, sounding vaguely disappointed, "yeah. So . . . you have anything in mind?"

"I want to start small, you know? See if I like it?"

"Sure." Another layer of disappointment.

"I want a fly."

"Like a zipper?"

"No, the insect." Although the memories of his first stolen tattoo were gone, the image of the actual ink was there in his mind. And he had dozens of photos of it taken that first night with his cell camera. Even a video of him holding his hand up and turning it this way and that. Owen had studied the vine and leaves, but they were of little interest. He thought the mantis was too stuck-up looking, and he had no interest in bees. The fly, though . . . that one caught his eye. He'd done an image search online and found out that it was a blowfly. Properly, a Calliphoridae, and sometimes called a carrion fly, bluebottle, greenbottle, or cluster fly. He preferred *blowfly,* though. It had a certain charm to it. Shakespeare was the very first writer to use that name, in *Love's Labour's Lost,* and later in *The Tempest.*

Owen dug his phone out of his pocket and showed several pictures of that insect, saved from nature websites.

"Just that?" asked Malibu Mark.

"For now, yes."

"Okay . . . but it's not going to take very long time. Couple hours, tops. Sure you don't want something bigger, more of a statement piece?"

"No," insisted Owen, "just the fly. And I want it here." He pushed up his sleeve and touched a spot on his forearm near the crease. "A big one. Life-size."

"Cartoon or real?"

"Photo-real."

Malibu Mark studied him for a moment, and Owen was never sure what he thought or what he read, but he nodded and explained the procedures, the costs, and everything Owen needed to know as a first-timer.

Owen had read up on what to expect and watched endless YouTube videos. Even so, he was surprised how much it hurt.

He was not at all surprised at how good that felt.

55

Malcom Crow lifted a single blind and watched Monk Addison pull away from the curb. When the car vanished in the distance he let the blind drop and left the doctor's lounge and drifted up to the injured woman's room, to where one of his officers, Kait, sat guard outside.

He indicated the patient on the other side of the door with an uptick of his chin. "She say anything?"

"Not a lot," said Kait. "Keeps telling everyone who goes in that she's fine, it was all an accident and that she wants to go home."

"Accident," said Crow, and sniffed eloquently.

"It's weird, Crow, 'cause I talked a bit with Dr. Argawal and he said that the bruises on her face are the wrong size and angle for someone to have whaled on her. He thinks they're self-inflicted. Said he can't pin down who inflicted the other stuff, but it's likely she did those, too."

"What about that smiley face tattoo on her hand?" asked Crow. "The one over the one that's kind of faded."

"She says she did that herself while drunk. You believe that?" asked Kait.

"Not sure what I believe, yet."

"Sure, but she's supposed to be this top pro tattoo artist and that new tat looks like it was done by a five-year-old."

"Five or thereabouts," murmured Crow vaguely.

"Definitely not what a pro would do is my point," said Kait. "Like maybe someone did that to her."

"Yeah," said Crow, "that had occurred to me, too."

"It's messed up, either way."

"Yup."

They looked at the closed door to the private room.

"I'm heading back to the office," Crow said after a few moments. "Call me if there's anything. Oh, and Ms. Trang's friend, the big guy with the tats? He doesn't get in. Nobody tells him anything, not even the time of day, until I decide it's cool."

"He our bad guy?" asked Kait, lifting an eyebrow and revealing a predatory gleam in her brown eyes.

"To be determined."

She cocked her head. "Horseback guess?"

Crow smiled, and as he often did, turned the question around. "What's your call?"

Kait was in her mid-thirties and had—as she called it during her interview for the job—"been around the block a time or two." She was on the hopeful side of cynical and had good reasons not to like most men. Even so, she shook her head.

"I talked to him for only a second," she admitted. "But he asked darn near everyone in the ER staff about Ms. Trang. Could be concern for a friend, but . . ." She shrugged. "He's guilty of something, but I don't know if it's this."

"Bad guy?"

"Dangerous," said Kait after some thought. "A little scary, too."

Crow nodded. "That's my read, too. Stay sharp and pass along what I said to Cooper when he comes on shift."

"Gotcha, boss."

Crow left the hospital and stepped out into the sunlight. There was a well of golden light spilling down through a ring of clouds that—so far—was hanging back. Crow didn't trust those clouds even a little.

The police station was only three blocks away, so he walked. He had a slight limp from some old damage to his hips and lower back. No amount of physical therapy could edit it out, so he settled into the pace that didn't aggravate it. The day was lovely and cool, and despite the heavy rains last night the trees hadn't been stripped of their leaves. That was something he loved about Pine Deep. The same storm in Doylestown or Easton or Hatboro would have punched all the autumn colors from the trees, giving everything a faux-winter appearance. But not in Pine Deep. No, here those leaves—the reds and oranges and yellows in ten thousand subtle shades—held on well into November. The riot of colors was breathtaking, and he never got used to it. Never became jaded by it. There was something about those colors that stoked the furnace of his optimism.

Faces peered at him through the windows of the stores along Corn Hill. A lot of them were new, but there were enough long-time residents to make him feel less like an outsider in his own town, which had started to be a thing. The population of Pine Deep was in a strange flux. Before the Trouble there had been close to twenty thousand people, divided between town and the farms. Like a lot of farming communities, the square acreage of the town was out of proportion to the population density. Those twenty thousand lived in an area a good deal larger than Manhattan, which gave the area a small-town feel. Then there was the Trouble; 11,641 people died, more than half the population of the town, marking it as the worst disaster in American history. Since then many of the surviving residents had moved elsewhere. Anywhere but Pine Deep, leaving barely four thousand to rebuild.

Since then, the town had come back to life a bit, like a cancer patient. Remissions and relapses. Three years ago the members of the new Fringe community started moving in, and in considerable numbers, though the overall population was still less than five thousand. They brought money and youth and energy. Good for the financial well-being of the town, but they were all outsiders, and some of them were extreme. The townies—known familiarly as the locals—were hard sells when it came to anything new and different.

The part of town where a lot of these newcomers settled was one that had been virtually obliterated during the Trouble. During reconstruction new streets and neighborhoods had been created. The main drag through that part of town was Boundary Street, though Crow could never quite figure out what it was a boundary of, or between. If there was a meaning to it, then only the nutbag who kept posting fake street signs understood the joke. It was lost on Crow.

"Just kind of came to me in a dream," the planner liked to say. "Woke up and there was that name in my head."

Boundary Street it became, and over time it became an actual boundary. The Fringe—as the new neighborhood was informally called—was on the other side of it, and pushed itself away from the town proper into municipal scrub that had never been developed. New stores, some nightclubs, and other businesses sprang up with surprising speed, and the Fringe took on its own unique personality. More like the way Chelsea had been in New York City in the late 1960s, New Hope, Pennsylvania, in the late seventies, or 1980s South Street in Philly. Some of the locals called the new residents freaks and geeks, or some variation of that. But since none of the Fringe-dwellers caused any problems, they became part of the Pine Deep landscape. Their stores and clubs brought in a new wave of tourists, and although these visitors spent the majority of their dollars in the Fringe, there was spillover to all of the town's businesses. Nothing, in Crow's experience, created a bond like increased income in a financially distressed town.

That said, there were a lot of raised eyebrows at the type of businesses in the Fringe. A retired drag queen bought an old grain warehouse and turned it into a burlesque club featuring male and female dancers, including a strong contingent of body-positive performers. Then a lesbian couple opened a bar with the best selection of craft beers in the county. A former Amish guy and his boyfriend opened a signature pizza place. Other clubs sprouted up seemingly overnight, bringing with them the kinds of stores that supported their themes—clothing boutiques, piercing studios, electronics stores, vape shops, art galleries, and more.

What was unusual was that most of these Fringe groups— even the ones that in other cities did not necessarily mix— seemed to cluster together in the new community. A second wave of newbies—mainly hipsters, some tech start-up guys, and artists—were drawn to Pine Deep's new vibe, but they went more for integration with the locals. Many bought the big farmhouses left empty by the Trouble, getting them for pennies on the dollar from distant relatives of the deceased, or at public auction for back taxes.

Crow's wife, Val, owned the biggest working farm in town, but it was framed on three sides by farms that grew nothing except wildflowers and unharvested pumpkins and wild corn. If people wanted to stop and pick any of that stuff, the residents usually just smiled, waved, and told them to have at it.

Even so, there wasn't a lot of mixing with most of the

newcomers and people who'd lived through the Trouble. Crow knew that the newbies were aware of it, and of that tragedy years ago. Hell, everyone in the country knew about it. The story—the government's official version—had been the only news for weeks. Reporters made careers and won Pulitzers on the Trouble. Books had been written—nonfiction and fiction; there were movies and one series on Netflix that lasted four years. Everyone knew of it, but no one talked about it. Not in town. The longtimers never ever said a word beyond using the Trouble as a chronological reference point. Something was either "before the Trouble" or "after the Trouble." None of them spoke about the Trouble itself. No, sir. Not here and not ever. If one of the newbies ever broached the subject the longtimers would go cold and silent and without saying as much told the newbies to go fuck off. Mostly the newbies did, in fact, fuck off. The two populations intermingled when they had to, but otherwise it was like two towns superimposed over one another without ever being actually one unified thing.

If anything, Crow mused as he walked, he and his officers were the only people who had to move and interact with both groups. Nature of the job.

He reached his office and went in, jangling the little bell above the door. Gertie was at the dispatch desk, obviously bored, playing Angry Birds or some shit on her phone. She gave him the briefest of looks.

"Nothing's happening," she said. Gertie was forty-something, but had looked fifty-something since high school. She was very tall and thin and angular and Crow thought she looked like a stick bug who'd semi-evolved into a human being. Her clothing choices shuttled between pastel yoga pants with heavy sweatshirts or leggings with heavy sweatshirts. Even in summer. She did not—nor had she ever, as far as Crow knew—attended a yoga class. Her hair was a taboo subject. For the last few weeks Gertie had been going to one after another of the hair salons along Boundary Street. Instead of coming into work rocking some cool color—Crow loved all the dynamic hues he saw on the streets—she kept her own mousy brown but sported a series of bizarre styles. The current 'do looked like a bed of hair in which weasels had been having ugly makeup sex. Crow was getting mouth scars from biting his lip.

"Okay," he said. "Hey, is there coffee?"

"If any's left," she said, not looking up again from her game.

Crow mouthed *kiss my ass* silently.

"I heard that," said Gertie.

"No, you didn't."

"I did."

He went over to the coffeemaker, saw that the pot was almost empty and cold. He manfully resisted the urge to fling the carafe at her, and instead cleaned it and made a fresh pot. Just to be pissy he made hazelnut, which he knew she didn't like.

Above the coffee station was one of a dozen different inspirational posters Crow bought once at a police convention. They were intended to encourage best practices. After years they had faded so thoroughly into the background that no one took notice. Except now. The one Crow stared at as he rinsed out his mug read: NOT ALL CRIMES LOOK LIKE CRIMES (THINK OUTSIDE THE BOX).

He stared at those words as if seeing them for the very first time.

He put a plastic stirrer in his mouth and chewed it thoughtfully for a few moments.

When the coffee was done, he poured a cup, added three

packets of sugar, all the while considering those words. then Crow went to his office, left the door open, turned on his laptop, accessed a couple of interjurisdictional databases, and did a very thorough background check on Patricia "Patty Cakes" Trang and Gerald "Monk" Addison.

56

Home. Kind of.

Monk had only been to the place three times before. Twice with a realtor, once with Patty. Most of the paperwork was done at the realtor's office in Doylestown. Monk wasn't sentimental about the place. It was a house and the odds were pretty sucky that it would ever become a true home.

It was at the edge of town, off Corn Hill, down a crooked lane, alone on a cul-de-sac. That's what the realtor called it. Fancy name for a dead-end street.

He turned around and carefully backed the U-Haul to within a foot of the garage door. Installing an electric opener was on his to-do list, right behind "give a fuck." He killed the engine, rolled down the window, and sat for a few moments, listening to the day. Getting a sense of it. There were four other houses on the street, but they were clustered by the main drag. Everything in between were vacant lots where homes had burned down during the Trouble. Those lots were thick with uncut grass, weeds, shrubs and hedges run wild, scrub pines, and the ubiquitous maples that always seemed to spring up when lawn-care crews took a five-minute break. Older trees, the ones that survived the fires, stood crooked and dispirited.

The nightbirds were in the trees already, as if they'd flown ahead to wait for him. Anyone else would have been freaked by that, but Monk accepted their presence. He knew those kinds of birds. Or their cousins in other places he'd been. Not places exactly like Pine Deep, but places that were wrong in their own kinds of ways.

"What the hell are we doing here, Pats?" he asked aloud. Dust motes, silent and unhelpful, swirled in the weak sunlight beyond the windshield. He leaned forward and followed the slanting beams up and watched as the last holes in the clouds closed, leaving a complexity of gray covering everything.

Monk sighed, got out, and spent the next several hours unpacking and arranging. There was already some Ikea furniture here. Stuff he'd had shipped. The realtor had accepted some cash to have someone here to let the delivery guys in. None of the stuff was assembled. Monk wondered how much bourbon it was going to take for the Ikea assembly instructions to make sense. He had plenty, though. His drinking buddies back in New York had sent him off with a six-pack: Knob Creek 100, Maker's Mark, Elijah Craig Small Batch, I.W. Harper, Henry McKenna Single Barrel ten-year-old, and a lovely bottle of Elmer T. Lee Single Barrel. Good stuff, but it made a statement. Disposable gifts for a disposable friend. In a year he'd be nothing more than an anecdote for them to tell one another, and in two years he wouldn't even be that.

He found that the fridge was already turned on and the automatic ice maker had filled the plastic tray. Monk unpacked a box of drink-ware, found a chunky tumbler, dropped two cubes in, cracked the seal on the Maker's Mark, and poured three fingers. He stood in the kitchen and took a sip, letting it soak his tongue, enjoying the full-bodied oakiness, then getting those hints of the caramel and vanilla notes. Then the spicy burn made itself known, which is when he swallowed. That burn went all the way down to his soul.

The first sip was for him, and maybe for the house.

Then second sip, though . . .

He raised the glass for a moment. "Love you, Patty Cakes," he said. "Don't you fucking leave me. Don't you fucking lose your shit and leave me all alone. Don't you do that."

He pressed the glass to his chest so tightly he could feel his heartbeat. On his skin the faces watched, the way they did. Around him the ghosts of the murdered stood watching him. Every now and then one of them opened its mouth and screamed. Monk listened for the voice of a little girl amid the shrieking. She was there, on his chest. One of his oldest tattoos. He thought he heard her weeping.

Or maybe it was himself he heard.

He drained the glass.

Thunder rumbled again, but far away. Monk refilled the glass, took only a small sip, set up his laptop and loaded a playlist of Nawang Khechog on Tibetan flute, and picked up the damn instructions.

57

Her name was Tuyet.

Or so everyone told her.

Patty cowered under the blankets, glad the female cop was gone. Glad to be alone. Terrified to be alone. Wishing Monk were still there. Glad he wasn't.

Because of Tuyet.

Tuyet.

Her left hand was swathed in bandages. That helped. She could not see the crude smiley face she'd drawn. Patty told everyone—the doctors and nurses, the cop—that she didn't remember doing that new tattoo, but that was a lie. In her mind she crouched naked in one of the barber chairs in her studio, a pot of ink open, the needle buzzing like the open line of an old-style phone, sending only noise after someone else hung up.

The memory of that was as clear as memories associated with the little girl were hazy and fleeting. Everything connected with Tuyet was as splintered as pieces of a broken mirror on the floor of her mind. Drawing over the other face. Trying to use new lines to trap the little girl's face as it faded. Too drunk, too crazed to do it—or anything—right. Failing. Feeling her memories and perceptions shift like furniture in a house caught in a mudslide. As that sensation grew worse and the alcohol polluted her blood, her skills failed. Going a bit crazy. More than a little. The little girl's face warped, became distorted by her new lines, and then there was a time of blackness when she must have turned the attempted cage of lines into that stupid, ugly, mocking smiley face.

There was nothing after that until she woke up on the bathroom floor.

The memories of Tuyet were still fading, becoming nothing more than a plaintive voice crying in her thoughts. On some deep level, though, Patty knew that her attempts to save her memories was successful. Partially. Enough? She didn't know and with each hour she was losing hope that she could cling to at least some of the memories of. . . .

Of . . .

What was the name?

Tuyet. Yes. That was it. Tuyet.

Her daughter.

On the drive to the hospital Monk had kept talking, explaining Tuyet, clearly hoping to say something that would be the key that opened the lock on whatever box or chamber held those memories. He was crying, too. Monk. Crying. Tuyet had been murdered, he said. Monk had killed the killers. He'd been with Patty through the process of identifying the body, and then burying the little girl and Tuyet's own grandmother. Patty remembered her mother, remembered that she'd been killed. But not why. And there was nothing in any box, or room, or anywhere. The memories were gone. Something had opened her head like an October pumpkin and scooped out every last bit of who Tuyet was, leaving her only the awful knowledge that she could not remember a single thing about her only daughter. It was worse than rape, worse than being stabbed through the heart.

"Tuyet," she murmured and hated herself—deeply, passionately loathed herself—because she barely remembered that poor little girl who'd died half a world away.

"*Ám ảnh tôi*," she begged. "For God's sake . . . *Ám ảnh tôi*."

The minutes dragged past with cold indifference.

Ám ảnh tôi.

She said it again in English. Pleading.

"Haunt me."

In the wintry graveyard of her memories the only sound or movement was an empty wind that had no voice with which to speak.

58

Crow got a lot of information about Patty Trang and Monk Addison, but no insights. Her backstory was a lot of nothing details—driver's license, immigration, naturalization, work history. Crow sent requests through Interpol and directly to the police in Tuyên Quang, Vietnam, asking for details about the murder of Trang's mother and daughter. That would take time.

For Monk there was less than there should be. He was able to confirm that the man had been born in New York, enlisted in the army at eighteen, ran with the Airborne Rangers for three years and then with Delta Force, and received an honorable discharge eleven years later. His service record read like the fiction it had to be. According to what Crow could find, Monk's MOS came up as 63W, a job code that meant he was a wheeled-vehicle repairer. He'd been a sergeant and a mechanic? Crow smiled. Sergeant he could buy, but that was about it.

His guess was that the military occupational specialty on record was horseshit. Everything about Monk screamed special ops. And not an obvious branch like the Green Berets, because the database Crow was accessing would have said that. Could Monk have been Delta? Those guys were cagey about what personal details were ever revealed. There was a guy Crow knew named Joe Ledger who was some kind of black ops and background checks on him were fiction, too, and unbreakable.

Was that what Monk was?

Maybe, Crow thought. Monk had hinted he'd also been a PMC, but those companies were even more squirrelly when it came to revealing employee information. Safety concerns, sure, but a lot of it was hidden behind walls built by the various intelligence and military agencies who hired private contractors. Even if Monk was in custody for a provable crime, none of those agencies was going to share data with a small-town cop.

As he dug deeper he was able to confirm that Monk really did work chasing bail skips, and Crow actually laughed out loud at the name of one of the firms who had him on retainer: Scarebaby and Twitch.

The company was owned by J. Heron Scarebaby and Iver Twitch. Actual names. Crow sniggered all the way to the coffeemaker and back. How fucking unlucky do you have to be, to be hung with names like that? Did their parents hate them? Were both families cursed by witches?

"What's so funny?" yelled Gertie.

"Nothing," said Crow.

"You better not be laughing at my hair, Malcolm Crow. I told you about that before."

"I'm not laughing at you, your hair, or anything in that whole corner of the office."

"You better not be."

"Hand to God."

Gertie lapsed into the kind of silence where it was clear she did not believe Crow and was going to be listening for validation of her suspicions. Her hair really did look like weasels were committing unspeakable acts in it.

Crow called the bond firm and got Mr. Twitch on the line. Scarebaby was, according to his partner, at another fat farm and hadn't bothered to bring his phone. Crow murmured a sympathetic noise and asked about Monk Addison.

"Why?" asked Twitch. "Is he is trouble again?"

"Again?"

There was a pause as Twitch probably suddenly realized what he'd just said to a cop. "Just a joke," he said quickly. "Monk's great. How can I help?"

"Doing a routine background check on him," said Crow. "Confidential."

"Uh huh. Is he okay?"

"He's fine. This is just routine and—"

"I'm an attorney," interrupted Twitch. "Criminal law. Don't talk to me like I'm a tourist."

"Is Mr. Addison your employee or your client?"

"He is both," said Twitch with a touch of asperity. "So, again I ask, is he in trouble?"

Crow drummed his fingers along the side of his WORLD'S GREATEST DAD coffee cup for a moment. "He is a person of interest in a matter we're investigating."

There was a soft *hmmm-hmmming* from Twitch, then he said in a quick rapid-fire, "You're Pine Deep PD. Monk just moved there. Pine Deep is where the Trouble was. Pine Deep is a notoriously weird little town. I've read the articles. The Most Haunted Town in America. What's your advertising slogan? 'Visit America's Haunted Holidayland'?"

"Past tense," said Crow. "We're pretty chill these days. Arts and crafts. Gearing up for our first fringe festival."

"Uh huh," said Twitch in exactly the way someone would say "bullshit." "What's Monk into?"

"I can't comment on an active investigation."

"Is Monk in custody?"

"No."

"Is Patty okay?"

Crow paused. "You know Ms. Trang?"

"Patty Cakes, sure."

"Can you tell me, please, about the nature of her relationship with Mr. Addison?"

"Is Patty okay?" Twitch repeated, leaning on it a little harder. And there was something in the tone that made Crow wonder if Twitch already knew the answer. Had Monk called him? Probably, he decided.

"She was brought into the emergency room of the Pinelands Regional Medical Center," explained Crow. "She's in stable condition."

"What happened to her?"

Crow said, "I'm going to be frank with you, Mr. Twitch . . . Ms. Trang came in with bruises on her face and body, a variety of small cuts, and a minor head injury. She claims that this is all self-inflicted during a drunken blackout, which is also the story Mr. Addison tells. Her blood alcohol content was .34, so that bears out some of it."

"What about other drugs? And, before you stonewall me, Chief, Patty's my client, too, and I'll get any test results I might need."

"I didn't call to stonewall you, Mr. Twitch, I'm looking to make sense of this. So, no, there are no traces of cocaine or other drugs. No Rohypnol, either, but I have some concerns about Mr. Addison and—"

Twitch's sharp snort of laughter cut him off. "Fuck me to tears, Chief, but if you think Monk Addison beat up Patty Cakes, let me set you straight. Monk only looks like the kind of guy who would cut your liver out with a dull spoon and make you buy it back while thanking him. He's a big, scary, deeply dangerous son of a bitch and that's me, his friend and lawyer, saying it. But—and this is a big twerking *but*—Monk is one of the good guys. Not a nice guy—God, don't ever get that impression—but if he has your back, then you never need to look over your shoulder."

"As you said, you're his lawyer . . ."

"Sure, you think I'm hyping him because he pays me. Sure, sure, and no. I know Monk. Not as well as Patty, but well enough. And, let me say this, if someone in your freaky-deaky little town has hurt Patty, then you do not want to get between that unfortunate asshole and Monk Addison. No, sir, you do not. Monk has this thing about people putting hands on women and kids. Let's call it a zero tolerance policy."

"So he's what? Captain Hero?"

Twitch laughed again and it sounded genuine. "Tell you what, Chief Crow," he said, "you go ahead and investigate all you want. If you like Monk for what happened to Patty, knock yourself out trying to sell that. It's your time to waste. But once you realize that he's the one person who is never going to be a legitimate—and I'll use your phrase here—person of interest—and start looking for the actual asshole who might have done it? When you get there, take some friendly advice and just step out of Monk's way."

"I think we can handle ourselves, Mr. Twitch."

The lawyer was still laughing when he hung up on Crow.

The chief sat at his desk and frowned at the phone. Then at the computer screen. And finally down into the depths of his coffee. There were no answers anyway. He got up and walked over to the big picture window and stood looking out at the day. The words PINE DEEP POLICE were written in big, fancy silver and black letters across the glass and he stared out through the O.

Where there had been sunlight not an hour ago now there were storm shadows. Every store and building across the street was painted in bruise colors.

"Going to rain soon," he said aloud. Not really talking to Gertie, though she answered.

"It rains every day now," she said. "Probably that climate change stuff."

No, thought Crow, I don't think so.

59

Monk lay on the couch, his whiskey tumbler resting on his chest, eyes staring at the jumble of half-empty boxes, packing material, and newly assembled furniture. Seeing none of it.

He was only half awake.

Maybe less than half.

Most of him stood at the edge of a dream, and in that dream he stood at the bottom of a long hill. The road was steep and crooked and shrouded in dense shadows that clung like weeds to the path. Far, far above him there was a place of light and movement. He could hear beautiful melodies floating down on the night breeze, but they were indistinct and he could never quite place the tune or hear the words. He knew that if he could they would tell him so much. They would open doors for him. They would turn keys in the shackles he wore.

But he was down there in the fetid darkness, and they were way up there. Up that impossible hill. He knew that he could not climb all that way. Others could. Others had. Better people than he. There was a woman named Rain Thomas, a sort of client from back in New York, who made it all the way to the top. Patty had been there, too. She told him about it sometimes, after she'd dreamed her way there in the Fire Zone. Tuyet was already there, if she was anywhere at all. She deserved to be up in the light.

For a while, after Monk had torn himself loose from the blood and gunfire, the screams and fire of his former life as a soldier and private military contractor, he thought he would be able to make it there. During those years he followed the mystic's road from temple to temple, from priest to shaman to healer on six continents, Monk thought that he would earn his way there. He used to think the shadows were the world and the light was some kind of heaven, but he knew better now. The light was chaos. It was a fire that burned away who you thought you were and let you forge who you wanted to be.

That's why he wanted to go. People called him "Monk" because of his journey. He took the nickname and used it, hoping that it would be his ticket for a ride across Boundary Street and up that hill.

So far, though, the weight of his crimes was too heavy a burden for any form of transport. And so he stayed down in the darkness. Looking up.

Looking up at the multicolored lights of the Fire Zone.

Outside his house, on the porch rail and eaves, in the trees and on the roof, the nightbirds, lashed by rain and shoved by wind, stood witness to his dreams, seeing everything. Mourning with him.

60

Night came to Pine Deep like a thief.

It stole in behind storm clouds, quiet and sly, and it crept onto rooftops and along alleys and peered into every window. Dressed in threadbare clothes of shadow, it pretended to be mundane and ordinary and not at all like the villain it was. But this was night in Pine Deep, and it has never been anyone's friend.

Some people—longtimers who had lived through a couple of the Black Summers—understood this. Surviving blight and heartbreak opens doors to certain insights. These people bought little charms at the right shops. Not the knockoffs, but the real ones. Corn crosses with a ball of garlic pressed in the crosspiece. Spikes of thrice-blessed hawthorn they drove into the wormy dirt on all sides of their homes—not in the four directions of east, west, north, and south, but where the ley lines cut across the troubled land. Little stone figures of old gods set in shrines framed by holly and wild rose. Fairy homes that did not look at all like dollhouses—not to anyone who had eyes to see.

Night and the threat of a new storm lay heavily over Pine Deep. The wise locked their doors and kept the lights on. The unwary lay down and bared their throats to the night.

61

In her dreams Patty Cakes often went to the Fire Zone.

That's what the place was called. She knew that without knowing how she knew it.

It was a place she kept trying to find when she was awake but could only ever find in dreams. That never deterred her, though, because at her best and most lucid waking hours she was absolutely convinced the place existed. Not as a metaphor or some cryptic symbolism, but as stone and wood, as neon and asphalt, as flesh and beating hearts. The Fire Zone was out there somewhere. All that she needed to do was find the way when she was awake, but that path always eluded her,

In dreams she knew the way, though. It was a simpler journey.

Those dreams always started with her down in the shadows along Boundary Street. The version of it here in Pine Deep; the other Boundary Street in New York. And the one back in Tuyên Quang. Always a Boundary Street. Always shrouded in shadows, as if they defined the people who lived there. Like her. Like Monk.

As the dream began to unfold, Patty began climbing a long hill up to where the lights from the Fire Zone shone out. She sometimes ran up the hill, even though it was steep and hard. There was Music up there. Music with a capital *M*. Music that was alive, awake, aware. There were also stores and libraries and nightclubs. Lots of clubs. Café Vortex, where people danced on air. Torquemada's, owned by the Bishop, where you could actually die right there on the dance floor. And Unlovely's, where the beautiful Mr. Sin helped you find whatever it was that you lost, as long as you were willing to risk everything to get it back.

During that long night in the hospital Patty Cakes climbed the hill and stepped from shadows into the swirling, multicolored light. That first step always tore a gasp from her. Being pulled from the water at the very edge, the very last twitch, of drowning and clawing in a breath of air. It hurt in exactly that way. It was terrifying and beautiful in that way.

Going to the Zone was only partly for that breath of clean air. Mostly it was to escape.

Her dreams in that hospital bed started out sick and sad and then turned vile. She couldn't bear to look at the bandage on her left hand. She remembered the stupid cartoon face she'd drunk-inked onto it last night. But it was so fucking hard to remember why.

Fragments came back to her, and then dragged her down the hill and across oceans to a town in the jungle. To a memory of a little girl. Not of her daughter, which was maddening. But about her. About that morning the police knocked on her door to say they'd found her little girl. *Found.* That was what they'd said.

"Ms. Trang, I'm sorry to inform you that we found your daughter."

Found.

As if they were talking about a missing dog. *We found her and here she is, have a happy day.*

They found her. They found Tuyet.

Someone named Tuyet.

This morning, at home, Monk had yelled at her, telling Patty that Tuyet was her daughter. That it was Tuyet's face inked so carefully by Patty's own hand, that had been marred by the cartoon image. He snatched up pictures and showed them to her. Pictures of Patty with a little girl.

Tuyet?

We found your daughter.

The police had found her that day. Monk could find pictures everywhere of her. But as for Patty . . . she was certain she'd lost her. When she opened her head and heart and looked in, shining her brightest flashlight of introspection, there was no little girl hiding, waiting to be found.

There were shadows. There was a smudge of blood. A discarded shoe. Stained underwear. A broken bracelet.

But there was no one named Tuyet anywhere to be found.

So, Patty climbed up the hill and stepped into the neon glow of the Fire Zone clubs, looking.

Hoping to find a little girl named Tuyet amid all the swirling color and movement and hope.

62

When Crow was finished chasing down every last crumb of information on Monk Addison and Ms. Trang, the sun was down and the clouds were strangling the last bits of twilight from the sky. The weather report said that it was already raining here and there across the sprawl of Pine Deep, but there were only indifferent patters against his window. Even without stepping outside to smell the air Crow knew it was going to be another bad storm. The day had that kind of vibe. A slow threat, like walking around a tiger who was nowhere near as asleep as he pretended to be.

There was a stack of accident reports on his desk from tourists who for some reason forgot how to drive when two drops of rain fell. That was a Philadelphia metro-area thing that always perplexed him. Philly was a humid and rainy city and always had been, but as soon as it started drizzling people acted totally surprised and, he was sure, lost forty IQ points at the first crack of thunder. Snow was even worse. Didn't matter if there were a dozen measurable snows the previous year, a half-dozen tiny flakes would make them all lose their damn minds. There would be fender benders all the way to the closest convenience stores, to which the citizens were hurrying for milk, bread, and toilet paper. God only knew how many—if any at all—would survive an actual catastrophe. Crow was sure this was Darwin in action.

Luckily no one in Pine Deep had killed themselves on the roads. Worse injury so far was a guy who had cracked his head on his windshield after hitting a cow. Crow only glanced at that, saw Mike had handled the incident, and left it, figuring Mike would tell him about it over dinner or breakfast. Mike was Crow's adopted son as well as his senior patrol officer.

He looked around the office. Gertie was gone for the day and the night shift operator, the ancient stick figure that was Mrs. Langston, sat at the desk reading a battered old copy of Truman Capote's *In Cold Blood*. She was always Mrs. Langston. Never Joan. Never anything else. In terms of personality she was the exact opposite of Gertie in that she almost never spoke except to handle dispatch duties, wasn't chatty, had zero personal warmth but also zero animosity. Mostly just zero. A monotone robot would be a cheerier office companion. Crow knew that Mrs. Langston had buried three husbands and both of her children and figured that life had crushed the chattiness out of her.

"I'm heading home," said Crow.

No answer.

"I'll lock the door on the way out."

Nothing.

"Have a wonderful evening filled with joy and rollicking laughs," he said.

Nothing.

"There's a live pterodactyl in the break room."

Mrs. Langston lowered the book and looked at him without expression as she turned the page, then the book rose to cover her face again.

"Right," said Crow. He grabbed his umbrella, tugged a Phillies cap down over his salt-and-pepper curls, and went out into the windy street. His car was a vintage 1970 Buick Gran Sport 455 Stage 1, a classic muscle car that had, at some point, been painted an absurd shade of puce but was otherwise in superb condition, with 400 horsepower and 510 pound-feet of torque on tap. He'd bought her from a dealer in Levittown and named her Middy in celebration of the midlife crisis he did not try to hide. She sucked gas but could run a quarter mile in 13.38 seconds at 105.50 mph. Not that Crow, chief of police and pillar of the community, ever exceeded the posted speed limits. At least not outside of the jurisdiction of officers whose paychecks he signed.

Middy roared to life and as soon as he was out of town and into farm country he opened her up and let her bash her way through the storm. But almost at once the rain stopped. In a reversal of its recent pattern, the storm was squatting down over the town but hadn't yet stretched out over the farms. Crow was okay with that and put the pedal down.

As he drove he mulled over what little he'd learned today. There was plenty of information in the various databases he checked, but at the end of the day what did he really know about Monk and Trang? Apart from Mr. Twitch vouching for Monk—which as his lawyer and employer the man was bound to do—there wasn't a lot there to help Crow shape an opinion.

And the hospital staff was no help. No one who spoke with Ms. Trang held the belief that she had been abused by Monk Addison. The staff shrink didn't even think the Trang woman had attempted suicide. The whole thing might dwindle down to a borderline-anorexic woman drinking way too much and doing some self-harm during a blackout. There wasn't even much to justify holding her overnight, let alone for much longer. The head injury, minor as it was, gave the docs the small leverage they needed to convince her to stay in for observation.

"What about her memory loss?" Crow had asked the psychiatrist assigned to the case.

Dr. Maddie Wolfe explained about traumatic amnesia, the memory loss that can occur after a blow to the head or other systemic shocks. "Most likely those memories will return. Could happen overnight or it could take months. She should see someone, though. I'll print out a list of names of therapists."

"What's going to happen when those memories come back?" asked Crow. "What with her having defaced the portrait of her daughter?"

Wolfe had looked truly pained. "It's going to be awful for her."

Yes, thought Crow, no doubt about that at all.

He wished Wolfe had gotten the chance to talk with Monk Addison. Her insights on him would have been useful. Crow wasn't actually sure he believed Monk was a danger to the woman.

But the man was dangerous. The potential for violence clung like a bad smell to the guy. He was the kind of man cops would always take note of. What they used to call a "cronky" way back in the day. Someone who had been in trouble, was in trouble now, or would inevitably be in trouble sometime soon. Now, whether that made him a bad guy or a good guy who flitted close to a dark flame was uncertain.

The Trang woman's story clawed at Crow's heart. He and his wife had buried two children. His wife had tattoos of her own to remember them. What fires had to be raging inside a mother's head to make her want to deface a memory tattoo of that special kind? What level of hell was Patty Trang walking through last night when she did that?

He topped a rise and below he saw the near edge of the vast sprawl of the farm owned by his wife. The Guthrie Place. Endless stalks of tall corn blowing in the wind. Garlic and pumpkins and other crops. Lush from all the rain. Still standing despite the storms. Every time he caught this glimpse it sent a wave of emotions flooding through him. So much of his childhood was spent on that farm. First making comic book and soda pop money working alongside the migrant workers picking corn. Later, after he and Val became friends, the two of them and their friends sitting on the porch, listening to Oren Morse—an itinerant worker and blues singer—fill the later afternoon air with song. Blues and soul, and even old folk. Maddie Wolfe's father, Terry, had been in the little pack that Val and Crow ran with. Crow's older brother, Billy, too. And some others.

And, as it always did, the memories of those harvest nights turned a knife in Crow because everyone else from their crew was gone. Billy died during the Black Autumn of 1974, killed by a serial murderer—a monster, really—who lived in town. There was a wave of slaughter that year and Val's uncle was one of the victims. The same killer nearly got Crow, but Mr. Morse—who everyone called the Bone Man because he was so skinny—saved him. Morse discovered who the killer was and murdered him down in Dark Hollow. But because the killer was a wealthy white landowner and Morse was a homeless black man, it was easy for the blame for all the murders to be laid on Morse. A vigilante group beat him to death and hung him on a scarecrow post.

Then, thirty years to the day when the original murders started, there was a fresh wave of violence. The Trouble. Before it passed it claimed the lives of Mayor Terry Wolfe, Val's father and brother, and thousands of other residents and tourists.

Those memories were always there. As real as if they were happening again right now. As vivid as if they were tattooed on Crow's flesh.

He rolled down the long slope and drove along the fence line.

There were good memories, too. Falling in love with Val. Losing their virginity together out in the cornfield. Getting married and building a life there. The children.

That twisted the knife even harder.

They had four biological kids and one adopted child. Mike Sweeney, of course, was the first to join their family. Then Val had four babies. The twins, now fifteen, Henry and Faith, and then Terry followed Abigail. The younger two were buried side by side beneath the sheltering arms of an ancient oak tree that guarded the front of the house.

With a flash of prescience, Crow knew that's where he would find Val. It was that kind of night. Had been that kind of month.

He punched the cassette player and ended the music as he turned off A-32 and onto the private drive ending in a gravel road that wrapped around the patch of grass where the oak stood. He stopped, switched off the engine, and sat for a long moment. The only sounds were birds in the trees and the tinkling of the cooling engine. Val was over there, seated on a canvas folding chair, hands clasped between her knees, strong back slightly stooped. Crow got out of the car and closed the door quietly, then walked across the grass to her. She'd brought his chair out, and beside it was a thermos of coffee. Crow did not kiss her head, touch her shoulder, or say anything. He knew her. Knew her needs at the moment.

He removed his wallet before he sat down and flipped through the glassine photo sleeves until he found the two pictures. Terry and Abigail. Their faces had all of Val's strength and beauty and Crow's grin. It was taken on Christmas morning. The last Christmas before Terry got sick. The last Christmas when they were all together, and healthy. And alive.

Crow placed the wallet on the grass so that they could both see those beautiful, smiling, perfect faces.

After a while Val reached over and took Crow's hand. They sat there for a long time and even the storm, vile as it was, did not attack until that vigil was done.

INTERLUDE ELEVEN   THE LORD OF THE FLIES

Owen stopped more than twenty times on the drive from Malibu to his apartment in Oceanside. To stare at the tattoo. He didn't dare do that while driving, because the image entranced him.

All along the way he thought he saw real blowflies whip past his windshield. At the rest stop near Camp Pendleton he saw a whole cluster of them crawling over the carcass of a dead crow. Owen froze in his tracks halfway to the men's room and stood there, staring.

Then his jaw fell open as the flies—at least three dozen of them—stopped their busy scurrying and turned toward him. To look at him.

The fly on his forearm throbbed with a sensation that was exactly half the distance between pain and pleasure. He shoved his sleeve up and stared at the ink. His heart lurched to an abrupt stop in his chest. The fly rendered by Malibu Mark was far more than photo-real.

It was real.

As he stood there, watching it, and aware that all of those flies were watching him, the inked fly trembled.

The tiny wings fluttered.

Owen did not even try to tell himself that he was imagining it. He seldom drank, hadn't done any drugs since getting off the antipsychotics, and wasn't nearly exhausted enough to be hallucinating. The fucking fly was moving its wings. He saw it.

He felt it.

And . . . he heard it.

"God almighty," he breathed.

The buzzing of the fly increased, and all of the other flies—the real ones—began buzzing, too. Owen's words seemed to echo in the air, sewn into the fabric of the moment.

God almighty.

Was he talking about himself?

The buzzing grew louder and louder and . . .

63

The storm killed business at the store and Ophelia let everyone go early.

Dianna debated driving to Wegmans, loading up on cake, risotto, and a big bottle of cabernet and maybe binge-watching something that did not involve too much rain, creepy clients, lost time, and problems with expensive tattoos.

It was a good plan, but that's not what she did.

Instead, she popped a very large umbrella, angled it into the wind, and pushed her way through the rain as she hurried along Boundary Street. The stores were going dark but the clubs lit the gloom with a hundred colors of neon and LED lights. Dianna sloshed past Othello's, where some of the leather boys were smoking under the big awning. Past the open doors of Pallbearers, where the plaintive self-lament of Armor for Sleep's "Car Underwater" was losing an argument with the thunder. She wasn't in an emo mood. It was too early for Tank Girl, which always had good dance music once the dinner crowd moved out.

What was left?

Halfway down the block was a big neon sign that jutted out almost to the curb, and on it was the stylized silhouette of a beautiful woman in a torn white dress with wild hair. The heavy breeze conspired to give the tatters of cloth and tendrils of black locks the appearance of actual movement. Very effective. La Llorona, a coffeehouse by day and wine bar at night. Across the front of the store was a marquee with OPEN MIC POETRY SLAM in black block letters.

Part of her wanted to flee from the thought of poets baring their souls on a night when she wanted to just forget everything. But that part of her didn't win the debate. She hurried down the street and slipped in out of the rain.

Inside it was warm and dark and the air was scented with coffee, whiskey, and baked goods. There were about two dozen people at the tables, filling nearly half the place. A bearded waiter in a lumberjack shirt was bringing drinks on a wooden tray while behind a small counter a woman with shocking magenta hair made drinks. Dianna found a table halfway to the stage but set aside from anyone close. She ordered a sake and gin martini and took her first sip as the manager stepped into a small circle of light in which was a wooden stool and a mic on a stand. He had a clipboard with the open mic sign-up sheet and called the next name.

"Let's welcome Leza Cantoral." There was real enthusiasm in the applause, suggesting the poet was either well known or had her entourage on deck. The woman who stepped into the spotlight was a short, curvy Xicana with wheat-colored hair over intentionally dark roots. Intense eyes that were a deep brown and accented with eyeliner that slashed backward, giving her a decidedly feline look. Very full lips and a strange little smile, as if she'd just told herself a joke but didn't want to share it. She wore a black T-shirt with a hand-cut deep V-neck and with this on the front: I Was a Witch in Every Lifetime.

She removed a folded piece of paper from her jeans pocket, opened it, took the mic, and then looked out at the audience for a moment, letting things go quiet. Dianna reached out a bit with her senses and tried to get a read on the poet, and found a lot of darkness. Not negative, not born in her, but wrapped around the woman. As if she'd been through strange emotional landscapes and survived, but had memories and scars. Dianna could certainly relate. She sipped her drink and waited out the fall of silence in the place.

"This one's about obsession," Cantoral said in a slow and husky voice. "About how we can't let some people go. Even I'm doing it with this poem. I'm obsessing on the way people obsess over Marilyn Monroe. We're all necrophiles in our own ways. This is 'A Series of Images to Convince You That She Is Dead.'"

Those dark eyes looked around, then the poet nodded to herself and began reading.

"A series of images that show her naked body in various poses . . . back when she was in the movies . . . some candids, outtakes, the ones that did not make the cut,

the ones with a big red *X* drawn across them . . . in red marker—her way to *X* out her imperfect selves."

Cantoral's voice was like smoke, coiling around the meanings and images.

". . . this is a movie . . . you are watching it . . . it is old scratched film . . . Super 8 film. You are drinking. You are drunk. You don't know why you are watching this."

A breath in an otherwise silent room.

". . . her eyes seem very alive . . . bright black in that projector glow . . . she is in a scene with other people—mostly men . . . but some women. There are a lot of bodies . . .

but it is somehow difficult to make her out, between the flesh and the ropes and the whips and the dogs, but then you start to recognize her body parts."

A flash of those eyes.

"Cut to a morgue . . . and she looks different. Her face—deflated. Dimples gone . . . skin pale . . . more pale even than before."

Cantoral's lip curls in disgust.

"Back to the glamor shots—early ones, from before she was famous, before she bleached her hair . . . and became the movie star. Full bush, scared but bold eyes . . . a smile to hide the pain."

Another breath.

"You think if you had loved her . . . if you had known her . . . you would have saved . . . protected her. But really . . . how?"

Cantoral's eyes glittered like jagged pieces of obsidian. Sharp and dangerous.

"What was her alienation that wrapped her up like a thousand scarves . . . pulling and pushing her from intimacy . . . holding her body as a shield between herself . . . and anyone . . . absolutely anyone . . . because it hurts more to be hurt again . . . than to be alone, with familiar wounds. You still can't believe she is dead though . . ."

There was a long moment before the applause began. Dianna glanced around and saw that the poem had hit some people more deeply than others. The ones who seemed indifferent to it, or who were possibly conjuring exactly the wrong kinds of Marilyn images, were fewer in number than those who seemed to get what the poet intended. Or, at least, get something deep for themselves.

"Damn . . ." breathed Dianna.

She finished her drink and stared into the empty depths of the glass. As she did so, her fingers absently—very absently—rubbed the place on her forearm where the beautiful rose had nearly faded away.

64

On the most distant outskirts of Pine Deep, near Songbird Bridge, a homeless man huddled into the doorless husk of an old refrigerator, an old rug pulled over him and newspapers lining the insides of his clothes. His name was left behind on a dusty road down south. The path from where he'd been when life turned on him to where he was now that life was nearly over was on some map that had long ago been thrown away.

The other homeless wanderers called him Aqualung, after an old song from when they were young. Sometimes they'd mock him by singing the first few lines of the song, but they mostly got the lyrics wrong.

Aqualung shivered, partly from the cold, and in his dreams he spoke names he did not know. They were not his dreams, and that was his problem. Ever since he was a boy his sleeping thoughts were filled with other people's dreams, and other people's nightmares. Unwanted, unbidden, unbearable. Tonight it was worse, because he knew the things that haunted him were stolen and it was like he was strapped to a chair and forced to watch the ugliest and most graphic pornography. Not sex, but naked emotions, stripped raw and laid bare, and all of it set to a music score of buzzing insect wings. Ugly and unnatural in every sense of those words.

Aqualung tried to wake up, but he could not. The darkness pressed down on his chest like a nightmare hag, and he was too far away from any house for anyone to hear his screams.

The wind carried those cries with them, and if ears could not hear them, hearts could.

65

Leaving the house was a huge step for Gayle. Up until the moment when she gripped the doorknob in one sweaty hand she was positive that it would be an impossible act of stealth and subterfuge, requiring ninja skills she didn't possess.

Scott was playing Gridiron Champions on his Xbox and only barely noticed she was leaving. He grunted something, maybe at her or possibly at the screen. The kids were in the playroom doing homework. Even the cat was indifferent, entertaining himself by licking his ass. There was a statement of some kind there, but Gayle didn't feel like decoding it. Things sucked enough as it was.

"See you," she said to a house that barely acknowledged her at the best of times. Closed the door, heard the lock click, and then she was in the Honda and accelerating out of the cul-de-sac like she was driving a getaway car.

Her house was on the northwestern corner of Pine Deep and driving to the Fringe was a short trip, though between the old and rather odd layout of the town and the newer, even less orderly pattern of streets, it took fifteen minutes to drive a handful of miles. Traffic slowdowns from the rain as well as vast puddles added to it, but when she saw TANK GIRL in slowly flashing white neon, her heart jumped.

She drove right past the club.

Three times.

Circling the block while having increasingly acrimonious discussions with herself. Her personal parasite—a passive-aggressive little bitch that sounded a lot like her mother—whispered in her mind that she was betraying her husband, endangering her marriage, putting her kids' peace of mind at risk, and generally acting like a slut. That part of her mind was unkind and unflinching. It nearly won, too, because after her third time circling the block she had her flashers on to head away. To go to the Panera up in Crestville and kill the evening doing nothing of value on her iPad.

The light turned green and she began to make that turn.

Then her fingers curled with unexpected strength around the wheel and wrenched it to the right, away from the exit route, into another circle around the same block.

"If there's no spot in front I'll just go," she said aloud to herself and her parasite. "That'll be a sign."

There hadn't been a single space on either side of the street the last three loops. It looked just as full this time, and Gayle's heart began to sink. To accept.

But then a car pulled out thirty feet ahead of her, angled into the flow of traffic, and left a big spot. Exactly in front of the door.

As signs from the universe go, it was eloquent.

Gayle pulled in, took four minutes of debating before she turned off the engine. Ten more minutes before she got out. The rain was moving along the street in lazy waves, like the tail of a big koi, the drops painted exotic colors by the neon.

"This is stupid," she told herself.

And got out.

66

Burleigh Hopewell, last surviving member of one of the town's oldest families, stepped out onto his porch, pipe in hand, eyes narrowed as he scanned the last of the twilight. The yellow porch lights pushed at the shadows, but then seemed to accept defeat and grew dimmer instead of brighter. Beyond the rail, past the gravel turnaround, the corn stood whispering, whispering.

Hopewell used his index finger to press the 4 Aces tobacco deep into the briar bowl, used his thumbnail to pop a stick match alight, and took long breaths to pull the flame through. He worked at it for a while until the pipe was drawing well, then he leaned a hip against the rail and watched the big stalks sway. They rustled as if something was moving through them. A careful deer or a sly coyote, perhaps.

He waited, listening, looking. Seeing nothing except the movement of leaves. The house behind him was empty, all of the migrant workers gone for the day. None of his regular help lived here, and there were no more Hopewells left in Pine Deep. The Trouble had taken his wife, his sister, and both of his kids. He'd been spared because he was at a growers conference in Pittsburgh, all the way the hell on the other side of the state. He was having a beer in the hotel bar, watching the Pirates get their asses handed to them by his own team, the Phillies, when they broke in with a news report. Something terrible happening in Pine Deep. Hopewell called home immediately and was relieved when his wife answered.

"Burr," she said in a voice that was oddly dreamy, "when are you coming home?"

"Belinda, what's happening? I saw on the news—"

"When are you coming home, sweetheart?" she'd asked, cutting him off. Her tone so soft.

"Are you okay? Are the kids okay? God, Belinda, they said the whole town's burning."

"We're all fine, sweetie," said Belinda. "We're home waiting for you. When are you coming home?"

"Honey," he said, "you sound funny. Are you okay?"

"I'm wonderful, Burr. Come home to us."

She sounded drunk. No, drugged, maybe. Like she'd taken too many Valium and was floating. The way she was when she overmedicated after writing checks for the bills they couldn't really afford to pay.

"Is Abby there?" he asked. "Put her on for a sec."

Abby was their oldest girl and was very much her father's daughter—practical, grounded, always clearheaded. When he was away, Abby ran the farm.

"Abby's here," said Belinda dreamily. "She's waiting for you, too. We're all waiting for you, Burleigh. Come home to us."

And then the line went dead.

He'd called back dozens of times, but there was no answer. There was never an answer.

Later, during the official investigation, they asked him about that call. He went over and over it, and even showed the call log on his phone. The officials glanced at one another and they stared at him. If it wasn't for the call log he knew they'd have dismissed him as confused, drunk, or so grief-stricken that he only imagined talking to his wife.

The call he made matched one received on Belinda's cell phone. The log on both iPhones listed the call was made and received at 8:19 on that evening. The call lasted for two minutes and ended at 8:21. There was no way to refute that the call had been made. What no one could ever explain to Burleigh Hopewell was who had answered it, because Belinda Hopewell had been one of a group killed when a bomb went off during a magic show that was part of the town's massive Halloween Festival. Abby and her brother, Trace, were found murdered that same evening, likely victims of either the white supremacists blamed for the terrorist attack or victims of people driven out of their minds by the hallucinogenic drugs in the town's water supply. The only thing the authorities could agree on was that none of the Hopewells took that call.

We're all waiting for you. Come home to us.

Burleigh Hopewell knew different. That had been Belinda on the phone. There was no doubt at all about that. He pushed up his sleeve and looked at the ink above his wristwatch. A small heart—red in the center but a morose gray around the edges, and in a circle around it were the names of his wife and family. The flesh beneath and around the tattoo ached. A dull sensation, like a bruise so deep it didn't purple the skin. But the heart looked strange lately. Not as vibrant. Paler. As if the ink had faded. Maybe it was time to have it redone, he thought.

"Yeah," he said aloud, waving at a fly that buzzed near his face. "I'll go to that new place in the Fringe."

The breeze through the darkened corn seemed to whisper a low and sneaky, "Burleigh . . ."

And it said that in Belinda's voice.

He clutched the hot bowl of his pipe and tried not to cry. He failed, as he failed every single night. The ache beneath the tattoo throbbed.

67

The bar was dark as pockets.

Flashes of lightning outside stole Gayle's night vision and she had to feel her way from the door to the bar. Tank Girl was semi-crowded, but most of the women there were huddled together in conversational envelopes, voices hushed, faces only marginally lit by tea candles. The music was loud, but deliberately so, forcing people to lean in. Gayle didn't recognize the singer or the song. A woman singing about standing on the ledge of a building, wondering if she can fly. Hoping she could because she was taking that step.

Gayle's paranoia meter was banging it at a solid ten and she was sure every eye was on her, judging her, criticizing her clothes, her weight, her right to even be there.

She slid onto a seat at the far end of the bar, with her back to a corner of a wall around which were the bathrooms. Tucked in there, with a sight-line to the exit.

"What can I get for you?"

Gayle turned, yipping a bit in surprise because the bartender had apparently materialized out of nowhere. A thin, tall, broad-shouldered Latina with a drop-fade crew cut and amused eyes.

"Um . . . I . . ."

The woman smiled, and the amusement turned to warmth. "You're new here."

"Yes," said Gayle, taking the question as multilayered and answering the same way.

The bartended nodded, her eyes shrewd but kind. "Don't worry, sister. This crew's pretty well behaved. Mostly guppies, a few sharks. No one gets out of hand."

Gayle laughed self-consciously. "Does it really show that bad?"

The bartender laughed, too. "Yeah. It's cool, though. If anyone messes with you, I'll set them straight. I'm Juana. Now . . . what can I get for you? Thinking of starting slow? A draft or some white wine? Or are you looking to kick it some?"

"What's in the middle?"

"How about a gin and tonic with lime?"

"Gin can sneak up on you."

"I know."

Juana nodded and mixed it. Gayle noticed that the pour was modest. Juana was not trying to work her or set her up. That was a comfort.

Gayle sipped her drink and listened to the music and—as her eyes adjusted—looked at the women. There were no men at all, not even straight or gay BFFs with their female friends. Only women. Gayle tried to decide who was a lesbian and who was bi, or bi-curious, but she had no real idea. Only a few of the women would have registered with her as obviously or possibly gay before she walked in. She was pretty sure there was a big blinking neon sign above her own head, though.

When an hour passed and no one seemed to even glance her way, Gayle checked herself in the mirror behind the bar. Her long hair was straight and glossy, the natural mahogany highlights showing through the black. She'd applied her makeup with subtlety. She wore a dark-brown Italian silk–merino wool

V-neck sweater with a ruffle from the top right shoulder down across the body almost to her left hip. The sweater was nicely fitted to accentuate her curves and show some cleavage, but with long sleeves because it was cold out. And she wore the tight black skinny jeans. A russet-colored scarf was draped around her, which Gayle kept pulling down to reveal her curves and then jerked back into place to hide them.

"You're going to pull a muscle doing that," said a voice and Gayle once more jumped half out of her skin. Were all lesbians freaking ninjas? She turned and then her mouth went totally dry.

It was her.

The black woman from the clothing store. Owning the space she stood in. Dark hair and dark eyes and very red lips. A wicked little knowing smile. Lots of silver jewelry and energetic stones. Black knit top with lots of subtle patterning. Black tights.

"I . . ." began Gayle and failed utterly to find a way to complete the sentence.

"You bought those jeans," said the woman. "Nice. They fit you so well. Is that seat taken? Good. My name's Dianna."

And that fast Dianna was seated next to Gayle, who was absolutely unable to utter a coherent sentence.

68

In her dream Patty reached the top of the hill and stepped from the shadows of Boundary Street across the line of light and into the Fire Zone.

The Music hit her like a wave. Harsh at first, but then everything she was, was suddenly aligned with what it was. The Music. Capital *M*. Sounds and songs that had been played so long, so well, with such insight and profound understanding that they had come alive, achieved consciousness and awareness and wisdom. The Music wrapped itself around her and kissed her and welcomed her to the Fire Zone.

Patty felt herself moving forward, along the street toward the avenue where thousands of people were laughing and dancing. The people around her seemed completely insubstantial, wisps of color in the shapes of men and women, and of children. With each step, though, each shape became more defined, more real in every way. Deeper, wider, brighter, hotter, infinitely complex in the way stars are. When Patty looked down at her own body she gasped to see that she, too, was dressed in rags of light. Shimmering and alive in ways she could never be back down in the shadows.

Dance with us, said a voice, and she turned to look, but instantly understood that the voice had come from inside her own mind.

"I don't dance," she said.

Everyone dances. It's how we are alive.

"I stopped dancing a long time ago."

Why? asked the voice, and it was as if the voices of every dancer around her spoke at once. Not in some overwhelming way, though. It was a perfect harmony, in time with the Music. Many of the voices were familiar. Many were not. All were her family, though. Soul family.

"I forgot how to dance," lied Patty.

No, said the voices. *No one ever forgets. We are made of star stuff, infinite and in constant motion. The universe moves within us and life itself is a dance.*

Patty tried to turn away, to hide her shame and her truth, but she realized with a shock that she was deep within the Fire Zone now. Completely surrounded by ten thousand shining faces.

Beyond the crowds rose the facades of the nightclubs where she used to dance in her dreams. Grim Torquemada's, with the massive bloodred neon hand flashing on its white wall. The swirling spike of silver and turquoise that was Unlovely's. Beyond that, Café Vortex, with a real spiral of wind that sucked up the dancers and sent them laughing into the night. And others. Too many to count. Dance clubs everywhere. Dancers and the dance everywhere.

"I don't want to dance anymore," protested Patty. "I'm not allowed."

The next voice spoke beside her and she turned to see a very tall woman with masses of red hair. Her body was ripe and lovely, dressed in a tight gown of shimmering green, and there was an emerald in her forehead. Not on a circlet—it seemed to grow out of flawless skin. But beneath the jewel and arching brows were smooth panels of flesh in which there were no eyes at all. And yet, on some instinctual level that reached all the way down to her soul, Patty knew that this woman was called Lady Eyes, and she saw everything.

Every.

Single.

Thing.

Who has told you that you are not allowed to dance?

Patty felt the tears on her cheeks burning like spilled lamp oil. "I forgot her name," she said with a sob. "I forgot her face."

Whose face have you forgotten?

"Tuyet . . . I forgot everything about . . ."

Her words trailed off as she realized she'd just spoken her daughter's name. Spoken it with surety, with a mother's unbreakable confidence.

Lady Eyes reached down and took Patty's hand, lifting it so

they could both look. Around them many of the dancers turned
to see. Their eyes were filled with fire. Lady Eyes used two very
long fingers to pluck away the bandage. There, on the back of
her left hand, was the face of Tuyet. The other tattoo, the crude
one, seemed to hover above the surface of Patty's skin, glow-
ing with a faint yellow light. A warning light, maybe, offering a
choice: stop now or drive faster.

She is right there, said the lady.

"She's leaving me," cried Patty. "He took her. He has her."

Who has her?

"Him!"

The Music seemed to suddenly become muted, distorted,
even ugly. There was a frenetic buzzing in the air that made it
hard for her to think.

Speak his name, urged the lady. *Names have so much power,
little sister. Don't you know that?*

"But I don't know his name. He stole her. I have no idea who
he is."

Yes, said Lady Eyes, *you do.*

"I don't, I don't, I don't," wailed Patty. The buzzing grew
louder and louder as if ten million insect wings fought the Music to own the Fire Zone itself. "He stole his name, too."

*Your daughter is with him, but she's also with you, Patty. Speak
his name.*

"I can't . . ." She fell to her knees, weeping, screaming, bleeding. Maybe dying.

The buzzing was a towering sound now. Patty touched her ear
and her fingers came away slick with bright-red blood. Around
her some of the dancers were wincing and drawing back. The
Music fought to be heard. All at once Lady Eyes raised her hand,
fingers wide, and in a voice louder than thunder yelled, *STOP!*

The buzzing stopped.

Just like that.

A thing like a shadow of light fell across her and the Music was back, soft and sweet and so powerful.

Speak his name, my love, said Lady Eyes.

With snot running from her nose and blood clogging her ears, and her tears mingling with spit from slack lips, Patty mumbled seven words. They hurt her mouth like punches.

"He is the Lord of the Flies," she whispered. The terror in her voice was vast and bottomless.

A moment later she felt the softness of lips pressed gently against her forehead.

Tuyet is your daughter.

And then Patty Cakes woke up, looking at the hospital ceiling. Around her the nighttime hospital was silent except for the hiss and ping of machines attached to the lost.

69

Monk couldn't sleep, so he trudged outside, ran through hard rain to his car, and drove to Patty's to double-check that he had, in fact, locked up that morning. He had. Her keys were still in his jeans pocket, so he opened up and wandered through the rooms. Seeing the things she'd unpacked—the tools of her trade, her iPad, some clothes—and the stacks of boxes left untouched. Art, old-fashioned photo albums, stuff from Vietnam, stuff from New York, books, pots, and pans. He debated unpacking for her, setting the whole place up, maybe giving it a good clean, lighting some cleansing incense. But when he found the framed picture of Patty with Tuyet, taken at the hospital where the little girl was born, he stopped.

He took the picture over to one of the barber chairs, slumped into it, and stared at the image for a long time. How in the hell could a mother forget her child? Fathers? Sure, some of them could let it all go, but they hadn't spent nine months sharing existence with a new life. It was always different with mothers.

How could Patty forget?

How?

He wiped tears from his eyes and stared at the tiny baby in Patty's arms. So newly alive, so full of potential.

"Goddamn it," he breathed.

INTERLUDE TWELVE   THE LORD OF THE FLIES

He went back to Malibu Mark five times. Each time he had one new fly tattooed on a different part of his body.

On his fourth visit he contrived to accidentally brush Tink, the receptionist's, arm with the backs of his fingers. His knuckles made the briefest contact with a tiny black and white semicolon. Owen mistook it for two small insect tattoos, but when they appeared on his arm later that evening he saw what the design really was. He was disappointed for nearly forty minutes.

Until the memories ignited like burning phosphor in his mind.

Instantly he was Tink—little Tinker Bell—at age eleven. A tiny waif of a girl cringing against the headboard of her bed, pillows and blankets pulled up to her chin as if they were armor enough against the monster who came into her room night after night. Uncle Harry. Big, fat, with a thin mustache and wet teeth that glistened as he smiled in the glow of the My Little Pony night-light. Teeth that glistened as he unbuckled and unzipped. Night after night after night.

Then he was Tink at fourteen. On the street, living in cars, in crack houses even though she didn't use. Blowing strangers for food money. Fucking truckers for enough cash to buy the antibiotics that killed what they gave her. Living like a ghost that haunted her own life.

Tink at nineteen, standing on the wooden kitchen chair in a tiny apartment she shared with three other women. The chair wobbling as she fitted the electrical cord around her neck and then around the ceiling light. Smiling for the first time in years because there was no tomorrow, and that was a beautiful, beautiful thought.

Tink at twenty-two. Assisting now in the Survivors of Suicide that met Tuesdays and Fridays at the Methodist church.

Tink meeting Malibu Mark at the group. Comparing war stories. Comparing scars. Getting inked by him with the semicolon, the symbol used by people like her. Because that symbol was used when an author could have opted to end a sentence with a hard stop, but didn't. Because now she was the author, and the sentence was her life . . . and she had finally come to the place where she understood there was more story to tell.

The memories burned through him. He screamed as he was raped, stifled her screams as he sold himself, wept for joy as he tightened the electrical cord, and shouted in triumph when he accepted life as the best next chapter. He. Not Tink. Owen. Because it was his story now, his life's experience, his memory.

His ink.

When he went back to Malibu Mark for his fifth tattoo, there was another receptionist at the desk. A black woman with a shaved head. A stranger.

"Where's Tink?" he asked, making it sound casual. The woman's eyes shifted away, but as they did he saw how wet they suddenly got. How filled with grief.

"Tink left," said the woman, and then changed the subject.

Inside the studio, as Malibu Mark worked, Owen asked the same question. The needle paused in its work, the buzz-saw sound filling the air. The artist looked away, just as the new receptionist had. Then he took a deep breath, held it for a moment, and exhaled slowly.

"Some people can't swim all the way upstream," was what he said. Only that, and nothing more.

Owen found the obituary online. It did not say suicide, but he'd read enough of those things to know. He'd taken her memories and she could not live without them.

Owen never went back to Malibu Mark for more flies.

He didn't need to. Now he understood how it worked.

Like a fly following the scent of spoiled meat, Owen went elsewhere, and the flies went with him.

70

"Crazy weather," said Gayle.

The beautiful woman sipped her drink and looked amused. "Yes," she said, blotting her lips with a paper napkin. "Rain. Been a theme here lately."

Gayle flushed, immediately hating herself for having resorted to talking about the damn weather. She fished wildly for something else to say. Small talk was never her thing, and starting conversations with strangers was at the bottom of the list of her skill set.

"I saw you at the store," said Gayle.

"Yes," agreed the woman. Amusement continued to sparkle in her eyes, though whether it was mockery or a sense of fun at Gayle's discomfort was impossible to tell.

Gayle looked around, seeing the same faces, the same hunched figures, the same arrangement of chairs and tables. None of that was helpful.

"Do you, um, come here often?"

The woman laughed out loud. "Oh my god," she said, "you're really bad at this, aren't you?"

"I . . . what . . . ?"

"I mean, like, awful."

Gayle felt her entire face and throat flare with heat. She was certain her blush was going to light the entire bar in a lurid crimson glow. "Um," she said weakly. "Thanks?"

The woman chuckled softly and laid a hand on her forearm. "Honey, I can spot a visitor from a foreign country at a hundred yards, and you are a classic example of the species. All you need is a tourist visa and a guidebook."

Gayle started to say something, stopped, looked down into her glass, and then raised her eyes and smiled sheepishly.

"That bad, huh?"

"Worse. I mean . . . the weather? You were in real danger of asking what my sign is."

"Ouch."

"Yeah," said the woman. "But don't worry, I'll let you off the hook. Let's start with the basics, okay? I'm Dianna Agbala. And you are . . . ?"

"Gayle Kosinski. Gayle with a *y*. And an *e*."

"Hello, Gayle with a *y* and an *e*. I'm Dianna with two *n*'s. Yes, it's raining. For the record, I'm a Scorpio. And, yes, this is a real-life lesbian bar and I will bet a stack of shiny nickels you've never been inside of one before."

The heat on Gayle's face increased. Scorching.

"I'll take that as a no," said Dianna. "And I'm guessing you're a Libra."

"How . . . ?" Gayle gasped.

"You look the type. And," said Dianna quickly, still smiling, "before you freak out . . . I'm a professional card reader, astrologer, and sensitive."

Gayle didn't quite know how to respond to that. She fumbled for a moment and then said, "I don't mean to be rude, but I'm not sure I believe in any of that stuff."

"It's not a requirement. But you are a Libra."

"Well . . . yes. . . . but . . ."

"And your drink is almost empty. Let me get the next round," Diana said and tapped the rim of her glass with a silver ring. Juana sauntered down, her eyes clicking back and forth between Gayle and Dianna.

"Same again?" she asked, got nods, and went away to do her magic.

Gayle had no map for how to navigate what she was doing, but Dianna's frankness was emboldening her. So, she decided to try frankness, herself.

"It's my first time here," she said. "Or anywhere like this. And by *here* I mean anywhere like . . . like . . ."

"Like a queer bar?"

"Um . . . yes." She paused. "Excuse me, but I thought *queer* was a bad word. Like calling a gay man a faggot."

"Oh, it's okay to use here, but we tend to not dig it if straights use it. If they use it because they're trying to relate— you know, an LGBTQ ally—then we give them a pass. Heart in the right place and all that. But when used as a pejorative . . . then, hell no."

"So, is it more like using the N-word if you're not black?"

"About that . . . black folks kind of hate it when people say 'N-word.' Either say 'nigger' when talking about racist terms, or skip the subject. 'N-word' is a slippery way of saying 'nigger' while trying to be PC. No, don't worry, I'm not offended, and you get a pass because I think your heart's in the right place."

The new drinks arrived and Gayle gulped a third of hers, choked, coughed, and soothed her throat with a smaller sip.

"This new terminology is a bit of a challenge," she admitted. "I mean, I'm getting used to going to conventions where people have their pronouns on their name tags, but . . ."

"When's the last time you had a conversation with a lesbian?"

"A few months ago," admitted Gayle.

"In person?"

"No."

"Didn't think so," said Dianna. "You don't know how to have this conversation, do you?"

"No," admitted Gayle weakly, "I really don't."

"Pretend—just for a moment—that lesbians are totally human beings and go from there."

"Ouch," said Gayle.

Dianna sipped her new drink and winked at Juana, who was washing glasses a few yards away.

"So tell me, Gayle," said Dianna, "if we were meeting casually at a Starbucks, or in the checkout line at a grocery store, then what would you talk about?"

"I . . . don't know . . . I rehearsed a bunch of lines but. . . ."

"I'm not talking about you having a lesbian conversation with a lesbian at a lesbian bar. Take that word out of the equation. We met at the clothing store. We're about the same age. We live in Pine Deep. We visit the Fringe. And we know the weather sucks.

None of that needs to be commented on. It doesn't tell either of us about the other."

"I guess it doesn't."

"Then what kind of conversation do you, Gayle, want to have with me, Dianna?"

Gayle felt like she wanted to flee. The conversation was off its rails and she didn't know how to get it right. "I really don't know."

"Okay, that's fair. How about we start somewhere in the middle, then? Between 'gosh, it rains a lot' and 'I'm not sure about my sexuality.' What's in the middle for you?"

Gayle thought about it. The first drink was already working on her and the big gulp of the second was softening the edges.

"My life, I guess. My kids, my job."

"And your husband?"

Gayle's gaze flicked away for a moment, but then she made herself look at Dianna.

"Yes. Him, too."

Dianna nodded slowly. "Let's work up to that. Start slow, stay in the middle lane. Tell me about your kids and your job."

71

Monk locked Patty's place up and drifted down Boundary Street, discovering the Fringe. Even in the rain it looked like a happening place. Much more alive—or alive in a less disturbing way—than the rest of the damn town. The shops were nice, but he wasn't in the mood to buy anything. The clubs were too loud for the mood he was in, so he began driving the side streets. There was a shithole of a beer joint off the main drag. He parked and headed in. A sign above the door read JAKE'S HIDEAWAY. Pretentious name for a place this nasty, dark, and dirty. Maybe thirty people in all, broken into little gangs that clustered around different parts of the place. But the beer was cold and the first glass tasted so good he had three more.

He called the hospital and got the same female nurse he'd pissed off the last time he called.

"I'm sorry, Mr. Addison," she said in a way that said she was not sorry at all, merely pissed. "As I believe I told you last time, hospital policy prohibits us from sharing patient information with anyone except relatives."

Monk looked around for a place at the bar, couldn't see one, and stood there, trying hard not to go bang his head on a wall. He was never good at being stonewalled.

"Miss . . ." he said slowly, "I'm not asking for details. I just want to know if she's okay."

He heard her sigh. Long, caustic, unfriendly. "Mr. Addison, I don't know how many ways I can say this—"

He hung up.

A truck driver–looking guy got up from the bar, tossed a five down, nodded to the bartender, and ambled away. Monk made a move but someone tried to cut him off and take the seat. The guy actually put a hand on Monk's wrist as if to pull him away from the only available seat. Monk looked down at the hand and then up at its owner.

"Fuck off," he said in a way that handed out credible promises.

"Um," said the man, clearly running the numbers in his head and not digging his odds. "Sure. Fucking off." And he did.

Monk shrugged out of his leather jacket, hung it on the back of the chair, and sat. A bemused bartender came over and took his order for a Jameson's neat and a draft of Big Black Voodoo Daddy, a stout with serious balls. The bartender nodded approval and brought the drinks.

Monk shot the Jamie's. "Fucking hick-town hospitals."

A voice beside him asked, "If you're talking about Pinelands Regional Medical, I can't argue."

Monk turned to see a white guy on the younger side of middle age, and almost dealt him a fresh "go fuck yourself," too, but didn't. The guy looked like Monk felt. Lean, harried-looking, hollow-eyed, with a Band-Aid on a bruised forehead. Even so, Monk said nothing, letting the other guy deal the next card.

"Sorry," said the man self-consciously, "I heard you talking to Nurse Hitler on your cell. If it's the one I'm thinking of, she's a real piece of work. Tall brunette, eyes like she works in a Chicago slaughterhouse and enjoys it. Mean as a snake."

"That'd be the one," agreed Monk.

The man touched his bandage. "Spent some lovely hours with her." When Monk didn't ask how or why, the guy explained, "Hit a cow on the road. Well, the car did. I hit the windshield."

"Cow?" asked Monk distractedly.

"Long story; I'm Duncan." He nodded to the faces peeking out from Monk's push-up sweatshirt cuffs. "Hey, you're into tattoos . . . mind if I ask you a question?"

"Depends on the question."

"Sure, sure, and it comes with a weird little goddamn story."

"Try me," said Monk.

Duncan signaled the waiter and then forked two fingers down at his glass and Monk's. Refills happened as the guy told Monk the story about his missing tattoo. At first Monk wasn't really listening, but then the details caught up and slapped him across the mouth.

"Whoa," he said, "wait, go back and tell that part again."

"Which part? Oh, right, sure." Duncan showed him the faint

scar and then picked his cell phone off the bar, scrolled through the pictures, and held it up for Monk to see.

"So, you had it removed . . . ?" said Monk uncertainly.

"No, that's what I was trying to tell you. I never had a tattoo at all, but the picture—and my wife—say I did. So either the world is fucked up, or I hit my head worse than I thought, or . . . or, well, something. It doesn't make any sense to me at all. I mean, how could I have a tattoo I don't ever remember getting, then somehow lose it with no memory of getting it removed? And, worse, how come I can't remember why I got it? My wife's cancer . . ."

Monk studied Duncan. The man's eyes were bright with tears but behind that there was a terror that was close to the screaming point.

"I came in here," said Duncan, "and spent the last couple hours scrolling through photos. That tattoo is in dozens of them. Here, let me show you. See? There it is, clear as day. I even went through my emails and found the receipt from a tattoo studio in Doylestown I never heard of. And I found so many"—and here his voice broke high and wet—"emails and text messages from my wife about her cancer. Emails from the doctor, from relatives, from friends, all talking about the cancer. The remission. All of it. Like three, four hundred messages."

Monk stared at him. "And you don't remember any of it?"

Tears fell down Duncan's face as he shook his head. "It's insane, man. I mean, this never happened. If it had, I'd remember something, right? *Right?*"

72

Gayle stood—not sat—in a toilet stall at Tank Girl. Hiding. Wondering how the night had gone this far wrong.

She and Dianna had talked and talked. In response to Dianna's request, Gayle showed pictures of her two kids and even a vacation photo of her and Scott taken at Disney last year. She also showed photos of herself at the school where she worked in administration four days a week, and more of herself at conventions receiving awards or giving speeches. Then, while scrolling to find a photo of herself at a party, she accidentally stumbled on a couple of photos she had thought long deleted.

Selfies she'd taken for Carrie. One was of her in pajamas with the top unbuttoned but only her sternum exposed, which wasn't too bad; but the one after that was of her standing in the bathroom wearing only pink underpants. Gayle gasped and yanked the phone back, hastily scrolling away from those.

"Oh my god," she said sharply, "I'm so sorry."

"It's all good, honey," said Dianna, laughing. "Nothing I haven't seen before."

"No, I thought I'd deleted them and . . . oh, god, I'm so embarrassed."

Dianna touched her hand with the pads of two fingers. A very light touch. "I'd like to see them again. One in particular." When Gayle could meet her eyes, she added, "Please?"

Not cajoling. Not begging. Merely asking.

It took a whole lot for Gayle to scroll back to find the pictures. She hesitated a long time before finally angling the phone to privately display the bathroom nude. But Dianna shook her head and used one finger to move to the previous picture. The pajama one.

"This is so lovely . . ." she murmured. "Your eyes are full of light."

Gayle looked at her, then down to the photo. Despite the unbuttoned top, the focus on the image was more than a promise of skin to be revealed. It was a statement of both vulnerability and trust. Not even a promise of more. It said, *See me. Me. Not my parts. Me.*

Her face was hot again, but not from embarrassment. Gayle couldn't have put a label on the emotion seeping through her.

That's when she had exited the image file, excused herself, and fled to the bathroom. She didn't need to go, but it was quiet in the stall. Gayle leaned against the closed door and tried to remember how to breathe.

What am I doing here?

She heard someone come in. Heard the faucet and then the paper towel dispenser. Then silence.

I have to get out of here, Gayle told herself. I have a husband. I have kids. What if someone from school sees me here?

She banged the back of her head on the door. Once. Twice.

Then she pushed off, straightened her clothes, took a deep and steadying breath, and left the stall.

And froze.

Dianna was right there, resting a hip against the sink, arms folded beneath her breasts, a small and very wicked little smile on her lips.

"I . . ." began Gayle and once more words failed her.

"As I see it there are three options," said Dianna casually. "Option one is you can leave right now. Go brave the storm, drive home, step into the costume you've been wearing since you were a girl. You can forget this place, or maybe chalk it up to 'research.' Go be who everyone already thinks you are."

Gayle licked very dry lips.

"Option two," continued Dianna, "is we go back to the bar and chitchat some more. We haven't discussed your stock portfolio, your husband's golf handicap, or your kids' favorite teachers. There's sooooo much small talk to be had."

It took a lot for Gayle to ask, "What's . . . option three?"

Dianna stood straight, walked past her, and locked the bathroom door. Then she turned and leaned back against it.

"Option three is you kiss me."

INTERLUDE THIRTEEN   THE LORD OF THE FLIES

While taking classes at a community college in Tucson—his eighth place of residence in as many years—Owen began to wonder if he was a vampire. Granted, he didn't suck blood—and that sounded disgusting anyway—but he knew for sure that he not only fed on memories, he thrived on them.

He did some Net searches on vampires and made a very interesting discovery. Several discoveries, in fact.

Only a third of the vampires in world folklore actually fed on human blood, and even some of those mostly fed on animals living near human villages and towns. Livestock and pets. Another group of vampires ate the flesh of corpses, and a smaller group fed on living flesh. Like zombies from those "living dead" movies or those TV shows—*The Walking Dead*. One show, *iZombie,* was pretty close. When the woman who played the coroner ate the brains of murder victims she was able to step into their memories and relive them sufficiently to get clues useful in solving those crimes. But it was fiction, a TV show based on a comic book, and not even from actual belief systems. Though there were some people—the Fore people of the Okapa District of the Eastern Highlands Province, Papua New Guinea—who fed on the brains of their fellow tribesmen because they believed this allowed them to preserve their memories and strengths.

Close, but not the same.

Then he read a book by a famous folklorist named Dr. Jonatha Corbiel-Newton. It was one of a whole list of books she'd written, but that one in particular was called *Deep Hunger: The Essential Vampire in World Culture.* In it she described a larger class of supernatural predators called "essential vampires." Owen had encountered that label before on websites. He ordered the book from a local bookstore and when it came in he spent all day in a Starbucks reading it. Two passages really struck him. The first was about the nature of these kinds of creatures:

> There are two forms of psychic vampires, one is human and the other is decidedly not. Human psychic vampires are people who either deliberately or, more often, subconsciously use passive-aggressive or codependent behavior to drain others of emotional, mental, and psychological energy. You've met them in the office, or in the PTA, or maybe one of them is your mother-in-law. Supernatural psychic vampires are creatures whose physical bodies have been destroyed or have completely putrefied or turned to dust. What is left is a kind of ghost whose presence pollutes an entire region. Psychic vampires often manifest as Nosferatu and spread disease and pestilence. Psychic vampires can create other vampires at will by causing the bodies of any sinful people to rise from the dead, and these newly created vampires are generally your typical blood-drinking revenant.

And the second riveted him to his chair.

> If any vampire type is to be accepted as a possibility, as something that may have existed, or might still exist, then it is the essential vampire. We know from the preponderance of published studies by psychologists and

psychiatrists, as well as supporting evidence by neurobi-
ologists, that concepts like true empathy and toxic empathy exist. What some pop culture subgroups refer to as a
"psychic vampire," someone who by some means appears
to feed off the emotions, particularly negative emotions,
their presence engenders in others. Some of the more
radical theories suggest that passive-aggressive behavior
is an aspect of psychic vampirism. If this is ever provable,
then contemporary science will need to take a closer look
at the concept of the essential vampire and measure it
against the mountain of case studies of abnormal behavior which have not yet been comfortably classified.

Owen read and reread those passages, and the whole book;
then dove deep into Dr. Corbiel-Newton's other works, her
magazine articles in both inscrutable trade journals and mass
market magazines. Looking for himself. Looking for what
he was.

He made one more discovery that startled him, and ultimately changed the direction of his life. The good doctor was
married to another writer, Willard Fowler Newton, author of
less scholarly and more sensational books about vampires. His
nonfiction book, *Hellnight: The Truth Behind the Destruction
of Pine Deep*, was made into a movie that Owen watched a
dozen times. It was about vampires and werewolves attacking
a small town in eastern Pennsylvania. Although the movie was
an over-the-top horror film with lots of CGI, the book it was
based on was published as nonfiction. Much like that voodoo
film, *The Serpent and the Rainbow*, with the guy who played the
president in *Independence Day*, was a fictionalized version of a
serious scientific study.

Owen bought a copy of Newton's book and rewatched the movie. Both were scary as hell. But now there was something whispering to him as he read and watched. He began to believe they were true. He began to believe that vampires were totally real. He marked a passage in Newton's book:

> Why did all of this happen in a town as small as Pine Deep, Pennsylvania? There are a lot of theories. There are always a lot of theories. My guess aligns with the oldest of these . . . a belief that was common to the original residents of that area, the Leni Lenape people, now a nearly extinct Native people. The stories passed down generationally speak of the region that is now almost entirely within the boundaries of the farming town of Pine Deep, and the tellers of those tales marked the area as bad. Not merely the negative charge that seems to linger in some old buildings in folktales, but an area they believed had always been evil. A place where darkness is exalted, and where the personal darkness in each human soul is fed and made stronger. It is a place of unquiet ghosts; a place that calls to people who are already wrestling with their own corruption and makes them stronger.

That sounded like home to Owen Minor.

When he finished that semester he gave his landlord notice, packed up his car, and moved east.

73

Alexa Clare was collecting scalps. That's how she thought of it. Not clumps of skin and hair, but virginity. Since ninth grade she had popped the cherries—so to speak—of eleven boys. Now, in eleventh grade, a day after her eighteenth birthday, she was going for an even dozen. She loved watching their faces when they went inside of her for the first time. Hell, she loved their faces when she put the condoms on, fitting them over the heads of their trembling cocks and then rolling them down with long, slow strokes. One boy back in tenth grade was so turned on he came before she could finish adjusting the Trojan. He was not one of the eleven, and Alexa had no idea where, or even if, he had another go at the whole lovemaking thing. It wasn't with her, that was for sure.

She hadn't mocked that boy. Alexa was not cruel and did not consider herself any kind of tease. She simply loved sex, and loved first sex.

Her own first had been with Will Hamblin, whom she'd loved since second grade. He was the first boy she'd ever held hands with. They'd shared a first kiss in fifth grade. He gave Alexa her first-ever orgasm in sixth grade, just by kissing her breasts. That orgasm had been so big it scared them both—and then they'd laughed about it. All through seventh and eighth grade they got together as often as they could, and they learned how to kiss—really kiss, with subtlety and style and generosity—and experimented with oral sex until they were able to make each other come. They always kissed after, because she'd read in a book that sharing a kiss with her wetness on his lips and his semen on hers was what the French called "lovers' wine." That was beautiful and sophisticated and it felt real. The first time they shared that exotic taste was when Will told her that he loved her. She broke down into uncontrollable sobs and Will held her. On the night before eighth grade started they lost their virginity together in his bedroom while his parents were at the movies.

Nothing had ever been so sweet. Will had been so gentle, so

careful. He later admitted that he'd read up on it. On what to really expect. He'd watched some porn, but that had told him more about what not to do, and how not to treat a girl.

He'd bought a pack of Trojans and they put one on him together, her hand over his. When he entered her there was only a little pain and discomfort. No blood—her hymen had been lost to his fingers months before. He was not particularly large, at least not by Internet porn standards, but bigger than his fingers. It took a while, but it was nice. And then it was more than nice. It was beautiful. She came first, and it was a big, sudden, clawing, screaming thing that scared them both. Will nearly stopped, but she clung to him, nails threatening to rend him if he pulled out. Her intensity, and the genuineness of it, toppled him over the edge. They bucked and gasped and shrieked as the tidal wave crashed down on them.

How many times in life can it be like that?

Alexa wondered that then, and so many times since then.

That night they'd marked the moment with tattoos. Not good ones. Not professional, because they were both too young to be allowed to get those. Instead they'd looked it up on the Net and then scrounged for the items needed for a stick-and-poke kit. One of Will's father's diabetes needles, ink from a Bic ballpoint, antiseptic, Saran Wrap to use as a medical surface cover, and the rest. They traced the design—a simple circle—over each other's hearts. Circle for completeness, totality, wholeness, original perfection, the infinite Self, the infinite, eternity, and the timelessness of their love. She joked that it looked like an O. For *orgasm*. They laughed and kissed and sunk the ink.

Four days later Will was in his side yard, using a heavy jack to raise the corner of his uncle Nick's farm truck. He had earbuds in, listening to Bauhaus. His uncle stooped to pick up the spare while Will worked the flat tire off the bolts when Nick saw his nephew lurch forward and smash his face against the fender. Will dropped to his knees and then fell sideways. Nick stood there, frozen by the kind of stupid incomprehension that true astonishment creates. He later said that he thought he heard a bee or fly buzz past his ear. Investigators speculated that this was the passage of the bullet that killed Will.

The cops figured it out: an out-of-season hunter considerably more than a mile away, using rounds too hot for taking down a deer. Forensics and ballistics sorted out the details and did the math. The bullet had been a reload of a .458 Winchester Magnum, fired from more than a mile away, almost certainly by someone illegally hunting on protected lands with way too much gun for the available game. The fact that the bullet had not hit a tree in all that distance was considered a fluke.

"These things happen," said one detective, as if that made it somehow okay.

Someone else said, "Stranger things have happened round here, and going way back."

Will's death destroyed Alexa.

Absolutely destroyed her.

There was that black period of time where she could not remember anything. Nothing at all. All she knew was that her throat was torn raw by screaming, and it had never entirely recovered. She spoke in a whisper. Guys found it sexy.

Then there was another space of time where all Alexa could do was sit and stare out the window. For days.

That was when they started giving her pills. And shots. It was when they made her go to therapy. Sometimes she talked. Sometimes she didn't. They gave her more pills.

Days passed. Weeks. She lost weight. She lost friends who couldn't carry the weight of her grief. She lost herself.

Then Will came to her in a dream. Alive. Whole. Beautiful.

She felt his presence while she was deep in a nightmare, running from ugly things she could not name, fleeing through a maze of cornfields that were laid out like that labyrinth in Knossos in that old story. She ran and ran and ran, stumbling, weeping, lost and helpless, and then she rounded another of the endless series of corners, and . . .

Will was there.

His face was as bright as if it was lit from within. One hand was placed flat on his chest over his heart and the other was stretched out toward her.

In her dream, Alexa screamed his name. Even to her own ears it sounded like the cry of a lost seagull. Will smiled a smile that brightened the entire world and took her into his arms.

He kissed her and undressed her and they made love right there, nestled down in the sweet grass, his cool hips between her sweaty thighs. He entered her without a condom and moved inside of her with a slow, inexorable, timeless rhythm. He felt bigger than before, but his skin was so cold. Even his lips were cold. But that was okay, because she was overheated from running.

"I love you," he whispered, his lips brushing the outside of her ear. "I love you forever."

Then he came inside of her, filling Alexa with a cold darkness. When she looked at him, though, she saw that the circle tattoo was gone from his chest, leaving only a faintness like a scar. But not a scar.

When she woke the next morning her thighs were slick with wetness. It smelled of seawater and damp earth. Alexa lay there, daubing the wetness with her fingertips and then licking it off. Over and over and over again.

And when she went into the bathroom to brush her teeth, she barely noticed that her own tattoo was gone. It was so completely gone that its absence did not register with her senses. She never dreamed of Will again after that night.

A week later she coaxed sixteen-year-old Howard Reston into her car. Howard lived in Newtown, miles away. He went to a different school. They met online and this was the first time they'd ever met in the flesh.

They went to a movie and had pizza and then drove out to a spot along the Delaware where huge oak trees draped everything in dense shadows. Alexa had to do a lot of the work to even get Howard to kiss her. She was his guide in everything. Schooling him on how to kiss. Showing him the easiest way to undo a front-closure bra. Teaching him about giving and receiving oral sex. And then putting the condom on him. Helping him do it, really.

The sex was awkward for him, and he was earnest but clumsy. And he came too fast. But she held him after and told him it would be better the next time. It was. He had been the first since Will. Her first scalp, as she came to think of it.

Tonight she was with Gary Felton. A thin, tall boy with a kind face and poet's eyes. He had kissed before, and gotten blowjobs before, but was still a virgin. He'd explained all this during long hours of texting. She'd driven down to meet him at a burger joint in Feasterville, and then they drove around until they found a big industrial parking lot where they could hide her car in the shadows between two silent semis.

Gary was less awkward now with most things, but there was

always a learning curve when it came to intercourse. Alexa knew how to guide without appearing to take charge too much. She used encouragement and gasps to let him know he was doing things right. He was able to hold out for a while before he came, and she faked an orgasm so they would have that golden moment of togetherness.

They lay together for a long time, gently kissing, feeling their sweat and juices dry.

"That was really beautiful," he said softly. "You're beautiful, Lindsey."

Alexa smiled. Lindsey was the name she used with him. Last time it was Kaitlyn, and before that it was Jessie. Going all the way back to Alice. Next time she would be Molly. Orderly, following the alphabet.

"You were good," she lied. "You were really good."

"You're amazing, Lindsey," said Gary.

"With you, I guess I am," she said and smiled.

And slid the blade of the oyster knife between his ribs and into his heart so quickly he was dead before he knew he was dying.

Alexa—for now she was herself again—held Gary's body for a long time. Feeling his muscles slacken and relax. Then she wormed her way out of the back seat, reached back to find her clothes, dressed, took a blanket from the trunk to cover him, and then drove back to Pine Deep. There was already a grave waiting. She'd dug it that afternoon, in a neat line with the others. The barn was on a farm that had been abandoned during the Trouble but never bought since. No one ever came out there that she was aware of. No one had in all this time.

It took hours to drag him out of the car, roll him in the plastic Tyvek sheeting, coat him with powdered lime, drag him into the barn, topple him into the grave, and fill it. The extra dirt was removed by wheelbarrow and scattered in the overgrown fields. Back inside, she patted the ground flat. Then she used a rake and broom to smooth away all traces.

Alexa went home, took a shower, and climbed into bed. All through what was left of the night she lay awake and listened to the night wind. It had an odd buzzing quality. It sounded like the frenzied wings of thousands of blowflies.

74

It was a very good kiss.

It did not stop the world.

It did not transport Gayle into a realm of orgasmic bliss.

It was not a kiss for the ages.

They were, after all, both half drunk and kissing in the bathroom of a bar. Given that, though, it was a very, very good kiss.

Dianna's lips were full and soft. And she cupped the back of Gayle's neck without too much force. Her other hand grazed Gayle's cheek in the moment before she probed gently with her tongue.

At first Gayle had no idea what to do with her hands, and it felt like she had too many of them and that each one weighed fifty pounds. She finally anchored them on Dianna's upper arms. Not as a caress, but for lack of any other plan that seemed to fit the moment.

She was aware of so many things during that kiss.

She and Dianna were almost the same height.

They both had large breasts, and those breasts were pressed together.

Dianna was very curvy and had broad shoulders, but she was much smaller than Scott, who was a big man. The difference in size was a little jarring.

Dianna's lips were softer than any man's Gayle had ever kissed. And her tongue was much less insistent.

There was no groping. Scott, and virtually every man before her, had groped. Usually hands went straight to her breasts. Not now.

Dianna kissed with her eyes open, though her lips were almost closed. A sleepy, dreamy expression. Gayle shut hers because she didn't want to make eye contact. The moment was already strange enough.

Dianna's breath smelled of gin and dirty olives and a little bit of mint.

The kiss probably lasted twenty seconds. A long time for a first kiss. Very long. Though it felt both shorter and much longer.

Dianna ended the kiss but did not move away. Gayle opened her eyes and they stood there very close, still holding each other, both of them breathing hard. Gayle, perhaps, nearly panting.

"You are very sweet," murmured Dianna.

"Th-thank you," said Gayle, tripping on it. Meaning it on several different levels.

There was a knock on the door, but neither of them responded to it.

Dianna stepped back and it was as if she was deliberately withdrawing her energy from the moment. She moved over to the sink and checked her hair. Her smile was constant. Small and amused.

Thunder boomed hard enough to rattle the whole building and then came the barrage of heavier rain hitting the roof.

"It's going to rain like this for hours," said Dianna. "Maybe all night." She unslung her purse, dug into it, and removed her phone. She looked up, one eyebrow raised. "May I have your number?"

"Um . . . yes . . ." said Gayle, and gave it.

Dianna tapped the keys. She came over and kissed Gayle on the cheek, and left the bathroom without saying another word.

A blond woman, looking annoyed at having found the door locked, brushed past and went into one of the stalls. It took Gayle quite a while to compose herself enough to go back out to the bar, but was dismayed to find Dianna gone. She lifted her coaster in hopes of finding a note, but there was nothing.

She sank down on the chair and stared at her drink, feeling more heavily disappointed than she would have imagined. She'd kissed a woman. A beautiful woman. And it was lovely.

What, she wondered, would have made it perfect?

Every bit of the answer to that question involved her. It was nerves and surprise and insecurity that were responsible for any flaws, of that she was certain.

Her phone pinged with the chime for an instant message. It would be Scott, of course.

Except it wasn't.

It was a phone number she did not recognize. And an address three miles outside of town. No other note.

Nothing else was needed.

Gayle settled her bill with Juana and was driving through the rain in less than two minutes.

75

Mike Sweeney turned in his cruiser and climbed onto his bike, a 1953 Indian Chief, one of the very last such machines ever made. It was beautiful and despite its power the engine purred rather than growled, and it devoured the road. The bike had been a gift from Crow and Val to celebrate Mike's graduation from the police academy.

Its name, WarMachine, was painted on the fuel tank. It made Mike smile, though faintly. When he was a kid he'd had a bicycle of that name. Childhood had been a horror show for him, but the WarMachine always made him feel free.

Then and now.

He fired it up and drove out of the department lot, but paused at the first intersection. He didn't care much about the rain, even liked it, cold and angry as it was.

There was no destination in mind, no real plan. He simply drove. Mike lived with his adoptive parents, Crow and Val, out at the Guthrie farm, but town seemed to call to him tonight, and so he drove along Corn Hill. Thinking about things. It was a strange year, and getting stranger. Last winter had been cold and snowy but overall ended without incident. No blizzards, no traffic deaths, no homeless people freezing to death. Spring came late, but when the flowers bloomed they rioted with colors of such drama that it even trended on Twitter. #PineDeepColors and #PineDeepFlowers. Beautiful at first, but the flowers persisted in an odd way. Even cut flowers stayed bright and cheerful for a few weeks. It bothered Mike, because it felt only as real as a clown's smile, and he was no fan of clowns. Mike was suspicious of anyone who smiled too much or too often. Even Crow, who was a legendary goofball, didn't go around grinning all the time.

Spring spilled over into summer like a bunch of drunks falling out of a bar. The flowers stayed bright until that one week when the temperature spiked to over one hundred and just stayed there for day after scorching day. Then everything withered, even those damn flowers. Sports games were canceled left and right, and farmers began to worry about their young crops—both what was already growing and what needed to be planted. You could see heat shimmer up from every stretch of road, and the pavement was too hot to even walk dogs.

The heat dropped, took a breath, and came back harder than ever. There were a few days where it hit 110 and only dropped into the low nineties at night. Old people on social security skimped on air-conditioning and died in their beds. There were some suicides, too, including a murder-suicide of a pair of newly-weds who set themselves on fire. Hell of a damn way of going out.

Crime stats shot up, of course, because that's always worse when it was hot. Mike had to bust some heads here and there. And he started having run-ins with the Cyke-Lones, a biker gang that had settled into that part of eastern Pennsylvania and New Jersey. That problem hadn't gone away when the summer finally wound down. If anything, there seemed to be more of them, and Mike knew he'd have to do something about them. That was likely to be messy.

When fall came, it came big and it brought cool temperatures and rain. A whole lot of rain. The skies always seemed ready for a downpour at the drop of a hat. There was some kind of rain every day or night, and several big storms, like the one that had smashed down last night and seemed to be building tonight.

Mike drove past the hospital and glanced at it, wondering how that couple, the Duncans, were doing. When he'd last seen the husband he was sitting on the edge of a gurney in the ER scrolling through photos long ago uploaded to his Facebook and Instagram pages. Photos that showed his tattoo. The missing tattoo. The poor bastard kept saying the same two words over and over again.

I don't . . . I don't . . ."

Never finishing the sentence because, really, where could he go with it?

It was one of two things that day involving tattoos, the other being the old vet. Crazy days, he mused.

At the corner of Corn Hill and Boundary, Mike turned right and rolled along past stores and clubs. Eyes turned toward him, and he knew that he didn't fit in here. Not in this world and not anywhere. He was huge, still dressed in uniform pants but with a bomber jacket over it. Not much of a smile because any smile that found its way onto his face rarely stayed. Mike knew that about himself. He was not a smiley kind of guy.

Eyes followed him, and he knew it. Conversations tended to falter when people became aware of him. He knew that it wasn't just because he was easy to spot as a cop. No, it ran much, much deeper than that. It was because of who and, more to the point, what he was. Even if they had no trace of a clue, and not many people ever did, they could all sense that they—the collective *they*—were one species and he was obviously something else.

Mike was a realist. He accepted that.

It was one of the reasons he liked the newcomers to town, the people who lived and worked along Boundary Street and the side lanes. The Fringe. They were all outsiders as far as the town was concerned, and none of them seemed even a little apologetic about it. They were who they were, and the level of overall acceptance within their community was huge. Everyone was aware of the strangeness or uniqueness or personal definition of each of the others and took it as normal. That's what it was. Different was normal in the Fringe.

That bit of insight made Mike smile.

There were signs everywhere for the Fringe Festival, and although Mike had to work it, he was hoping to maybe make some friends there.

He drove on, eventually turning onto a feeder road and

following it out of town. Road became road, way turned onto way, and the evening shed its town clothes to become country. Out there the darkness was deeper, the air cleaner, the road empty. It was not safer than town, though. The countryside, especially at night, was so deceptive. So many things could hide in the trees, concealed behind the corners of empty farm buildings, crouched down among the cornstalks, wriggling through the wormy soil of pumpkin patches. And all around the farmlands were the arms of the vast Pinelands State Forest. All those acres where a tourist could get lost within a hundred feet of the road. He knew, because Mike had found some of those bodies.

Besides, down in Dark Hollow there were shadows so dark they could not be explained by geography or weather. Mike knew all about that kind of darkness, too.

He drove on, feeling the internal shift move from random to specific as he headed to the farm where he lived. Right there, pressed up against the forest and edge by Dark Hollow Road.

Home.

As they whipped past his visor, Mike thought he heard something. A voice?

He slowed, looking to either side of the road. Nothing. Even when he stopped, cut the engine, and took off his helmet all he could really hear was the wind. Just the night wind. Only the exhalation of a storm hungry to take another bite.

Only that.

He sat there, still as a statue for more than two minutes. Doing nothing except listening, trying to interpret what the night was trying to tell him. But if there was a message then it was whispered in a language too strange even for someone like Mike Sweeney to understand.

The engine came to life and now it did seem to growl. Mike

growled, too, low in his throat. He did not like that murmuring wind. Not at all.

He drove home, feeling as if the night was in close pursuit.

INTERLUDE FOURTEEN   THE LORD OF THE FLIES

Owen Minor moved to Pine Deep and settled in. He enrolled in school, finished his degree, and got a good-paying job. He worked extra shifts in order to save money and vacation days to fly all over the country to attend tattoo conventions. There were a lot of them. Often they were the same people—artists, tattoo junkies, artists' groupies, a few celebrities—and he cruised the edges of that world. By now he had forty blowflies on his arms and chest and stomach. And one each on his upper thighs whose wings brushed his hairless testicles.

Owen volunteered his services at the conventions. Very few of the cons had any kind of medical staff on hand, though they should have. Regulations for those events were sketchy, leaving hygiene and first aid up to the individual artists. Most of those artists were conscientious enough to handle things themselves, but things happen. Accidents, newbies who panic when the needle begins grinding, people who bleed too freely. A registered nurse volunteer was a godsend. Everyone was happy to see him. And Owen was always careful about who he touched, and when. He listened to the stories people told as they browsed the various stalls. If they were merely looking for novelty or impulse-buy ink, Owen could not have cared less. Those memories were worse than trying to find decent nutrition by gorging on cotton candy. Empty memories rather than empty calories.

Patience and paying attention helped him find the right targets. A broken heart, a lost friend, a buried child, failed hopes. Grief, survivor's guilt, shame, regret, bittersweet nostalgia—those were the choicest cuts. Bloody and juicy.

He wore nitrile gloves, but on certain days there were tiny holes in the pad of one or two fingers. Only for a few minutes, only long enough to make a touch. And almost always on the last day, before the con broke up and people scattered back to their lives.

Owen would also head back home, too. To Pine Deep. To the new Fringe neighborhood that was growing larger and more interesting every day. To his job at Pinelands Regional Medical Center. To that abode of ghost stories and urban legends, of darkness and despair.

To the only real home he'd ever known.

76

Val built a fire while Crow got plates and silverware for the take-out delivered by a soggy, disgruntled Grubhub driver. Indian food spicy enough to eat its way through the cardboard containers.

He offered to open a bottle of wine for Val, but she shook her head. They were years past the point where she felt obliged to drink nonalcoholic stuff around him, but she rarely drank anyway. She drank spring water and he washed his pork vindaloo and phaal curry down with three bottles of Yoo-hoo.

Solomon Burke was crying the blues via the Echo speakers, and the fire cast a golden carpet of warmth over them as they ate sitting on the floor. The twins had come home, turned up their noses at what looked way too much like the parents being romantic, and fled upstairs to wait for pizza delivery. Crow over-paid the same driver, now even more bedraggled, and handed over the pizza to the twins, who once more escaped any chance of being around romance. Particularly of the parental kind. Loud hip-hop created an impenetrable barrier to the third floor.

With the detritus of dinner around them and the logs chuckling in eloquent denial of the storm outside, Val and Crow sat wrapped in a blanket, their backs to the couch, watching the flames dance along the burning cherrywood.

They talked about a lot of different things. She told him about how her staff was managing to reduce damage from rain and flooding. He told her about Patty Trang and Monk Addison.

Val's face went white as paste. "She forgot her own daughter?"

"At least for now. Argawal said it could be head trauma."

Val got up and walked over to the window and stood for a few long moments looking out at the storm-lashed trees. It was warm in the living room but she hugged herself. Crow watched, waiting, knowing where her thoughts had gone. To two small graves under the big oak. To names that Val sometimes could not say out loud. To the iceberg of memories to which her ship of sorrow so often sailed.

"Whatever it is," said Crow, "it'll probably pass. She'll get her memories back."

"What if she doesn't?" asked Val without turning. Lightning painted her in blue light that made her look like a ghost.

"Hey, come on, nothing can take away all of her memories. Not sure that's medically possible. Not for one specific aspect of her life. What she's going through is probably just the result of alcohol abuse, malnutrition, and some minor head trauma. They scanned her for brain tumors and she was clean. Same for an aneurysm. She's clean there, so there's no reason those memories won't come back."

Val looked over her shoulder. "If it was her short-term memory, or recent memories from just before that Monk person took her to the hospital, then that wouldn't bother me as much. Forgetting memories from all those years ago. Forgetting her little girl . . . that's so . . . so horrible."

"Right, right," said Crow, "but there are a whole bunch of things that can futz with long-term memory. Sleep deprivation, smoking, depression, stress—all of which pretty much describes the Trang woman. Not to mention prescription drugs. Antidepressants, antihistamines, antianxiety meds, muscle relaxants, sleeping pills, tranquilizers, and painkillers. I'd bet you a six-pack of Yoo-hoo she has more than a passing acquaintance with prescription meds."

"Mm," she said, noncommittally.

"But, like I said . . . I'm sure those memories will come back," Crow assured her. He held out his hand and after a moment's hesitation Val came over, took the hand, kissed it, and sank back down next to him. Crow pulled a big fleece from the couch and wrapped it around them both.

They were quiet for a bit, during which he could feel her relax by slow degrees. Logs shifted comfortably in the hearth, Then Val came back to the story of Patty Cakes and Monk Addison.

"Do you think he abused her?" she asked, brow furrowed and jaw set.

Crow shook his head slowly. "I . . . really don't think so. I mean, if you saw the guy you'd immediately put him on some kind of watch list. But I've been checking him out and he's just that kind of mook. A big, scary sumbitch who looks like the kind of guy who does what he does. That said, he has no criminal record, and I got in touch with a couple of cops up in New York. This one detective, Anna-Maria Martini, had a lot of things to tell me about how much she dislikes Monk, but when I asked her if he was the kind to put his hands on a woman, she laughed at me."

"Meaning no?"

"She said about the same thing the lawyer, Twitch, said. Monk won't put his hands on women or kids, and don't get between him and someone who does."

"Reminds me of someone else I know."

"Thank you, my dear."

"I was thinking about Mike," she said.

"Ouch."

"But you're pretty okay, too."

"'Pretty okay' will not get you laid tonight, Ms. Guthrie."

"Will this?" she asked and began unbuttoning her blouse.

"Egad, woman . . . there are young and impressionable children upstairs."

"Yes," said Val, "and they know that once we have a fire going down here and some sultry blues playing, they would rather be eaten by ginormous rats than come down and see anything. More or less direct quote from Faith."

"Sounds like her."

Val's fingers lingered on the button just above her heart. "I can stop if you're too much of a prude."

He set his Yoo-hoo bottle aside and sidled closer. "No, ma'am, not a prudish molecule in my body."

She cocked an eyebrow. "Call me 'ma'am' again and your body will be found in a ditch."

He kissed her and they fell sideways in exaggerated slow motion until they lay cuddled together, lips touching gently, hands very busy.

77

They drove in separate cars.

It was the strangest drive of Gayle's life because every single street corner she approached seemed to beckon as an escape route.

What am I doing? she asked herself a hundred times.

She even glanced at her own eyes in the rearview.

Her inner parasite gave her no answers and the look in her reflection's eyes was that of excitement. Interest. Hunger.

Yes.

All of those.

The house looked old but was one of the faux Victorians that had sprung up after the Trouble. Beautiful and ornate, with turrets, dormers, and a wide wraparound porch with decorative railings and turned posts. And everywhere outside was lovely trim work, including gingerbread cutouts and spindle work. They ran up onto the porch, both of them laughing because the rain was so fierce and cold that hiding under umbrellas was a complete waste of time.

Dianna unlocked the door and held it open for Gayle to enter first.

The place was clean but not neat, with stacks of magazines and books everywhere, untidy shelves of crystals, musical instruments from cultures Gayle couldn't even name, and an improbable number of cats. They seemed to be everywhere and of every species—smoky gray, orange stripes, calico, and one named Noapte, which Dianna explained was Romani for *night,* and who was midnight black except for a white heart-shaped patch on her throat.

Dianna took her wet coat and hung it up and offered her a towel.

"I'm soaked to the skin," said Gayle, and then flushed because it was obvious to both of them. Her silk sweater clung to her and the cold made her nipples stand out in undeniable points.

"I can get you a robe," said Dianna, and went off to do that before Gayle could protest. She came back with a thick dark blue terry-cloth and indicated the guest room where Gayle could change. It was done without a hint of suggestion about anything that might follow, and as Gayle undressed she wondered if she'd read the whole thing wrong. Despite the passion of the kiss at Tank Girl, there had been no understanding that they were going to make out.

She realized that's all she was thinking about. Making out. She caught a look at herself in the mirror—soaked, bedraggled, and in her underwear—and had to laugh. Her hair hung in rattails and she was covered in goose bumps.

"Oh, yes," she said to her reflection, "total sex goddess."

She debated leaving her bra and panties on, but they, too, were soaked. So she took the plunge and stepped out of them, hanging everything on the shower curtain rail and towel racks in the en suite bathroom. Then she pulled on the robe and cinched the belt tightly around her waist, taking care to tie a knot that wouldn't just pop open.

There was a soft knock and she opened the door to see Dianna also in a robe. Hers was purple and had embroidered tulips on it. Her hair was back in a ponytail and she'd washed all the makeup from her face. Her skin was a medium brown and there were some small acne scars from long ago. A real face, without a trace of pretense.

They stood for a moment, looking at each other without sound.

Then Dianna touched her own cheek. "Me in factory settings," she said. "Don't be scared."

"No," said Gayle quickly. "No . . . God, you're beautiful."

They stood a yard apart, but Dianna smiled faintly and said, "Come here and say that."

Which Gayle, after only a moment's hesitation, did.

They made love in Dianna's big bed.

It was very sweet and very slow and very strange for Gayle.

At first it was merely tender, with them holding each other and kissing. Rediscovering and deepening the rhythm of the kiss from an hour ago. They wore their robes and Dianna did not touch her in any sexual way. No, she left that door for Gayle to open. After fifteen minutes or more, Gayle touched Dianna's cheek and then let her fingers drift down along the side of the woman's neck and over her collarbone and along the V neckline of the robe. There was another pause—a mere heartbeat—and then she flattened her hand and ran it very lightly over one full breast. When her palm brushed over the cloth tented over the nipple, Dianna shivered. So did Gayle.

Their kisses continued while that hand rested there, unmoving. Gayle was almost afraid to break the spell. She had come this far, dared this much, but was she really ready to go further?

Dianna hooked a finger in the collar of her robe and pulled it open so that Gayle's hand now touched her bare skin.

"Yes," murmured Dianna. She leaned over and kissed the soft flesh below Gayle's ear. It sent an electric thrill through Gayle's whole body. Once upon a time Scott used to kiss her like that. In some other century, in some other life. Dianna's kisses were quick, with small bites.

Gayle continued to caress Dianna's breasts and, try as she might, she could not help comparing this woman's body to her own. It was maddening. Dianna had larger breasts and her nipples were paler, pinker, with smaller areoles. The flesh was shaped differently and the surface rippled with each of Dianna's deepening breaths. It was surreal, because Gayle kept expecting her own breast, her own nipple, to feel what she was doing to Dianna. As if this were her touching herself.

She realized, too, that she was tensing for the moment of pounce—when Scott would climb on top and use his knees to part her thighs, spreading her for penetration. Her body had become conditioned to that as the inevitable next stage.

But Dianna lay there and kissed her.

And soon Dianna's hands began caressing her. She found all the places that sent electric thrills through Gayle, but it was alien. Just as she had been struck at how different it felt to kiss another woman, or to hold one in her arms in a passionate embrace, it was equally strange to be touched by one. There was a gentleness that was in no way weakness. There was a knowingness in each caress. Dianna doing to her what she knew felt good to a woman because she was a woman.

When Dianna went down on her, it was absolutely beautiful and Gayle nearly broke into tears. Her body writhed like a snake, and she gasped when Dianna slid a finger inside while her tongue flicked and danced.

It was nearly perfect.

Nearly.

But not.

And the fault, Gayle knew, was in no way Dianna's.

This was so different. Much different than she expected, much different than she dreamed about. Despite all of the wonderful, beautiful things this lovely woman did, she was unable to fully relax. There was a gradual rise toward climax, but the orgasm eluded her. And after a while both of them knew it.

Gayle almost—almost—faked an orgasm, but did not. It would be an ugly thing to do. A lie in the midst of discovering truths.

When she went down on Dianna it was beautiful and delicious, and for a while Gayle was completely lost in it. Doing to Dianna what the woman had done to her. Dianna's orgasm, when it came, was intense. She turned her mouth and bit a pillow and screamed, her hips bucking as Gayle fought to hold on, to maintain contact so as not to spoil the orgasm before it ran its course.

Afterward they kissed again. And touched. And went down on each other again. Gayle did not come. Dianna did, but it took more effort. Maybe because second orgasms often do, or maybe it was because of the burden placed on the moment by Gayle's inability to come at all.

Eventually it was just sweetness and quiet. Neither of them saying much at all. Listening to the rain. Dianna held Gayle tenderly against her breast, stroking her hair and her back and occasionally kissing the top of her head.

The only words spoken throughout their time in that big bed were said as Gayle was getting up to get dressed to go home. Dianna watched her rise and put on the blue robe, but before it was belted, she said, "You are beautiful."

That made Gayle cry and she wheeled and fled to the guest bedroom where her clothes waited. Where another version of Gayle waited to be put on like a garment and worn for the ride home.

78

Monk left the bar well before midnight, feeling too much stout and whiskey sloshing around in his gut, and too many ghosts in his head. But what he'd learned at the bar kept him on the icy side of sober. The story Andrew Duncan told him scared the piss out of Monk.

Another missing tattoo? Another set of memories gone?

He stood in the rainy darkness and shivered. Not from the cold but from bad thoughts and shapeless uncertainty. He'd been in Pine Deep less than two days and already knew the place was wrong, but wrong *how* was beyond his understanding. A sound pulled him from that thought and he looked up to see the nightbirds clustered together on the rooftop of the vape shop across the street, looking like refugees at a closed border. It was too dark to see their eyes, but he could feel the weight of their stares. He wondered, not for the first time, if they could see the ghosts around him. Real ghosts, not just the bad thoughts in Monk's head. Those spirits were always there. They traveled with him. Some of them screamed at him all through the day, all through the night. Mostly at night. He could see them, hear them, feel their various degrees of coldness all the time. A little less so when he was hammered, as he was now.

Could these birds see them, too?

As if in answer, one of the nightbirds cawed softly. It was such a sad, lonely, lost sound that it came close to breaking his heart.

Were these things even birds at all? Or, he wondered, were they as lost as the ghosts who haunted him? The birds rustled but gave no other cries, and for a moment all of the souls around Monk fell silent as a wet storm breeze blew past. He turned into the wind. Far down the street, along the edges of the coming storm, the night was thickening like a chest filling with air. Monk shifted his stance, widening his legs, balancing his weight onto the balls of his feet as if bracing for a wave. Or a punch.

But the wind blew wet and long and did not attack.

Monk closed his eyes and blessed the night, aching to set the ghosts free, to unchain his own longing and let it flutter like a piece of torn cloth on the breeze. He wanted to find the end of night and place his many hurts on the altar of dawn and be forgiven for all the harm he had ever caused. Especially the deeper injuries inflicted every time he tried to do good in the world. The GPS of his good intentions was faulty and there was no road map through this landscape. Not in this half of his life.

"Help me, mister."

The words came from behind him and Monk whirled.

The street was empty except for parked cars. No one walking. No one anywhere in sight. He walked a few paces to change his perspective, but there was nothing. He heard the words as an echo in his mind.

Help me.

The voice was female. Young. And . . . familiar?

Monk fought to place it. Not Patty's voice. No, this was a girl.

"Is someone there?" he called, his right hand touching the zipper of his leather jacket. He could unzip and draw his gun in a heartbeat. He'd done it many times.

There was no answer and his words died in the damp air.

Monk took a few careful steps in the direction of where he thought the voice came from.

Nothing.

There was a sudden sharp pain in his chest. Not deep, though. Not his heart. This was on the surface of his skin. Like a scrape or cut. It was intense, but fleeting. There and gone.

"That fuck . . . ?" he asked the night.

The nightbirds rustled nervously on the rooftop.

"If you're playing some kind of joke, kid," Monk called, "then you're making a bad choice. Trust me on this."

"Please, mister . . . help me."

Once more it sounded like it came from behind him and once more he spun, this time pulling the heavy automatic. He raised it into a two-hand shooter's grip, finger laid ready along the trigger, but there was no one to threaten. The clouds began spitting at him.

Help me.

This time the echo felt very close, like a damp whisper in his ear, clammy as the grave. The pain flared once more in his chest. Monk shifted the pistol to his left hand and let it hang at his side. With his right he rubbed the spot on his chest. Beneath the fabric of his sweatshirt he could feel the tattoo. One of many faces he wore. It seemed to ripple and writhe, as if the inked mouth was trying to open. To scream.

Or . . . to whisper.

Please, mister, help me.

The drizzle turned to rain and Monk Addison stood there, touching his chest, knowing that it was the voice of a girl long dead who spoke to him. Who begged for help.

He pulled down the neck of the sweatshirt, yanking it, tearing it so he could see the face, just to the left of his sternum. He knew the name of every face on his skin. Each name, each life, each death.

"Angie," he breathed.

The rain fell on the face of Angela Bailey. Fifteen. Raped and murdered eleven years ago. Dismembered and left like garbage in a dozen public trash cans. Angela. Angie.

Hers was the third face Patty had inked onto him and the eleventh face overall. Sweet little Angie. Torn to pieces and thrown away.

He stared at her face.

Her dead eyes were open.

Her dead lips moved

Help me, she screamed.

But it was not Angela Bailey's voice. Looking into her eyes, he knew that. She was screaming, but hers were not the screams that filled the air around him. No, those were made by another voice. Younger. With a heavy accent. Or . . . speaking in another language.

He touched Angela's face and then the bare spot next to her. There was no tattoo there.

Except there was.

There should be.

He pressed his fingers into his skin, scrabbled at a mark, a swirl of muted colors that faded even as he looked at it. Eluding his attempt to hold onto the memory of it.

Whose face had it been? He fought to remember. A name was almost there. Almost. Not Angela. Whose?

The rain ran down his chest and smeared the remnant tattoo, washing away the features, washing away the name.

And the memories.

He watched in total horror as the tattoo faded from his sight, from his experience, from his mind. Disappearing.

Monk spun, looking for her ghost among the crowd that surrounded him.

"Đừng để cô ấy quên tôi!"

Those words filled the air and each one hit Monk in the chest.

Don't let her forget me.

"Little girl!" he roared, calling her that because all traces of the name were gone. Not a first letter, or the number of syllables. Nothing.

He strained to hear her in the wet darkness around him, but now even her ghostly voice was gone.

What was her name?

What did she look like?

He spun wildly, counting specters, but there were no ghosts missing from his entourage. He looked down again, straining to see that spot on his chest. Directly over his heart. There should be a tattoo there. There had been one. An old one. One of the first of that kind he ever got, or . . . maybe the first.

"Đừng để cô ấy quên tôi!"

The words made the bare spot throb with pain. Not sharp. Dull, like a bruise fading to nothing.

"Don't let who forget you?" he yelled. He staggered toward the nearest car and squatted to see his chest in the sideview mirror. The skin looked unmarked. Only a faint blur, like some of the other places on his body where he'd had old military tattoos lasered off.

There was no face in that spot on his chest.

There was no . . .

Monk stood in the rain, touching a dead spot on his chest. An empty spot. A place that connected his thoughts to no one. He waited for the voice to speak, but it was totally gone now. He sagged against the car as a sob broke from deep in his chest.

The pistol fell from his left hand and clattered on the concrete.

Around him, the other ghosts screamed. All of them. Every single ghost screamed. And he did, too.

79

The rain was steady but not aggressive. Gayle drove away from Dianna's house, turned at the corner, went two blocks along the street, and then pulled over.

It was one of those residential streets without sidewalks or lights, with two homes on one side and a public park on the other. One house was totally dark and the other had a single light in an upstairs room. The light was a pale blue that flickered. Someone watching TV in bed.

Gayle left the engine running but turned off the lights and wipers, then sat with her hands resting on the upper curve of the wheel. Remembering. Cataloging all of the details of what had just happened. And the consequences.

She had just had sex with a woman. Her mind resisted calling it lovemaking because that came with heavy baggage.

She and Dianna had shared intimacy in a way Gayle had not since she'd first married Scott. No, that was wrong. In a way she had never experienced.

It was good. It felt right, but it also felt wrong.

The right parts—and some were truly right for her—were right because of the freedom. The moments that had allowed her to be entirely herself. No lies, no false fronts. The fact that she hadn't completely opened up was separate and personal. That was all about her fear and awkwardness, not because the door was shut and locked. It was too new and too strange for her to have relaxed enough to completely enjoy the experience. She hadn't had an orgasm. Not that Dianna hadn't tried. The woman had skills. But Gayle had been more nervous tonight than when she'd lost her virginity in her senior year of high school. Back then, the conventions she had been sold as "right and normal" provided a framework so that all she and the guy in question had to worry about were contraception and basic mechanics.

Not tonight. The world had gotten a good deal larger tonight. More so than she anticipated when she began looking for a "first date" with a woman. More so than when she and Carrie swapped carefully worded notes of passion and a few pictures.

Carrie had been freer than Gayle, her photos and notes more explicit. Maybe if they'd followed through to have a night together it would have had more of the safety net of familiarity. Maybe Gayle would have been a better lover and been more fully receptive. Maybe, maybe, maybe.

Had Dianna's orgasm even been real? Or had she thrown Gayle a pity fake of the kind she herself gifted Scott with when it seemed like he was really trying? On those rare occasions.

Lightning flashed and Gayle flinched. Somehow the flinch and the starkness of the light made her think of home. Of Scott and the kids. Of what he would say if he ever found out. Of what he would do.

Yes, he had originally agreed to let her go on a date.

No, he had never agreed to Gayle sleeping with another woman.

Yes, he had wanted a threesome with another woman.

No, he did not want to share her. Not really. Not when it became clear that her desire to spend time with another woman had nothing at all to do with him, and that he would never be invited into that new connection.

What would he do if he found out?

There would be yelling. That was certain.

What else would happen? Scott would be hurt, betrayed, afraid. Would it drive him away? Would he go straight to a divorce lawyer?

Did she want that?

"No," she said aloud.

No. But . . . why? Sex with Scott was nothing. Rough, dehumanizing. She was a receptacle for his sperm. She was breasts and a vagina. She was a cook and a paycheck and child care. She cleaned the house and was a good hostess. But was she even a person to him anymore? Did her needs, her wants, her reality, truly register with him? If not, why?

If not . . . what next?

The rain seemed to soften, to whisper along the street and wash, rather than pummel, the windshield.

Gayle thought about Dianna's tattoos. Before they got out of bed, when the frequency had shifted completely away from sex, they'd discussed a number of things. Dianna's job reading cards and providing spiritual guidance using her gifts of sensitivity and intuition. They also talked about Dianna's tattoos. The pride rainbow was the oldest of the woman's skin art, and the most obvious. On her left ankle was a small labrys, the double-sided ax associated with the goddess of the hunt, Artemis, and the harvest goddess, Demeter. A symbol of enduring female strength and independence; a severing of the connection to—and need for—male strength and protection. On Dianna's right ankle was a small black triangle, which had originally been used by the concentration camp Nazis to mark certain female prisoners known for *arbeitssc¬heu*—antisocial behavior that included feminism, prostitution, and lesbianism. And, along Dianna's spine, from the coccyx to the top of the thorax, were the phases of the moon. Dianna explained how the tattoo artist, Patty Cakes, scolded her about that because exploring her lesbianism was not a phase of her life but a defining quality.

"Maybe I should get that one," said Gayle. "I think I'm still more straight than anything."

"Yeah," said Dianna diffidently, "or maybe wait to see what happens. You might surprise yourself."

"I don't think so," said Gayle, and Dianna didn't push it.

The last of Dianna's tattoos was one on the inside of her forearm—a green vine from which roses budded and bloomed. But that one looked old and pale, faded to faintness.

"What's that one for?" asked Gayle, and for a moment the other woman just looked blank. Then she frowned and shrugged.

"It's nothing. I kind of forget why I even got it."

Gayle touched her arm, running her fingers along the smooth, pale skin. Touching each faded rose. "The roses look withered. Was that intentional?"

Dianna shook her head. "I don't know. It was a long time ago."

Now, sitting in her car, she touched her own arm. Imagining more there. Imagining art there.

Imagining meaning there.

She sat for nearly twenty minutes more, and then she started the car and drove home. Scott was asleep in front of the TV, the kids were in bed. There was no way for Scott to even know when she got back. Gayle went to the bathroom and, despite having showered at Dianna's, cleaned up again. She put on her pajamas and then went down to the living room to wake Scott.

He blinked bleary eyes at her, saw those pajamas.

"Hey," he said and smiled in a way that reminded her of how he looked when they first started dating. A sweetness, an innocence. "How long have you been home?"

"Oh, for a while," she lied. "Didn't want to wake you, you looked so peaceful. So I took a shower and read for a bit. But then I thought about how your back gets sometimes when you sleep too long in the La-Z-Boy, so I figured I'd wake you. Is that okay?"

He rubbed his face and got heavily to his feet. Sighing a lot.

"That's sweet of you, Gayle," he said and kissed her cheek. "You're the best."

He stumped up the stairs, and Gayle followed. He was burdened with weariness. She carried much heavier baggage. He fell asleep as soon as his head hit the pillow. Gayle did not sleep at all that night.

Not one wink.

80

Owen Minor lay naked on his bed.

Spread-eagle, erect, panting, bathed in sweat.

The tattoo on his forearm burned as bright as a spotlight, catching blowflies in flight, throwing their shadows against the wall.

His body was in the room. His mind was not.

Everything that defined him was miles and miles away. At the edge of town, down a country lane, around past Davy Peach's organic produce store, near Pine Walk Park. In a house with a big porch, past a door hung with corn dollies, up a flight of stairs, beyond a half-closed bedroom door, past a trail of clothing—black tights and black jeans, a silk sweater, a wool tunic, two bras, one thong, and one pair of Victoria's Secret highwaist underwear—and onto a bed where one body lay naked in the velvet darkness. The woman was covered only by a sheet, and barely by it. The temperature was turned up and the room was warm. A scented candle guttered in its Mason jar. Music played on an Echo Dot.

That was where Owen Minor was.

Inside the house, inside the room, inside the skin of the sleeping woman.

Inside her mind.

Feeling the crystal clear echoes of very private experiences. The touches and kisses. The tastes and pungencies of natural oils. Hearing and sometimes uttering the cries and gasps.

Owen relived each moment.

The recent memory of Gayle, new and fresh, but fleeting. Used up and gone, leaving only a fading scent of passion. But the deeper he went into Dianna's tattoo the more he found stored there. The real nourishment came from older memories. Of Dianna and the first woman with whom she had made love. Not just kissed or fondled, but the first person who had ever taken Dianna up above the normal, out of her skin, and into a light so pure that it still burned. He fought to capture that person's name.

Andrea.

Yes.

Years and years ago. When Dianna was seventeen and Andrea was nineteen. It was a defining moment. It was the first time sex had become lovemaking. An act of beauty. A thing of purity.

Owen Minor lay on his bed and remembered every kiss, every touch, every flutter of a heartbeat. It was so wonderful. So delicious.

And in his secret, private darkness, he fed on it and was well satisfied.

Later . . .

Much later.

Owen forced himself to let go of Dianna Agbala, to leave some of her tattoo there. On him and on her. The woman was so rich in experiences—good and, to his delight, bad—that he did not want to use her all up. Not yet.

She would feed him for weeks, he thought. Maybe months.

But he was still hungry.

That was the problem . . . the hunger was always there now. Always. It no longer faded like it used to. There were none of the gaps of months, or weeks, or even days anymore. The hunger was massive and it followed him and owned him.

He had to feed it.

There was no option B. He fed it because he must.

And so, he got out of bed and staggered to the bathroom, turned on the yellow light, and stared at his nakedness. He had a dozen tattoos that he hadn't yet unlocked. Some of them belonged to an old Vietnam veteran. He wasn't in the mood for those tonight. Nor was he in the mood for the despair of the farmer, Burleigh. He needed to give that a rest and taste something new.

There was a big full-length mirror on the back of the bathroom door and Owen turned, looking over his shoulder at the images on chest and ribs and back; on thighs and buttocks; on his arms and even one between the cheeks of his ass. Tattoos stolen here and there. A menu.

But even as he studied each image, he knew which one he was going to pick.

The new one.

Brand new. Stolen without notice and now fully formed on his chest, right over his heart. He stepped close to the mirror and studied it. Several curious flies landed on his shoulders and neck and crawled down toward the image.

"Mine," he said, and they did not touch it with their little black feet.

In the mirror, the small tattoo of a young girl's face stared at him with wide, frightened eyes. Asian eyes. Those eyes looked at him. Saw him. And knew, with the bitter wisdom of experience, what he was going to make her do.

Owen touched the tattoo, caressing the cheek.

"Show me," he said.

The mouth of the tattooed face opened into a wide and silent scream.

"Show me, Tuyet."

No one else could hear the little girl's scream.

No one except Owen Minor.

81

Monk Addison sat on the front porch of his house. He vaguely remembered driving home, but he had no idea where his keys were now. The door was locked. His handgun was gone. The car was locked, too.

He sat on the Ikea rattan chair, his head in his hands, shuddering from time to time. His ghosts stood around him. Silent now. Shocked and frightened. As he was shocked and frightened.

Monk touched the bare spot on his chest.

It took him a long time to make his brain work right. To reconnect with the patterns of logic, of cause and effect, that defined him. There had been the guy at the bar. Something Duncan. Maybe Arnold or Andrew. The guy who lost the tattoo celebrating his wife's remissions from breast cancer.

And there was Patty. She'd lost a tattoo, too.

But . . . of what?

It was a face, too, but it was gone. Whose face was it, though?

A name floated just beyond his ability to hear it.

The storm was worse now, and the wind slashed him with cold rain. That was good. That was fine. It felt like punishment. It felt deserved.

Though for which sins, he was not sure, and the night refused to share its secrets.

He caught movement out of the corner of his eye. A thick fly walking along the arm of the other chair. Bold as brass, the little fucker.

Monk's hand moved at the speed of his fury and smashed the fly to paste.

"Fucker," growled Monk, wiping his hand clean on his jeans.

Twenty minutes later he got up, walked through puddles down his side yard, and kicked in his back door. He propped it closed with a kitchen chair, stripped out of his clothes, and let the various pieces lay where they fell. He stood in the hottest shower he could bear for almost half an hour. Then crawled into bed and fell asleep almost at once.

PART THREE

Wine dark lips
In it for the Night
In it for the forgetting—morning
Waking the monsters
With the sunshine—
tangled around me around you

"TANGLED" LEZA CANTORAL

The Devil doesn't have a face.
He has a hundred damn faces.

"DEVIL IN THE WOODS" OREN MORSE

82

Morning is a lie in Pine Deep.

It explodes with light and color, laughing the clouds away and shouting among the many-colored leaves. The lingering raindrops on the grass sparkled like jewels and birds sang happy songs in the trees.

The morning was sneaky like that. Manipulative. It insisted you accept the fiction that all was right with the world and each new day was, indeed, filled with the promise of good things and happiness. Those people who moved through life with little awareness, barely noticed, because they had not really taken note of the intensity of the darkness the previous night, nor the harshness of the storms. They sleepwalked through their days and got lost in TV or computer screens at night and were some-how armored against the world as it was.

For the others, though, the ones who counted more than five personal senses and who were wired into the nervous system of the town, the lie was obvious. Some took the reprieve from shadows and storms, accepting it with the gratitude of the beaten, who bless the moment when the bully takes a breath. For some the morning offered at least a chance to shuffle the cards and maybe deal a better hand. And for those special ones who could not unsee the things that moved behind the curtains of either day or night, the bright sunshine was a joke, a deception, a crocodile smile.

Dianna Agbala got out of bed and stood by the windows, shiv-ering despite the heat turned high last night. Even the bedroom carpet felt like ice beneath the soles of her feet. She stood rub-bing the place on her arm where the tattoo had been fading, where the roses had withered. She was not aware she did that.

She thought about Gayle. About the things they talked about, the things they shared. The sex was the least of it. Gayle had been sweet and earnest, but too uncertain and self-conscious to be a good lover. Maybe she was in her hetero life, but she did not yet understand how to make love as a woman with a woman. Dianna wondered if there would be a second time for her, or if last night had gotten it out of her system. Her instincts said that a door had been opened, though, and maybe couldn't be closed.

A mockingbird drew her attention for a moment and when she returned to thoughts of last night they were oddly vague. As if it were something that happened months ago rather than hours.

"Christ," she said aloud, "how drunk was I?"

It annoyed her because she had to fight to reconstruct the face of the woman she'd slept with. Grace? Or Greta? Something like that.

She waved a fly away from her face and the action broke her concentration. She did not return to thoughts of last night. Not even for a moment.

The streets were still wet and the morning sunlight painted impressionistic landscapes with colors borrowed from the trees. It was easy to behold such rampant beauty and forget that there were shadows in the world. In moments like that Dianna even forgot about the tattoo on her arm. When she shivered, she smiled and dismissed it as the last of the storm breezes.

Andrew Duncan sat on the bed of the motel room where he had slept badly. He wore boxers and a tank top and stared for hours at the scarred spot on his arm. His wife had called her sister and gone to her place in Easton. There was no invitation for him to follow. She'd even blocked his number.

He stared at the faded scar on his arm and wondered if the local bars were open yet.

Down a crooked farm road, Alexa Clare sat cross-legged on her bed, all the lights out, rubbing at the spot between her breasts where a circle once connected her to the world, to her first love, to her sanity. She used the pads of forefinger-and-index fingers and made circles with such consistent force and pressure that the skin was abraded, raw. Tiny droplets of blood tickled down her stomach, but she didn't notice.

She tried to remember what she did last night, but could not. There was a room somewhere in her mind where certain thoughts were hung. Alexa was aware of its existence, and knew without doubt that there were times when she went in there and put on those thoughts like a second skin. In her dreams there were some vaguely erotic images, seen as indistinctly as shadows on the other side of a drawn shade. No real details. And a lot of lost time.

She rubbed the spot on her chest and wondered why it hurt. And wondered what it was.

She was not aware that she had a new tattoo in the center of her back, at the angle where the eye does not usually fall. There, in her skin, the blowfly trembled and waited.

Gayle Kosinski lay alone in bed. Scott was gone—up and out to play golf with his friends. The kids were still, mercifully, asleep. She lingered at the edge of wakefulness, recalling bittersweet fragments of a dream in which she had gone prowling in bars along the Fringe and found a beautiful woman. They had talked, and laughed, and kissed, and made love in a big bed. It had been so good, and Gayle came over and over again. But then the dream changed as she tried to bring this new lover to orgasm. She tried and tried, but nothing worked. Not fingers or tongue. After a while the effort fatigued her own muscles. Her jaw ached and she started getting a headache from the position, lying face-down between the woman's thighs. It was also uncomfortable for her breasts because there was a fold of the top-sheet beneath them and Gayle didn't dare stop what she was doing to move it. Then the woman reached down and pushed her fingers against Gayle's forehead, breaking the contact, pushing her back, and in a cold voice laced with disapproval, said, "You're useless."

That's when Gaye looked up, past stomach and breasts, to the woman's pinched and shrewish face . . . and saw her own. Saw that this woman was her. That the only woman she could ever meet, ever seduce, was herself, and even in that she had failed.

She lay in bed, her hands clenched to fists, pulling the blanket over her body so that even she didn't have to look at it.

It took her hours to remember what actually happened last night, and when it all came back she sat up sharply, gasping, confused. The strangest thought popped into her head—that it was not her own memory that was faulty, but that she was somehow being forgotten. Which made no sense at all.

Miles away, Malcolm Crow sat on the edge of his bed. Val, sweet and smart and strong, slept next to him, twitching as if something in a dream stabbed her. Memories, Crow knew. Like the ones that had pulled him awake. The birds singing outside were hateful and noisy. He leaned his forearms on his thighs, hung his head, and felt lost.

Val slept on her back and wore a thin white camisole. It was not sheer, but just translucent enough so that he could see the faint outlines of the ladybug and the lightning bug on her sternum. He wondered if she was aware of how many times a day she touched that spot.

Seeing those tattoos shoved his mind in the direction of their meaning and of Patty Trang. Forgetting a child, even if that was the result of stress, head trauma, or some other cause, was truly appalling. Crow was in no way a religious man, but it felt like a sin.

He got carefully out of the bed and walked over to the window that looked out at the oak tree and the two headstones.

"We'll never forget," he promised his children. His babies. The lost ones.

There were dozens of nightbirds hidden among the leaves

of that ancient tree. They all cawed in a soft, plaintive chorus. Closer to the house, blowflies buzzed as they looked for a way inside.

In a hospital bed at Pinelands Regional, Joey Raynor lay staring up at the ceiling. He wanted a drink so badly that tears ran from the corners of his eyes and soaked his thin pillow.

As he lay there he ran his hand over his chest and stomach. Over the smooth artless skin. He had his eyes closed and was barely aware that his fingers stopped here and there and there . . . each time lingering where a tattoo had been. It was not memory exactly, not on the surface anyway. It was deeper than that. A habit of awareness. His deepest mind, his truest heart, was aware of the absence.

But an absence of what?

He wept alone in the darkness of his hospital bedroom.

Monk Addison lay on the floor of his living room. Sprawled where he'd fallen when the alcohol in his system flooded the control room and short-circuited all awareness. The loss of that tattoo on his chest was awful for him. He wasn't scared of much in the world, but the few square inches of bare skin terrified him.

Truly, deeply terrified him.

He was already drunk when he walked in the door and grabbed the rest of the whiskey bottle he'd started that morning. He'd been mad at Patty for poisoning herself with too much alcohol, but he outdid her by a mile. Good bourbon was a velvet cudgel and he let it smash all his lights.

It was not the morning light or the chorus of songbirds that woke him. It was the ringing of his cell phone. It took him so long to make sense of the sound. Longer still to climb up that dark, steep hill to awareness. His punctured hand spider-crawled to where the cell lay, found it, grabbed it, scuttled back to press it against his face.

"What?" he croaked in an old man's voice.

"Monk?" said Patty Cakes. "They're letting me go. Can you come get me?"

INTERLUDE FIFTEEN   **THE LORD OF THE FLIES**

It was in Pine Deep that Owen Minor discovered something about himself he did not know.

On a warm spring morning, while he was sitting in the Scarecrow Diner eating liver and onions and reading about some new special effects tattoo techniques, he saw a man come in and sit down at the counter. Even if he hadn't been wearing a sleeveless denim vest with CYKE-LONES MOTORCYCLE CLUB embroidered on the back, Owen would have pegged him as a biker. The nickname "Slider" was stitched below the emblem. He reeked of pot, testosterone, and violence. The whole place went quiet, like a saloon in an old Western when the evil gunslinger pushed through the batwing doors. Two people at the counter even got up and moved to a booth at the far end of the diner.

The biker, Slider, looked around with an expression of practiced contempt on his craggy features. He even gave a clichéd snort that was an eloquent dismissal of everyone and everything in the place. While waiting for his order, the biker turned on his stool and studied the bustlines on two high school girls, who colored and looked at their phones; at a brawny farmworker who suddenly found something interesting on his plate; and then at Owen.

"The fuck you looking at, you bald faggot?"

Owen quickly looked down. He felt his testicles crawl up inside of him and his hands went cold with fear. In that instant Owen did not want to steal this man's tattoos or peer into his memories. What he wanted to do was flee. To get up and get out of there and maybe never come back to that diner.

However, as he thought that he suddenly felt a shiver ripple along his skin. Not goose bumps rising. No. It was the flies. Their tiny wings fluttered in agitation. Not in fear, not sharing Owen's discomfort. It was a totally different reaction. The flies were angry. Mad as wasps. Buzzing, buzzing with hate.

"I wish you would just fucking die," said Owen, but no one else heard him. Certainly not the biker. "I hope a truck grinds you into paste."

And then he saw something that nearly tore a cry from him. A fly crawled out from under the cuff of Owen's shirt. A blowfly. One of his blowflies. Not merely buzzing on his skin but somehow—impossibly—alive. Separate from him. Moving with total independence. Real. And yet . . . it was a thing of ink and pieces of borrowed flesh, torn from Owen's own skin.

In terrible fascination, he watched the fly's wings become a blur as it lifted off his wrist and soared into the air. It swerved uncertainly for a moment, moving as awkwardly and sloppily as a newborn ripping free from its maggot husk. Within a few seconds, though, its flight became more deliberate, more controlled. It soared up to the ceiling and landed upside down, crawling over the acoustic tiles. Then it dropped down again and lit on the back of the man's biker colors, high, near the collar. Slider was now leering at the waitress, who was arranging a plate of Salisbury steak and potatoes in front of the man. The fly, silent as a shadow, crawled up to the collar, poised on the edge of the material, and then vanished inside Slider's shirt.

Owen sat for a long time, fingers clamped around his coffee cup, feeling it go cold, shaking his head when the waitress offered a refill. The biker ate his food, farted, laughed at the expressions of the patrons, tossed a twenty on the table, and walked out. Slider paused to look down at Owen's cup, then bent and stuck a dirty index finger in it, studied the wetness, and wiped it clean on Owen's sleeve. Then he left.

The waitress hurried over with a clean cup, but Owen barely noticed, instead staring with his whole being at the biker, who walked across the street to where his bike was parked under a tree. Slider mounted, fired up the bike, but did not drive away. After four minutes of sitting on the rumbling machine, he got off, turned to watch traffic, and, when a truck heavy with four tons of harvested pumpkins came rolling fast to try and beat a yellow light, walked right in front of it. The truck was going forty miles an hour. More than fast enough to smash Slider into red jelly and hurl his broken body ten feet into the air. Everyone inside and outside of the diner screamed. Even Owen.

They all rushed outside, and Owen, dazed, followed along. The flies on his skin buzzed with a crimson joy.

I wish you would just fucking die.

The flies on his skin buzzed.

I hope a truck grinds you into paste.

That night Owen checked his body and saw the empty place where one fly was no longer inked. He touched the smooth skin.

"What . . . ?" he asked aloud. It took him forever to fall asleep.

When he did, he was the biker. He was actually Slider. He was not inside the biker's memories. Not really. Not the way he was when he was feeding on pain and grief and loss. But he was Slider. He was that crude man as he stepped into the street and was smashed to ruin.

I wish you would just fucking die.

That memory did not vanish after Owen took his first bite.

Or his second.

I hope a truck grinds you into paste.

He relieved those few moments a thousand times that night, crying out in orgasmic delight each time the grill of the truck crunched into flesh and blood. Each time, the remaining flies on his skin buzzed so loud it tore holes in the night.

83

Mike Sweeney lived in a suite of rooms in the back of the big Guthrie farmhouse. The rooms were big, lined with bookshelves floor to ceiling, and private. He even had his own entrance.

As for Crow, he was also cracking jokes, even when things were at their worst, but a lot of that was reflex. An old survival habit learned when Crow was a kid and being knocked around by a drunken father. That was a territory Mike knew well, though he had gone deep inside instead of trying to lighten everyone's mood. Scars take all sorts of forms.

Val's survival skill was throwing herself into work. She owned the largest farm in Bucks County, thousands of acres that included some of what had been neighboring farms before things went bad. For a while the primary crop had been garlic—hardnecked German White variety, with scattered patches here and there of elephant, wild, Rocambole, softneck, Silverskin, porcelain, artichoke, and purple stripe. For ten years after the Trouble, garlic was the region's biggest crop. That changed over time, and Val was back to her father's profession of corn farming, with large fields of pumpkins, hay, soybeans, oats, potatoes, tomatoes, beans, and cabbage. All of which smelled better than garlic, and it had taken years for the stink to fade.

Mike was a creature of habit. He woke precisely at six in the morning, every morning unless he was on night shift. He rolled out of bed onto the floor and did four sets of fifty push-ups, alternating with slow-burn and speed crunches. Then he did two kung-fu forms—the Yang Tai Chi long form and then Wing Chun's Biu Jee. Sometimes he did one of the more difficult Shotokan-karate katas, either Gojushiho Sho or Unsu. Then he put on sweats and ran seven miles through the forest, following deer paths, much of it done in sprints. After that he showered and came through into the main house for breakfast, dressed in a freshly ironed uniform, with creases so sharp they could draw blood.

The kitchen smelled of breakfast.

Val was a truly awful cook, one of the worst in North America—a fact she readily agreed with. Crow wasn't much better, but he could scramble eggs and toast bagels. And there was always coffee brewing, with mugs for any of the hands who wanted to come in for a cup on a cold morning.

That morning, it was just Val and Crow in the kitchen. She was going through harvest reports and Crow was doing a crossword puzzle. A chafing dish heavy with eggs sat next to a plate of bagels. There were tubs of country butter and local-made cream cheese.

Crow looked up over his reading glasses, amused at the mountain of eggs Mike ladled onto his plate, and nodded his approval.

"You were out late," said Val, bringing Mike a steaming cup.

"Yeah," said Crow, "hot date? You finally ask that psychic lady out? What's her name? Diane?"

"Dianna, and no. She's gay."

"She is?" asked Crow, surprised.

"Very," said Val.

"Well, how 'bout that," said Crow. "I'll stop shopping for wedding gifts for you two crazy kids."

"Ha ha," said Mike, who had—in fact—asked Dianna Agbala out a few months ago, and gotten a very polite no. Accompanied by a courtesy explanation that Dianna did not have to provide, but for which Mike was grateful. He'd tried to apologize for his presumption, but Dianna just laughed it off and told him he was a handsome hunk. Just not her cut of meat. They'd since become friendly acquaintances. He stuffed a massive forkful of eggs into his mouth.

"So what were you up to last night?" asked Crow.

"Not much," Mike said, his cheeks puffed like a squirrel's. "Just cruising the Fringe."

"In the rain?" asked Crow.

"Sure. Felt nice."

"You're insane, you know that, right?"

Mike pointed to Crow. "Pot." And then to himself. "Kettle."

Val sat and poured Splenda into her coffee. Mike privately wished he could find someone like her. His age, of course, but with her intelligence and toughness. She was lovely, but cold and hard, too. Everything she'd ever endured was just there behind the hard blue of her eyes, and etched in lines around her mouth. Crow called them laugh lines, but they weren't. She was his adopted mother, but Mike would always be a bit in love with her.

"Yesterday was a pretty weird day," Mike said aloud.

Crow snorted. "In Pine Deep? You shock me."

"No, I mean about that tattoo thing at the hospital."

"Oh, yeah." Crow finished a clue and set his pen down. He sipped some coffee. "She seemed so certain."

"The wife? Sure."

"No," said Crow, "the tattoo artist."

They looked at each other for a beat.

"Wait, what are you talking about?" they said at the same time.

"The woman from that new tattoo shop on Boundary Street," said Crow. "Isn't that why you were in the Fringe?"

"No. And what woman?"

"The woman with the missing tattoo."

"No, you got it wrong," said Mike, "it was her husband who had the missing tattoo."

"Husband? You mean Monk Addison? He's not her husband."

Mike blinked. "Who's Monk Addison?"

Another beat.

Val said, "I hate to interrupt but this conversation is going sideways. Each of you has something to say. Maybe take turns instead of turning this into an *SNL* skit."

Crow took a bagel from the plate, picked up his knife, scooped some cream cheese, and pointed the knife at Mike. "You first."

So, Mike told them about the Duncans and the husband's pink ribbon tattoo and his wife's cancer remission dates. Then he explained about the vet whose entire chestful of tattoos had gone missing. Crow had begun spreading the cream cheese but stopped and stared open-mouthed throughout the narration. When he was done Crow finished preparing his bagel and ate a bite, chewing slowly and thoroughly before he spoke.

"Crow . . . ?" prodded Val.

"I'll see your cancer tattoo and inked vet," said Crow slowly, "and raise you a tattoo artist in the ER last night." With that he launched into his story about Patty Cakes Trang and Gerald "Monk" Addison. When he was done, the three of them looked at each other without speaking for nearly a full minute. Mike saw Val's hand stray to her sternum and he knew that she was touching the ladybug and lightning bug tattoos that kept her heart beating.

"Can't be a coincidence," said Mike. "I mean . . . seriously, it can't."

Val looked at him with her cold blueberry eyes. "This is Pine Deep."

"Sure, sure, this is Pine Deep. We all know that. Town's weird. Hell, I'm weird."

"Truth in advertising," agreed Crow, and Val whacked his wrist with her coffee spoon.

"But this is weird even by our standards," continued Mike.

"Yeah," said Crow slowly. "It's kind of freaking me out. I mean . . . it's just so weird. So . . . hell . . . I don't even know what to call it."

"*Weird* works," said Val under her breath. The lines around her mouth were deeper and now there two vertical lines etched between her brows.

Mike ate another forkful of eggs, shaking his head while he chewed and swallowed. "Where do we even go with it? It's not actually a crime. And the injuries—Mr. Duncan's head, that Tran woman's injuries, and that Monk character's hand—those are incidental. No bad guy here. What now? Do we react to this? If so, how? What's the play?"

Crow got up and poured himself more coffee, sat back down, and stared deep into the brown depths as if there were some oracle there. He shook his head and glanced at Val.

"Open to suggestions," he said.

Val raised her eyebrows. "Don't look at me. I'm just a humble farm wife. I have cows to milk and hay to bale."

"We don't have any cows," said Crow. "And you have thirty-six employees."

"Doesn't change the fact that I don't have any idea. I joked about this being Pine Deep, but maybe it really is a coincidence. No, don't look at me like that. When you told me about Patty Trang last night it freaked me out. I know her. Kind of, I mean. We've met. I talked to her about adding something to . . ." She touched her sternum. "And she knows Dianna—and, Mike, you could have asked me about her. I've known her for ages."

"Oh," said Mike and Crow at the same time.

"But this tattoo thing," continued Val, "that's not just weird, it's freaky weird. Three separate cases, all on the same day. That's scary."

"It's weird," agreed Crow, "but, as you said, this is Pine Deep. Let's keep some perspective. It's very strange, but it isn't anything dangerous. It's not like the Trouble is starting up again."

"Might be worth poking at it some," said Mike softly. "Ask around."

Val nodded. "Maybe so."

Crow nodded. His cell rang and he made a face when he looked at the screen.

"It's the evil bitch-queen of the universe," he said, then punched the button and leaned back in his chair. "What's up, Gertie? Did I forget to clean the coffeepot again?"

Mike and Val watched him as he listened. Crow sighed heavily and then cursed under his breath.

"Okay," he said into the phone, "Mike and I will head over now and check it out."

He set the cell down carefully, as if it were eggshell fragile.

"What's wrong, honey?" asked Val.

"Mort Peters and his daughter went up to the Crestville

Bridge to fish for rainbow trout, and . . . well, damn . . . the girl—little Maddie—sees a body. Guy either fell or jumped, but he splashed himself real good on the rocks."

"God," said Mike, "that's a horrible thing for a kid to see. Maddie's what? Ten?"

"Eight," said Val, looking stricken. "Poor kid."

Mike looked down at the eggs still on his plate, then shook his head and pushed it away, his appetite gone. "That tattoo thing can wait, I guess," he said.

"Yeah," agreed Crow. "Let's go."

84

Dianna stared at her phone, mouth open, totally perplexed by the text that just popped up.

Last night was beautiful.

You are the gentlest, sweetest and most beautiful woman.

Thank you for everything.

They came in from someone named Gayle.

But . . . she did not know anyone by that name. Not that spelling, and the only other Gail she knew was an old friend who now lived in San Jose.

She almost deleted the text and blocked the number, thinking that it was some kind of scam. She got as far as loading the screen that allowed her to block.

Did not, though.

Instead she scrolled up from the text from this unknown person. And nearly screamed. There were other texts. From Gayle.

And texts from her.

A lot of them. And they were from last night.

She read and read and read. Over and over, piecing together an encounter that started at Tank Girl and ended in her own

damn bed. There were photos of Gayle, taken at—apparently—
Dianna's request. A lovely nude of a beautiful white woman
with dark hair and a nervous smile. And a reciprocal photo of
Dianna, also naked, touching her fingertips to her sternum over
her heart, lips puckered as if blowing a kiss.

The sheets on which Dianna lay were the ones on the bed
right now. New sheets, bought less than a month ago. She'd put
them on fresh yesterday morning.

She whirled and ran upstairs and stared at those sheets, and
the blanket. She bent and sniffed, capturing the fading scents
of perfume and sex. Dianna backed away from the bed, stumbling, gasping as if all the air had been sucked out of the room.
Her back thumped against the dresser. Her knees, already weak
from shock, buckled and she sat down hard on the floor. The
bed seemed to crouch there, sneaky and full of secrets that
made no sense.

Dianna had no idea how long she sat there. A minute or an
hour. Her mind was reeling and she kept her palms flat on the
floorboards to keep from falling off the edge of the world.

"Gayle," she said. And a moment later whispered the name as
a question. "Gayle . . . ?"

There was something there. Buried so deep it was barely a
shadow. A face filled with hope and self-consciousness and
need and desire and fear. Soft lips speaking her name in the
night, then brushing against her cheek. Inexpert hands, used
to different kinds of curves, discovering the art of touching another woman.

"Who are you?" Dianna asked aloud as panic flared in her.
She could feel her heart hammering and the room was suddenly
too bright.

Why can't I remember?

There was a momentary flash of horror as she wondered if she'd been drugged somehow. Date rape was not exclusively a hetero thing. Dianna knew women who had been raped by other women. Was that what this was?

She searched her heart and also her insights, the part of her that was able to peel back the ordinary layers of perception. She focused everything that made her who she was on the question.

"No," she said aloud. And believed it.

Not rape. Not a roofie or some other drug.

Then . . . what?

The bed, with its rumpled sheets, and the text messages on her phone remained immutable, challenging the emptiness of her memories with their truth.

And it was then, in that moment, as she was reaching for the phone, which had fallen from her hand when she hit the dresser, that she saw her forearm. Saw the tattoo.

Saw what was left of the tattoo.

Suddenly her mind was gone. Shifting hard away from the absolute moment and into something approaching a fugue state. The room vanished. The three-dimensional reality faded. She stood, naked and terrified, in the bedroom of someone she did not know. A room she'd never been to.

A man lay naked on the bed. Pale, ugly, lumpy, hairless. Tattoos of flies covered his flesh. The air in the room was fetid and smelled of yeast, sweat, anger, and the wrong kind of sex. The ejaculate engineered through hate rather than a cleaner form of passion. There were stains all over the sheets, and more flies—real ones—swarming above the man. Dianna took a tentative step forward, repelled and compelled in equal measures. But there was something on the man's skin. Images.

Tattoos. Not only those of flies. Faces. Symbols.

And . . .

A green vine, delicate with the sweetness of early spring, sprouting from a blue vein near the wrist. Curling up the forearm, sprouting roses in dozens of shades, each flower larger and more vibrant than the last, and also subtly different—more realistic, more defined—until a final rose whose lush petals brushed against the tender inside of her elbow. Not a flower in transition, but one that was so clearly itself that seeing it was a celebration of joy.

The tattoo seemed to writhe on his skin as if struggling to break free of him. It was very rich in color, but only in places. Some of it was pale, and there were pieces missing except for the faintest of outlines.

She looked at her own forearm, at the same design, faded to a ghostly outline. Nearly gone.

The man lay there on the bed, sweating, flesh wobbling, eyes glazed in ecstasy, chest rising and falling rapidly. Then he froze and gasped. His eyes instantly sharpened and he jerked his head toward her. Eyes locked on her. Seeing her. Actually seeing her.

She watched his expression change from startled fear to something else. The eyes crinkled, the nose wrinkled, and the mouth widened into a wide, wet, leering grin of absolute delight.

"They're delicious," he said, spit flecking his chin, his hand beginning to move again. "They're so goddamn delicious and you can't have them back. You can never have them back."

Dianna screamed her way back to her own bedroom.

85

Owen Minor laughed as he came.

The look on that psychic's face. The horror. The understanding. It was absolutely delicious. Perfect. Priceless.

He looked at the vine and delighted in its vibrancy. This one was going to be a keeper. It was tied to that woman's whole life. Not a single incident, like a stillborn child. Those memories went all the way back; they peeled back so many layers of Dianna Agbala. The woman as well as the professional psychic. They revealed so much.

So much more than she ever told anyone, including her therapist.

The doubts and fears, the image issues with race, with weight, and with the need for acceptance. The mockery about her outing herself as a sensitive, card reader, and spiritual healer. The process of fighting through the gender identity roles imposed on her by family, church, and community. The climb up that long ladder to find a version of her own skin she was comfortable wearing. Becoming the Dianna Agbala who liked being her.

All of that was tied up in the buds and budding flowers on that tattoo. Patty Cakes had done an exceptional job. There was some kind of real magic in that ink.

And now it belonged to him.

He lay there, smiling at the flies buzzing overhead.

But he was still hungry. If he couldn't have more of Dianna right now, then why not go to the other tattoo that had Patty's unique vibration on it. The face he'd stolen from the man covered in faces.

It intrigued Owen that this was the same little girl's face that was on Patty's hand. The one that would not entirely transfer over to his. That face as a mother would render it—smiling, happy, beautiful.

No, the one he'd stolen from the big man was that girl at the end of her life. Terrified, broken, violated, dying. It was there . . .

right in the center of his chest. Waiting for him, like a fright-ened kid in a closet waiting for the punishment belt.

Owen ran his fingers across the silently screaming face.

And woke her up to him.

86

Monk was really damn glad there were no traffic cops bothering him on the way to the hospital. The body processes alcohol at the rate of about an ounce an hour, and even fumbling with fuzzy rec-ollections he figured there had to be something like a pint of whis-key sloshing around in his system. He didn't actually hit anything, but there was some horn-blaring and four-, six-, eight-, and ten-letter words shouted at him. He dared not let go of the wheel long enough to either wave an apology or flip anyone the bird.

He veered into the ER lot, parked crookedly in a slot re-served for ambulances, ignored something a security guard said, and staggered inside. Patty was waiting for him in a wheelchair and the sight of her jolted him into a shocked so-briety. She looked tiny, withered, deflated. Her complexion, generally a pale tan, looked jaundiced and she sat slumped. Her eyes, though, had a shifty, feral quality to them, darting at him and away, back, and away again.

Monk squatted beside the chair and took her right hand and held it against his cheek. She leaned over and rested her fore-head against his.

"I'm sorry," she said.

Monk kissed her hand.

"Get me out of here," she whispered fiercely. "Please, Monk, take me home."

Which he did.

87

Owen lay facedown on the bed.

Gasping.

Weeping.

His throat was raw from screaming.

There were bloodstains on the sheets. A lot of it. From where he had tried to claw the tattoo off his chest. There was piss and shit on the bed, too. The bedroom stank like an outhouse, pummeling him with shame.

He could heard his mother's voice, screeching at him for having soiled the bed again. It didn't matter that she was bones in a box in a cemetery whose name he'd totally forgotten. Her screams, her icy voice, and her knuckly fists, and the swish of the flyswatter with which she enforced her ever-increasing set of house rules—those things were as real as if she were still alive, still with him. Still filling the room, the house, the world, with the force of her glacial, implacable disapproval.

Owen lay tangled in the soiled sheets, unable to move. Unable to do anything.

Then he thought of the things he had down in the cellar. The knives. The scalpels. The acid. Surely they would save him.

On his chest the little girl's face screamed and screamed and screamed. And, as if somehow standing behind her, was the face of the man from whom he'd stolen that tattoo. The big, ugly man with the muscular shoulders and the air of ragged violence. The face of that man leaned toward him, emerging from the shadow of the tattoo-inspired dream, but also seeming to lean into his bedroom. Owen turned away, not wanting to see it, but it was there in every corner, smiling at him in such an ugly way. A dark smile filled with the wrong kind of magic.

"Mine!" cried Owen, clapping his hand over the tattoo. But then he instantly snatched it away, hissing at the pain. He stared at his fingers and palm, watching as his skin puffed and then swelled with blisters. There was blood on his fingers, too, from where—in the heat of madness—he'd tried to claw it off his skin.

The flies buzzed around, agitated, angry. Frightened, too.

You're a perverted little piece of shit, snarled his mother's ghost.

Mommy, don't forget me, wept the little dead girl.

"Mine," said Owen weakly.

In his mind he could see the knives, the acid, and the scalpel down in his workroom so clearly. So very clearly.

88

Mike had to help Crow down over some of the rocks. He did it without comment, knowing that Crow's old hip injury had to be acting up with humidity this high. They reached the riverbed and walked along to where a pair of EMTs stood beside another cop, Rowdy Sullivan, who was a freckle-faced ex–high school football jock who joined the department when the college scouts all passed on him. Built with the narrow hips and broad shoulders of a tight end, but too short for college or pro.

Rowdy already had yellow crime scene tape strung from trees along the bank, enclosing an area of about forty feet by fifteen. A body lay sprawled on a cluster of big chunks of broken granite and smoother river rocks. His arms and legs were spread wide, but his head was bowed forward, chin shoved against sternum by the impact that had utterly smashed the skull. The rocks were painted with red that spattered outward in a textbook pattern consistent with a fall from the bridge. Crow looked up at the gray metal struts and down at the corpse.

The victim was dressed in old, dirty clothes—sneakers and jeans, a flannel shirt, and a fleece jacket with a flag patch on the left shoulder and a round U.S. Army emblem above the heart. On the right, where a name was usually embroidered, the cloth was torn and the name missing. The jacket was two-tone, with the arms and a band across the chest originally navy or black, but faded now to a dusty gray, and the torso in olive drab.

"Not a regulation jacket," said Mike.

Crow shook his head. "Custom. Danbury Mint used to sell these. This one's Desert Storm." He glanced at Rowdy. "You check for ID? Wallet, cell . . . ?"

"All he had was about four dollars in ones and change, pack of gum, pack of tissues, pack of Camels with three left, and what's left of a book of matches." Rowdy held out a plastic evidence bag. "Looks like he's homeless." He paused. "Was," he added, but not unkindly.

"You recognize him?" Crow asked, but the two younger cops and the EMTs all shook their heads.

"You document the scene?" asked Crow, and Rowdy nodded, holding up his cell phone. "Took about a hundred pics and uploaded them to the department server. Took measurements, too, and I tagged the pics with GPS coordinates."

"Good job."

"There was no sign of a scuffle on the bridge," said Mike, who was bending over the man.

"No," said the older of the two EMTs. "And no obvious bruising or marks of violence except for the head trauma. ME will know better, but I've seen jumpers before and that's what this looks like."

Crow said nothing. He studied the dead man for a while, then glanced up again at the bridge.

"What?" asked Mike.

"I'm seen my fair share of jumpers, too," said Crow slowly, "and a few right here."

"But . . . ?"

Crow ran his fingers through his curly salt-and-pepper hair. "Can't recall a single one of them who fell backward like this. They do that in movies because it looks dramatic or artistic or some shit. But not a real jumper."

They all thought about it, and talked about other suicides they'd dealt with. Jumpers were not all that rare in the country. The Crestville Bridge was the only one of the several spans around the town that was high enough to guarantee death. Even the Songbird Bridge, which went over the Delaware into New Jersey, was lower. But Crestville, on the other side of the river, was—true to its name—built on a high crest of rocky land, formed by some shifting of the earth millions of years ago. Other suicides in the area were more likely the result of drug overdoses—Oxycontin was a problem—car wrecks, and handguns. Once in a while someone went very old school and hung themselves.

"Guess he didn't want to see it coming," said Rowdy.

Crow grunted. "That, or maybe he was going for the effect he got. Back of the head's a lot more fragile than the forehead and face. Quicker, too."

The EMTs nodded.

"Okay," said Crow, "let's bag him and take the poor son of a bitch . . ." His voice trailed off and he stepped closer and knelt beside the dead man. The others watched as the chief pulled on a pair of black nitrile gloves. He hooked a finger in the V of the man's flannel shirt, which was buttoned to the clavicular notch, and gently lifted the material. He gestured with his other hand for Rowdy to move out of his light and all five of them looked at the exposed skin of the victim's upper chest.

"Looks like an old burn," said the younger EMT.

Crow ignored him and glanced up at Mike, who slowly lowered himself until he was sitting on his heels.

"Not a burn," said Mike.

"No," agreed Crow.

There, partly exposed, was an area of skin that looked melted or smeared, and which was faintly stained, as if there had been a colorful image there that had been nearly—but not completely—erased.

"Jesus Christ," breathed Mike.

89

Owen Minor was sick.

He tumbled out of bed and vomited on the floor. His skin was slick with sweat and there was a pain on his sternum hotter than fire. The bandage hid the spot where he had excised the tattoo of the little girl's face.

It wasn't the first time he'd been poisoned by a memory, but that hadn't happened for years. Many years. What truly alarmed him was the fact that it was nine hours since he'd removed the image and the skin had not regrown. There was still a shallow and bloody patch. Four ragged square inches. The dressing kept the blood from running down his belly, but he could feel how raw the wound was. The pain was like a fresh burn.

"What the fuck?" he asked his reflection in the bathroom mirror.

Owen Minor was almost never frightened about anything.

He was terrified now.

The flap of skin was in the trash down in the cellar. Wrapped in wax paper and shoved down under the other debris. Later he planned to dispose of it far from his house.

Minor could feel it. He could almost hear it. The flies buzzed in long traffic patterns, around him, down the stairs, through the house to the basement stairs, down and around the trash can, and then back. Over and over again. They were frightened, too.

They were angry as well.

Minor was more than angry. He was furious.

That motherfucker Monk Addison. This was his fault.

"You're going to goddamn well pay, you bastard," he growled, then winced as a fresh wave of pain shot through him.

He thought about sending one of his flies to find Monk and make him do something awful. Maybe force him to go stick his hands into a wood chipper. That sounded fun. But he hesitated. Even the flies seemed reluctant. There was something about Monk.

Only once before had the flies refused to target someone Owen disliked. The big cop with the red hair. Owen had seen him flirting with Dianna outside the store where she worked. Owen wanted to do something bad to that big man. Partly because Owen lusted for Dianna, and partly because the cop scared him. Like that biker had scared him. But the flies absolutely would not go near him. And the one fly Owen sent to follow Monk to his house had never come back.

"You fucker," he snarled, but the snarl turned into a sob.

He got dressed very carefully, filling his pockets with extra sterile pads and tape just in case the bandage leaked. Then he crept downstairs, moving like a man in a minefield until he reached the trash can by his workbench. The flies buzzed and swarmed and screamed in his mind.

He knew that he had to get the tattoo out of his house.

He had to do it now or go totally mad.

90

Chief Crow was at his desk, clawing his way through a mountain of expense reports related to the extra security his department would need to provide for the Fringe Festival. Because of threats and rumors of threats about the Cyke-Lones planning on causing some trouble, Crow was trying to conjure extra money from his budget for overtime as well as shift work for cops borrowed from Crestville and Black Marsh. Math was not his strong suit, so when the phone rang he lunged at it like a hungry bass.

"Crow?" said the familiar voice of April Chung, a friend in the FBI. "I have some info for you on your John Doe jumper."

Crow leaned back in his chair. "Another blank?"

"Actually," said Chung, "no. We got something substantial. You know my niece runs the FDDU, right?"

"Yes . . ." Crow said cautiously. The Federal DNA Database Unit was notorious for dragging their heels processing requests from small-town police departments. He'd waited as long as three months for results in the past.

"Well, little Violet would like her favorite aunt to cosign for that house she wants to buy. So, she's been kissing my ass quite a lot. Mind you, that stops once she signs the lease, but until then she's my minion. Anyway, she ran the sample you sent and we got a hit. The vic is Lester Mouton, originally from New Orleans."

"Did he serve in Desert Storm?"

"Wait, you already know him?" asked Chung.

"No, but he was wearing one of those Danbury Mint fleeces."

"Ah, gotcha. And, yes. Honorable discharge in ninety-two.

Worked a bunch of odd jobs here and there, according to tax filings, but he dropped off the edge of the world around 2002. One arrest for vagrancy in 2003, but nothing after that, so figure he was homeless."

"That fits," said Crow. "You get anything else?"

"Not much. No relatives except very distant cousins. Never married, no kids."

"Rats. But this is great, April. Gives me a place to start."

"I have to ask, though," said Chung, "why did you want a rush on a suicide of a homeless guy? I mean, don't think I'm hard-hearted but it's hardly a capital crime. Is this related to something else?"

"I think it might be." He explained about the rash of missing tattoos. There was a long silence on the other end of the call.

"Okay," she said, "this is going to sound really freaky—"

"I'm chief of police in Pine Deep," he said.

"—but I think I heard about something like that."

"Wait . . . what?"

"Yeah, you know how agents will talk over drinks? The freaky stuff. Everyone wants to story-top with some kind of *X-Files* bullshit. Well, about two years ago someone was talking about that at a Christmas party in Quantico. . . . Crap, I can't remember the details. Let me go dig it up."

"Okay, but—"

And she was gone.

91

It was raining. Again.

There was no open spot near Patty's store, so Monk double parked with his flashers on and hustled her inside. Somehow helping her—and the need to truly be there for her—was sobering him up fast. The effect might not last, and he was likely to crash hard later, but he was okay with taking the short-term lift.

Once inside, Patty went immediately to one of the barber chairs and sat down as if the effort of walking from the car to there had sapped what little strength she had.

"Beer me," she said, waving a hand in the general direction of the fridge.

Monk stared at her. "You out of your mind? You drank a whole case of—"

"Give me one now or I'll just wait until you go."

"Patty—"

"And you look shitfaced yourself, Monk. And don't even get me started on how you smell."

The standoff lasted for half a minute. It felt longer, and Monk knew he was going to lose unless he ankle-chained her to the bed. Chief Crow would love that. But there was nothing in the box except a Diet Dr Pepper, a tub of hummus, and a mass of leafy greens that was evolving into something vaguely threatening.

"Sorry, Pats," he said, "but you're dry."

"Will you go get me something? There's a beer place a couple blocks down."

Monk went over and sat in the adjoining chair. He looked around the place, seeing it in daylight, listening in his head for an echo of the vague feeling of threat that was there yesterday. That sense someone was watching, or waiting. It wasn't really clear if that feeling was gone because there was never a reason for it to be there in the first place, or because whatever it had been was no longer there. Or no longer looking. He said nothing about it, though.

"Look, I saw a pho place on the way into town yesterday, I could get us something."

"I want a beer."

"Well, that's just tough," he said frankly. "Christ, Pats, look at yourself. Have you eaten, like, anything since you came here? You were borderline malnourished before you bugged out of New York, but now . . . shit . . . I'm surprised they kicked you loose from the hospital. Kind of expected them to put in a feeding tube."

"You know how to charm a girl."

He snorted.

She looked away. "I don't want pho."

"Chinese?"

"No. You going to run through the whole of Asian cuisine?"

"What do you want, then? Pizza? A steak? Every other store around here's a takeout. Or we could go to that big diner, what's it called? The Scarecrow? Get some eggs. You need a protein hit and a crap-ton of carbs."

"And you need to stop being my mother."

"Okay, fine. Skip the food for now. How about we sit here and talk about what happened? How about we talk about Tuyet?"

She gave him a withering look. "You can really be a cruel bastard sometimes, Monk."

"And you can be evasive as fuck. How 'bout we stop playing games?" He stabbed a finger in the direction of her bandaged hand. "Let's not forget that I was there when you inked Tuyet's face on your hand. I was there for all of it."

"Don't . . ."

"I know what that art means to you, what it's always meant to you. You can spin some bullshit to the cops and the doctors, Pats, but you can't lie to me. Not to me. We don't do that. Neither of us. Ever. That's the deal and we don't break the deal. Not once in all these years."

She looked down at the bandage on her hand. Time seemed to stall. Monk sat there, watching her, watching the way her shoulders painted a picture of total defeat. When he glanced at the wall clock he was surprised that time was actually passing. Outside it was raining again. Was that all it ever did in this town?

Patty said, "Monk, do you love me?"

It was a sudden question. Full of sharp edges, and yet spoken in a voice that was completely calm.

"You know I do," he said, not moving from where he sat.

She nodded.

"I know something's wrong with me," she said after another long silence.

Monk did not dare speak. He did not dare contradict or try to make it better with some encouraging bullshit. Patty was telling her truth and they both needed him to be her witness.

"I'm not going to kill myself," she said. "I wouldn't. I wasn't trying to do that yesterday, in case you're wondering. The shrinks at the hospital grilled the hell out of me and they let me go because they can tell I'm not a danger to myself. Well," she glanced bitterly at her bandaged hand, "not to my life. Turns out there's no actual law to prevent people from banging themselves up. I got Twitch on the phone to explain that to them. Even so, they wouldn't have let me out unless they believed me. You can believe me, too. I'm not going to kill myself. Not now or ever. And me not eating isn't some kind of subtle slow suicide. Nothing like that."

"Okay."

"But I'm not okay, either." Patty wiped at her eyes and studied her fingers, looking a little surprised to find them dry. "I know this is killing you, baby. You want to save me and I don't know if I can be saved. If I'm worth the effort—No . . . no, let me finish." She cut a look at him, saw that he was merely sitting there. She nodded. "I went to the Fire Zone last night."

Monk's heart jerked sideways in his chest, but he held his tongue.

"I went looking for her. For . . ." She paused and had to take a breath before she said the name. "For Tuyet. It was so weird, because we could hear and see people. Laughing, talking, singing with the Music. I saw this woman. Lady Eyes." She told him about the encounter. "But then there was this sound. A buzzing. At first I thought it was my ink gun, like some kind of flashback to either me doing that original tattoo or what . . . I, um . . . did last night."

"Take it slow, Pats. It's okay."

She nodded and sniffed. She was panting as if she'd run up three flights of stairs. "The more I heard that sound, the harder it was to even remember why I was there. Who I'd come to look for, you know?"

He nodded.

"And that lady kept asking me to say a name."

Monk leaned forward. "What name? Tuyet's?"

"No. She wanted me to say someone else's name. And—you're going to think I'm crazy here, but . . . I think it was the name of the person who . . . who . . ."

"Give me a noun, kiddo."

"She wanted me to say the name of the person who stole Tuyet." She cut a pleading look at him. "Am I crazy?"

Monk managed a smile. "Patty darlin', I'm an ex-soldier who has dead faces tattooed on his skin and who sees ghosts. You do some kind of weird magic with your tattoo gun, and more than half of what's inked on me is stuff you did. Somehow your most precious tattoo, the one with five thousand times more meaning than anything else, has started to fade and it's taking with it memories of your little girl. Crazy? No, sweetheart, the world is bugfuck nuts and we're stuck in the madhouse."

Patty started to say something, but he held up a hand.

"There's more," he said and told her about Andrew Duncan. Patty's eyes grew wider and they filled with a deep, deep dread.

"What . . . what . . . ? I mean . . . what?" she stammered.

"And it gets worse," said Monk. He stood up and shucked his jacket and grabbed the hem of the Minor Threat T-shirt he wore. He had to steel himself to do what he did next. Then with one abrupt move he pulled the shirt over his head and dropped it on the chair, standing naked to the waist in front of her. The eyes on all those faces were open and awake as they always were when he was alone with Patty Cakes.

"I don't . . ." began Patty, but then Monk touched the bare spot over his heart. Her face slowly lost all color, all muscular tone, and she slid slowly—very slowly—out of her chair and onto the floor. Monk caught her before her bony knees could hit the hard tiles. He pulled her close to him and held her.

"They stole her from me, too," he said.

They held each other, clung to one another. Patty screamed and Monk wept and their heartbreak filled the whole world.

92

Mr. Pockets had a route he liked to follow. The pubic trash cans on Corn Hill, always good for half a sandwich, down the street from the Pinelands Brewpub, or some crusts out of the Dumpster behind Peace-a-Pizza. It never mattered to him what he ate, as long as he ate, and he was always hungry.

Always.

Deeply.

He was digging for a bite of anything when he found the tattoo.

He'd seen a lot of things over the long years of his life, but Mr. Pockets had never once found a tattoo. With two immensely filthy and very delicate fingers he plucked it out from beneath an empty soda cup and held it up. The thing drooped, so he pinched two corners and raised it to the weak sunlight. It was still soft, a little damp. Takes a while for a slice of skin that thick to harden into something like parchment.

The tattoo was that of a face. A little Asian girl. Pale, beautifully rendered. More like a photograph than something done by an artist. The eyes were open and stared at him with a horror so bottomless that it made his groin stir. The mouth was open, and Mr. Pockets turned his head and leaned close to see if he could hear the scream.

It was there. Faint. Like someone crying out at the bottom of a very deep well. A child's shriek and the sound matched the age of the face. Very young. Still a little girl when she died.

And that made him cock his head to one side, appraising the excised tattoo. This was the face of a dead girl. He could feel it; knew it for certain. She'd been pretty up until she died, and then had died ugly. Ruined by someone.

Who'd tattooed her on their skin?

He didn't think it was the girl's father—and this was definitely male skin. Middle-aged. Caucasian. But it was odd skin, too. Pale as a mushroom and sticky, the way insect feet are sticky.

Not from the blood, either. Mr. Pockets sniffed it. This slice was new but the skin smelled old.

Thunder boomed overhead and it began to rain. Mr. Pockets neither noticed nor would have cared if he had.

He debated eating the piece of skin, but instead opened his dirty fingers and let it drop into the can. There was a dead mouse in the litter and he ate that instead. Fur, bones, and all.

93

April Chung called back in less than an hour and sounded excited.

"I was right," said Chung, "there's a story floating around that a lot of people have heard. One of those things people dig because it's cool but no one really believes. Or admits they believe."

"What've you got?" asked Crow.

"So there's this agent named Chuck Richter who worked out of the Los Angeles shop but then transferred to the East Coast as he was coming up to retirement. Worked a lot of oddball cases, cold cases, scut work, like that. Never a first-chair field man but still had some chops. Anyway, we were all at the big Christmas party a few years ago and he's the kind of guy who can't bear to be outdone telling cop stories. You know the type. He starts talking about a case he was on that looked both weird and hot but petered out. Started with a woman named Tina Bellamy, known as Tinker Bell or just Tink, who was a receptionist in this swanky tattoo place called Malibu Mark's. Richter interviewed the owner, who said that he came in and found Tink crying her eyes out and saying crazy stuff about not being able to remember who she was. It wasn't that she forgot her name, but big chunks of her memory were gone. Very important chunks."

· "Jesus Christ," breathed Crow.

"Malibu Mark told Richter that the memories Tink lost were the ones that explained who she was to herself. Not happy stuff, because apparently that wasn't in the cards. Bad home, sexual abuse, drug addiction, possibly some prostitution. A long run of bad stuff, but then she came out of it, got clean, did the work the therapists gave her, and had that receptionist job making good money. Now, you'd think that having the bad stuff suddenly gone would make her happy, but it didn't."

"No," said Crow, "it wouldn't. Those kinds of memories are a measuring tape for the distance traveled. They remind us about what the world tried to make us and who we built ourselves to be."

"I know," said Chung. "You told me about your dad. The fucker. Mine was no peach but all he did was yell and criticize."

"Abuse is abuse. It's relative and it always hurts. Always leaves a scar."

"Yeah. And the kicker is that Tink had one of those semicolon tattoos, the ones suicide-attempt survivors sometimes get? Except that when she showed her arm to her boss, the tattoo was gone. Not completely, but mostly. And Malibu Mark swore that he'd seen it the day before. Hell, he was the guy who inked it for her as a birthday present. He was proud of her, for all she overcame."

"So, you said Richter got this from Malibu Mark? Not from Tink?"

"No," she said, "and that's part of why your suicide triggered me. Tink went out for lunch that day and never came back. Malibu Mark got worried when she didn't come in the next day so he drove over to her place. She'd swallowed enough sleeping pills to kill an elephant. Left a message on the wall that said 'I am nobody.'"

"Goddamn."

"The case was marked suicide because that's what it was, but it always bothered Richter. For the same reasons this stuff in Pine Deep is turning dials on you, Crow. Richter couldn't leave it alone and over the next few years found a bunch of other cases—suicides and murders—that seemed to connect. People claiming to have lost both tattoos and memories. He poked at it, but couldn't actually find a crime, so he eventually dropped it. Still bothers him, though. And, hey, look, I asked him to send his notes to you. If it helps, maybe you can send him a bottle of something for Christmas. He likes good tequila."

"Done. This is great, April. You're the best."

There was a pause. "Crow, you know that I know some of what really happened in Pine Deep during the Trouble. It keeps me up some nights. Makes me go to church, you know?"

"Yes," said Crow. "I do know."

"Is this going to be something like that?"

Crow took a little too long in answering.

"Damn," she said and hung up.

94

Grief is a monster. It wins so often and so easily.

It's sly and cruel and persistent. Like most scavengers it is opportunistic.

Monk and Patty held on to each other as the black waves of it rose and fell. Alone they might have perished and been swept away into darkness.

But Patty held Monk with every ounce of who she was, and that was a substantial anchor. Monk was her rock in turn. They trembled and shuddered as the waves fell, but they were still there. Battered, nearly broken, but there.

Slowly, slowly, the dark seas of grief subsided and something equally powerful began to rise. First in her. In her mother's heart, which had been looted but was not empty. She pushed Monk back and looked into his eyes. No, she glared. With heat so intense it was nearly palpable.

"I know his name," she snarled. "I know the motherfucker's name."

Monk gasped and sat back hard on his ass. "You what?"

"That lady in the Fire Zone made me say it. She forced me to say it out loud."

"For Christ's sake, Patty, tell me."

Patty hesitated, though, her fires hot but her confidence flickering.

"It's . . . it's not really a name, though. It's the name he calls himself. It's how he thinks of himself."

"Tell me anyway," said Monk, bracing for disappointment.

She licked her lips. "He's the Lord of the Flies."

"Flies . . ." echoed Monk.

"You think I'm stupid, don't you?"

Monk shook his head. "No," he said. "No, I don't."

"Do you know what it means? Flies . . . flies . . . there's something about that. It's buzzing in my head but I can't . . ." She growled in frustration as tiny fragments of thought, of memory, flitted away. "Shit."

Monk wiped his eyes with his fingers and stood up, then gently pulled Patty to her feet.

"We're in the middle of something really out there. Out there even for us."

"Yes."

"Look, we don't have enough to go on except the tattoo thing. You did your tattoo and mine, but Duncan's was inked by a guy in Doylestown who has a place off of Main Street."

"Spider?" asked Patty, brightening.

"You know him?"

"Yeah, I see him at conventions a lot. He's good. A little intense. Got some PTSD and maybe some other shit going on. Decent guy, though. Knows his game."

"You have his number?"

Patty got her phone, located the number, and sent the contact details to Monk's cell. He called, but there was no answer.

"It's early," said Patty. "Maybe he's not open yet."

Monk nodded, chewing his lip for a moment. "Yeah, yeah. Let me think for a sec." He began pacing around the shop while Patty sat in her chair and watched. "This whole thing is Freaksville and we're reacting like victims. Fair enough, we are. But fuck if that's the agenda. I need to grab whatever this is by the balls."

"How you going to do that?"

"Well . . . my skill set is pretty focused. I'm a hunter, right? So I'm going to hunt."

"How? Talking to Spider?"

He shook his head. "That's step two because he's not answering his phone. No, I think I'll make a call to our friend the professor."

"Jonatha?"

"Sure. Who better to ask about something like this?"

Patty nodded. Jonatha Corbiel-Newton was a professor of folklore at the University of Pennsylvania and the author of more than forty nonfiction books, most of which dealt with myths, legends, cultural beliefs, and religious accounts of the supernatural. She was a frequent talking head on the History Channel and Nat Geographic for shows dealing with vampires, werewolves, ghosts, demons, fairies, and other creatures belonging to what she called the "Larger World."

"Let's hope she can help," she said, though the doubt in her voice was evident.

"And then I'll maybe head to Doylestown and see this Spider."

"Looking for what?"

"Fuck if I know. But I got to start somewhere. I mean, do you want to let this stand unanswered?"

That volcanic heat was still there in her eyes. "I need you to find this person. This Lord of the Flies cocksucker. I want you to—"

"Kill him? Oh, you can count on that."

"No," she snapped, "I want you to bring him here. To me."

They stared at each other with all the meaning in her words filling the room, crowding it, forcing mercy out the door.

Neither spoke for a long time, and then Patty's eyes softened. When she spoke her voice seemed far away. "I always loved going to the Fire Zone in my dreams. She was always there, you know. Always. I could always find her there."

She. Not *Tuyet.* It stabbed Monk through the heart that Patty was slipping back to where she was yesterday.

"She wasn't there. That's how I found the Fire Zone in the first place. She took me there in a dream. I remember that much. That part. But not . . . I mean, I can't really remember . . ."

Patty pressed the bandage to her mouth. It was all she could manage for a long time. The rain strengthened, turned, blew almost horizontally past the window. There were pops of white seeded in with the gray drops. Hailstones, big as pearl onions. They popped and pinged against the cars. The flashers from Monk's car painted every other one red.

"I can't see her face," said Patty, her voice nearly buried beneath the weight of pain.

"Say her name," urged Monk gently. "Say it aloud. Keep saying it all day."

Patty braced herself and forced the two syllables out.

"Tuyet . . ."

She touched her lips as she repeated the name, feeling the shame of it. Frowning, frightened. But also hopeful.

"It'll come back," promised Monk. "She'll come back. Tuyet isn't gone."

"You lost her, too," said Patty.

"And we'll both get her back."

"What if we don't?"

Monk had to bite back the answer to that. There was one thing he hadn't told Patty about Tuyet. About their shared understanding of the little girl. He wanted to tell her but was afraid to, because if he was wrong, then maybe she was lost for good.

So he kept his secret for now.

He went over to her, took her hurt hand, kissed the tips of each finger without touching the bandage itself. "We'll get her back. Believe that. Hold on to it. And we'll find whoever did this to us."

Patty Cakes studied him, searching his eyes, then slowly nodded.

"Good," he said and released her hand with a final kiss. He stepped back. "Look, can I trust that you won't do something crazy while I'm out?"

She nodded.

"Kind of need to hear you say it, Pats."

"I'll be okay," she said with exaggerated exasperation.

"No beer? No mad dash to the liquor store?"

"I promise."

"If I order food from Door Dash, can you at least try to eat something?"

"I'm not hungry," said Patty.

"Not what I asked," said Monk firmly. "Will you eat something?"

She sighed. "I'll try."

He gave her a look.

"Jeez, you're a bully," Patty said. "Okay, okay, I'll eat something. Hand to God."

"That's a start," said Monk warily. "No drinking, either." He loaded the food delivery app on his cell, searched for an Italian place, and ordered salads, sandwiches, a pasta bowl, eggplant parm, and garlic bread. He ordered enough for ten meals, looking her in the eyes while he did it. He topped the order off with ten bottles of water and a bunch of sports drinks. The ones with the salt and electrolytes. Then he paid by credit card and added a tip, upping it to 25 percent because of the rain. That way all Patty had to do was open the door for the delivery guy.

"Whatever you don't eat goes in the fridge," he said. "No sneaking it into the Dumpster and then lying to say you binged."

"You're a bastard," she said bitterly, then softened and offered a weak smile. "But I love you anyway."

He kissed her forehead, caressed her cheek, and then went out.

95

Patty sat in the chair for a long time after Monk left, one foot braced against the counter where her inks were stored in rows, slowly moving the chair sideways and back. Outside the wind was blowing like the end of the world. It must have whipped through someone's yard and snatched up all the clothing off the lines because there were pieces of colored cloth sailing past. She saw blue jeans, a violet padded bra, socks in a zebra pattern, a man's royal-blue sweatshirt, a lacy thong. Then they were all gone. The rain intensified until it smeared the windows' specific images.

Like the scar of a tattoo.

She could feel something behind her eyes. Not more tears. Those had turned to dust. Nor was it a migraine. No . . . this was something else. It was as if she could feel the place where the memories had been cut out of her. Not the memories themselves, just the wound. Bleeding awareness of loss.

Patty slid from the chair and landed with a thump on the floor. It hurt the bones in her ass, but she didn't care. Sometimes pain was the best sensation. The rain blew and she sat on the floor and time moved at its own moody and abstract pace.

Her iPad began singing to her and Patty turned to look at it. She hadn't touched it, and was positive Monk didn't turn it on when he was here. But the music filled the air of her shop. An old song. "I Will Take You Home." The saddest lullaby in the world, sung by the Grateful Dead. Sung from the point of view of a father telling his frightened daughter that nightmares can never hurt her because he will always be there, he will always guide her safely back to her bed and to his protective love. The song had been cowritten by Brent Mydland, and sung with heartbreaking honesty, his dedication to the promise absolute. Two years later the singer was dead from a drug overdose. The video of Mydland's little daughter joining him onstage, sitting beside him on the piano bench as he gave his oath to her, was unbearably sweet, and unbearably tragic.

Her iPad, cruel and insightful, played the song for her.

On some level she was frightened that it was playing by itself, but she didn't care. Making sense of things belonged to yesterday, or the day before. She listened to it play, and then the music fell silent.

It took her a lot to get to her feet. It cost more coin than she wanted to spend. The account was seriously overdrawn.

"Please," she asked of the air, or maybe the storm, but the word just hung there.

Patty went over to the iPad and checked the playlist. That song wasn't cued up. Of course it wasn't. It probably hadn't played at all. It was just her sliding farther down the toilet pipe. She picked something nondescript. Some indie pop nonsense. Then she walked through the rooms, not at all sure what she was looking for, or looking at. Rooms with boxes, with the tools of her trade, with books of tattoo art, with clothes, with old stuff she'd carried from one apartment to another. The kinds of things she took out and put on shelves or in closets but never really looked at. Books she would never read again. Little figurines from a religion she'd left long before she emigrated from Vietnam. Photo albums from the days before digital pics.

Patty Cakes was not at all aware of what her hands did with the photo albums. Her mind slipped out of gear and into a fugue as she lifted them, carried them to the tiny second bedroom, and put them on a shelf that was mostly hidden whenever the door was open. She stacked them in a row, with all of the ones from Tuyên Quang closest to the wall. Unless she closed the door and turned to look at the shelf, she would never see them. No part of her surface awareness was part of this process. That consciousness slid back into gear when she was in her bedroom, rooting through a box of winter clothes. The transition from awareness to fugue back to awareness was seamless.

She found a pair of old leather gloves Monk bought her years ago when they'd had motorcycles and drove from New York to Canada, following the smallest lines on the map. She sat on the edge of the bed, kneading and working the gloves to soften the leather, and then took a pair of fabric shears and cut off the fingers. She let the severed canvas fingers lay where they'd fallen.

She pulled the gloves on. The left took effort because of the thickness of her bandage, but she managed.

Then she got up, walked into the store, flipped over the sign and switched the neon on. COME IN!, it said. WE'RE OPEN.

She turned away but then heard the door open and the bell above it tinkle.

"Patty . . . ?" asked a tentative voice.

Patty turned back to see a woman standing there, her eyes filled with tears, her arm held out, sleeve pushed up, to reveal a tattoo that was almost completely faded.

"Help me?" begged Dianna.

96

Crow paced like a caged animal in his office. He could feel his blood pressure rising but didn't care. The information April Chung shared with him was setting his brain on fire.

Missing tattoos.

Missing memories.

He stalked over and stared at the sign over the coffeemaker again.

NOT ALL CRIMES LOOK LIKE CRIMES
(THINK OUTSIDE THE BOX)

"Holy shit," he said. A few moments later he said, "Holy God."

Then he called Mike Sweeney.

"Where are you?"

"Usual place, boss," said Mike, "looking for speeders and being bored out of my mind."

"Do you know if that old vet with the missing tattoos is still in the hospital?"

"Sure. The nurse said she'd call me if they were going to cut his discharge papers. Why?"

"Because a weird week just got a whole lot weirder. Meet me at the hospital."

"When?"

"Now."

Crow hung up and started to turn then saw another of the signs, this one over the row of file cabinets. Like the other it had become virtually invisible to him over the years, but now stopped him in his tracks.

A GOOD COP IS ALWAYS READY BECAUSE
A COLD CASE CAN CATCH FIRE AT ANY TIME

He grinned at it. "No shit, Sherlock."

And was out the door.

97

Monk went to the Scarecrow Diner and approved of it at once. He was a diner snob and this one was a classic. Lots of stainless steel polished to mirror brightness but showing scars from the lives and years that had passed through the place. There were twenty swivel stools at the counter, each with brown vinyl seats. Some diners had the traditional red, but this was farm country and it was a Halloween town, so pumpkin orange was perfect. What made it better was that the seats were patched, worn in spots. Not a trendy choice to give them a faux distressed look—time and a lot of asses had stressed them out just fine, thanks. The counter was Formica made to look like Carrara marble. And there were high-backed booths reaching away from the well-lit counter into the softer shadows on either side. The place smelled of coffee and bacon and that weird but yummy yellow gravy they put on diner turkey platters. The very nature of the place was a balm to his frayed nerves.

A sign told Monk to seat himself, which he did, heading to the booth farthest from anyone else. There were maybe thirty people in the place, but it was big and they were scattered, creating a feeling of privacy. You could talk about anything in a place like this.

A waitress appeared. She had a brown uniform dress with orange piping, an apron, a paler orange cardigan with a couple of cloisonné pumpkin pins on the left breast, and a tag that read BRENDA. Perfect.

"Getcha?" she asked. Brenda had scrambled yellow hair, a few little scars high on one cheek that looked like someone had been unkind to her a long time ago while wearing a ring, dark-red lipstick, and perhaps the kindest gray eyes Monk had ever seen.

"Coffee with milk."

"Whole, two percent, or skim?"

"Whole. And whatever's the special. If it's a meat dish, bruise it but don't kill it."

"Sec," she promised and vanished only to return almost at once with a big porcelain cup, saucer, cutlery setup, and a little metal pot of whole milk. The coffee was perfect. There was no coffee anywhere in world better than diner coffee from a real goddamn diner; of this Monk was certain, because he'd drunk coffee on six continents. And really good coffee could anchor you to the moment. It made so much sense that it clarified a lot of things. Not everyone knew that consciously, Monk was certain, but people like him did. People from the storm lands.

While he waited for his food, Monk made a call. Four rings and then a voice said, "Monk . . . ?"

There was always a bit of caution when Dr. Jonatha Corbiel-Newton answered his calls. A bit of unease. Sometimes she didn't answer, and he figured at those times she saw his name pop up on the screen display and did not have the personal bandwith to deal with whatever he wanted from her. That was fair. He didn't call her often enough merely to shoot the shit. He called when he needed something for one of his cases. Not the bail skips . . . but the ones related to the faces he wore on his flesh. She was one of the very few people who knew about those faces, and about some of his more extreme gigs.

"You alone?" he asked out of the blue, as if there hadn't been radio silence between them for almost ten months.

A beat. A sigh. Then, "Yes." It was a single word but it had a whole lot of *Christ, now what?* in it. Again, fair enough.

"I got something freaky going on," he began.

"Freaky by normal standards or your standards?"

"Definitely the latter."

"Ouch," she said. He heard her take a steadying breath. "Tell me."

He did. Patty, the Duncans, and his own missing ghost. He gave her every single detail he could remember. "Any of this ringing any bells with your sort of thing?" he asked when he was done.

"Honey, you're my sort of thing," she countered, "and I mean that in a purely academic sense. You're a bit of grumpy real-world folklore. I could—and probably should—write a book about you."

"Which you won't," he said.

"I never made that promise," she said. "All I'll grant is that I wouldn't use your name."

"Whatever."

Jonatha laughed.

"Okay," Monk said, "do you have any clue to what's going on here? Something or someone who steals tattoos?"

"Is that what you think is happening here, Monk?"

"Sure, I just told you that—"

"No, I mean, are you sure it's the tattoos that are the point?"

"I . . ."

"Sounds to me like something is stealing memories."

"But—"

"Memories for which the tattoos are a cue, a mnemonic."

The waitress arrived with his food. A thick slab of steaming meat loaf covered with melted Cheddar, diced scallions, and sides of roast potatoes and steamed broccoli. Monk leaned down and inhaled the smell, nodded, smiled at the waitress, and accepted a refill on the coffee. She left him with a smile but did not interrupt his conversation.

"Who or what steals memories?" asked Monk when he was alone again.

"Well," said Jonatha, "that's tricky. There's nothing I know of that specifically does that, but if you're seeing this accurately, then we may be looking at some kind of psychic phenomenon. A psychic vampire of some kind."

"Oh, for fuck's sake," said Monk, cutting a piece of meat loaf and stuffing it in his mouth. "I don't want to hear about vampires."

"We're not talking about Dracula or Lestat," said Jonatha quickly. "No fangs and opera cloaks. Nothing that sparkles. No beautiful immortals lamenting eternity."

Monk chewed and swallowed. "Well, that's a relief."

"Not really," she said. "Psychic vampires are a theory. There's no actual documentation. And most of them are charismatic types who more or less feed off of attention."

"Yeah, we elected one a few years ago."

"I didn't elect shit," said Jonatha crisply. "Be that as it may, we're talking about real people with various kinds of emotional disorders. These are sometimes called 'energy vampires,' and they're part of psychoanalytic science not folklore. There are martyr types who cast themselves as victims and feed off either guilt or excessive sympathy. There are narcissistic vampires who lack the capacity for empathy and feed on attention in which they are cast as the central figure in any situation. There are dominator vampires who act as if they are alphas but really crave validation from people who view them as leaders. Then there are melodramatic vampires—drama queens—who seek out a crisis because it allows them to be the victim. The judgmental vampire subtype feeds on bringing other people down with what they call 'brutal honesty' but which is really an attack on the insecurities of others. And, of course, the innocent vampires, the ones who appear to be so fragile or vulnerable that others will leap to protect them in words or actions. They drain everyone around them."

"Not what we got here."

"I know. I'm thinking out loud."

"Are psychic vampires—"

"'Psi vampires' is the common nickname."

"Are psi vampires an actual thing?"

"Documented? No. Not in the way you're asking. Psi vampires and energy vampires are mostly pop-culture nicknames for different kinds of charismatic manipulation that is often pernicious but not always. The British occultist and author Dion Fortune wrote extensively about this kind of predation in her 1930 nonfiction book *Psychic Self-Defense*. In her view—and I'm paraphrasing here, not quoting—it's somewhere between a parasitic attack and a symbiotic relationship, often requiring some conscious or subconscious participation on the part of the victim. A folie à deux, or a shared psychosis."

"This isn't Patty thinking she lost a tattoo, Jonatha—"

"Let me talk, damn it. I'm trying to work my way through what I know to see if there's anywhere to get firm footing," she said. "Where was I?"

"In the middle of a lecture?"

"Hush now. Okay, good old Anton LaVey is actually the one who coined the phrase *psychic vampire* as part of his Church of Satan. This is in the 1960s, mind. His take was that psychic vampires are actually emotionally weak or deficient people who feed on others to make up for some natural lack in themselves. And it was, of all people, violinist Graham Smith who coined the term 'energy vampire,' though he was talking about how much fans seem to take from performers. Bottom line is that there are a lot of people in the vampires' real-world, nonsupernatural communities who believe very heavily that they, or people they know, are psi or energy vampires. Some people in the BDSM community are even subs to dom psi vampires."

"Okay," he said, stabbing a potato with his fork. "Whatever floats your boat."

"But if we're talking the actual ability to steal a tattoo from a living person in order to feed off of the attached memories, then . . . gosh, Monk, that's a new one even for me."

"So what's it mean? That I'm seeing this wrong?"

"I didn't say that. I'm saying this is something I haven't personally or professionally heard of. That doesn't mean no one has. I'm research girl, so let me dig around, ask some colleagues, poke through the literature."

"Why do you sound happy about that?"

"Well, not happy for what's happening with you and Patty," she said quickly, "but if this is something new? Or something old that hasn't been documented, then . . . hell, I can see myself publishing a juicy paper."

"I'm so fucking tickled that this is making your day."

"Oh, bite me, Monk. You know what I mean."

"Yeah, yeah."

"In the meantime you should see if you can put together more information. Apart from you and Patty, is there something that links either of you to Mr. Duncan? Or his wife? Maybe there's a local connection there in New York and—"

"We're not in New York anymore," said Monk. "Didn't I tell you? No . . . I guess I skipped that part. We're actually in your husband's old stomping grounds."

There was an audible gasp on the other end of the call. "Wait, wait, god . . . you're saying this is happening in Pine Deep?"

98

Mike Sweeney stood behind the single visitor's chair in the single room at Pinelands Regional Medical Center. Crow sat, forearms on his thighs, a coffee cup cradled between his palms. He rolled it slowly back and forth.

"Take your time," said Crow gently. "No stress, no pressure."

On the bed, Joey Raynor, the old homeless veteran, seemed to crouch beneath the thin hospital sheets, as if terrified of the conversation. He was hooked up to machines that monitored his vitals but told no one anything of real value about the man. Despite the fluorescent lights overhead there were shadows huddled in every corner and the whole room seemed washed in an unhealthy yellow-gray.

The Veterans Administration had responded to Mike's information request and said that the physical description he provided matched that of Alan Joseph Raynor, born in 1946, formerly a resident of Philadelphia. Served five years with the air force. Honorably discharged, but subsequently treated for PTSD, depression, alcoholism, drug addiction, malnutrition, and other illnesses related to a life lived on the downward slopes of poverty and disenfranchisement. He was eligible for medical care and also qualified for-as-yet-unclaimed disability benefits related to frequent exposure to Agent Orange and other chemicals. The last official record of Raynor visiting a VA office was in June 2012, and until now he had been presumed dead by his caseworker.

Joey Raynor lay huddled into a ball of trembling tension on the narrow hospital bed as the two cops waited for him to speak. Silence was a fist closed around the three of them, broken only as Mike fidgeted in slow motion, shifting every now and then from one foot to the other, his leather gun-belt creaking for a moment. A fly crawled without sound on the metal headboard a few inches above the vet's head. Mike wanted to swat it, or snatch it out of the air and crush it in his fist. The fly was fat and bloated, loathsome in its indifference to this old man's pain. But Mike didn't want to do anything to scare the poor guy.

The old man did not look at either of the officers when he began to speak. His voice was creaky and dusty, but he spoke clearly, even with eloquence.

"I got my first ink in 1966, at a place on South Street in Philly. It was a music note. A G-clef. You see, I was the lead singer in one of those old Philadelphia a cappella bands. The Seventh Sons. Doo-wop versions of old blues stuff. Muddy Waters, Howlin' Wolf, Willie Dixon, Albert King. My old man called it 'nigger music,' but we didn't. His generation was back from World War Two and Korea and they were way behind the curve when it came to stuff like civil rights. My buddies and me were cool with everyone. Black, white, brown—it didn't matter as long as they were into music. That was our race, our religion. It was all about the tunes."

He paused and sighed, and even though he was turned away he seemed somehow to have grown younger as he spoke.

"There were five of us," said the old man. "Me, Tommy Murphy and his little brother Dan, Pat Reilly, and Stan Pulaski. None of us were seventh sons, though. That was just from the songs, from the blues." He paused for a ragged breath, eyes still averted. "We started singing in seventh grade. Not in school, but that's where we met. Sang on street corners, holding a Coke bottle over our heads like it was a microphone, and all of us in a circle. I'd start a song—I think it was a Lightnin' Hopkins tune—and sing it with that doo-wop slow rhythm. Dan would add falsetto and Stan would be the bass. Pat and Tommy sang harmonies and you never heard better. They could follow me anywhere, and if I fell off the note they'd bring me back. Tommy had perfect pitch and he always shined a light on the right key. I got good at runs, and if we'd stayed together we might even have done some soul. We all liked Ray Charles, but he was more up-tempo. We were poor kids from the worst part of Philly. Kensington. Factories, row homes with no room to breathe and every family with five or seven kids."

He paused and stared at the shadows in a corner of the room, as if they were a window to the past. Mike found himself holding his breath.

"We all knew there was a lottery for the draft," the man continued, "but we also knew that none of us were going to come up with exemptions. None of us were ever getting into college. Our folks didn't have influence or the money to protect us. We all knew a bunch of guys who'd gotten drafted into the army and sent to 'Nam. None of us wanted to shoot anyone. We used to joke about being lovers, not fighters. And that was true, though what we loved was singing. Making music. We even cut an LP with a small company in South Philly. Fourteen blues a cappella songs, and even got radio time with 'Hellhound on My Trail' and 'Born Under a Bad Sign.' But we knew the clock was ticking on us. So I had a plan. I went to the air force recruiting office on Kensington Avenue and asked some questions. I figured, it's the soldiers and marines who get killed. Not the navy and not the air force. Dan had a fear of drowning, so that's why I picked the air force." He made a soft, sick sound of derision. "I went in there thinking I'd get straight answers. After all, I was coming to them. Being a patriot and all. That recruiting sergeant never stopped smiling. Told me that 'sure, son, you and your friends can enlist and we'll keep you Stateside.' He promised that. Gave it to me in his own handwriting, signed and all. If we signed up together they'd train us to repair trucks or drive motor-pool. Not near home, he said, he couldn't promise that, but down south somewhere, most like. Worst-case scenario was we'd all do a year in Germany or Okinawa. That wasn't too bad. See the world, meet some foreign girls, have some adventures, and then come home. When I told him we had a group and were on the radio, he said that made it even better, 'cause the air force had a lot of officers' clubs and they always needed entertainment. That's what he said and he was smiling the whole time. I guess crocodiles and sharks smile just about the same way."

Crow turned and glanced up at Mike, who gave a sad shake of his head. Neither spoke.

The man in the bed wiped at his eyes. "You can guess what they did. They sent us straight to Vietnam. Not with the USO or anything like that. Not motor-pool, either. They put us in the 819th Red Horse Squadron. Civil damn engineers. We went to Da Nang and then Pleiku to build bases, repair fences, put up housing. Then they thought of better uses for some of us. For me and my friends. They'd drop defoliant on some forward area and then send the Seventh Sons in with a platoon of soldiers to watch our backs while we built helicopter bases. We were sucking Agent Orange every day, but we wouldn't have cared much about that even if we knew what it was." He paused for a long time, maybe a full minute. "Dan went first. We weren't even out of the jeep when he took one in the right cheek. Blew half his face away. His teeth and tongue hit Tommy and stuck to his face and shirt. The force of the impact knocked one of Dan's eyes out its sockets but with all that damage he wasn't dead. I remember sitting there, staring, unable to move a finger as he reached up and tried to put his eye back into the socket. His fingers were rock steady, like this was nothing. Blood pouring down and all of us screaming. Then he started choking. Drowning on his own blood. We sat like idiots and watched him die, bullets zipping through the air all around us. I remember hearing them and thinking how bad the flies were. That's what I thought. Then the army guys grabbed us and pulled us out of the jeep and we all huddled in the mud, heads down, watching the infantry fire a couple thousand rounds into the jungle. Monkeys screaming in the trees."

He finally turned and looked at the cops. The pain in his eyes was almost too much for them to witness.

"Help me sit up," he said, holding out a hand. Mike began to move, but Crow waved him back and stood. He took the hand and steadied the veteran as he sat. The vet turned away again, presenting his back. "Untie this damn gown."

Crow untied it and the man shrugged out of it and let the fabric fall to reveal a scarecrow body. Sallow skin covered in old scars and new scabs. What drew the eyes of Mike and Crow, though, were the tattoos on his back. From the trapezius muscles to just above the waist, and from armpit to armpit, the man was covered with tattoos. Scores of them, interlocked or merely adjacent. Some of the colors were vibrant, others badly faded. None of them, though, was erased, like those on Mr. Duncan or the suicide victim under the bridge.

On the exact center of his back was the red knight chess piece emblem of Red Horse Squadron. Surrounding it, spiraling outward, were other tattoos. The screaming face of a tiger and the coiled evil of a bamboo viper; a flurry of musical notes peppered with bullet holes and strung with creeper vines crawling with insects. A swarm of Jolly Green Giants—the Sikorsky HH-3E utility helicopter that defined the 'Nam jungle experience. The faces of four young men—three with distinctly Irish faces and one with the blond hair and blue eyes of a Pole. Below each was a date of birth and the date when they died. The dates were all within five months of one another. There was a picture of the Virgin Mary—looking distinctly Asian—bending over them, arms stretched as if to gather their souls to her breast. There were burning villages and skeletal ghosts in torn BDUs. There were babies and little children who had Irish faces and Vietnamese eyes, but they were all weeping, or reaching for helicopters retreating into the distance. His entire back was the story of that conflict, from heartbreak to heartbreak.

Mike and Crow exchanged a look. Neither had served in the military, but both of them had been through a war of their own. The Trouble. Although neither of them wore their stories on their skins, they understood what they were seeing. They could perceive the truth of it.

Raynor half turned, grunting with the effort, as if memories and arthritis conspired to make every movement painful. He said, "That's where I came from. That's what I carried. And I always wanted those tattoos on my back because even from the jump, from when the first of my friends died, I wanted to remember them but walk away from the pain. The . . . horror of it. If it was inked onto my back then it was always behind me. Do you . . . do you understand?"

Mike was unable to speak. Crow cleared his throat and answered for both of them. "Yes."

Raynor nodded, then he pulled the rest of the gown off and let it puddle around his waist. He lay back on the bed and looked at the cops as they looked at his chest and stomach.

"I did three tours in Nam," he said. "I kept going back because I had some stupid idea that my friends were still there. That it was a joke, some kind of cosmic hide-and-seek and I was too high to realize it. The chaplain finally figured out just how messed up I was. Something I said, I guess, and they shipped my ass back home. I spent the last few months doing clerical. They wouldn't even let me have a hammer. Guess they were afraid I'd do myself an injury, or—worse—someone else. But they were wrong. I'd already done all the damage I was ever going to do in this world. At least to others. You see, it was me who went to the recruiting office. It was me who talked my friends into enlisting. It was me who killed them all. And, no, don't try to say different. I've been through all that with shrinks at the VA and more twelve steps than I care to count."

The room was quiet.

Raynor nodded and continued, "Then my time was up and they kicked me out. You know that old saw about how the military trains us for war but not for peace? Yeah, well, that's even true of civil engineers. I never once pulled a trigger in anger, but I went in as a green kid and came back a killer. I hit the ground and ran right for the bottle, and then the spike. Really, anything that would sand the edges off and give me a little peace." He laughed. "Peace. Yeah well. I tried. See this here?"

He touched the skin over his heart.

"First day I got clean—and by clean I mean the first day I woke up without a screaming ache inside me for a drink or a needle—I went out and had my six-month chip tattooed. You know what that means?"

Crow said, "I've been going to meetings for a long time."

Raynor gave another nod. "Okay. You remember that first really clear day? Not those stupid days when you lie to yourself that you're never going to want to use again because you're cured. Alcoholism can't be cured. You're always an alcoholic, so the rhythm is to make a decision every morning not to drink."

"One day at a time," said Crow faintly.

"Yeah. And sometimes one hour at a time. One minute. But there was a day, maybe five months in, when I knew that I wanted a drink but I didn't need one. You dig that?"

"Yes," said Crow. Mike put his hand on Crow's shoulder.

"I was a month out from earning my chip, but I had the tattoo done and because it was on my chest with every step—every clean step—I was walking toward it. That's why I put it there. That's why all of these were there." He touched his right chest. "My family. My mom was alive when I had this done in Brooklyn. She never turned her back on me, even after I stole money from her for crack. I knew that I was going to get back to see her one day. Clean and sober. I did, too. Best day of my life. She hugged me and we cried for so long I thought I was going to break apart. And here? This is my sister and her kids. I swore I'd be a good brother and a good uncle. Someone they could be proud of. I did, too."

He touched over twenty spots on his torso and told the stories of how he climbed out of the pit. His eyes moved back and forth between Mike and Crow, and his finger was unwavering as it sought exactly the right spot. The right memory.

But there were no images on his skin for anyone to see.

It was obvious that the old veteran had been as comprehensively tattooed on the front of his torso as he'd been on his back. And there were hints of color, vague shapes, spoiled lines. That was all, though. It was like a sand painting done by either a Navajo healer or a Tibetan monk, because after those paintings were completed they were then erased. In both of those cases, though, the erasure was part of the ritual, part of the healing or the uplifting of the soul.

Not here.

No.

What was left looked like something smeared by a malicious hand. At a glance his skin looked melted, like a burn victim's, but it was smooth. Like a child's skin before life put its mark on it.

"How many tattoos did you have there?" asked Mike.

Raynor brushed his hand from collarbone to navel, the fingers fluttering. "Twenty-six. The first was my chip and the last one I got was my mama's face."

"I thought that was an older one," said Crow.

"The first one was."

"I don't—"

"I had it redone when that first one went away. Same spot. Based on the same photo. Even the same tattoo artist. Coney Island Joe."

"You had it redone after it faded?"

"Three times," said Raynor. "Last time was at a tattoo place in Doylestown. But then I kind of . . . you know . . . stopped trying. I guess I stopped trying to do anything. I had a job back then and a couple of bucks in the bank. Tapped an ATM on Main Street in D-town and went into this little bar across the street. Haven't gone too many days without a drink since then, and those were days when I was out of cash."

"What happened to the tattoo?" asked Crow. "What made it fade like that?"

"I don't know. I asked Coney Island Joe, but after the third time he kind of got freaked out. Didn't want to try again. Didn't want me back in his shop. Even refunded my money. By then a bunch of the other tattoos were going away. Not the ones on my back, just the ones that mattered, you know?"

"When did this happen?"

"First time?" Raynor had to think about it. His eyes were a little glazed from fatigue and pain. "First time my mama left me was sometime in 2000. Don't remember the date. After that Y2K thing, but not long after. Maybe March."

"What about the last time?" asked Mike. "When did the last tattoo disappear?"

Raynor looked down at the empty place on his chest. "Last one faded out on me a couple of days after I came here to Pine Deep. That was—let me think—it was in the middle of summer. There was a carnival and I was cruising the edges of it, you know." He rubbed his thumb and fingers together in the time-honored symbol for money. For him that meant panhandling. "And I picked up some extra money sweeping up and collecting trash after everyone went home. But I slipped on some ice cubes someone dropped. Hit my head and they brought me right here to this same hospital. Just the ER then. Wasn't a concussion, nothing broken, so they didn't keep me. Hitch-hiked back to the carnival and finished cleaning up. Took most of the night because I wasn't feeling very good. When I was done it was still early and no one was around yet, so I stripped down to my boxers and hosed off. Felt great, too. It was hotter than hell and that hose water was so cool. But then I happened to look down and saw that Mama was gone. So were some other little ones I had. Lucky charms, and some saints. Gone."

He stopped talking and just shook his head.

"I never tried to get the chip put back. What's the point? I was cursed, I guess. Damned, maybe, for what I'd done to my friends. I ain't walking toward anything anymore except maybe hell. Yeah . . . guess that's where I'm going, with all those troubles on my back pushing me."

With that he turned away and did not say another word.

99

Jonatha Corbiel-Newton had Monk go through it all again. Every incident, every conversation down to the tiniest detail. She'd come to Pine Deep in the days leading up to the Trouble, invited by a local reporter named Willard Fowler Newton who had recently broken a huge story.

To most outsiders, the Trouble started when a gangster and murderous psychopath named Karl Ruger, fleeing from a deadly gunfight with a Jamaican drug posse, had crashed his car in the town. That seemed to ignite a series of calamities that included mass murder, missing persons, arson, poisoning, brutality, and—ultimately—an attack on the Halloween Festival by white supremacists. Those events made Newton a huge star in journalistic circles and, later, in the darker side of pop culture when his nonfiction book on the violence became a runaway bestseller and then a hugely popular movie. The movie went into the lurid direction of suggesting that the white supremacist violence was merely a front for an attack by a horde of the living dead. Vampires. Naturally that version of the story was universally derided by all official channels. Vampires were absurd, fictional, at best echoes of older and since discredited folk beliefs.

The harder the government hammered at that version of the story, the stronger the rumors on the conspiracy theory whisper chain grew. Even now, a decade and a half later, papers and websites across the country ran DID YOU KNOW . . . ? stories every Halloween, and in the towns around Pine Deep the movie, *Hellnight,* was played on a twenty-four-hour cycle. Few people openly admitted to believing in monsters, but in anonymous polls the number of believers was at least equal to nonbelievers.

Ask anyone in Pine Deep the question and they either sneered or changed the subject. Few locals ever directly gave an answer.

Jonatha and Newton—an incredibly unlikely couple—had met and fallen in love during the Trouble, and later married. It was a relationship on a par with Beyoncé falling for George from *Seinfeld*. Nevertheless, it worked. They got rich off his movie, and the subsequent spin-offs and a highly fictionalized Netflix series.

Jonatha once told Monk about the Trouble, but even she had been a bit vague, playing up the fact that the town's water supply had been laced with LSD and other hallucinogens. When asked if she'd been high, Jonatha was evasive.

Now, she queried him. "Monk," she said, "go back to the part where you said some smartass local cop grilled you about Patty. Tell me, was his name Malcolm Crow?"

"That's the guy. Little SOB, but he looks like he might be almost as tough as he thinks he is."

"He's tougher," said Jonatha. "Believe me when I tell you that you don't want to get on his bad side."

"Lot of people have bad sides," said Monk quietly.

"Hey, I know you're all scary bad. Patty's told me stories. But Crow is in a different league." She paused. "Have you met his son? Well, adopted son. A very big young man with red hair."

"No, why?"

"He's even scarier than Crow."

"I can handle myself."

"No," she said flatly, "you can't. Maybe—and only maybe— with Crow, but not with Mike Sweeney."

There was such certainty in her voice that it gave Monk serious pause. "Okay," he said, "I'll make sure not to piss on their shoes. But at the same time I'm going to look into this and they better not get in my way. I'd take that amiss."

"This isn't a penis-measuring thing," she said. "Crow is dangerous because he's actually one of those really high belts in jujitsu, and he has a lot of very practical experience."

"Noted," said Monk. "Same with the Sweeney guy?"

"No," she said sharply, "Mike's different."

"Different how?"

She paused. "Different in the way that I define it, and by that I mean as a world-class expert on the paranormal and supernatural. Mike has . . . gifts. Not the right word, but it's the best I can phrase it without breaking any confidences. But hear me, Monk—don't cross him and don't get in his way."

"I'm a licensed investigator and a professional bounty hunter, Jonatha," he countered, "that gives me a certain freedom of action."

"Sure, and you can use them however you like when it comes to conducting an investigation through channels. What I'm saying is about what would happen if Mike thought you were a bad guy. Someone getting in the way of him finding out who hurt a woman in his town."

"What exactly would happen to me?"

"You'd die," she said. "Badly."

They were quiet for a moment. Monk looked down at the remains of his meat loaf. The cheese had long since congealed.

"Well . . . fuck," he said.

"Look," said Jonatha, "I know Mike and Crow. We . . . bonded during the Trouble. Like family. Let me give Crow a call and tell him you're okay."

Monk sipped his coffee, which was tepid. He winced. "Sure, vouch for me," he said, "but you can't tell him everything. You can't tell him about my tattoos."

She thought about that. "Okay. Look, try to get to know him. Crow's one of the good ones. Don't be fooled by his jokes. There's a lot more to him."

"He wasn't all that funny yesterday."

"Let me call him."

She hung up and Monk sat there, moody and confused. He ate the rest of the food but didn't have much appetite for it anymore. When Brenda came back to fill his cup Monk didn't even glance at her. He sat there staring out the window, watching the rain. Then he paid his check and stepped outside, pulled his collar up and trudged to his car.

100

Owen Minor was very afraid.

That tattoo he'd stolen from Monk Addison had shaken him all the way down to his marrow. It punched a hole in what had been a thrilling few days, and polluted his enjoyment of the Tuyet memories.

Owen was also pissed off that he could not get all of Patty's memories of Tuyet. She'd done something to prevent it.

"Fucking witch whore," he said aloud every time his rage surged up past the fear. No one was ever able to stop him before.

He debated sending a fly to her, to take control of the witch and make her do something really bad to herself. Maybe stab herself with her own tattoo needles.

The thought drifted around in his thoughts, taking shape, feeling right.

It would also eliminate a possible threat. Not Patty herself, but her friend. That big oaf Monk. Owen's victims always forgot his name and face. That was part of how it all worked, and it'd kept Owen safe all these years. Now, though, the process had fractured. With Tuyet's tattoo still partly on Patty's hand, could he ever be sure she'd forgotten his face and name?

No. He couldn't be sure of that at all.

"Witch," he spat.

And what about Dianna. She was a goddamn psychic, after

all. He had hoped feeding on her memories would give him some kind of doorway into her clients' memories. A cascade of goodies. But that had been a big freaking mistake. What at first had seemed like a great opportunity now felt both foolish and a stupid risk.

She was another witch. Maybe she'd gotten way too much insight into him.

"Whores," he snarled, but there was fear in his voice and he could hear it. So could the flies. They flew erratically and too fast, their flight paths warped by agitation.

And as for Monk . . . the face Owen had stolen was similar to all of the others inked on Monk's ugly hide. Were they the same kind of thing? The faces of ghosts? The faces of murder victims? How was that even possible? The fact that Owen stole tattoos and fed on memories was totally natural to him now, but whatever Monk Addison did was unnatural.

What did that make the man? A male witch? Or was it a warlock? Owen wasn't sure. He racked his brain for something that would explain Monk and surprised himself by remembering a reference in one of Jonatha Corbiel-Newton's books. Something called a *varð-lokkur,* a word that was either Old Norse or Old English—he couldn't remember which—that meant "caller of spirits." Was that what Monk Addison was? Some kind of medium?

He wasn't sure, but thought it might be close to the mark.

All of these thoughts raced through his head while he stood in the bathroom of his old house. The buzzing of the flies was constant, and that, at least, soothed him.

Witches and spirit callers, he mused, then he met his own eyes in the mirror. Flies crawled over his eyelids and nose and lips. The temptation to send the flies out, despite his trepidation, was very powerful. But the risk was too great.

On the other hand, he thought, the flies don't have to land on them. No. No, sir, they did not. There were other ways to use the flies. Other people they could land on, people who would do whatever Owen wanted. He'd done it many times before, starting with the Cyke-Lone biker Slider—though never exactly like this.

Not like this.

In his mind he could hear the roar and thunder of a whole army of motorcycles.

Would it work?

Owen chewed on that.

He noticed his reflection beginning to smile.

101

Dianna sat in one of the chairs, openly weeping, while Patty stood holding her arm. The delicate tattoo work of vines and roses was as faded as a painting left outside for a dozen winters. The richness of the colors was gone, turned to thin cheapness; the precision of line and the curve of the buds and blooms looked traced and phony.

Without letting go, Patty leaned forward and kissed Dianna on the forehead. Then she released her and stood, panting slightly, shaking.

"It's more than the tattoo," she said, watching distress turn to fear in Dianna's eyes. "You lost some memories, too."

"What . . . ? How—?"

"You have, haven't you," said Patty softly. "Memories tied to that image. Tied to what it means to you. About your identity as a woman, as a lesbian, as free and strong and whole. Some or all of that is gone, too, isn't it?"

Dianna recoiled from the words as if they were the vilest accusations. Vicious protests rose to her lips, but died there. Patty watched the fight Dianna had with her own emotions, with her terror, with the truth. She knew that fight probably felt like being beaten and savaged to the woman, but it was heroic to watch. And heartbreaking to see. She gave her as much time as she needed, and Dianna needed a lot. Finally, after nearly two full minutes, the woman was able to speak in a nearly normal tone.

"I was with someone last night," said Dianna. "A woman. Someone I just met at Tank Girl. Gayle. Gayle . . . something. She came to my house. To my . . . bed. We made love and then she left."

Patty waited.

"I know this because of texts on my phone. I called Juana at the bar and she confirmed it. She joked that I must have been more drunk than I looked because how else could I forget such a pretty woman? I laughed at her joke and made up some lie and hung up. Then I sat down on my living room floor and cried. I think I'm going crazy, Pats. I came here because the tattoo you did is fading along with that memory, and with a lot of other things. All I have are some pieces. Women I've known. Women I really cared about, or loved. Or still long for. Places I've been while I've been breaking away from what my family tried to make me and become who I really am."

Her dark eyes were fever bright and there was such desperation in them despite the calm way she spoke. That amount of control was beautiful but also frightening, because Patty knew powerful oak trees break if the storm winds blew hard enough.

Dianna took a breath, her fists balled on her lap so that the knuckles were pale against the warm brown of her skin.

"Patty . . . how did you know I forgot some things? How?"

"Because it's happening to me, too." Patty pulled off the fingerless glove and peeled back the bandage, then held out her fist, palm down. Dianna looked at the faded tattoo and the crude stick-figure face over it and her eyes slowly grew wider. She looked up at Patty.

"Tuyet?" she whispered.

"My . . . my baby is nearly gone," sobbed Patty. "Someone is stealing her from me. They took her once and killed her body. Now . . . God help me, Dianna, I think they're trying to kill her soul."

102

Crow and Mike drove over to the Scarecrow Diner and settled at a four-top. They brought their case notes and spread them out, careful not to get coffee on them.

"At the risk of being obvious," said Mike, "but what the actual hell?"

They'd gone back to Raynor's room to take an official recorded statement, and Gertie—under protest—had typed it. Statements by Andrew and Corinne Duncan and the hospital statements by Patty Trang lay overlapped with Crow's own detailed notes from his interview with Monk Addison and his conversation with April Chung. They also had a preliminary report from the coroner about the dead homeless man, Lester Mouton, and Agent Richter's notes—also courtesy of Chung—on the woman named Tink and several similar cases. Chung had forwarded photos of the victims, focusing on the areas of missing tattoos. Those were on Crow's iPad.

All through a long lunch they went over every single detail, creating a chronology of incidents.

"We have more than we had this morning," said Crow.

"We have more information but no actual insight. We don't know what this is."

Crow sipped his coffee, leaning into a corner of the booth and staring at a point above Mike's shoulder. He sipped, stared, sipped until the coffee was gone, then signaled the waitress for a refill. Once it was poured he leaned forward and his eyes found Mike's.

"Make a statement," he said.

"What kind of statement?"

"Whatever comes to mind. Tell me what we know for sure. Lay out the facts, okay? Big or little. Let's start there."

Mike took a big piece of carrot from his salad, chomped a piece, chewed as he thought, and eventually said, "The obvious stuff first. Including Agent Richter's notes and the four people here in town, we have eleven possible victims. Each apparently has or had missing tattoos. From those victims able to give a statement there seems to be a consistent phenomenon of missing memories."

"Keep going."

"Joseph Raynor claims to have pieced together memories of what his missing tattoos were, or probably were. Kait and Gertie are making calls to places where Raynor believes he may have gotten those tattoos. So far we have corroboration on two of the missing images, Raynor's mother and his six-month sobriety chip. Each was done by different artists from different states, respectively Coney Island in New York, and Cape May in Jersey. The Jersey one was done at a convention, though, at the Cape May tattoo artist's booth. The reason these were easy to find was because those same artists had done some of the ink on Raynor's back, too."

"So, where does all this leave us?"

"I really don't know," said Mike, shaking his head. "Not even sure this is a case. I mean . . . what's the actual crime? Theft of tattoos? How is that even possible? And before you give me the 'this is Pine Deep' stock reply, this isn't ghosts or monsters. This is missing tattoo ink."

"Is it?"

Mike blinked. "Of course, that's what we're talking about."

"O young Padawan, you are actually in danger of missing a key element of crime detection. Something that's pretty much page one of the Crimestoppers' Handbook."

"Then enlighten me, O Jedi master."

"Let me ask you a question . . . if we got a call to investigate three downtown businesses with their back doors kicked in, should we assume the intent was to damage doors and locks?"

"Ah," said Mike. "Assumptions."

"Ah," agreed Crow. "Ass. U. Me."

Mike took another bite of carrot and chewed thoughtfully. "The fact that the tattoos are missing is only an element of the crime—if it's a crime."

"What is the more important element?"

"Three of the four victims have lost memories."

"Yes. And can we form any theories about why the fourth victim committed suicide?"

"The loss of an important memory?" suggested Mike. "Something he couldn't live without. Or didn't want to live without?"

They thought about that for a moment.

"Yes," said Crow slowly. "Imagine what might have happened to Ms. Trang if Monk Addison hadn't come by."

JONATHAN MABERRY

"Glad he was there." Mike ate a piece of cucumber. "You still thinking of him as a bad guy in this?"

Crow shook his head. "Nah. He's bad news for someone, but not for us, and I don't think he's bad news for Ms. Trang."

"Okay, so are we investigating a crime? I never saw 'theft of memories' in any list of felonies."

"Statutory crime?" mused Crow. "Probably not. Morally? If this was somehow a deliberate act—and do not ask me how because I have no freaking idea—then this is definitely an infliction of real harm. You know, Mike, I've been thinking about what it would be like if someone stole Val's tattoos and her memories of the kids."

"Jesus Christ," said Mike sharply, then his eyes went hard and cold. "This is rape. Of a kind, I mean. Someone's taking something precious that the victims do not want taken. Maybe not by force, but . . ."

He trailed off, the point made. They drained their cups and took one last refill. Outside the rain fell and the distant thunder mocked them with its deep laughter.

Crow's phone rang and he looked at the screen display. Both of his eyebrows rose and he showed the phone to Mike so he could read the name. Then he punched the button and said, "Well, well, Jonatha . . . you're just the person I was thinking about calling."

"Let me guess," said the professor, "it's about memories and ink, isn't it?"

103

Monk drove out of Pine Deep and turned onto serpentine Alternate State Route A-32, which took him through farm country and past the place where he'd spent the other night in his car. There were two bridges branching off—one crossed the Delaware into Jersey and the other spanned a canal and emptied onto Route 32, which ran like a knobbed backbone from Easton all the way down to Point Pleasant. It was longer than cutting immediately over to 611, but it was prettier and Monk needed something pretty. The trees along the way were almost too fiery to look at, and the roadside grass was still a deep summer green. The cold of autumn seemed unable to sink its claws into the landscape. But that changed once he turned southwest onto 232. It seemed the farther he got from Pine Deep the more the season was successful in leaching colors from the leaves. By the time he reached Doylestown everything was brown and all the grass was dead and withered.

He wasn't sure what to read into that. Pine Deep was a colder, older, and demonstrably creepier place but managed to look like fucking Narnia, while the saner and more welcoming parts of eastern Pennsylvania looked like the suburbs of Chernobyl.

His phone rang as he approached the outskirts of the town's busy business district. It was Twitch. Monk punched the button.

"I'm rolling into D-town right now," he said by way of answering. Not precisely a lie.

"Okay," said the lawyer, "but that wasn't why I called. Two things. First, how's Patty?"

Monk gave him the lowdown. Twitch made sympathetic noises.

"She really doesn't remember her kid?"

"Not totally, but enough that it's going to wreck her if it continues."

"And it's not a concussion? Traumatic amnesia, something like that?"

"Doctors say no."

"Well . . . hell. And no idea what happened to her tattoo? She spill some kind of chemical on her hand that dissolves ink? I'm fishing here, not even sure that's a thing."

"It's not a thing," said Monk. "It's not laser surgery, either."

He did not mention his own missing tattoo or the rest of the mystery. Twitch was not in the circle of trust of people who knew Monk's secrets. Not those kinds of secrets anyway.

"You should go talk to some other tattoo artists," suggested Twitch. "It's a community of sorts, right? Somebody might know something."

"That's what I'm doing right now," Monk said. "You said there were two things . . . ?"

"Oh, yeah, I had a call from Pine Deep Chief of Police Malcolm Crow." He gave Monk the bones of the conversation. "I asked around and he gets a clean bill of health when it comes to corruption. Stand-up guy, my sources tell me, but they also said he's a bit of a weirdo."

"Pine Deep," said Monk.

"That's pretty much what people say. They should make that a meme. Anyway, I just wanted you to know that they also say he is not to be fucked with."

"So I've been told."

"Whoever said that is someone you should listen to."

After the call, Monk wormed his way through crooked streets that seemed to have been arranged with no actual plan. Duncan had said the tattoo parlor where he'd gotten his tattoo was called INKredible. Might have been amusing on any other day.

He found it and pulled up out front, but the windows were dark and there was a CLOSED sign hanging crooked between drawn blinds and glass. He went over to knock anyway, in the hopes the owner was in there somewhere. No response. Monk cursed under his breath and started to turn away, but stopped and turned back. Something was niggling at him but it was so small that it barely registered. He leaned close and placed his ear to the door glass. Nothing. He knocked again, three sharp raps; listened more.

There it was. A faint buzzing sound, hard to hear, and it took him a bit to decide if it was the sound of an artist's ink gun. It wasn't. Close, but . . . no. Then he realized the sound was both closer and smaller than he thought. He raised his eyes and saw that a couple of fat flies were caught between the blinds and the door glass, their tiny wings making the buzz.

"Shit," he said and stalked back to his car. There were no posted hours, though when Monk checked the INKredible website on his phone it listed hours from ten to eight. Nothing about being closed, or opening late. It was less of a mystery than it was a pain in the ass.

He decided to wait for a while, but didn't relish another vigil in his car. There was a bar two doors up and on the other side of an alley that led to a parking lot.

The bar was called The Dog. There was no picture of any breed of dog on the sign or window. Those windows didn't look like they'd been cleaned since Hector was a pup, and most of the neon beer signs were dusty and dead. As he approached he could hear the thump-thump of a bass from inside. Canned music.

He went in.

The place was dark as pockets and smelled of old beer, testosterone, cleaning products, and fried meat. It wasn't the kind of place to have a doorman or require a cover. No live music, no dancers. Just a bunch of lumpy guys hunched over beers or shooters, heads bent forward in conversation or leaning into their own murky thoughts. Monk had been in a thousand places like this in countries all over the world. There was an undercurrent of anger, disappointed dreams, and frustration, and the cleanup guy every night would likely be mopping up tears and blood as much as spilled beer.

He went to the bar and was pleasantly surprised to see a very pretty Mexican woman wiping the counter. At first glance he thought she was late twenties but as she stepped up he added fifteen years. Good years, in terms of how fit and lovely she was, but every day of those years was there in her dark-brown eyes. Her red lips smiled but there was pain in her eyes so old that it was a defining characteristic. Some small scars, too, and a bit of challenge.

"Thirsty?" she asked, then a half beat later added, "Or on the prowl?"

He sat on the stool farthest from anyone else—an old man who appeared to be asleep, nodding over a schooner of dark beer, and a biker type methodically punching a message into his phone.

"You got any IPAs with bite?"

"You know Albatross? Out of Pittsburgh." When Monk shook his head, the bartender poured him a sample. Monk tried it and it was hoppy as all hell. He nodded and she pulled a tall glass for him. Her hands went through the motions automatically, but those dark eyes kept flicking back to Monk. Trying to read him. He liked her enough to keep his eyes steady and let her figure out whatever she could. He was impressed she'd already pegged him as being on the job.

She came and stood in front of him, with the bar-top between them. Dozens of beer mugs and shot glasses drying on a rack, stacked bowls for nuts and pretzels. Big jar of pickles—something Monk hadn't seen in a tavern in years—and a stack of food-stained plastic-coated menus.

"You here to cause me some trouble?" she asked.

"You? No."

"I work here. Need the shifts and the tips and I can't get either if you bust the place up or shut us down."

Monk sipped his beer and shook his head. "No badge."

"Chasing a skip?"

"Most days, but not today," he said. "Came to see the guy who runs INKredible, but his shop's closed."

The woman grunted. "Spider? Yeah, well, he's a little weird. Semiretired, so he isn't always nine to five."

"He's closed now."

"Give it time." Her eyes narrowed. "What do you want him for? He in trouble?"

"Nah, just following up on something," said Monk. "Thought he might have something I could use for the case I'm working. Not here for anything else."

One of her eyebrows rose a tenth of an inch. "Really? Nothing else?"

They smiled at each other.

"Name's Monk," he said.

"Sandy," she replied and offered a small, cool hand. Strong, though. She was a petite woman, but not frail or delicate. She wore a silver blouse with the bar's name on the right breast, and a pair of very tight black stretch jeans over sneakers. Lots of intricate and symbolic silver jewelry. Great lines, and a lot of tone. Moved well, stood easy.

Monk found that he liked Sandy. More than her looks, too.

There was a kindred thing that Monk was always sensitive to. This Sandy was another child of the storm lands. Like Patty. Like him.

He thought he saw the awareness in her eyes, too, but she didn't lower the drawbridge. If he was a woman in this fucked-up world, he wouldn't, either.

"It's weird. Spider sometimes keeps crazy hours, but he's here more than not. If he's closed up it's usually for a bathroom run or shopping. Or eating over here. Mostly, though, he's in the shop," she said. "Ever since his wife died a few years back that place is his whole life. Even on slow days he's open. Or he hangs a note for people to come in here to find him."

"That's brave. Telling people to find a needle-jockey in a bar."

Sandy laughed. Musical, but rich. Despite the hurt in her eyes, she knew how to laugh and there was some freedom in it. Her pain, he thought, lived in her skin but did not own her.

"Actually, Spider doesn't drink. He goes to meetings sometimes, you know? And before you ask, he comes in here for the fish and chips. I brew a pot of decaf for him and he sits right here at the bar. He has a lot of friends here. Local guys and such. And he picks up work here from those bikers."

She leaned a little on the word, and kept her voice low. Monk nodded. He'd spotted four customers with biker colors when he came in. One sitting at the bar and three at a table in the far corner. All of them Cyke-Lones. He filed that away as useful because Gus, the guy Twitch wanted found, rolled with them sometimes. The fleeting hope arose that there was a connection between Duncan and Gus, but it dissipated. Nothing in life was that convenient. He tried it on Sandy anyway.

"Hey, you know a guy goes by the name Gus? Sometimes Dirty Gus. Runs with the Cyke-Lones."

He watched her face, saw the shutters drop behind her eyes. "You trying to game me, Monk?"

"No," he said honestly. "I asked because I have another case and it involves this guy Gus. He's a biker and you got cats from the same club here. Taking a long shot."

She considered that and her reserve lifted a tiny bit. "I heard of him."

"Heard of him or know him?"

She shrugged. "He comes in sometimes. Not here now. He's mostly here late on Friday or Saturday, so I don't think you'll see him."

"Ah well," said Monk. "Had to ask. Maybe I'll come back on Friday."

"Maybe I'll be working, too."

Sandy took a rag and wiped at a spot on the counter that didn't need wiping. The jukebox was by the door, so the sound of Korn screaming "Freak on a Leash" didn't drown out the conversation they were having. When she spoke, she did it without raising her voice and without looking at him.

"It's not Dirty Gus or even just Gus anymore." Her eyes flicked to the other patrons at the far end of the bar, but the old man was still asleep and the biker was now talking on his phone, arguing with someone about a late child support payment he insisted had been dropped off in cash.

"Okay," said Monk quietly.

"Goes by Earl."

"That's his middle name."

"He's not the brightest person I ever met," said Sandy, a small smile there and gone. "Comes in here now and then. Not a regular." She paused. "You're a lot more likely to see Spider walk through the door. Stick around, Mr. Monk, and I bet he'll be here soon."

Monk took a chance. "Should I stick around?"

Now her eyes rose to meet his. There were questions in them. There was uncertainty and some fear, too. But something else as well. The question she asked took him off guard. It was so layered and insightful that it cut him to the heart. It was the right question to ask of someone like him.

"Am I going to be sorry if you do?"

Monk didn't smile because he knew he wasn't good-looking enough to make a smile look charming. Instead he let her take a second, longer look into his eyes.

"I hunt bad guys, Sandy," he said, "and that's all I hunt."

Again he caught a lot of different things flickering in her eyes. Some people had eyes like that—deeper than you could swim, but often worth drowning in.

"Then stick around," she said.

104

Gayle was working late, sorting through lesson plans submitted by the teachers and enjoying the utter stillness of the school when everyone was gone.

Her phone vibrated, and when she saw the number her heart jumped. It was her. Flash images of Dianna exploded in her mind—those dark eyes and the side of her throat, the shape of her lips, and the cool touch of her fingers.

She cut a look to make sure her office door was closed and then answered the call.

"Hi," she said in a voice that was more hoarse and husky than intended.

"Is this Gayle?" asked a stranger's voice. Accented. Asian?

"Who's calling?" Gayle said, forcing herself to suddenly sound official. She double-checked the number on the display and it was Dianna's phone.

"My name's Patty Trang," said the caller. "I own the tattoo shop on Boundary Street. You know the one?"

"I do. Why are you calling me on Dianna's phone?"

"She's here with me," said Patty, "and we're hoping you can come to my store as soon as possible."

"Why?" asked Gayle, all of her defenses up.

There was a rustle and a new voice came on the line. "Gayle?"

"Dianna? What's going on?"

"Gayle, I need your help and I need it right now. Can you get away? Are you home?"

"I'm at work, at the school . . ."

"Oh, really? Okay. Can you get away, though? It's important."

"What's going on? You're being weird and it's scaring me."

"I'm scared, too, Gayle, but . . . after the other night . . . after we . . . you know . . . do you trust me? Can you trust me?"

It was such a strange thing to ask and the practical side of Gayle wanted to end the call and block the number. Whatever this was had nothing to do with her, of that she was sure. And yet . . .

There was such a deep vulnerability in Dianna's voice.

"Are you safe? Are you in trouble? Should I call someone? Nine-one-one?"

"No," said Dianna quickly. "They can't help. This is not that kind of thing."

"Then what is it?"

"Please," begged Dianna. "Please come over."

Gayle had a dozen reasons to say no, all of them practical, sensible, and safe.

She said, "I'll be right there."

105

Monk nursed a second beer and let the minutes burn off. He wanted a cigarette and didn't think Sandy would yell at him for smoking, but he hadn't bought a fresh pack and was half-ass glad of that.

Half an hour in, his phone rang. He saw that it was Jonatha, so he told Sandy he'd be right back and stepped outside to take the call.

"Hey, Professor," he said, leaning a hip against his car. "You got something for me?"

"Nothing and a lot," said the folklorist.

"Meaning?"

"Meaning that there is nothing in the literature that matches what happened to Patty."

"Well, shit, 'cause it's not just Patty. It's other people and it's me."

There was a pause. "Yes, I spoke with Malcolm Crow. There may even be some you don't know about. You should really go talk to him. You're both pulling at different ends of the same thing. That's what I meant by 'a lot.' This is a bigger case than you think, and if it is something paranormal or supernatural, then it's new. Or at least unrecorded, and believe me when I say I searched."

"Maybe I will," said Monk grudgingly. "I'm in Doylestown right now following up on a tattoo artist who may be involved."

"I'm serious . . . talk to Crow."

Jonatha ended the call, which left Monk feeling frustrated as hell. He drank his beer and went through every detail again in his mind. Nothing wrong with his memory—except for the stolen memories of Tuyet. Unlike Patty, who—thank god—still clung to something of that poor little girl, Monk felt as if she was really gone from him. From his life, his experience. It stabbed him with knives of grief.

It also made him very damn angry.

He stood up, told Sandy he'd be right back, and went to check on INKreadible, but the CLOSED sign was still there. He came back to a fresh beer and a bowl of mixed nuts. He drank, he crunched, he thought, and he fumed.

Sandy came over a few times and that part was nice. And he needed something nice to think about. Monk was fascinated by her. From the jump he could tell she had some history, and he picked up clues as they chatted. No rings. She flirted but not in a guilty way, so Monk didn't think there was a boyfriend. Or girlfriend. He'd watched the bartender watching a woman in tight jeans who'd come in for a drink with a construction worker. Sandy watched her, not him. But the same controlled interest in her eyes was still there when the woman left and Sandy looked at him. That was okay with him. Straight or bi, she was who she was, and she was lovely. He wondered if he was going to ask for her number. He wondered if she'd give it. He liked his odds betting on both.

Which was weird. Monk wasn't a good-looking man. He knew that. His face had been hit too many times with great enthusiasm and from too many angles. He had boxer's gristle on one ear, a nose that wandered this way and that, scars that didn't come from anything nice. He was the kind of guy cops and bouncers always took note of. He was the kind of guy that encouraged decent folks to cross the street, lock their car doors, and avoid eye contact with. Fair enough.

The fact that Sandy seemed to like what she saw said a lot. She was okay with rough trade, or at least rough packaging. She wasn't afraid of how he looked but had other kinds of caution lights blinking.

He watched her deliver a pitcher and glasses to two utility company repairmen and she caught his eye as she strolled back to the bar. That's what it became—a transition within two steps from brisk business walk to a stroll that invited him to observe. It was such a clear invitation, too, that Monk didn't feel awkward looking at her curves. She was petite, but every inch of her was lush. She gave him a small slice of a wicked little smile.

Nice.

Earl did not come in.

Monk had a third beer, checked five times to see if Spider had opened his shop, ate the nuts, ate a plate of fish and chips, and felt like there was a big clock ticking in his head.

Finally Sandy came and leaned on the bar. "Shift is over in ten."

"Okay."

She leaned farther.

"For god's sake, Monk, ask."

He grinned. "Okay . . . can I get your number? Maybe take you out for some food sometime?"

She rolled her eyes. "You are actually corny."

"I—"

"I think that's sweet. The world could use a little more corny." Monk said nothing.

"I get off in nine minutes. I need to eat. You have two choices."

"Which are?"

"You could take me to the nicest restaurant that would take someone who looks like you, and let's face it, that limits the choices here in Doylestown, No offense."

"Truly, none taken."

"Or, if you're not fussy, I could reheat the lasagna I made the other night. We could watch a movie on Netflix, maybe." There was a beat, and her smile widened. "Oh, you so get points for not making a 'Netflix and chill' joke."

"I'm not actually an asshole."

"No," she said, giving him an appraising look, "I don't think you are."

"Thanks. You want me to leave first and meet you?"

"I'd rather you walked me to my car."

"I can do that."

"Good. Let me cash out, wash my face, and I'll be back."

Eighteen minutes later they left the bar. Eyes watched them, from the squinty-eyed night bartender to several of the customers. There was envy in those eyes. Good dollop of hostility. No one said shit, though. Smart choice.

Monk checked the tattoo parlor, knocked really loud, and called the number from the website. Zilch.

"He must be away somewhere," said Sandy. "Which is weird, because he usually asks me to feed his cat when he goes off to a convention or something."

"Short of kicking down the door," said Monk, "I'm out of options here."

Sandy glanced around and asked what he drove, and when Monk pointed to his rust bucket of a car, she laugh-snorted. "Sweet baby Jesus."

"It runs."

Thunder rumbled and a few fat drops splatted on the pavement.

"God. Let's take my car," she said, then turned and ran down the side alley as lightning forked the sky. He followed and found that her car was actually a hefty Ford Expedition. Huge, and new. She popped the locks and they got in just as the drizzle turned into a downpour.

Sandy shivered and wiped drops from her face. When she saw him checking out the sleek interior, she said, "Divorce settlement. At least he was good for something."

"It's cleaner than anything I've ever seen in a showroom."

"I like clean."

He nodded, getting it. Big car was protection. New car was a statement about self-worth, especially after a bad divorce. Clean car was imposing her will over aspects of her life. He upped his appreciation for her even higher because he was pretty sure she was aware of all that and deliberate in how she played the cards dealt.

She was also a good driver, which earned her more Monk points.

Sandy made a couple of backstreet turns and then found a road that took them into the suburbs, but the rain was getting as bad as it was the night he'd driven to Pine Deep. The streets metamorphosed from gray to purple to black, with walls of water falling like iron bars. She slowed from road speed to a crawl.

"I think we need to pull off and wait until it eases up," she said. "I haven't seen rain like this in years."

"This is nothing," he said as she pulled off into an empty parking lot. "You should visit Pine Deep."

"That place? No thanks."

"I just moved there."

She cut him a look. "Why?"

"Long story."

The parking lot was ringed by big oaks and pines and wrapped around a big old church that had a sign out front saying that the whole location was for sale for commercial development. A dead church. Monk wondered what had killed it.

Sandy drove around the building and pulled in between the back entrance and a big construction Dumpster, both of which created a natural shelter from the winds. The rain still hammered down, though.

She left the engine on, put on some music—some Goth stuff that Monk half-ass knew. No metal. Nothing harsh. He watched her unbuckle and then turn to him and pick up his bandaged left hand. "What happened? Pop a knuckle in a fight?"

"Nah," said Monk, making it casual. "Mishap with a tool. Nothing to tell."

Sandy did not immediately let go of his hand.

"I have to ask a question," she said. "And it's important. I'll know if you lie."

"Ask me anything."

"Will you hurt me?"

Monk looked into those brown eyes. Seeing the colors. Seeing her.

"No," he said softly. "I won't ever do that."

Sandy sat there, reading his eyes. Seeing him, too.

She reached out and took him by the jacket lapels and pulled him to her. Maybe she was just nervous, or maybe it was something else, but she pulled him with a lot of force.

He came willingly.

106

Gayle looked at Dianna and Patty, then down at her hands, and finally out the window. The other two women waited in silence. Inside her chest her heart was pounding hard enough to break. And break it might.

Forgotten.

Everything . . . just gone.

She took a tissue from her purse and pressed it to her eyes. Fighting for control. Feeling her face burning with borrowed shame. This wasn't her fault, but it felt that way. It was like school, when boys made crude jokes about her breasts and the girls just walked past her in the hallway as if she were a piece of dog shit on the ground. No, worse than that. Like she was nothing at all to them. Like she did not exist, and if she died they wouldn't even pause in their day to notice. It felt like that.

Like some part of her had died. And that somehow she, not Dianna, was to blame.

Gayle wanted to leave. She even looked at the door, but did not get up or move toward it. She needed to be out of there, to be somewhere with enough air. Somewhere neither Dianna nor this tattoo artist, Patty, could see her.

Forgotten. Every awkward moment. Everything that was said and shared. Every secret. Each kiss. And what they had done together in bed. Forgotten, as if it were nothing. As if she were nothing.

Just get up and go, she told herself. Just say fuck this, tell Dianna I never want to see her ever again, and go. Go back home.

Home.

Gayle got to her feet. The room swayed, but she managed to keep her balance.

There was a shopping bag on the floor by the barber chair in which Dianna sat. Gayle went over to it, removed one of the big magnums of white zinfandel, and studied the label without really reading it. The wine had a screw cap and Gayle twisted it off.

"I'll get you a glass—" began Patty but Gayle silenced her with a stare and took a very long drink from the bottle.

Gayle used her foot to nudge Dianna's chair until they were eye-to-eye. "And you really want me to believe that you don't remember a thing about that night?"

Dianna shook her head.

"Nothing?" insisted Gayle. "Not one moment of one of the most important nights of my life?"

"I'm sorry."

Gayle took another heavy pull. She had no head for wine and welcomed the punches it was going to throw.

"Sorry? Well, imagine how I feel."

"I can."

"Oh, why? Because you're a psychic?" Gayle shot back.

Dianna looked hurt. "No," she said, "because I have a smidgeon of actual compassion. Empathy, too."

She held out her hand for the bottle. Patty watched the drama, her heart racing. Gayle wanted to throw the bottle at Dianna. She wanted to scream and kick her. There was an ugly ringing in her head that was probably blood pressure and hurt and shame coming to a furious boil.

"Why did you even bother to have me come here?" Gayle demanded. "What's the point? You just punched a big hole in everything. My self-confidence, my sexuality. All of it. Why would you want to rub it in my face?"

"Because," said Patty, "this isn't something she did to you. This is something someone did to her."

Gayle paused, the bottle halfway to her lips. "What's that supposed to mean?"

"She means," said Dianna, "that someone stole my memories. They stole some of Patty's, too."

"Stole?" echoed Gayle, half smiling. "How does someone steal a memory?"

"That's what we're trying to figure out," said Dianna. "Patty and I are victims. You're a victim, too, in a way. Whoever did this stole from all three of us. We've been violated in a way I can't even properly describe."

"And you want me to believe that?"

"Yes," said Patty.

"Yes," said Dianna. "I need you to. From the texts you sent and I apparently sent before I . . ."

"Before you forgot me," finished Gayle.

"Yes. From what we shared in those texts someone stole something very special and very beautiful. But they stole a lot more than that, Gayle. They stole my whole life as a lesbian. They stole everything that defines who I am . . . and I am so terrified I don't know how to even be. I thought you being here might help trigger something, or give me some insight into what I lost so I can get it back."

Gayle's hand tightened on the bottle. "Do you want it back?"

"Yes. God, yes, I do."

The room was quiet except for the rain on the window. "This is all insane, you both know that, right?"

They said nothing.

"I don't believe in ESP, channeling, Atlantis, astral projection, tarot cards, astrology, or any of that crap."

Patty and Dianna were silent.

"I'll listen," Gayle said. "That's all I can promise. And then when we're done here I don't think I ever want to see either of you again."

Gayle took another long drink and handed the bottle to Dianna.

107

Owen Minor lay in darkness as the storm raged.

Bedroom door closed, lights out, window open ten inches. Rain slanted in and pooled on the floor. The cold wind raised gooseflesh all along Owen's thighs. His body trembled and shuddered, but not with orgasm. No, he felt the flies moving inside his skin. Not under it. Inside it. They were only as deep as the ink that had created them. Even after all this time the movement felt strange. Almost an itch. Almost uncomfortable.

Always exciting

All those other times, with Alexa Clare, Burleigh Hopewell, Slider, Eileen Sandoval, and dozens of other drones over the years, it was a different kind of excitement. Sure, he'd made them do bad things. Delicious things. Exciting things. Some of them anyway. Others he just fed on their despair, because that emotion was so firmly anchored to specific memories. Alexa was his favorite because on some level Owen was sure she enjoyed killing all those boys as much as she enjoyed banging them. The others were just random murders, and with a fly in their skin Owen got to be right there. Not memories but actual in-the-moment experiences.

So hot.

Tonight was different, though. Tonight he was not just sending out a single fly to create a single drone.

Tonight he was going wash Pine Deep in blood.

Tonight Owen Minor was going to war.

108

Crow and Mike drove over to Monk Addison's house and got there as that night's storm was in full swing. They found the U-Haul parked in the driveway and a locked door; no one answered.

"Check the windows," said Crow. "See if he's inside."

"His car's not here," said Mike.

"Check anyway."

Mike checked, peering through the windows as he tried to

see. The blinds were angled wrong, so all he got was a fragment of a view of packing materials, boxes, and part of a couch.

"Nothing," he said and straightened, then saw something on his left palm. At first he thought it was a dead bug and started to wipe it on the porch rail, then stopped and peered more closely. "Hey, Crow? Take a look at this."

They both studied the gunk on Mike's hand. Two cops frowning at a smear of black and purple, red and green.

"I thought it was a bug," said Mike.

"I think it is," said Crow dubiously. "A wasp or fly, maybe. I think."

"Not a real one, though."

Crow touched it with the point of a pencil he took from his shirt pocket. Some of the purple mess and a bit of black that looked like an insect leg clung to the point. He angled it toward the thin orange light coming from the streetlight.

"Is it some kind of paint?" asked Mike.

Crow sniffed it. "I don't think so. More like . . ."

His voice trailed off and the two of them stood and stared at each other.

Neither of them said the word, but it was right there, and in that moment it made a weird kind of sense.

Ink.

109

Monk and Sandy wound up in the back seat. They got soaked getting there, but that didn't matter.

They kissed for a long time. It began with a kind of junkie urgency, on her part, now his. But the way he kissed her back changed the rhythm. His kiss was soft, gentle, respectful. He did not pull her to him but rather brushed her cheek with his fingers, doing it very softly. That sent a ripple through her and in the space of a heartbeat her kiss stopped being an attack and became a conversation. *This is me,* it said. *This is who I am.*

And he responded in the same language.

Their lips met and there was that awkward moment—very fleeting—as they became familiar with tastes and textures, with resistance and acceptance. When their tongues met, it was as tentative as opening eyes on a spring morning. Then the kiss built from there, rising and falling with intensity. Learning, exploring creativity and generosity, until they were breathing the same heated breaths.

He did not touch her first. He knew that he was allowed to, that was evident in the tensions he could feel in her kiss, and in her hands on his chest. But he was willing to wait, to yield power so that she understood how safe he really was.

The kiss went on and on as the rain fell. The windows were smoked dark already and a night full of rain probably made the car invisible, especially tucked away back here. Why would anyone come looking?

Sandy trailed her fingers down his chest, over his flat stomach, and onto his thigh. She paused, leaning back an inch to force eye contact. Then she took his right hand and kissed it—the knuckles, the hollow of his palm—and placed it over her heart. In any other circumstance it would have been trite, too romantic a gesture to be anything but a come-on. And there was some of that there, sure, but she wanted him to know something. That she trusted him.

The whole thing was about trust.

Monk kept his hand there while he bent to kiss her again.

Time became meaningless.

He undressed her in the back seat. She was the kind of woman who was made lean by clothes, but naked she was riper than Monk expected. Her breasts were full and high, and her nipples were an exquisite chocolate brown. He bent and exhaled hot breath on each before taking them into his mouth. She cried out and arched her back. His big, scarred hands discovered the landscape of her. She had many scars on her stomach and back, and Monk could feel vibrations of the evil things done to her. The guy part of him wanted to do ugly things to whoever had hurt her, but that was macho bullshit. The man in him accepted her as she was and on her own terms, offering neither pity nor bravado. She required neither from him.

She settled back as he slid onto his knees in the rear footwell. He lifted one of her legs over his shoulder, kissing the cream-pale skin from knee to hip. Then he breathed another hot breath on the bud of her clitoris before bending closer still.

When she came she punched the back of the seat, the roof, and even his shoulders. She screamed so loud. She thrashed. Monk knew that it was not really about how well he'd gone down on her. She was releasing things that had nothing to do with him. He was her safe bridge from there to here.

She came again seconds later, one orgasm flowing into the next.

She did not call his name. She did not call God's name. She said, "Please."

Over and over again.

Afterward he held her. Naked, small, curled into him.

She wept against his chest for a long, long time. He didn't own any of those tears and did not need to know who did. Sandy required a witness, and that's what he was.

Then, her fingers touched his hardness through his jeans. He had shucked his jacket but was otherwise dressed. She sniffed and reached for his zipper, but Monk touched her hand.

"No," he said.

"But I can't leave you like that," she said in a tiny voice. "You need to—"

"I don't need a thing, Sandy."

"But guys—"

"No," he said. "Guys don't need to come. There's no such thing as blue balls. Any guy who says different is hustling you."

She gave him a quizzical look. Her eye makeup was smeared by tears, her lipstick gone, her black hair in disarray. "Don't you want me to . . . you know . . . help you?"

"As an obligation? No. And definitely not right now. Let's just be for a minute, okay?" He kissed her. "I have the taste of you on my lips and that's all I want right now."

She settled back against him, wriggling closer still. Monk was deeply aroused, but all of his instincts told him to stop where and when he had. Maybe there'd be another time with her. With them. Right now, though, the echo of those tears filled his mind, and he wondered when the last time was that someone had been kind to her? Had valued her above their own hungers?

The night was so black that he couldn't even see the rain beyond the windows. Monk leaned over and kissed her head, nuzzling in her hair.

110

Gayle, Dianna, and Patty sat for hours. Telling impossible stories, drinking wine, crying. Sometimes laughing. Frequently terrified. They talked it all out. Gayle had to walk Dianna through the steps of what happened at Tank Girl and after. She was deeply embarrassed to do so and flushed a furious crimson. She was also devastated that Dianna didn't remember more than fragments.

Dianna went through the story from her side, including the fugue where she saw a pale man in ecstasy as he fed on her memories. She also told them about the tarot reading and what it meant.

The Ten of Swords.

The Magician.

And the Tower.

"He's the Magician," she said. "He's the one who's come here to destroy the town. Maybe not the brick and stone, but . . . us."

No one called her a liar. No one said that this was New Age woo-woo stuff. Not even Gayle. Somewhere in the middle of the second big bottle of wine and Patty talking about Tuyet, a lot of that resistance crumbled away.

And Patty told as much of Tuyet's story as she could, mostly quoting Monk Addison. She opened boxes and pulled out photos, weeping when she saw some she ached to remember.

"We have to tell Monk," said Patty.

"Do you think he can find this man?" asked Gayle. "This . . . fly pervert?"

"The Lord of the Flies," said Patty and Dianna at the same time.

"Fuck," breathed Gayle, and shivered. Dianna wrapped an arm around her shoulder, and then Patty came and wrapped her thin arms around both of them.

The storm raged outside, but they were safe inside. With each other. Three women, three violations. Three horror stories to share as the thunder tried to bully them and the lightning attempted to burn the whole world down.

It was a long road until dawn.

111

"Want to come over?" asked Sandy. She almost whispered it, and there was remembered passion but also need there. Not desperation, but a genuine desire for more of him. More of them. "For the night, I mean?"

It was so tempting. It was an offer made with trepidation and caution, but wrapped up in her pride and her history of being harmed. Monk knew that this was an offer rarely made, and it was all the more appealing and lovely for that.

But he saw Patty and Tuyet in his mind. He saw pain and horror, and he saw his own anger thrown like a goblin shadow on the wall. He came to Doylestown for answers and so far had none, and he was feeling guilty for the time spent with Sandy. Monk did not want to paint this moment with those colors.

"I can't tonight," he said, trying not to wince. "I gotta get back to Pine Deep. This thing I'm working on . . ."

She looked immediately hurt and suspicious, but Monk took her hand and kissed it very gently.

"Listen to me, sweetness," he said softly, "you're amazing. I'm not joking. You have no idea how long it's been since I met someone like you. You're beautiful, smart, funny, and sexy. If you're asking if I want to spend the night, then yes, I really do. I think it would be something of real beauty even if all we did was curl up together and sleep. But this case I'm on is doing real harm to my friend. She's an old friend. Not a girlfriend. We're family. Another one of us who've been through the Valley of the Shadow. You'd like her, I think. She just got out of the hospital today and she's a mess. I need to make sure she's okay. You can understand that. I know you can." He paused and dug a card out of his pocket. "This is my cell and my email. Text me so I have your info. And as soon as this shitstorm is done, let me take you out on a real date. Not joking. You put on your pretties and I'll—so help me God—wear a tie. Maybe we'll go down to Philly and catch a concert. Or we can hit the movies and find a really nice place for dinner. Somewhere they'll wait on you and treat you like the queen you are. We can—"

She stopped him with a kiss. And that turned into a smile and then a laugh.

"What's so funny?" he said, pulling back an inch.

"You are so corny, so old-fashioned," she said. "So sweet. I don't think I know any guys like you. You might even be the real deal."

"I'm never going to lie to you and never going to hurt you," he said, and he meant it. There was no way to look into those dark-brown eyes and tell anything but the God's honest. "I give you my word."

She kissed him again and was still smiling as she put the big Expedition into gear and drove him back to his car. He stood on the wet pavement and watched her go, rain falling on his shoulders. His cell vibrated and he glanced at the screen. She must have stopped at a light around the corner. The text said two words.

White Knight.

Below that was her phone number.

"Sandy," he said to the night.

There was a faint cawing sound and he turned to see that

the nightbirds he thought he'd left behind in Pine Deep were standing in dense rows along the rooftop of the one-story building that was INKcredible. Dozens of them. Scores.

Monk studied them, trying to read something from the way they stood, from the agitation of their oily black wings.

The tattoo parlor was still closed, the sign exactly where it had been before. Nothing was really different.

Or was it?

He went to his car and opened the trunk, unlocked the gun safe, removed the Sig Sauer, and tucked it into the back of his belt. He didn't feel like getting soaked by taking off his jacket to slip the shoulder rig on. Monk looked past the open trunk to the store, then took a few additional items from his gear bag: his leather case of lockpick tools, and an old-fashioned blackjack with its wafer of lead sewn between thick black leather. That went into his right front pocket. He preferred to use his hands in a fight, but there was something wrong about the energy. Those nightbirds were spooked, and that spooked Monk. The blackjack had a short, springy handle, and if used with the right flick of the wrist, transferred a lot of kinetic energy to that dense lead core. Lay it just so and he could daze someone and take the fight out of them; put a little more English on it, and it would shatter a wrist or a skull with equal precision. Cops used to carry them but too many were heavy handed, resulting in brain damage or death for their victims. Monk wasn't technically allowed to have one, either, but he operated on the philosophy that he'd rather be tried by twelve than carried by six.

He closed the lid and approached the parlor. The rain was steady but not hard, although it was icy cold and wormed its way down into his clothes. On his skin the faces of all those dead girls and women were stretching their mouths and trying to say something. He glanced around and saw their ghosts. He'd long along learned that even the dead can be frightened.

112

Out on Route A-32, just shy of the bridge to Crestville, was a tavern that nobody in their right mind ever went to. It was exactly that kind of place. Broad, squat, and ugly, looking like what it was—a biker bar. Twenty-six bikes were lined up beneath a long canvas tarp. The *thump-thump* of Alabama Thunderpussy playing "None Shall Return" rattled the windows and crashed like artillery in the night air.

Johnny Ray Kenton, a massive lump of a bald man six and a half feet tall, with a furious red-gold beard and a line of skulls tattooed across his forehead, sat on a stool just inside. He was the doorman and bouncer and kept an eye on the bikes.

Beyond him, spread out around a bunch of tables or in a hunched line at the bar, were the members of the Cyke-Lones. Not all of them. Not even half, but some of the more senior members. None of them even cared that they were stereotypes, with cliché biker nicknames or lifestyles that came straight from the Hell's Angels movies of the 1960s. To them this was living a legacy, and they lived it hard. The crew ran coke and crack up along I-95 and took laundered cash and bearer bonds down to other clubs who ferried it in links to the cartels. It was an old business that ran smoothly and with little change as the years went by. There were members who were designated to take falls for more senior riders. And there were some who had been born into the club and who considered it their true family.

They didn't care what anyone else thought because as far as they were concerned, fuck the world.

The place stank, but the barbecue was good, the beer was

cold, and most of them had wives or girlfriends. Old Lenny Snicks in the corner had this week's crack whore on his knee and his hand up under her blouse. Nogs and Panhead were playing liar's poker with two of the younger guys. It was a rinse-and-repeat night, with nothing new happening. They were chilling out until the next big shipment, and were amusing themselves by dropping hints or starting rumors that they were going to hit the Fringe Festival. Which they were not. Bragging on it meant that half the cops in the county were going to be in Pine Deep, while they were going to be in New Jersey, heading south on back roads until they crossed over in Philly and got on the interstate. Cops would be looking their own way and holding their dicks. Fucking cops.

None of them noticed that there were more flies in the place than usual and certainly more than were at all common on a cold night of wind and rain. There was a dressed buck hanging on a hook out back because Nogs liked to hunt and they were planning a venison roast if the rain ever goddamn stopped. Dead meat draws flies. Who cares?

The flies, however, noticed them.

And, far away, in his bedroom, a dreaming Owen Minor looked through dozens of multifaceted eyes, searching for the toughest, the meanest, the deadliest of them. Finding everything the Lord of the Flies desired.

113

Monk checked the street in all directions and then walked up to the front door of the tattoo parlor. He could still hear music from the bar where Sandy worked, but it was some old Guns N' Roses song. "Sweet Child O' Mine." Nobody gets worked up into a rage when that eighties stuff was on.

Once he was sure he wasn't being observed, Monk tried the door again, but didn't bother knocking. Above him the birds shuffled nervously.

"Yeah, yeah," he told them. "I can feel it, too."

Saying it made him realize that he actually could feel something. There was an odd feel to the door, to the whole place. He hadn't paid enough attention earlier, but now he was on high alert. He leaned close and put an ear to the glass.

No sound.

Except . . .

Except that wasn't exactly true. There was something in there. It wasn't so much a noise as a sense of something. He was spooked enough to imagine that as he listened at the glass, some alien ear was pressed against the other side listening to him. Listening to his breath, to his heartbeat.

He cursed under his breath, mocking himself for being stupid. The feeling, however, persisted. There was something in there. It was the same feeling he had when he came to Patty's place the previous day. That feeling of being watched, but not necessarily by human eyes. By something. By who? By what.

And that fast, Patty's voice echoed in his head. *He is the Lord of the Flies.*

Monk licked his lips that had suddenly gone dry.

His car was eighty feet away and he could be behind the wheel and hauling ass in under four seconds. To hell with this place and to hell with whatever was in there. This wasn't even his case.

Patty's voice was still in his head. Her, trying to say the name of her little girl. Trying to say . . .

Monk had to fight to remember the name, too.

Tuyet. All the ghosts on his skin whispered the name of their lost little sister.

Monk forced himself to say it aloud. "Tuyet."

He wanted to cry. He wanted to kill someone. He wanted to put his hands on something that would scream for mercy that he was not willing to give.

"Tuyet," he said again as he fished his lockpicks out of his pocket. The lock was a good one, made to resist burglars. Monk heard the tumbler click and then the door sagged inward on its hinges. Not much, a half inch.

He stuffed the lockpicks into his pocket and drew the black-jack as he pushed the door open and went inside. It swung on hinges that made no sound. Oiled and smooth. He took a breath, let it out, and moved fast, going in to the left, crouching, turning to scan the room, trying to capture flash images in his brain. Assembling the whole place.

Like Patty's place there were barber chairs.

Like her place there was a long worktable with pots of ink, boxes of gloves, books of art samples, and several kinds of tattoo guns.

Like her place there was art on the wall.

After that . . . there was nothing that connected Patty's studio of art and beauty to what filled this place.

The walls were painted with dark colors. Blacks and purples that Monk knew were tinted wrong by shadows. When lightning flashed outside he could see the real colors. The scarlet. The crimson. The red of death and pain.

He saw that each of the barber chairs was occupied. By something.

They had been human once, but virtually everything that

defined them as human, as people, was gone. Stripped away. Carved down to horror. In an irrational fragment of thought he wondered why they were tied to the chairs if they had no hands or feet. Or skin.

The floor was a lake of blood.

Lightning flashed again and in the middle of that lake, naked, legs spread wide, body painted the same color as the walls, stood a man. Sixty or so. Hair wild and caked with blood. Lips hung with pendulous beads of drool. He held a tattoo gun in one hand and a butcher knife in the other. Black flies crawled over his face. His eyes were wide and staring, and there was nothing human or sane in them.

With a howl like a demon from the deepest pit of hell, Spider came rushing at Monk, teeth snapping and blade flashing as thunder tore the night apart.

114

The man was older than Monk but he was fast as the deeply insane are fast. A sudden rush propelled with a mad fury that tightened the entire body into a fist. The impact slammed Monk backward against the arm of one of the chairs with crushing force, driving air from his lungs and exploding pain in his lower back.

Monk was starting to turn, to try and slough off the force of the rush when Spider hit, and it was enough to keep those teeth from his throat. They banged together an inch from Monk's windpipe. Hot spit spattered his throat and chin and lip. Spider was bizarrely strong and Monk felt himself being bent further backward over the arm of the chair and onto the lap of a skinless dead man. Flies erupted from the corpse and spiraled in the air like vultures. There was a strange sound mingled with Spider's animal growl—a harsh, high-pitched buzzing. With a swift and terrible insight Monk realized that the tattoo gun the madman held was turned on. A powerful battery-operated device dripping with red ink.

No. Not ink.

Monk's injured left hand shot out and caught Spider's wrist, stopping the needle as Spider tried to stab him in the eye. The act of grabbing hurt like hell, but it made Monk grab even harder. Desperation takes weird turns.

"Stop it, you crazy fuck," he roared, but the man was beyond understanding. The lights that burned in Spider's eyes were kindled in some other world than this.

Monk tried to hit him with the leather sap, but the angle was bad and the weapon bounced off the bunched meat of Spider's deltoid. Spider head-butted him, catching mostly cheekbone but bashing enough of Monk's nose to detonate white-hot pain.

"Fucking hell," cried Monk and brought his knee up between Spider's thighs. It was an awkward angle but the man was naked. He crumpled, uttering a high whistling shriek. Monk twisted and tumbled sideways off the chair, falling to hands and knees but immediately hurling himself forward into a sloppy roll. Had he not done that the tattoo needle would have stabbed him between the shoulder blades. The groin kick had slowed the maniac, but did not stop him. Spider charged at him, aiming a kick at Monk's chin.

This time Monk was set and he whipped the blackjack sideways, using all the muscle of his shoulder, arm, and wrist, and putting a heavy snap at the end of the move. The leather-clad lead disk struck Spider's ankle and exploded the bones. Spider shrieked, but there was more fury than agony in the sound. He collapsed forward onto Monk, driving him down onto the floor, his head darting in like a jackal's to bite into the meat of Monk's chest. In Monk's mind a ghost screamed so loud it threatened to break the world. Monk could feel the teeth breaking through his skin, tearing the face on his chest.

"No, no, nooooo," roared Monk as he whaled on the side of the man's head with the sap. The buzzing sound of the needle changed with every blow, becoming higher and thinner.

The blows should have knocked Spider out, but all they did was break the grip of teeth on flesh. The man canted sideways, his mouth smeared with fresh blood. Monk saw something on his throat and realized that, impossibly, it was a fly crawling slowly from collarbone to ear as if there were no savage battle under way.

Except that it wasn't really a fly.

It was a tattoo of a fly. Realistic, full-color. Ink and art. But it was moving. Crawling inside Spider's skin. Above and around them other flies swarmed. These were real, but the moment no longer was.

Lord of the Flies.

Monk pivoted on his hip and kicked out with both feet, catching Spider in the gut, lifting him, propelling him backward against the chair. Spider hit hard and dropped to his knees, and Monk was after him, grabbing a fistful of hair and jerking the man's head sideways as he brought the blackjack down with savage force. The edge of it caught the fly as it crawled over Spider's chin. There was a burst of colored light so bright it stabbed Monk's eyes and then Spider fell, battered to unconsciousness, his jaw crushed.

He crumpled to the floor and lay in a boneless sprawl, eyes rolled high.

On the side of his face was the crushed fly. The other flies swirled away, backward and up and then gone into other rooms or under cabinets. Hiding.

Hiding from Monk.

Hiding from what had just happened.

Monk, gasping and wheezing, bent over Spider, staring at the splash of tattoo ink in the shape of a smashed fly on the broken jaw of the madman.

He reached out with a trembling finger and touched the ink. It was dry. As if it were a real tattoo. Like it had always been there.

Monk staggered back until he thumped against the wall by the door.

115

The whole place was a red nightmare. What had Conan Doyle called it? *A Study in Scarlet*? Yeah. That. Outside Monk could hear the nightbirds screaming, even beneath the droning hiss of rainfall.

Monk stuffed his blackjack into his pocket and tried to figure out how much trouble he was in. His left hand was bleeding through the bandage and there was probably some of his own blood in the mix on the floor. He tore some electrical cords out of the wall and used them to bind Spider's wrists and ankles, and also checked his vitals. He was out and hurt, but alive. The swatted fly now appeared permanently inked, and the fact of that was freaking Monk out.

Monk forced himself to look at the three corpses, but there was not enough left of them to identify. He held his palm over the flayed skin, but there was almost no warmth left. They'd all been dead for hours, maybe all day.

He searched around for clothing and found a heap of rags in a corner, each item sliced by a very sharp knife. Amid the debris were wallets, and Monk was bemused to discover that one of the dead men was Dirty Gus.

How and why he had been selected as a victim was beyond understanding. Monk could not begin to construct a scenario that connected his hunt for the bail skip to this bloodbath. Or to what was happening in town. Nothing.

"The world is fucked in the head," he told the dead man.

The other two men were strangers, but Monk made a startling discovery as he went through their ID cards. One of them was named Alan Carney, but his business cards had the name Carnival Al on them, and an address in South Philadelphia. The other man was from out of state. Way out of state. California license in the name of Marcus P. Sanders. He also had business cards that gave his trade name. Malibu Mark.

Both of them were tattoo artists.

Monk was studying the cards when his cell vibrated. It was Patty.

"Hey, Pats," he said, forcing his voice to sound normal. "You okay?"

"No," she said quickly. "Nothing's okay. You need to get back here right now."

"I'm in the middle of something and—"

Suddenly there was a different voice on the line. "Mr. Addison? This is Chief Crow. I'm with Ms. Trang at her store. There have been some developments on her case and I'd appreciate it if you could come here right away. We stopped at your house and you were gone."

"I'm out of town," Monk said.

"How far out of town?"

Monk hesitated, but remembered what Jonatha had told him about this man.

"I'm in Doylestown," said Monk. "And . . . there's been some trouble."

"What kind of trouble?"

"The really bad kind and I'm not sure I want to tell a cop about it."

"Mr. Addison," said Crow, "it might be better if you think of me as an ally in this fight rather than a cop."

"And which fight would that be, exactly?"

"The fight to keep some kind of goddamn vampire from feeding on the memories of Tuyet Trang," said Crow. "The memories stolen from Patty and the ones stolen from you. How about we start there."

Monk closed his eyes and leaned against the wall. The storm was building again outside and it felt to him as if it were raging even more ferociously in his chest.

"Sure, fine," he said. "You want to know what's going on? How's this? I broke into a tattoo parlor in Doylestown and found three people tied to chairs. Dead people, and they'd been skinned by the guy who owns the place. That son of a bitch attacked me and I beat the shit out of him. During that fight I saw one of his tattoos moving—actually crawling—on his skin. How's that?"

There was a pause, then Crow said, "Was it a tattoo of a fly?"

The world was so still that even the storm seemed to hold its breath.

"Mr. Addison—Monk—I really do think you need to come back to Pine Deep."

"Yeah," breathed Monk. "But what about this shit right here?"

"Did anyone see you go in there? No? How about you do this: wipe down every surface you touched and get the fuck out of there. I'll call it in as an anonymous tip and make sure the right people show up to take control of the scene. These are all small towns in this part of Bucks County. Everyone watches everyone else's back. I can make sure none of this falls on you. So, clean up and get out of there right damn now. We need you here. Patty needs you here."

Monk looked around and took a ragged breath.

"Okay," he said.

Monk found a rag and began wiping down any surface he might have touched. His hands shook as he did this. And while he worked his mind spun furiously. What the hell was happening? As if in answer there was a crack of thunder so loud it seemed to split his head in half. Outside the rain was so heavy that he could barely see twenty feet. No one could see him, that was for sure. He turned his collar up, ducked his head, and ran like hell for his car.

Despite the storm and the wind, the nightbirds followed.

116

Mike Sweeney stood by the door of Patty Cakes's shop and watched the rain wash the streets clear of traffic. So far this was the heaviest downpour yet, which was saying something for a brutal season. Crow came over and stood next to him.

"Feel like I should be out there," said Mike quietly. "There are going to be lines down and accidents."

"Let the state cops handle the fender benders and PECO can fix the lines," said Crow. "We're exactly where we need to be."

Mike glanced at him and then over his shoulder at the three women. Patty and Gayle were seated in the two farthest chairs. Dianna was standing between them, but no one was speaking.

After realizing that the dead fly on Monk's porch was made from tattoo ink—a fact that jolted the day into a new and bizarre shape—they'd come here to talk with Patty. And found that she wasn't alone. Dianna was a friend of Val's, and had come here with her when Val had the ladybug and lightning bug tattoos done. Val often went to Dianna for spiritual readings and counseling. Gayle worked at the school where the twins went.

The three of them, each moderately hammered, poured out their stories of stolen tattoos and fractured memories. Mike had been deeply uncomfortable when Dianna and Gayle explained how they met, and that they'd slept together. Crow seemed to take it in stride, and Mike—not for the first time—thought that Crow was at his best when things were getting weird in town. He'd been a key figure in the town's survival during and after the Trouble. Crow had grown up knowing that Pine Deep was not like other places. He'd always believed that there were things going bump in the dark.

Mike's path was different. He'd been a victim of the Trouble in a unique way, and those events had changed the nature of who and what he was forever. As far as either Val and Crow—or Jonatha—for that matter, knew, Mike was absolutely unique in terms of his biological, spiritual, and existential nature. A lone wolf in very point of fact.

He touched Crow's sleeve. "Boss, after hearing all that stuff, and given all we've found out, what's the play here? I mean, if we come up with a suspect, do we arrest him? If so, on what charge? We're on really shaky legal ground here. And you just compounded a felony—a handful of felonies—with what you told that Addison guy to do."

Crow pasted on that smile of his. The strange one. That smile he never showed to Val.

"Kid, I have no goddamn idea what we're doing or going to do," he said just loud enough for Mike to hear. "I'm making this up as I go."

"That's not particularly comforting."

Crow nodded. "Wasn't meant to be."

117

Monk raced back to Pine Deep as fast as the storm would allow. The wind whipped sheets of rain at him and it felt as if the car were smashing through a series of plate-glass windows. His faith in the tread left on his old tires was failing.

"Come on," he breathed as he steered around massive puddles and veered away from cars pulled to the side of the road by more cautious drivers. "Come on."

Off to his right, appearing out of the midnight gloom, was a cluster of white lights. And he realized with amazement that they were motorcycles. To be out on a bike in this rain was suicidal. They were coming down from the north, maybe from Crestville or someplace beyond it, following A-32 instead of taking the smaller farm roads. They were looping around the town to come up from the southeast, a route that would dump them onto the road Monk was driving, but a few miles back. But all these roads were going to be lakes soon. Monk didn't want to have to pull over like he did a few nights ago, but if he had to he could drop down to fifteen or twenty and pick his way through. Those bikes were in real trouble.

"Should have stayed home," he said, though he might as well have been talking to himself.

118

Nogs was riding point, with Big Karl beside and a little behind. The rain and wind blew past them, pushing along the road as if it wanted them to reach the town.

The others were riding in loose pairs behind them, going

only as fast as the conditions would allow. Taking no risks beyond being out in a storm. Needing to get to where the Lord of the Flies wanted them to be.

A fly crawled across Nogs's face, its inky body flattened into the surface of his flesh. The biker's eyes were vacant but he wore a smile, as they all wore smiles, identical to that of the little man who was safe at home in his bedroom.

119

"He's not coming, is he?" asked Gayle.

"He's coming," said Patty, though she did not sound all that certain.

Dianna went over and stood next to Mike Sweeney, staring out at the night.

"He's coming," she said.

Thirty minutes later headlights flashed through the window as a car pulled a U-turn and parked badly, the front wheel up on the curb. The door opened and a big man with a battered face ran for the shop. Patty was there to open the door and she pulled him inside.

"Holy shit," gasped Monk as rainwater sluiced down his body. "It's like the end of the goddamn world out there."

Patty brought him a big mug of hot tea and a bunch of towels. Monk stripped off his jacket and shirt and toweled himself dry. He was acutely aware of everyone looking at his tattoos.

"Oh my god," said Gayle. "Those faces. I . . . I'm sorry, I don't mean to be—"

"No," said Monk, "a lot of people have that reaction. It's cool."

"Nothing's cool," said Patty.

Monk sipped his tea and looked around him. He nodded to Dianna and Gayle. "Who are you?"

Patty made introductions. "They're caught up in this, too."

Monk noticed that Patty wasn't wearing a bandage over her disfigured tattoo. Dianna held out her arm and showed the faded roses.

"Okay," said Monk, "you all got stories to tell. Let's hear 'em."

"We need to hear yours, too," said Crow.

"Yeah," said Monk as he sat down on the third chair, "we'll get to that. You first."

Everyone already knew Patty's story, so Dianna went next to explain what had happened to her and Gayle; then Crow and Mike tag-teamed to explain everything they'd seen and learned—Joey Raynor, Lester Mouton, Agent Richter, and other cases across the country. At one point Monk held up his hand.

"Whoa, whoa, stop there," he said, "go back to that last name. The guy the girl Tink worked for."

"Malibu Mark," said Mike. "What about him?"

Monk cursed. "I don't want to make a weird night weirder, but he's one of the dead guys back at Spider's."

They all looked at one another.

"Damn," said Crow.

"There's a little more of our stuff," said Mike, and he explained about going to Monk's house and finding the dead fly made of tattoo ink.

Monk got up and prowled around for a few minutes, chewing on his thoughts. He saw the shopping bags with one big bottle of wine left unopened. He twisted off the cap and tossed it in the bag and then chugged down at least eight ounces. He didn't like wine very much, and zinfandel not at all, but it had alcohol and that was fine.

"I think it's my turn," he said, wiping his mouth with the back of his hand. It was the bandaged hand, which tinted the sodden bandage a pale yellow. He studied them all. Dianna stood against the workbench, one hand clasped around a crystal she wore on a pendant. Gayle, seated nearby, simply looked freaked. Like *way* freaked. Monk wondered how much more of this she could actually take. Mike Sweeney stood by the door. Or rather, he loomed there. Kid was a moose, and there was something weird about him. Spooky weird, and it made him remember Jonatha's warning. No, in fact, he would not want to cross that son of a bitch. Crow wore the same shit-eating smile he had when they first met, and it was as false now as it was then. Like a plastic Joker mask that was starting to crack.

Then he caught Patty's eye. She gave him a small nod and even managed a fragment of her old smile. The sweet-sad one she wore every day. Her usual expression that was a shield between her and the reality of being the mother of a sodomized and murdered child. Everyone, he mused, had their defenses.

"Okay," said Monk, "you've all been through some weird shit. But I'm going to see your last couple of fucked-up days and raise you this." He brushed his fingertips across the inked faces. All of them staring. All of them way too real.

120   MONK'S STORY

I'm not like other people. I'm not like anyone you ever met.

Little backstory first. I went from high school into the military. Trained special ops and then went higher up the food chain to Delta Force. Worked a lot of bad jobs in a lot of shit places. None of it's going to earn my way through the Pearly Gates. Guys like me know that. And there was one gig that burned me out. Bad intel put us on a kill mission in a small village. We were told that there were zero friendlies and that it was what they call a target-rich environment, meaning if they aren't on your team then they were to be put down. But, like I said, the intel was bad and it turned out the village had only civilians. We killed them, but in a lot of ways we killed ourselves. I opted out and returned to the States when my tour was up. But . . . life likes to kick guys like me in the dick every chance it can.

My sister—the only relative I really cared about—got sick and her shitty minimum-wage job was part-time. No health care, and her medical bills were skyrocketing. I knew how to make some money, a lot of it, and so I became a PMC. Private military contractor. What they used to call mercenaries. I had a certain reputation and there are groups willing to pay through the nose for that.

I worked a bit for oil companies protecting their interests in the Middle East, then my team got hired to work freelance for Uncle Sam, for a department under the umbrella of the CIA. The Agency has very deep pockets, especially if they're drawing funds from the black budget. We ran ops all over the world. Some of it was for the good, too, taking down some cartel assholes, ripping up a human trafficking ring. But most of it was way into the gray area. Let's face it, if you're cashing checks from the CIA you are not wearing a white hat, no matter how much you want to think you are.

I was really good at what I did. Work flooded my way, and my sister's bills got paid. That's how I justified it, you see. The people I was taking down may not have been evil, but they were dirty. They were in some part of the game, and someone like me showing up in the middle of the night was a possible consequence. I took them off the board and kept my sister on her meds, paid for the chemo and the surgeries for someone who was clearly an innocent. A true innocent.

But then I was on a job in Taklamakan Desert region. Bunch

of small villages near poppy fields. The villagers swore up and down that they had no choice, that they were forced to harvest the flowers and process the heroin and opium. We felt sorry for them because we could see disfigurement from torture, and some of the women had that evasive look they get when they've been raped but aren't allowed to go to the authorities. The black marketers owned the cops, and any woman who made too much of a fuss would be either shot in front of her family or shot with her family.

We were trying to disrupt the drug flow and were spending weeks cultivating assets from among the villagers. But we had to fight through all that fear, and the certain knowledge that one day we'd leave and some other drug gang would come in and take over. We weren't affecting any long-term change. Not a chance.

Then one day this kid from our team was driving a couple of other guys out to relieve sentries when their vehicle blows up. I was asleep at the time and heard the bang. I didn't know what was happening, but by the time I had my pants on and was out of the place where I was staying everyone was shooting. The villagers were running all over the place as my team was hosing them with automatic fire. I saw teenagers throwing rocks at them and thought that this was the village rising up on the orders of the drug lords, and I started cutting them down.

How long did the firefight last?

I don't know. Two minutes. Maybe a little less. Two of my guys were dead, apart from the ones in the truck. One with a smashed head from a rock, the other stabbed with a bread knife.

And the vil?

We killed thirty-seven people in those two minutes.

Now here's the kicker. When we picked apart the wreckage

of the vehicle, we figured out what happened. Someone in that truck accidentally set off a grenade. Don't know how. Maybe just fucking around with it. But they killed themselves. My guys panicked and . . . I guess I did, too. The villagers fought back with knives and sticks and stones because what else should they do? Stand there and just die?

The CIA spooks came in and cleaned it up. That town is gone like it never existed. No charges filed, nothing on the news. Any lingering traces were made to look like the drug lords did it. Funny thing was, that probably helped them keep the other towns in line, so not only did we murder those people, we actually strengthened the strange hold those drug runners had.

And me? Well, I was done.

Twice now I'd been party to massacres, and more times than I can count there was blood on my hands that I knew was at least partly innocent. I mean, who am I to judge?

You hear people talk about burning out, about losing their shit? That was me. I'm telling you the short version, and believe me there is a lot more to the story, but after we slaughtered all those people I felt like I'd killed part of myself, too. Maybe the most important part. I felt gutted and lost, and I was drowning in guilt that ran so damn deep. I didn't even try to trick myself with the arguments soldiers use. I know every one of them, and I wasn't the audience for it anymore. I was nothing. I sure as hell wasn't former Staff Sergeant Gerald Addison. I was no one who mattered, and I was no damn good to anyone.

You see, I thought I was damned. There was just enough religion in my head to sell that. I believed it with my whole heart that day, and I believe it now. Maybe not as much, but enough that I'm pretty sure there aren't wings and a halo for me when

I finally go down. I think I'm going to fall, like one of Lucifer's angels. I'll drop off this world and fall forever.

So, I reviewed my options. The one that looked best in the moment was going out into the desert and sucking on the barrel of my gun. But . . . there was that whole damnation thing.

Option two was to suck it up, shut off all power to my empathy, and go back to the job. And maybe I would have, but there was enough in the bank to keep my sister going for a year or so, and some investments she could cash in if I died.

The third option was more vague. Basically, I dropped out of the world. I went away. Left my equipment and weapons and all of it and walked off. Don't know if they looked for me or just wrote me off as MIA, or more likely KIA. Don't know and don't care.

I spent the next few years looking for answers to how a man gets to repair his soul. Not some Sunday confessional whitewash, but actual redemption. We're not talking Christian, either, or at least not exclusively. I wandered through mosques and temples, prayer huts and sweat lodges, cathedrals and caves where silent monks sit year after year. I told my story to priests and pastors, rabbis and imams, shamans and witch doctors. I held nothing back. They heard the horror stories. Some of them passed judgment on me. Some of them actually told me to leave. Some, the better ones, sat with me and taught me how to let go, to allow, to strip away my ego and lay myself bare to whatever the universe needed from me in terms of balancing the checkbook.

That's where the nickname came from. I ran into a guy I'd known back in Iraq. He was on his own pilgrim road, and we talked. He started calling me Monk, and it stuck. Now it's who I am.

Which is where this circles around to the shit we're in now. I was working my way through Southeast Asia and found myself in Vietnam. I know it's supposed to be officially an atheist state. That whole Communism crap. Whatever. There are a lot of believers of one kind or another. Buddhists, Taoists, and Confucianists are the most common, but there are some older religions there, too. Way older. Caodaism, Hoahaoism, and some belief systems that don't have names. Religions that exist only in remote villages and predate the Hồng Bàng dynasty. Primal beliefs that don't get tied up in doctrine. I spent a few weeks with one old woman, she had to be a hundred if she was a day. She remembered the French and Americans and all the other soldiers who came through in the fifties, sixties, and seventies. She remembered Hồ Chí Minh and the Viet Cong. All of them swept through the land. They all raped and stole and brutalized. She'd been raped half a dozen times, and she'd buried children and grandchildren. I told her I was no better than any of them and said that if she wanted to cut my throat, it would be fair. I gave her my knife and told her to do it. Kill me, let me fall through the floor of the world. I mean, here I was, a killer like those other men, asking her for help. The audacity of it, the hubris. Fuck me. She was worth ten thousand of me.

She said that she didn't need revenge. She was too old for it. Killing me wouldn't bring back anyone she lost. I broke down. I grabbed the hem of her robe and begged her to tell me what I could do for her, to make even one thing right for her. That old lady gave me the sweetest smile I've ever seen. She took my face in her hands and kissed me on both cheeks, and said that there was a way. It was hard, very difficult, and it would hurt, but there was a way.

I told her I would do anything, and I meant it. Anything. No limits.

She smiled and took a piece of paper and a pencil and wrote two things down. One was an address of a family of tattoo artists living in the town of Tuyên Quang. Below that she wrote *huyền bí,* which means "mystic." She said go get that tattooed over my heart and the path would open to me. From then on I'd be following the road out of darkness. Then she took another piece of paper and wrote something on it and sealed it in an envelope, making me promise to give it to one of the women in that family. Made me swear I wouldn't open it, and I did swear. Then she gave me something so I could sleep.

When I woke, I was in a whole different part of the jungle and I knew that I shouldn't go look for her. I didn't. I hitchhiked my way to Tuyên Quang and found the Trang family. I showed the paper to Patty, who was the only one in the shop when I knocked. She said she understood and that it would take her a few days to get the right kind of pigment for the ink. I hung around. Patty and I had some meals, got to know each other. Became friends. The day I was supposed to get the ink, there was a huge commotion because a gang had broken into the Trang house. They killed Patty's grandmother and took Patty's little girl. Tuyet.

The things they did to the old lady were bad enough. But when they found Tuyet . . . God. You're all looking at me funny, because maybe Patty told you that I forgot Tuyet. And that's true up to a point, but other people remember her. They remember her story. I'll get to that in a second.

Before I walked the pilgrim's road I was a hunter and a killer. I'd said that I never wanted to hurt anyone again. Ever. But I saw the old lady and I went with Patty when she had to identify what was left of her daughter.

I stayed in the village for a while. Stayed with Patty. Helped her as much as I could. Doing stuff around the place. Being a shoulder and an ear. And I tried looking for the men who killed the little girl, but I had no way to find them. She'd been dumped on the road, and the cops didn't even know where she'd been held.

One thing that I skipped, and it's important, is that when Patty went to identify Tuyet, she brought along a few little glass vials. She asked me to guard the door, which I did. I watched her scrape up her baby's dried blood and mix it with water and then put it away. I didn't ask why. This was Patty's need.

I kept trying to find the men, and failed every time. But while I was looking I started feeling connected to the little girl, like I'd actually known her.

Maybe two months later Patty found the old woman's letter and remembered that she had the ink. I told her that I didn't want the word *mystic* tattooed on me. I said that I wanted Tuyet's face inked right over my heart.

Patty said she understood, and that she realized it was why the old lady sent me to her. She went and got one of the vials that had some of Tuyet's blood in it. She said that she was going to mix it with ink so that I would always have some of Tuyet with me. And maybe I would learn to laugh again, because her daughter had always been happy.

She mixed the ink and did the tattoo, and something happened. Something really goddamn weird. First off, it hurt. Not just in a physical way, but way down deep. I felt like my nerve endings were actually on fire. Worst pain I ever felt in my whole life. Savage pain, worse than getting stabbed or shot.

But that was just the start of it, because the moment Patty finished the tattoo, when the last detail was done, it felt like a massive hammer smashed me out of my own head. I was falling—literally falling—out of my body. And then I was in someone else's body. Connected to all five senses with hyper-awareness. It hurt even worse because I was being hurt. I was being beaten and raped. Over and over and over again.

You see, in that moment I was Tuyet. I was her as she was being tortured and abused. Every single thing that she felt, I felt. Every degradation, every bit of inhumanity inflicted on her was inflicted on me.

I can see from the looks on your faces that you don't believe me. Or don't want to. Either way I don't care. I was Tuyet. I was her from the moment the men abducted her to the last second of her living awareness, and when she died, I died.

Then I was me again. In my own body, in Patty's tattoo chair, writhing and screaming. Patty held me all through that night.

In the morning I went hunting. Those memories that had been forced into me were still there. Details the girl saw. Places, street names, signs, all of it. Tuyet's memories were my guide and I went to find those men. I have never hated anyone as much in my whole life as I did them. They destroyed that child. Fuck. There was no gray area here. This was evil.

I killed them in very, very bad ways. I won't ever tell anyone what I did. That's mine to know.

Now . . . I don't know if I chipped even a fleck of guilt off my soul by what I did to those guys. Almost certainly not. But I felt I had to do that. To honor the Trang family.

See this bare spot here? That's where Tuyet's face was. That's where it should be. She was the first face inked onto my skin. And these other faces? Most of them girls or women? They are other victims. That's what I became. Chasing bail skips pays the light bill, but this is the work of my soul. Funny, huh? A killer lays down his gun to go and find spiritual understanding and redemption, and the universe decides that this end is best served by making him keep on killing. And killing and killing.

How do I remember all this if the tattoo was stolen? See this face? And this one? And this one? All of these? They are alive in me. In a way. There's a price for what I do. Not one I impose, but it's there all the same. If I find the person or persons who killed someone—not for revenge but to keep that person from killing others—and I take them off the board . . . there's a price. For the dead one who comes to me and asks me to do this, and for me. They are stuck here. Ghosts haunting my life. I can see them right now standing all around me. There's an old lady who was murdered in Amsterdam standing next to you, Crow. And Dianna, maybe you're psychic enough to see the twin teenage girls on either side of you. They haunt me. They're always here. Murder, even if it's done to prevent more harm, is out of balance with the universe, and those ghosts and I share purgatory right here.

So, that's my story, and it's fucked up and if you don't believe me, who cares? I know it's true. Patty knows. And I think most of you, maybe all of you, actually do believe me.

We're all in this mess together. Someone is stealing memories, and maybe making people commit murders. Like what Spider did. Now, folks . . . what the hell are we going to do about it?

121

Monk looked around at the shocked faces that stared back at him.

"Yeah," he said, "y'all might want to take a moment with that."

122

Monk came over to Patty and gave her a kiss on the cheek, and she responded with a long hug. Gayle, who was closest, flinched away.

No one said anything for a long time, and then Mike Sweeney walked up to Monk and gave him a long up-and-down appraisal. Monk stepped away from Patty and faced the big young cop. There wasn't much that scared Monk, but this kid gave off all kinds of weird vibes. And even if there was something genuinely spooky about him—and Monk had his doubts—the kid looked like he could bench press a pickup truck, the way his biceps strained the shirt sleeves. And the hard and uncompromising look in the cop's eyes, like he'd both been there and done that.

Even so, Monk stood foursquare, ready for any play. "You got something to say, Big Red?"

"I do," said Mike, and he held out his hand. Monk stared at it for four full seconds before he took it and they shook.

"I . . . I don't even know how to . . ." began Gayle, but lost her way and stopped talking.

"Okay, okay," said Crow loudly, "we're shocked and appalled and maybe if we all say a collective 'what the actual fuck' we'll be able to get past the moment. No? Okay, take it as read, then." He clapped his hands together, rubbed them vigorously. "So, how 'bout we figure out what we know about what we know? Sound good?"

"Sure, Chief," said Monk. "You have an idea of where to start?"

"I do," said Crow. "When each of you was telling your stories about how you lost your tattoos you very pointedly omitted one detail. Same detail for each of you, and I'm pretty surprised none of you mentioned it."

"And what would that be?" asked Monk. "We know it's this Lord of the Flies cocksucker."

It was Gayle who answered. "No, Mr. Monk," she said, "I know what he means. None of you said who took them."

"I just said it was . . ." Monk's voice trailed off. "Oh. Yeah."

"Points to the teacher lady," said Crow.

"School deputy administrator," corrected Gayle.

"Sure. Patty, you lost yours first, right? At least as far as I can work out the chronology. Two days ago. And then Dianna the same day, and lastly Monk that night. That means our Fly Guy was in town on that day. For now we can eliminate Andrew Duncan, because he doesn't actually know when he lost his, and he and his wife hadn't ever been here before. They came here on a whim, doing some antiquing. Ditto for Joey Raynor and the homeless guy, Lester Moutan. So it's you three. What we have to do is figure out who each of you has in common. A neighbor. Someone you met on the street. Could even be a mutual friend. Something like that."

"Not a friend," said Monk. "Only person in town I knew before I got here was Patty."

"Then we need to find intersections in your day," said Mike. "Ms. Trang, you know Dianna and you know Mr. Addison."

"It's just Monk, guys."

"Dianna," continued Mike, "when was the last time you were here in the shop?"

"Five or six days ago," said Dianna. "I came in for a quick minute to see if I could schedule an appointment to get her opinion on changing my back tattoo. I have this island tribal thing that seemed really cool back in college, but I don't have a connection to it anymore. We talked about what Patty could turn it into."

"Was anyone else in the shop at that time?"

"No."

"Did you still have your rose vine tattoo?"

"Yes."

"You're sure?" asked Mike.

"Positive," said Dianna, and Patty nodded.

"Besides," said Monk, "first time I was ever in the shop was when I found Patty."

"Dead end," muttered Crow. "Patty, were you with Monk anywhere except here and the hospital?"

"No."

"Monk, were you at the store where Dianna works?"

"Didn't know she worked at a store," said Monk.

"Another dead end."

"That's not going to work," said Gayle. "Can you three remember when you first became aware you were missing your tattoos?"

Patty's face flushed and she cut a look in the direction of her bedroom. "Here. I woke up drunk on the floor by my bed."

"Yeah, for me," said Monk, "I was at some bar. Jake's Hideaway. That's where I met Duncan. I noticed the tattoo once I was out on the street. I, um . . . heard Tuyet calling my name."

"Fuck me," murmured Crow. Gayle got her purse and fished inside for a plastic packet of tissues. Handed one to Patty and used another herself. Crow looked at Dianna.

"I was at work. I was doing readings and I kind of went loopy. I think that's when it happened."

Everyone looked at her.

"When you say 'loopy' . . ." prompted Monk.

"Well," said Dianna, "it was weird. I'd just finished a card reading for a client, but I must have blanked out because Ophelia, the lady I work for, told me that I had a client waiting and the time was wrong. My first client should have been nearly an hour before that. When I mentioned that to her, she said my first client had gotten his reading and left already. I don't remember, though. Not a thing, really."

Patty made a small sound and now the eyes shifted to her. "I . . . I had something like that, too. Before everything, you know, happened. I had a client in to have some work done. But after he left I couldn't remember a thing about him, the ink, or . . . well, anything, really."

Dianna glanced at Monk. "Did the same thing happen to you?"

Monk shook his head, then began pacing. Thunder rattled the windows and the lights flickered. "No," he said slowly. "Not really. I didn't lose a block of time as far as I know. But I could feel the memories leaving me. It's hard to explain. I was very much in the moment with it."

"Maybe it was because the memory you lost is special," suggested Dianna. "*Mystical,* if I can use that word."

"*Mystical* is right on the money," said Monk, "and maybe you're right. The memories I lost fought to stay with me. Tuyet fought."

Gayle shivered. "Couldn't you . . . um . . . just, y'know . . . ask the other ghosts? And, that is the freakiest sentence I've ever uttered."

Monk smiled at her. "Oh, I wish I could, sis. That would make it all easier."

"We're nowhere," complained Mike. "We don't even know if this memory thief is a man or a woman."

"It's a man," said Dianna and Patty at the same time.

"What makes you so sure?"

"Because," said Dianna, "when I had that vision, it was a man."

"Describe it again," suggested Crow. Dianna did and in greater detail than before. A very pale man, hairless, obscene.

"Pale as in white or albino?" asked Mike.

"A white man. I couldn't see his face but I don't think he's older than forty. Not in good physical shape. And he has those awful fly tattoos."

"Christ," said Crow, snapping his fingers loud as a gunshot, "we're being really dense here. Dianna, your client was a guy, you said, right? And Patty, so was yours. Did either of you touch him? Or did he touch you? Was there any physical contact of any kind?"

"I don't usually touch my clients," said Dianna. "I don't want to interfere with their energy."

"I wear gloves," said Patty. "But . . . maybe he touched me. I kind of half remember something . . ."

Dianna licked her lips. "Yeah . . . maybe I do, too. Only it's kind of gone. No, that's not right. It's like I'm remembering something from a long time ago. A kind of *faded* memory, if that makes sense."

"It might," said Monk. "If a memory is being taken, then the clarity of it would diminish, right? It'd fade back, like it was old. But really it's just leavin'."

Gayle shivered. "God almighty . . ."

Mike asked, "Do either of you have credit card receipts? Or a scheduling book?"

Patty shook her head. "That was a walk-in, I'm sure of it." She checked her credit card app, but there was no sale that day. "He must have paid in cash."

Dianna chewed her lip. "You know, Ophelia prints out my client list every day. She keeps them, too, so she can work out what to pay me."

"We need that list," said Monk. "When does the store open?"

"Not until ten tomorrow."

Monk looked at the wall clock. It was three in the morning. "I don't want to wait seven hours."

"I have a key," said Dianna, grabbing her purse and digging out a key ring. "I use it for whenever Ophelia asks me to open, like if she has a doctor's appointment."

"Outstanding," said Crow. "Mike, why don't you go with her?"

"On it, boss," said the big cop. He and Dianna put on their coats and hurried out.

123

Monk picked up the wine bottle and offered it to him, but Crow declined.

"Why, 'cause you're on duty?"

"No, because I'm an alcoholic and I really, really want that whole bottle."

"Ah," said Monk, "That sucks." He twisted the cap off the bottle and took a heavy gulp. Then began pacing the room like a caged tiger. "This whole thing is weird as balls, but if this is about stealing memories, then it makes a fucked-up kind of sense. A logic, I mean. But flies that turn to ink when you smash them? What the hell does that mean?"

After a moment Gayle raised her hand like a kid in school, "Okay, so this is a very weird theory but hear me out. In her vision Dianna saw this guy covered in fly tattoos and also flying flies. Real ones, I mean. Well, what if they were all tattoos? What if he's somehow—I don't know, it's sounding stupid to say it out loud—but what if he's really in command of them? An actual lord of those kinds of flies? Maybe he can send them out to—and god, here's another crazy thing—do his bidding?"

"That would have sounded a hell of a lot crazier yesterday than it does now," grumbled Monk. He took another heavy swig and thumped the bottle down on the work counter. "If Fly Guy can send his tattoos out . . . why? What's he hope to gain?"

Gayle wrapped her arms around herself and shivered. "Spies? Is that possible?"

They stared at one another, but eventually each shook their heads. Not in dismissal of Gayle's question, but because none of them had actual answers.

"Why here in Pine Deep?" mused Crow. He sat on one of the chairs and rocked slowly side to side. "We know that this one artist, Malibu Mark, worked with one of the victims. Tink. And now he's suddenly in the area, at Spider's place. Why?"

"Hell if I know," admitted Monk.

"I do," said Patty suddenly. "The Fringe Festival! There are maybe sixty or eighty top tattoo artists going to be here. People from all over the country."

"So we're thinking Malibu Mark and the other two victims were hanging out with Spider because they're colleagues?" asked Monk.

"They probably were," said Patty. "Most of the pros know each other. Spider's place is next to a bar, so it makes some sense that they met to hang out."

"That part's easy," said Crow. "I think our boy is getting squirrelly. Maybe knows he's being hunted and is cleaning his back trail."

"It can't be that simple," said Gayle.

"Why not?" Monk said. "It's what I'd do."

Gayle was visibly shaking and her eyes were bright and wet. "This is freaking me out. We're talking about this like it's so reasonable, but there's some kind of monster stealing memories and feeding on them. How is that even real? I don't believe in any of this. I'm generally pretty grounded, you know? I don't believe in God, or angels, or spirits, or any of this. The world isn't like that."

Patty, Crow, and Monk looked at her.

Tears welled in Gayle's eyes and her mouth lost its firmness. "The world shouldn't be like this."

The difference in her last two statements came close to breaking Monk's heart. He opened his mouth to say something, to try and offer some words of comfort, but he never got the chance.

There was a roar from outside louder than the thunder, louder than the hammering rain, and suddenly the store was blasted with intense white light. Then the front window of the store exploded inward and a big wire-mesh trash can from the curb hurtled inside, dragging ten thousand shards of glass with it. Wind and rain howled in through the shattered window and the night was filled with the roar of two dozen motorcycle engines.

And everything went to hell.

124

A throng of bikers came charging through the window. In the flash of lightning they looked like Viking raiders tearing through the monasteries of Northumbria, or a horde of Visigoths roaring with murderous glee as they sacked Rome. There were so many of them; they were armed with knives and chains and pistols, and even a couple of pump shotguns. They howled as they charged. A wordless bellow of fury; and their eyes blazed with madness.

They began firing wildly, not really aiming, but shooting as if the very air of the shop was something they wanted to kill. Bullets smashed mirrors and punched through the backs of the barber chairs and tore into the art pinned to the walls. Torn paper, plaster, and porcelain flew everywhere, and a hundred colors of ink splashed the walls and ceiling.

Patty grabbed Gayle and spun her around and down behind one of the chairs, Crow dove for the far wall to avoid being slashed to ribbons. Monk backpedaled, but the storm of splinters caught him, chopped at him. He went down to one knee, clawing at his Sig Sauer, but before he had it out Crow was up on one knee, his big Beretta .40 in a two-hand grip, challenging the storm with lightning and thunder of his own. The heavy slugs took one biker in the chest and another in the mouth, but his third shot struck the barrel of a shotgun, throwing that weapon high as it fired and then ripping it from the man's hands.

Monk tore his gun free and dodged behind one of the barber chairs, firing an entire six-round magazine dry in seconds. He swapped in his second and only backup just as Crow's slide locked back. The chief's gun had a ten-shot magazine, but he had two full extras on his belt.

But before Crow could finish slapping in the new magazine the bikers were on him. Monk lost sight of him as three of the attackers swarmed in. Monk rose shooting, going for chests and faces at that range. Hitting everything he aimed at. But then he was out and used the butt of the Sig to smash into the visor of the closest man, then shoved him to send him crashing into the others. They were so densely packed that the force created a chain reaction, dragging four of them down and tripping the ones behind.

That gave Monk the only chance he had, and he took it. As one man stumbled over the legs of his comrade, Monk grabbed his shotgun and wrenched it free, using all of the strength of his hips to create torque. The jerk was so strong that Monk actually pirouetted in place, bringing the weapon up as he completed the turn. He tucked the stock hard against his shoulder and fired straight, aiming for the bobbing helmets and exposed faces. In the narrow confines of the tattoo parlor he could not miss, and the pellets sprayed outward from the barrel, doing awful butchery.

Suddenly there were new shots, but they came from behind him, and Monk pitched sideways, twisting as he fell, expecting to see the doom of all of them behind. But it wasn't more of the Cyke-Lones barging in through the back—instead he gaped in astonishment to see Gayle standing in a wide-legged shooter's stance, a small-frame Glock in her small hands. Her eyes were huge and full of shock at what she was doing as she pulled the trigger over and over again. Four of the bikers staggered backward or crumpled to the floor. None of them dove for cover, which was deeply weird in a situation where everything was weird.

Lord of the Flies.

A flash image of Spider provided the explanation, as well as the proof of their theory that somehow the bastard behind all this was able to exert some kind of freaky-deaky mindfuck on people. The bikers were more like drones or robots than thinking creatures. They could fight, drive bikes, use weapons, but that was all part of their imperative need to destroy the enemies of their master. There was no self-preservation in their actions. No unity of attack, either. With their numbers they could have already won, but they failed because each of them was attacking as an individual rather than with coordination was a flaw. A vulnerability. They were getting in each other's way to try and accomplish their orders, which encumbered the others.

Gayle's last shot rang out and one more biker fell, and then the others surged forward, still howling in that wordless challenge.

"I don't have any more bullets," she shrieked, and Monk saw Patty hook an arm around her waist and drag her away down the hall to the bedroom.

Monk dropped his pistol and pulled his two remaining weapons—the Buck knife and the blackjack—and flung himself at the killers.

Out of the corner of his eye he saw two of them fall sideways, one face turned into a red mask of ruin and the other clutching a crushed throat, and then Crow rose into sight. He was bleeding from a broken nose but he moved like a jungle cat—blindingly fast, lashing out with his open hands and with short, brutal kicks. Crow met Monk's eyes for a split second, and there was a hell of a lot said. In that moment they understood each other. Monk recognized Crow as a fellow traveler through the storm lands. A scarred warrior who did not and would not accept the possibility of defeat. If these bastards were going to win then they would need to earn it, and it was going to cost them far more than they'd want to pay.

125

Mike pulled his cruiser to a stop in front of Nature's Spirits with the passenger door curbside. There was a six-foot gap between car and awning, and Dianna opened the door and made a break for it. Mike hurried to meet her and stood watching the street while she fitted the key into the lock. The door clicked open and a thin wailing began.

"There's a security thing," said Dianna as she hurried over and punched numbers into a keypad on the wall. The wailing stopped and the store was plunged into silence.

Mike looked around, one hand on his holstered gun. He'd been in there a dozen times, including that time he came in to ask Dianna if she'd like to go to dinner with him. It was almost right where he was standing when she'd declined with a lovely smile and an explanation about her dating preferences. Mike had been surprised and disappointed, but had been cool with it. As the Fringe community along Boundary Street had grown, he'd long since learned to overcome the male view that lesbians were a "type." Dianna was one of the most beautiful women he'd ever seen, let alone known, and his regret was a wistful one. He also envied Gayle, though it was merely envy and not the more petty emotion of jealousy, which carried with it a false sense of ownership. Mike had his full share of issues, but jealousy and intolerance were not among them.

As if reading his mind—or sensing his emotions—Dianna touched his arm and gave him a sweet smile.

"You're a good man, Mike," she said. "I hope you know that."

"Trying to be," he replied, and they smiled at each other for a moment. Then he turned and pointed to the counter. "Is that where Ophelia keeps her client sheets?"

"Yes, there's an accordion file for payroll and other stuff," said Dianna as she hustled around behind the counter. She pulled the buff-colored file onto the countertop, located the pocket for time sheets, and pulled out a sheaf of papers. "Here!" she said excitedly.

She spread the papers out and pulled the one from the right day. They looked down at the name of the first client listed.

"Owen Minor," said Mike. He shook his head. "Never heard of him, have you?"

When Dianna did not immediately reply he looked at her and saw that her eyes had become strangely unfocused, as if she was looking inward instead of at him. Her lips formed the four syllables of that name. Once, twice . . . Mike stood very still, waiting.

Finally Dianna blinked her eyes clear and in that moment her expression fell into sickness and disgust.

"That's him," she said.

"You're sure?"

Her eyes hardened. "Yes. Now that I see his name? After everything I saw in that vision? Yes. Owen Minor is the Lord of the Flies."

"Outstanding," said Mike. "I'd better call Crow and tell him."

He made the call, but there was no answer.

"That's weird," he said. "Why would he have the ringer turned off?"

"Let me call Gayle," said Dianna, pulling out her cell. She found the number and hit the call button. It rang four times and just when she thought it was going to go to voicemail Gayle answered.

But she answered with a scream.

"Dianna! There's a bunch of psycho zombie bikers! I think he sent them. Oh my god, I . . . I . . . I shot some of them!"

And then the call abruptly ended.

"Stay here," yelled Mike as he ran for the door.

Dianna did not stay there. She was in the cruiser before he was.

126

Monk Addison tore into the Cyke-Lones, smashing arms and faces with his blackjack and slashing and stabbing with the knife. Blood filled the air like an explosion of rubies. Howls of rage became screams of pain that rose above even the mind control.

Ten feet away he saw Crow, who was twice his age and half his size, dropping bikers with some kung-fu bullshit that was frightening to behold. There was more than just survival in the frenzy of the small cop's moves. Maybe he was down on that animal level where a pack leader becomes a monster in order to defend the young of the pack. Or maybe he'd personalized the threat. What had he said during their first meeting? That he'd lost a couple of kids? Maybe he was inside Patty's grief about Tuyet, borrowing her outrage at the theft of life. Whatever was shoveling coal into his furnace it was burning hot as the sun.

But the man's face was flushed a bright red and he was streaming sweat. He might win this fight, but it looked like it was going to kill him.

He felt his own body tiring. There had to be fifty cuts all over him from when the windows shattered, and his own blood was pooling in his shoes. There were still bikers outside battling to get in. Monk and Crow were individually a match for any of them, but this was going to come down to a numbers game. The two of them might win a lot of battles but lose the war from blood loss, age, and fatigue.

That thought—and horror at what would then happen to

Patty and Gayle—dumped new fuel into his own engines. He pressed the attack, taking the fight to the bikers, letting the brutal soldier he'd once been come out of his cage. Saying *fuck it* and *fuck you* to the whole goddamn world. If this was where all of his miles on the pilgrim road were going to end, and even if that meant that he—unredeemed—was about to plummet through the bloody floor on which he fought and fall into the abyss, then so what? He would take as many of them with him. He would fight long enough for Patty and Gayle to get out of there. If he could save them by dying, then that was redemption enough.

The bikers howled as they rushed him, but Monk saved his breath for the killing.

127

Patty pulled Gayle down the hall toward the door to the basement.

"Run!" she yelled, and they both clattered down the steps. The basement was damp and there were puddles of rainwater. Old boxes of stuff left over by previous tenants moldered in stacks, and some had fallen over, blocking the back door.

"Help me," cried Patty as she grabbed one box. It was soaked and crawling with roaches, but she flung it aside. Gayle grabbed the next and in seconds they had the door free. And Patty jolted to a stop, staring at the lock. At the double deadbolt.

"Where's the key?" asked Gayle, terror rising in her voice.

Patty felt her heart sink. "It's upstairs." She could see it in her mind, a sturdy Yale on a ring hanging from a hook by the cash register. Up where the fighting was raging so loud it muted the thunder.

Gayle pulled out her cell and punched in 911.

Before the call even went through there was a massive *whump!* against the door. The blow was so heavy it shook the hardwood panel in its frame. Patty pressed her eye to the peephole and saw that the tiny yard was crowded with Cyke-Lones. One of them, a monstrous man with a bald head, a wild red-gold beard, and skulls tattooed on his forehead, had his foot raised for another kick.

Gayle was now screaming into her phone, but Patty knew it didn't matter. Even if the dispatcher sent every cop in town right now they would never get there fast enough.

They were going to die down here.

The image of a laughing little girl appeared in her mind. Faded but recognizable.

"I'm sorry, baby," murmured Patty. "Mommy's so sorry."

The next kick tore the whole lock out of the frame with a spray of wood splinters.

128

Mike drove way too fast. The tires hydroplaned across the surface of a black puddle and the cruiser swung around, the back end crunching into the door of a parked Mini-Cooper with bone-jarring force. Mike cursed under his breath, stamped the gas, and fought the wheel. Then an Amazon delivery truck came out of a side street, forcing Mike to jam the brakes, which sent the car into a complete three-sixty. He felt like the whole damn world was trying to prevent him from reaching the store. Mike was a man who seldom cursed, but he fired off a blue streak of particularly foul invective as he corrected again and plowed through the rain toward Boundary Street.

Beside him, Dianna was strapped in and had one hand on

the inside handle above the door, the other clutched around her crystal pendant, and a foot braced on the dash. Her brown face was shocked to a butter paleness and she was saying rapid-fire prayers to spirits or gods or angels. Mike didn't know which, but he hoped some of them were listening.

They splashed through another puddle, one that hid a pot-hole, and the jolt rattled Mike down to his bones. And then they rounded a corner and raced up a side street to the intersection of Main and Boundary.

Lightning flashed with showy drama, revealing a scene from one of the outer rings of hell. Motorcycles everywhere. Men with weapons crowding in through the shattered front window. More of them climbing over the fence to attack the cellar door. The flash of gunfire and the mad howls of attackers driven beyond sanity.

Mike slammed on the brakes, skidding half a block before the tires burned their way through water down to asphalt. The cruiser stopped hard and rocked on its springs.

"Get out," Mike ordered. "Find someplace to hide. Call nine-one-one. Tell them 'officer in need of assistance.'"

"No," she protested.

Mike grabbed her forearm. "Listen to me: something's going to happen right now. I don't want you to see what I'm going to have to do here."

He saw Dianna search his eyes and knew the moment when she saw his eyes change. Her nostrils flared as a scent filled the car—an odor that was in no way human. Something older, strange, primal. The scent of what he was beneath his skin.

"Get out," he said, and already his voice was deeper, harsher. More of an animal growl than anything human. It was the se-cret he guarded so closely. One that only Crow, Val, and Jonatha knew about. It was something tied to the complexities of his parentage, tied to his survival and his shame. He cared about Dianna, even if he could never have her, and he did not want her to see this aspect of him. Not now or ever.

Dianna unclipped her seat belt, then surprised him by leaning over and kissing his cheek.

"I love you," she said, and through his heartbreak he understood what she meant. And in her eyes he saw an understanding that ran very deep. She was psychic, after all, a sensitive, and Mike knew that on some level she understood him. It made him ache for her all the more.

Dianna jerked the handle and slipped out. He looked in the rearview and saw her duck behind a parked SUV, the phone already to her mouth.

Mike gunned the engine, spinning the wheels on the blacktop and then releasing the brake. The powerful Ford Police Interceptor shot forward, accelerating from zero to sixty in the eight seconds it took to reach Patty's store. As the change worked its way through him, he could hear, even at that distance, the sound of an active fight inside the store, not in back. If the Cyke-Lones got in the back they'd crush all four of the people inside between a hammer and anvil. So Mike angled his car toward the bikes parked by the back fence.

His cruiser was a missile when it hit.

Two big Harleys flew into the air and the car's grill wore a third one as it punched through the fence and smashed into the bikers in the yard.

Dianna Agbala peered over the hood of the SUV, staring in horror as Mike's cruiser crashed through the bikes and bikers. She was a nonviolent person by nature and didn't even like watching action movies. This . . . God, this was awful.

But then it got worse.

As insane as the last few days had been, as bizarre as tonight had become, those last seconds in the car with Mike had spun things up into the funnel of a tornado. She had actually seen Mike Sweeney begin to change. His eyes first, then his voice . . . and by the time she was getting out of the car, even the shape of his face was undergoing a fantastic metamorphosis. It was as if his bones were melting beneath his skin and re-forming into something else.

She knew what that thing was. Her insight told her, but even now, as she saw the hideous shape spring from the open cruiser door and hurl itself at the bikers, Dianna was afraid to think the word.

Because this was the world and there were no such things.

He could not *be* such a thing. Mike was a kind, sweet guy. A friend. A good person. However the creature that pounced on the Cyke-Lones was not any of those things. It was a beast, running on four legs, its massive muscles covered in stiff red fur, its ears raised to tufted points.

And the howl.

That awful howl of red delight.

She wanted to look away, needed to.

But that thing was still Mike Sweeney, and he was fighting to save Gayle and Patty, Monk and Crow . . . and maybe all of Pine Deep.

And so it would have been a failing of trust and a weakness of her belief in the Larger World to deny being a witness.

129

Monk Addison was barely able to stand.

Crow leaned against the wall, blood running from his nose

and mouth and from too many cuts to count. He looked like he'd aged forty years in five minutes.

Patty Cakes stood with her arms around Gayle, and both of them were white-faced and unable to speak. They kept throwing terrified glances toward the hall that led to the basement. Monk had heard strange noises down there. Shouts and screams and some kind of awful animal howling. Had the bikers brought a dog to this fight? If so . . . what happened to it and the Cyke-Lones who'd tried to come in through the cellar? From the looks on the women's faces he was pretty sure he did not want an answer to that question.

Not now anyway.

And where the hell was that big kid with the red hair?

The night was filled with flashing red and blue lights. Local cops, EMTs, state cops, and even the fire department. Swarming in, each of them trying to make sense of what had happened in the context of their own jobs. Failing utterly.

Dianna came in, escorted by the female cop who'd been outside of Patty's room. She looked as shocked as the other women. *What the actual hell?*

Monk sagged down and sat on the floor, hands dangling off his knees, head sinking down on his chest. He saw a flash of black and looked up to see nightbirds flapping in through the window. They lunged here and there and it took Monk a moment to realize what they were doing. Flies were rising from the bikers, from the living and the dead, and the ragged black birds were attacking them, snatching them out of the air with a ferocity every bit as savage as the human fight that had just ended. But each time one of the birds crushed a blowfly between its beak, there was a splash of color lit by a tiny burst of light, as if the life spark of the insects was detonating. And each time a bird killed a fly, it died, too. A sacrifice of a kind Monk did not understand. Not the science of it, or the magic, or whatever it was. But he understood the why of it.

He watched in weary, sick fascination as the birds devoured every last one of them. Then the cops and EMTs rushed in, scattering the birds, who squawked and flew back into the storm, leaving their fallen brothers behind.

Monk wept for those birds.

Then he let the tide of officialdom sweep over and around him and carry him away from this place.

130

Monk and Crow both wound up in the ER. Fifty-three stitches for him, forty-four for the chief.

Monk saw a tall, black-haired woman with an almost regal face with Crow. His wife? If so, he was punching way above his weight. It made him wish that Sandy was there for him.

Sandy.

They'd spent exactly one day together and already she was a seed planted in the strange soil of his heart. She was damaged goods, too, but really . . . could he ever expect to be with someone who wasn't? Sandy had a purity about her that shone through, and it felt like a beacon to him.

In the ER, Monk was bemused to find that he had the same doughy nurse, Mäsiarka, and the same ten-year-old doctor, Argawal. However, this time, Patty was there with him, as a friend and spokeswoman, taking charge and making sure Monk was given the best care. That seemed to amuse the doctor but annoy the nurse. Whatever.

"It's going to be okay," said Patty when they were alone in the ER cubicle, though her voice lacked all conviction. "We have his name now. Owen Minor."

"Never heard of him."

"Crow's people matched the name to registrations at more than thirty tattoo conventions. He was Dianna's first client that day. And I think that might have been the name he gave me when he came to my shop."

"Well . . . shit."

"And there's more," said Patty. "In the store, while the cops were taking our statements, I saw some drawings on the floor. They must have fallen out of my sketchbook. You know the one I use when I'm working with a client on a new tattoo? Want to guess what it was a drawing of? Want to guess what he had me tattoo on him?"

The nurse came in and injected something into his IV. "Something for the pain, Mr. Addison," he said. "Might make you a little sleepy. It's okay if you drift off because we're waiting for a room to open."

"Go for it, kid," said Monk. "Maybe give me a double dose because I am not digging being awake right now."

While the nurse worked, Patty shifted to a more neutral topic. "Dianna's a sweetheart. Since my whole place is a crime scene, she's going to let me use her spare bedroom. And Gayle called her husband and told him some story, so she's going to stay with me. Good chance we are going to get very, very drunk."

She cut a look at the nurse, realizing how that might sound after her last visit here, but the man smiled. "I don't judge. I give out drugs and empty bedpans. From what I heard it was a really bad night for you guys. I'm going off shift, but Karen will take care of you. She'll be in to take fresh vitals in a bit. Hope you all get some rest."

He nodded and left.

The painkiller was a doozy and Monk could feel it kick in. The narcotic—along with sheer physical exhaustion—was trying to push him over the edge into sleep. "Pats," he said weakly, "what happened down in the basement?"

She looked away, and it took her a long, long time to answer. "Mike happened," she said simply.

"Yeah, but what was that roaring?"

An even longer pause this time, and by then Monk was fading, slipping, falling.

"That was Mike," she said. There was more to what she said, but it made no sense. It was impossible, and so Monk stopped trying to hold on and let himself fall.

131

Patty Cakes stopped at the liquor store and bought wine, vodka, beer, mixers, and as much junk food as she could carry. Chocolate was a factor. Then she drove over to Dianna's place. There were two cars there already, and Patty assumed the other was Gayle.

She parked across the street and let some time pass, giving the two women a chance to have some kind of normal conversation. Maybe even a brand-new first kiss. It was so strange a thing that it was hard to think about, and yet the thought that there was maybe some tenderness going on inside comforted Patty. Tenderness belonged to the world she wanted to live in. She wished she were in that head space, but she'd tried relationships before, mostly male, sometimes female. None of them worked. Hell, even she and Monk had tried it, but they quickly discovered they were friends making love rather than actual lovers. She had some occasional one-night stands, but didn't think she could remember three names out of five if she were at gunpoint.

Last night's rain was done and the sky was partly cloudy, allowing some rays of light to slant down. Pillars of heaven, some people called them. But these were crooked, as if heaven was ready to tumble.

That thought plunged her into sadness.

"Tuyet," she said, and then the tears came.

As fractured sunlight glinted on the lingering raindrops of ten thousand leaves, each of a different shade of red, Patty Trang sobbed alone in her car.

Inside the house, Dianna and Gayle held each other.

They were dressed and on the couch. They had kissed, but it was tentative and strange, and Dianna knew that if they were going to ever be intimate again it would have to start slow. There was no guarantee that it would go anywhere, but if not . . . they were friends now and that was a beautiful thing.

There was a lot of silence going on. Things known but not said. Experiences that were miles away from being processed. Dangerous memories. Dangerous expectations, too, because the madness at the tattoo shop had all the drama of a finale, but it wasn't. It was only a battle, because the Lord of the Flies—Owen Minor—was still out there somewhere.

And fear.

So much fear.

Gayle's handgun had been confiscated as evidence. Dianna didn't own one. First thing she did when she got home was go around the house and check every window and door. Then, with Gayle watching, she got several knives from the kitchen, and a screwdriver from her tool drawer, and tucked them behind cushions and on shelves.

"Arming for war?" joked Gayle, but it fell flat. Of course she was arming for war. Gayle sat and watched, and then got up and helped.

After that they held each other for a long time on the couch. Not kissing. Sharing warmth and light and safety.

The doorbell rang and Dianna let Patty in. The tattoo artist's eyes were red and puffy, but no one was indelicate or dense enough to ask why. Dianna hugged her, and so did Gayle. Then they saw the shopping bags on the porch and everyone laughed as they brought the contraband inside.

"We need some actual food to go with this," said Gayle, inspecting the boxes and bags of chips, salsa, cookies, and chocolate assortments. "I can make a run . . ."

"Nah," said Dianna, reaching for her phone. "I've got delivery menus for every kind of food known to womankind."

They ordered Chinese. Dianna started a fire in the hearth, put on some John Legend, and they started pouring glasses of comfort. Outside the birds sang in the trees.

They did not notice the dozens upon dozens of nightbirds who sat in silent ranks on telephone wires and all along the roof of her house.

132

Mike Sweeney sat in his cubicle at the station with two desktop computers running and his laptop open. The printer was chugging out page after page of the names of those from the tattoo conventions who'd offered to cooperate without the requirement of a warrant. Privacy policies for events like that were internal and informal, and many of Mike's requests came in via local FBI offices. Besides, it wasn't like he was seeking political or medical information.

Mike was systematically going through the printouts while also running database searches to cross-reference information. The slowdown was that no two of the conventions used the same damn programs for registration, so there was a ton of cutting and pasting.

Work was therapy for him. He was in a lot of pain from last night. Only some of it was physical. Most was what Crow called an "existential freak-out." Gayle and Patty had seen a side of him Mike hated to show, and he was afraid Dianna had, too. He was deeply ashamed of that "other Mike." The animal Mike that was a legacy from the Trouble. It didn't matter—or, mattered a tiny bit less—that he'd risked that transformation for a good cause.

But it was a risk. His control in such situations was always a crapshoot. Although he'd never lost that control yet, he had to accept that it was a possibility. There were thousands of years of folktales arguing that real control was impossible.

He'd had to go all the way home like that, too, because his clothes were shredded rags in what was left of his cruiser. That was still something he'd have to explain.

Work was calming. Work was orderly and normal and even searching for a freak like Owen Minor had a comforting structure to it. It's why Mike liked puzzles. Sudoku, jigsaws, cryptics, nomograms, explicit and implicit math problems, Masyu . . . all of it. He scored exceptionally well on the kinds of IQ tests that skewed toward patterns and logical problem-solving. Less so on abstractions, but police work was mostly logical.

He found Owen Minor's name on an attendee list at a tattoo convention in Anaheim, California, more than a dozen years ago. When Mike cross-referenced, that he found that Malibu Mark had been at the same event.

"One down," he said aloud.

"What's that?" asked Gertie.

"Nothing."

"That wasn't me," she said. "There's old egg salad in the trash."

"I was talking to myself," he assured her.

Mike worked through the other lists and found no other mention of that name.

"Plan B," he said, but kept his voice too low for Gertie to hear. One of the most well-known things about people—criminals and civilians—was that when they picked a fake name for any reason there was a statistically high likelihood they would use either one or both of their initials. John Doe might pick Jack Dole, or something like that. Even though Web security people warned against this all the time, the practice was a mnemonic. People remembered easier when some part of their name, particularly their initials, was the same. So, he did a search on that and found a fair few *O.M.* or *M.O.* names, and worked his way through them, eliminating most by simple Net searches using interjurisdictional search engines.

A few oddities emerged and he added them to a special list. They included Orson Mouche, Orlando Mosca, Omor Musculiţă, Oliwier Mucha, Ohit Māchi, and several others. All specifically ethnic names. French, Polish, Bangla, Romanian, and so on.

Mike sat and looked at the list. There were seventeen names like that, scattered all across American tattoo convention records. Mike tapped a pencil eraser against his teeth and thought about it. Sure, tattoos were a worldwide thing, with long histories, but the pointedly ethnic names seemed wrong to him.

Contrived. When he checked, there was a smaller percentage of overall names at each convention that were ethnic in both given and surnames, with exceptions for Indian, Pakistani, Chinese, and Western European. Few of these names, though, fit into those categories.

So the next step was to match those names against Agent Richter's list of conventions where possible victims had attended as either guests or professionals.

By the fifth name he checked Mike could feel his pulse quickening. Four out of five. Then seven out of nine. Then fourteen out of seventeen.

"Holy smokes," he said.

"I'm not smoking," said Gertie curtly. "You know I gave that up."

He ignored her and began plugging those names into the police search engines. He searched all seventeen just to be sure.

He got three hits. The other fourteen were fake names.

Then he searched the surnames for clues, to see if there was anything there beyond an ethnic name that started with *O*. That came up with nothing useful. Then he tried the surnames.

The very first one he tried was Mucha.

And time seemed to stop.

Mucha was the Polish word for "housefly."

"God," he breathed.

He plugged in the Spanish name, Moscarda.

Blowfly.

The French name, Mouche.

Fly.

All of them.

Fly.

Lord of the damn Flies.

"Got you, you bastard."

"That's not a nice thing to—"

"Gertie," he snapped, "please."

She lapsed into a hurt silence, but Mike didn't care. He was onto something. He loaded a translation program and began searching for foreign-language words for *fly, horsefly, housefly,* and *blowfly.* And found every single name on his list of fourteen.

Mike was excited now and his fingers trembled as he began focusing his search. Looking for someone with one of those names who lived here in Pine Deep. He knew that Owen Minor used that name when booking a reading at Dianna's place and at Patty's, but he did not own a house under the name. He tried DMV, real estate and tax databases, and others.

And twenty minutes later he found the name.

He found the home address.

He found where the man worked.

Mike found everything.

He grabbed his hat and ran for the door, yelling orders to Gertie over his shoulder.

133

It took the three of them a long time and a lot of booze to get around to talking about last night. They came at it from odd angles. Dianna asked Gayle why she had a gun.

"It's one of the few things Scott and I do together," said Gayle. "We're both army brats, so we grew up with guns. We go about four times a year. Sometimes more often. He hunts, but I don't. Not my thing. At the range we're about the same in terms of target scores." She faltered and dabbed at her eyes. "I . . . can't believe I actually . . . shot someone."

"If you hadn't," said Patty, "Crow, Monk, and I would all be dead. You, too."

"I know, but . . . at the range it's just paper. I don't even use the targets that have the drawing of the robber on it. You know the one with the old-fashioned cap and Lone Ranger mask? Scott has some zombie targets, but that's him. I only use regular bull's-eyes, you know?" She shivered. "Shooting those men. Those poor men . . ."

"Those poor men were drug-running gangbangers," said Patty. "So, okay, they were under some kind of spooky mind control thing, but on any other day they'd have done every bad thing to you in the book. I know that type, believe me."

And later . . .

Dianna looked at Patty. "Did you really use blood for Monk's tattoos?"

"Yes," said Patty. "That's the only way it works."

"But how do you know that?" asked Gayle, sipping her second vodka and cranberry juice. Her words were already starting to slur. Not much, but enough that she had to make herself over-pronounce to keep from being mush-mouthed.

Patty shrugged. "It's hard to explain. My grandmother taught me the way, and her grandmother before her, going way, way back. It skips a generation."

"Had you ever done it before Monk?"

"No," laughed Patty. "Until him I don't think I even believed it."

"You used your daughter's blood?" asked Dianna.

Patty nodded gravely. "Yes." She reached into her blouse and pulled out a chain on which was a vial of pinkish liquid. Dianna recognized it from before, when Patty had showed her chest tattoo. The vial sparkled as if frequently polished.

"If he steals the rest of my memories," said Patty, "this will be all I have of Tuyet."

"Well," said Gayle slowly, "couldn't you use some of that to—I don't know—redo the tattoo of her?"

"No, that wouldn't work."

"Why not?" asked Dianna.

Patty stared at her, then at Gayle, and then at the vial.

"I—" she began and the doorbell rang.

"Hold that thought," said Dianna, springing up. "Actual food!" She grabbed her purse. "Can you guys get some plates and napkins? In the kitchen."

She was smiling when she opened the door.

Owen Minor's smile was even bigger.

<hr>

134

Monk Addison slept so deeply that there weren't even dreams down there.

He was asleep when they wheeled him to the room and only vaguely aware when orderlies helped him into the bed. He immediately dropped back down into that lightless, soundless place where even his ghosts couldn't follow. He had not been aware when Patty left.

Nor was he aware that a man in a wheelchair sat watching him.

"You are one strange cat," said Malcolm Crow. He was hooked up to an IV stand and had a bottle of Yoo-hoo resting on his thigh. A gift from Val. There was a cooler with more of them, and if anyone at the hospital had an issue with it, the hospital administrator was Val's best friend. So they could go piss up a rope.

Crow had an aluminum frame around his shattered nose and

his face was already beginning to look like a tropical sunset. And it hurt. A lot.

Karen, the shift nurse, came in and checked the readout on machines but did not try to wake Monk. She nodded to Crow, smiled, and left without saying a word. Crow wasn't sure why Monk had come here, but it felt right. Monk was strange, sure, but he was a good man, and Crow felt a kinship with him.

But the meds in his own system began to wear on him and he was dozing when another nurse came in. Not Karen. This one looked like a nursing assistant who might still be in school. Slim, pretty, but with zero personality.

"He's asleep," said Crow. "If you don't mind, can you get an orderly to help me back to my room?"

The nurse didn't answer. She bent over the side of Monk's bed and stared down at the sleeping man's face, her hands in the pockets of her scrubs. Crow frowned because she wasn't looking at the chart or the machines. Then he saw it.

The fly.

It was crawling on the back of her neck.

No. Crawling inside her skin.

"No!" cried Crow as she pulled her hand from her pocket. He saw light glint on the blade of an oyster knife and lunged for her.

One second too late.

135

Owen Minor punched Dianna in the stomach with shocking speed and strength. She was not prepared for it and it folded her, buckling her knees. Before she could fall he shoved her roughly backward. She crumpled to the ground, face purple, gagging and gasping.

"You fucking witch," he snarled and spat full in her face. He back-kicked the door shut and stepped over her. Gayle and Patty shot to their feet, but Gayle immediately lost her balance and sat back down with a thump. Patty instantly hurled her glass at Owen, but it was a long throw and he dodged easily. He was not a powerful or fit man, but he was filled with a towering rage. Adrenaline coursed through him, making him strong, giving him a total belief in his strength. He was a man and these were three women. Three whores. Three witches.

They were no better than his whore of a mother.

No better than the witches on the block where he grew up. So much for it taking a village to raise a child. They never gave a flying fuck about him. Not at her funeral and not after. None of them offered to take him in. They stood and watched and Child Protective Services took him away and fed him to the foster care system.

He hated them all for that, and hated them even more for what they were doing to him. Conspiring against him. Trying to spoil everything.

He had been at the hospital when they brought in Monk and Crow. Those pricks. God, how he'd wanted to slit their throats. Or, better yet, inject something nasty into their IVs. Hydrochloric acid. Bleach. Something fun. But they were both still in the ER when he went off shift. The funny thing was that neither of them—not the bounty hunter or the chief of police—knew that the person taking their vitals was him. The Lord of the Flies.

They looked at his name tag and stopped fucking thinking. Nurse Oeznik Mäsiarka. Ozzie to the staff. A nice Slovak name—a country Owen had to look up on the map after he found the name on one of those baby name sites. The site even gave the meaning.

Oeznik.

Butcher.

He grinned a butcher's smile at the women. Flies buzzed around him and on his skin. One crawled across his face, in one nostril and out the other. It tickled. It made him smile.

Gayle struggled to her feet and grabbed an unopened wine bottle. Patty just stood there with her hands opening and closing. The hatred on her face and in her eyes was so fucking delicious. Owen felt himself growing hard. Maybe he'd do more than kill them. Maybe he could do a lot more.

"You stole her," said Patty in a voice so choked, so raw that it came out as a whisper. "You stole my daughter. You stole my baby."

"Yes," he said, grinning.

"You're just as bad as those men who killed her."

"Oh, no," he said, "I'm ten times worse. She lives in my head, you stupid cunt. I get to fuck her over and over and over again every time I close my eyes. I'm going to fuck her every day for the rest of my life."

Patty's scream was a towering shriek of unbearable rage and hurt and horror and she launched herself at Owen.

His grin never wavered. He was expecting this, hoping for exactly this kind of delicious drama and even before she took a single step he reached into his pants pocket and pulled out a gun.

And then he screamed.

He spun and looked down in absolute shock at the screwdriver sticking out of his calf. Blood—his blood—pumped out over the bright-yellow handle. The pain was immense, bigger than anything he had ever felt in his real life. It was memory pain. Dream pain. Stolen pain. But it wasn't fun. It wasn't delicious.

It was awful.

It was so big that he was lost in that pain for two very long seconds.

Long enough for Patty Cakes to hurl herself like a panther at him. Long enough for Gayle, drunk as she was, to race over with the wine bottle held high. Long enough for Dianna to claw her way up the bookcase by the door and grab the knife she'd hidden there.

Two seconds was all the time in the world. His finger jerked on the trigger and the gun barked, but the barrel was pointing nowhere useful. He screamed louder than Patty had. He screamed so loud it tore blood from his throat.

He screamed for a long, long time.

Crow wrestled the nurse to the ground and she fought him with the same mindless ferocity as the Cyke-Lones had done at Patty's place.

She fought and fought.

And then she stopped fighting. All at once.

In the space of a single heartbeat she went from murderous monster to a teenage girl who was absolutely terrified. A girl who, as far as she knew, was being attacked by some strange man.

Nurses and orderlies and hospital cops came running.

It took a lot of time to sort out who the young woman was. Not a nurse at all. She was a high school student named Alexa

Clare, and the girl could not then, or ever, explain why she was in the hospital at all. No idea why she was dressed as a nurse. No idea why she had an oyster knife or why she had stabbed a patient with it.

Or why she had a tattoo of a fly on the back of her neck.

No one else could explain why the tattoo began to fade and was entirely gone by that evening. If Chief Crow had any explanations, he did not share them with anyone.

2

Monk Addison was rushed into surgery with a stab wound that tried very hard to kill him. Sucking chest wounds are like that. Mike Sweeney was one of the first on the scene, having been running to find Crow anyway. He applied pressure until the right people could hustle Monk down to the ER.

It was close.

Very close.

3

Val Guthrie answered her door very cautiously. She'd only been back from the hospital for forty minutes. Her husband had told her everything, because Val had been through the Trouble and had the sawdust to take anything.

She looked through the peephole and frowned, recognizing a neighbor standing on the porch looking a bit dazed and confused. Val opened the door as far as the chain would allow. She had the barrel of a Glock 26 pressed up against the panel, aimed right at the man's heart.

"Burleigh?" she asked. "What are you doing here?"

Burleigh Hopewell rubbed the back of his neck. "I . . . I really don't know, Val."

4

Monk Addison lay propped up in bed, holding the hand of a very pretty Mexican American woman named Sandy. When Crow came in to visit him and asked who his guest was, Monk introduced her as his girlfriend. It came out so naturally, but hearing it aloud seemed to surprise him and the woman. She kissed him for that.

"Can I have a minute with your, ah, boyfriend?" asked Crow.

"Sure," said Sandy, "but Monk . . . if he bothers you, just call me and I'll throw him out. Badge or no." She gave Crow a ninja death stare and then left the room. Both men watched her go. Everyone in the hall watched her go.

"Wow," said Crow.

"I know," said Monk and laughed. Then winced because every damn thing hurt. Except holding Sandy's hand. That hadn't hurt at all.

Crow lowered himself carefully onto the guest chair. He had been discharged from the hospital four days ago. But there was so much to do that this was the first time he'd been by to see Monk.

"World's stupidest question . . . how are you?"

"They tell me I'll live," said Monk.

"Nice to hear. Has anyone brought you up to speed yet?"

Monk nodded. "Mike Sweeney was here for a couple of hours this morning."

"So you know how it played out."

"Yeah. All of it."

They sat with that for a while.

"I've been all over the world," said Monk finally. "And there's this nasty bit of folk wisdom. You hear it in movie dialogue sometimes and there's a tendency to dismiss it as melodrama, but. . . ." He shrugged very carefully. "If a tribe or village captures someone, an enemy—a real son of a bitch, or someone from an army who thinks rape is a perk of being a soldier—if the community is merciful they cut the prisoner's head off or hang him. If they are not merciful, they gave him to the women."

"Yeah," said Crow, "I heard that."

It was all that really needed to be said.

5

They kept Monk for another week, and he spent two weeks at Sandy's doing nothing much except binge-watching stuff on Netflix and eating too much of the food she prepared. She was the kind who liked to cook and expected her guests to overeat. How she stayed so thin was a mystery.

Monk ate, and rested, and healed.

Mostly healed. Body first, then soul.

6

One month to the day he first rolled into Pine Deep, Monk Addison came into Patty's tattoo parlor. He was alone. Despite Sandy's food, he was thinner and he felt far older than his years. He wore his leather jacket over an Iggy and the Stooges vintage T-shirt. He carried a bottle in a paper bag and set it on the counter.

The place had gotten a makeover. New chairs, new window, new shelves, fresh paint. Val Guthrie, Dianna Agbala, and Gayle Kosinski had all helped. A coven of witches, and Monk had come to love and admire them all. Darkness, it seemed, was not the only power in Pine Deep.

Monk locked the door and switched off the OPEN neon. He lowered the double set of blinds. Patty watched him.

"You're really sure you want to do this," she asked.

"Yeah," he said, "I am."

"You don't even know if it'll work."

"Never will know until we try."

He shrugged out of the jacket, tossed it onto one of the chairs, and then removed the bottle from the bag. It was Laotian cobra snake whiskey, and there was a real king cobra floating in the amber liquid and it had a real scorpion in its mouth.

"How'd you get that? It's illegal to even import."

"Gift from Twitch," said Monk as he set about opening it. "He has odd friends."

"So do I," said Patty.

"I'll drink to that."

Which they did.

It tasted of ginseng and death and made their lips swell, but it had a mule's kick and that was damn fine for both of them.

Monk took off his T-shirt and sat down in the chair closest to Patty's equipment.

"Do it, Pats," he said. "We have to try."

He handed her a vial of blood diluted in holy water. She took it with a wince, like he was handing her a live scorpion.

"Where?" she asked.

"Anywhere I don't have to see it."

"Take your pants off."

He did.

Patty nodded and adjusted the chair so that it lay flat, and told him to lie on his stomach. He did. She uncorked the vial and mixed the contents with ordinary black ink, then loaded her gun and set to work. Before the needle touched him, he looked at the tattoo on the back of her hand. She'd had the crude smiley face lasered off. Soon the skin would be ready for fresh ink. Soon, but not yet.

Then the needle drilled into him.

It was a small tattoo, no bigger than a silver dollar, and she inked it high on the back of his thigh. It took her less than two hours to get it just right.

"Here it is," she said, "last line."

"I'm ready," he said and set his teeth for the pain.

She finished the face and Monk's whole body went rigid as pain slammed through every nerve ending. He yelled, but he welcomed the pain. His eyes went out of focus and suddenly he was not Monk. Not entirely. He was Owen Minor. Fully awake, totally alive, screaming in his mind. Ten thousand separate moments of Owen's life crashed through Monk. All of the memories he'd stolen. All of the things he'd done. His thoughts, his fantasies and desires. It felt to Monk like plunging his head in a cesspool. None of the other faces he wore had been evil. Some had done bad things, but nothing—absolutely nothing—like this.

And he could hear Owen Minor screaming in his head. Screaming . . . and laughing because he was awake and aware again. It was a madman's laugh. The laugh of a death row inmate who'd suddenly discovered he was invulnerable and immortal. The other faces on Monk's skin screamed in horror to share purgatory with this monster.

In his mind, Owen Minor sneered at him. *I'm with you forever, you freak. Everything you see, I'll see. Everything!*

And the madman in his flesh laughed and laughed and laughed. For joy. For victory. He was trapped, yes, but in the flesh of a tattooed man for whom memories were his trade. His curse.

I'm with you forever.

"Do the rest," gasped Monk. "Come on, Patty, for fuck's sake, do the rest."

Patty refilled her gun, this time with pure black ink, the darkest shade she had. She took another hit of the whiskey and set to work.

Inking black over every speck of white in the tattooed face. Filling it all in. Turning the face into an eyeless mask of nothing.

Monk clutched the arms of the chair and screamed as loud as Owen Minor screamed. There was no laughter now. Instead there was a rising horror as the truth dawned on him.

Yes, he would live forever in Monk's skin. But blind, unable to see anything. A sightless ghost staggering through forever. Around him the other ghosts howled in awful delight.

7

Monk lay panting on the table, bathed in sweat, nearly broken.

He tried to turn over, but Patty had to help him. His chest hurt and he was dizzy. Patty pushed a glass of the whiskey into his hand and he drank, hissing at the fire from alcohol and venom.

"Do . . ." he began but a fit of coughing stole his voice. When he could breathe he tried it again. "Do the other one."

He fumbled for her hand and pressed her fingers to the bare spot on his chest. Patty stood there looking and saying nothing. More than a minute passed, and Monk thought she was going to back out. Her eyes were wet with tears but they were hard for all that. She set her glass down and slipped the necklace off. She kissed the vial and opened it. Monk watched as she poured exactly half of the contents into a bowl and then added a special kind of black ink imported from her hometown. She capped the vial and set it aside, standing it on a stack of photos of Tuyet. Photos of the little girl smiling. Patty stood for a moment, looking at those smiles and glancing at her own hand.

Monk watched everything she did. He saw her lips as she mouthed four words in Vietnamese. *Mẹ sẽ tìm con.*

Mommy will find you.

He could feel his heart breaking. Not falling apart, but cracking open to let in some light.

Patty saw him watching, gave the smallest of smiles, said nothing. When she was done mixing she loaded the ink into her gun and handed him a short piece of thick leather.

"I don't want the belt," he said.

"It's going to hurt."

"Let it hurt."

"This will hurt worse."

"I don't care."

Patty nodded and began to work.

It hurt so goddamn bad. Monk took the belt and put it between his teeth to keep from screaming. All the faces watched her work. Around the chair the ghosts stood vigil as she worked.

Three hours later Patty said the same thing she had before, meaning something so completely different.

"Last line . . ."

"Do it," whimpered Monk. "God almighty, please do it."

She did.

Then she sank down to her knees, the needle falling from her hand. Monk lay like the dead in the chair. Even the ghosts held their breath.

After forever, Monk said, "Patty . . ."

She did not look up. She shook her head and buried her face against Monk's thigh.

"Patty," he said again, his voice hoarse from screaming. "Patty, please."

She kept shaking her head.

"I . . . I can see her," said Monk. He was crying now. And smiling. "Oh my god, Patty, I can see her. She's here, Pats. She's right here."

Patty raised her head, tears streaming down her face, her lips hanging slack with grief and fear.

"Patty," said Monk, reaching for her hand, "she's right here. She's standing right beside you."

He took her hand and raised it to the cheek of the small ghost who stood beside the chair. Patty felt nothing.

"Close your eyes, Pats," Monk said gently.

She did.

And when Tuyet moved to press her cheek against her mother's hand, Patty Cakes felt it.

She felt it.

She felt Tuyet's sweet face.

PATTY CAKES'S PLAYLIST

"A Thousand Kisses Deep"
  by Leonard Cohen

"Ballad of a Thin Man"
  by Bob Dylan

"Casey's Last Ride"
  by Kris Kristofferson

"Corey's Coming"
  by Harry Chapin

"Mad World"
  by Gary Jules

"Primemover"
by The Leather Nun

"A Certain Slant of Light"
by The Tea Party

"A Lesson Never Learned"
by Asking Alexandria

"All Around Me"
by Flyleaf

"All I Ask"
by Adele

"Bad Things"
by Jace Everett

"Barton Hollow"
by The Civil Wars

"Wish"
by Nine Inch Nails

"Blame It on the Kids"
by Aviva

"Broken Bones"
by Kaleo

"Broken"
by Amy Lee

"Burn"
by The Cure

"Bury Me with My Guns On"
by Bobaflex

"Change"
by Deftones

"Clap Hands"
by Tom Waits

"Closer to Believing"
  by Emerson, Lake & Palmer

"Come As You Are"
  by Prep School

"Creep"
  by Radiohead

"Crying"
  by Roy Orbison

"Dark Side"
  by Blink 182

"Darkness"
  by Disturbed

"Dead Flowers"
  by Dax Riggs

"Devil's Backbone"
  by The Civil Wars

"Down the River"
  by Chris Knight

"Every Day Is Exactly the Same"
  by Nine Inch Nails

"Eyes on Fire"
  by Blue Foundation

"Fade into You"
  by Mazzy Star

"Falling Away from Me"
  by Korn

"Fisherman's Blues"
  by The Waterboys

"Forever Autumn"
  by Moody Blues

"Forward"
 by James Blake and Beyoncé

"Gone for Good"
 by Morphine

"(Every Day Is) Halloween"
 by Ministry

"Hate Me" or "Black Orchid"
 by Blue October

"Have You Ever Seen the Rain"
 by CCR

"Hello"
 by Evanescence

"Heroes"
 by David Bowie (cover by Peter Gabriel)

"Highwayman"
 by The Highwaymen

"Hold On"
 by Tom Waits

"How to Disappear Completely"
 by Radiohead

"Howlin' for You"
 by The Black Keys

"Feel Alright"
 by Steve Earle

"I Grieve"
 by Peter Gabriel

"If It Be Your Will"
 by Leonard Cohen

"I'll Fall with Your Knife"
 by Peter Murphy

"In the Air Tonight"
   by Phil Collins

"Man in the Box"
   by Alice in Chains

"Innocent When You Dream"
   by Tom Waits

"Into Dust"
   by Mazzy Star

"It's a Dead Man's Party"
   by Oingo Boingo

"Jesus Christ"
   by Brand New

"Keep Me in Your Heart"
   by Warren Zevon

"The Killing Moon"
   by Echo & the Bunnymen

"Last Goodbye"
   by Jeff Buckley

"Love Will Tear Us Apart"
   by Joy Division

"Lullaby"
   by The Cure

"Mars, the Bringer of War"
   by Gustav Holst: The Planets

"Mercy Street"
   by Peter Gabriel

"Mondo Bizarro"
   by The Ramones

"Monsters"
   by Shinedown

"Moondance"
 by Van Morrison

"Moonlight Sonata"
 by Beethoven

"Nemo" or "Sleeping Sun"
 by Nightwish

"I'm Never Gonna Dance Again"
 by George Michael

"No Heaven"
 by DJ Champion

"Old and Wise"
 by the Alan Parsons Project

"Opus 194"
 by Stephen Rowe

"Outside"
 by Hollywood Undead

"Paint It Black"
 by Inkubus Sukkubus

"Perfect Day"
 by Lou Reed

"Promise Me"
 by Badflower

"Rags to Rags"
 by the Eels

"Red Right Hand"
 by Nick Cave & the Bad Seeds

"Reflections of My Life"
 by Marmalade

"The Road to Hell"
 by Chris Rea

"Rope on Fire"
 by Morphine

"Ruby's Arms"
 by Tom Waits

"Running Up That Hill"
 by Kate Bush (cover by Placebo)

"Sail"
 by Devildriver

"Self-Control"
 by Laura Branigan

"Shrug"
 by Queensryche

"Silence"
 by Beethoven

"Sleeping on the Blacktop"
 by Colter Wall

"Slippin' into Darkness"
 by War

"Something I Can Never Have"
 by Nine Inch Nails

"Sound of Silence"
 by Simon & Garfunkel (cover by Disturbed)

"South of Heaven"
 by Slayer (cover by Brides of Lucifer)

"Stand By Me"
 by Ben E. King (cover by Florence and the Machine)

"Susan's House"
 by the Eels

"Take the Pain"
 by Acroma 13

"Take Me Down"
  by The Pretty Reckless

"Tangled Up in Blue"
  by Bob Dylan

"Tears Don't Fall"
  by Bullet for My Valentine

"The Humbling River"
  by Puscifer

"The Last Call"
  by Sirenia

"The Man Comes Around"
  by Johnny Cash

"The Widow"
  by The Mars Volta

"Turn the Page"
  by Bob Seger (cover by Metallica)

"Voices"
  by Russ Ballard

"Voodoo"
  by Godsmack

"Wipe Me Down"
  by Boosie Badazz

"You Are My Sunshine"
  by Jamey Johnson

"Your Lucky Day in Hell"
  by Eels

"Zombie"
  by Bad Wolves

"Zombie"
  by The Cranberries

ACKNOWLEDGMENTS

Thanks to the many people for sharing your stories about your personal ink. Too many to list here, but I'm grateful to you all!

Thanks to Rhian Lockard, Rachael Lavin, Marie Whittaker, Rachel Maleski, and James Ray Tuck for their good advice.

DON'T MISS ANY OF THESE THRILLING TITLES IN THE *NEW YORK TIMES* BESTSELLING SERIES

 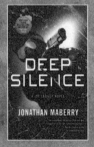  

"JONATHAN MABERRY

delivers plenty of action and intrigue."

—PUBLISHERS WEEKLY

JonathanMaberry.com

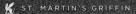 ST. MARTIN'S GRIFFIN

When all you have are memories, there is no greater horror than forgetting.

One day tattoo artist Patty Cakes, who has her dead daughter's face tattooed on the back of her hand, notices that it's beginning to fade, taking with it the memories she has of her daughter. Could this be real?

But she's not alone . . .

Monk Addison is a private investigator whose skin is covered with the tattooed faces of murder victims. He is a predator who hunts for killers, and the ghosts of all of those dead people haunt his life. Some of those faces have begun to fade, too, destroying the very souls of the dead.

The damaged people of Pine Deep are all experiencing this same phenomenon: having their most precious memories dragged and ripped out of their hearts forever.

Something is out there. Something cruel and evil preying on the damaged and lonely, feeding on their memories, erasing them from the minds of good people.

How do you hunt something you can't see? How do you forget something you can't remember?

For the people of Pine Deep, tracking down this memory thief will lead to the greatest horror of them all. Through the pain and suffering of memory, this supernatural thriller will teach you that there is no greater horror than forgetting.

PRAISE FOR JONATHAN MABERRY

"A waking dream, at once powerful and subtly sinister."
—CLIVE BARKER, *NEW YORK TIMES* BESTSELLING AUTHOR

"Nobody brings the pain in modern horror like Jonathan Maberry."
—SEANAN McGUIRE, *NEW YORK TIMES* BESTSELLING AUTHOR

"Maberry has done it again." —*SUSPENSE MAGAZINE*

"Grab *Rage* and thank me later." —*AIN'T IT COOL NEWS*

SARA JO WEST

JONATHAN MABERRY is a *New York Times* bestselling and five-time Bram Stoker Award–winning author of *Deep Silence, Kill Switch, Predator One, Code Zero, Fall of Night, Patient Zero,* the Pine Deep Trilogy, *The Wolfman, Zombie CSU,* and *They Bite,* among others. His V Wars series has been adapted by Netflix, and his work for Marvel Comics includes *The Punisher, Wolverine, DoomWar, Marvel Zombies Return,* and *Black Panther.* His Joe Ledger series has been optioned for television.

Cover design by Rob Grom and Nikolaas Eickelbeck

Cover photographs: woman © YouraPechkin/Getty Images; tattoo © AKV/Shutterstock.com; ink © joker1991/Shutterstock.com; faces (top and bottom): two men and women © oOhyperblaster/Shutterstock.com; faces (middle): women © OSTILL is Franck Camhi/Shutterstock.com

US $17.99 / CAN $24.50
ISBN 978-1-250-76588-8

51799 >

9 781250 765888

ST. MARTIN'S GRIFFIN
ST. MARTIN'S PUBLISHING GROUP
120 BROADWAY, NEW YORK, NY 10271
PRINTED IN THE UNITED STATES OF AMERICA

www.stmartins.com